Catch of the Day

Catch of the Day

Whitney Lyles • Beverly Brandt • Cathie Linz • Pamela Clare

BERKLEY SENSATION, NEW YORK

THE BERKLEY PUBLISHING GROUP
Published by the Penguin Group
Penguin Group (USA) Inc.
375 Hudson Street, New York, New York 10014, USA
Penguin Group (Canada), 90 Eglinton Avenue East, Suite 700, Toronto, Ontario, M4P 2Y3, Canada
(a division of Pearson Penguin Canada Inc.)
Penguin Books Ltd., 80 Strand, London WC2R 0RL, England
Penguin Group Ireland, 25 St. Stephen's Green, Dublin 2, Ireland (a division of Penguin Books Ltd.)
Penguin Group (Australia), 250 Camberwell Road, Camberwell, Victoria 3124, Australia
(a division of Pearson Australia Group Pty. Ltd.)
Penguin Books India Pvt. Ltd., 11 Community Centre, Panchsheel Park, New Delhi—110 017, India
Penguin Group (NZ), Cnr. Airborne and Rosedale Roads, Albany, Auckland 1310, New Zealand
(a division of Pearson New Zealand Ltd.)
Penguin Books (South Africa) (Pty.) Ltd., 24 Sturdee Avenue, Rosebank, Johannesburg 2196,
South Africa

Penguin Books Ltd., Registered Offices: 80 Strand, London WC2R 0RL, England

This book is an original publication of The Berkley Publishing Group.

This is a work of fiction. Names, characters, places, and incidents either are the product of the author's imagination or are used fictitiously, and any resemblance to actual persons, living or dead, business establishments, events, or locales is entirely coincidental. The publisher does not have any control over and does not assume any responsibility for author or third-party websites or their content.

First edition: June 2006

Library of Congress Cataloging-in-Publication Data

Catch of the day / Whitney Lyles . . . [et al.]— 1st ed.
    p. cm.
    Contents: Brides gone wild / Cathie Linz — Heaven can't wait / Pamela Clare — So caught up in you / Beverly Brandt — The wedding party / Whitney Lyles.
    ISBN 0-425-20986-5
    1. Love stories, American. 2. Humorous stories, American. 3. Weddings—Fiction. 4. Single Women—Fiction. 5. Bridesmaids—Fiction. I. Lyles, Whitney.

PS648.L6C38 2006
813'.0850806—dc22

                                                                                2006040738

PRINTED IN THE UNITED STATES OF AMERICA

10 9 8 7 6 5 4 3 2 1

CONTENTS

Brides Gone Wild

CATHIE LINZ

CHAPTER ONE

Maybe it was the full moon.

Maybe it was the five weddings that floral designer Pam Greenley had scheduled this first weekend in June.

Or maybe it was the fact that her lucky CUTE AND CHEERFUL T-shirt had gone up in smoke yesterday when she'd inadvertently stuck it in the oven instead of the washer.

The end result?

Brides Gone Wild.

Five normal women transformed overnight into demanding Bridezillas.

One wasn't happy with the size of her bouquet and wanted hers to be as big as the "honker" at the Hissie-Phitt nuptials two weeks ago.

Another was refusing to walk down the aisle because the all-white roses she'd insisted she'd wanted were "boring."

A third wasn't happy with the height of her centerpieces, while the fourth and fifth brides wanted to change their floral selections entirely.

Pam had never had so much go wrong so fast. But things went from bad to worse the instant she heard that Michael Denton was back in town.

This info was the last straw. It was now official. Her hometown of Serenity Falls, Pennsylvania, had morphed into Hysteria Heights.

"Really? Michael Denton?" Outwardly, Pam remained calm while inside she was totally hyperventilating. Not that she could show it.

After all, she was the proud owner of Bloomers Flower Shop and the employer of several assistants, including Jessica Schmidt, who'd just broken the "Michael news" to her.

For Pam to reenact Munch's famous painting, *The Scream*, hands pressed to her cheeks and mouth hanging agape, simply would not do for the newest member of the Better Business Association. Instead, she meticulously placed a single lavender rose in the midst of pink miniature carnations and gerberas for the centerpiece she was creating. "I thought he wasn't coming here from Chicago to attend his cousin's wedding."

"Yeah, well, I heard that the best man, like, broke both legs and an arm when he fell playing basketball," the nineteen-year-old Jessica informed her. "So Michael had to step in. Is there a problem?"

Yeah. A big one. "I used to go with him."

"You did?" Jessica frowned. "Like, when?"

"Like, when we were in high school together."

Jessica rolled her eyes and handed her a fresh batch of eucalyptus. "That was decades ago."

"Only ten years. *One* decade. Singular."

"Which means I was, like, nine when you two were going together."

"Thanks for sharing," Pam muttered. She didn't need reminding that she was rapidly approaching the big three-oh. Thirty had never seemed like a big deal until recently.

Pam checked her reflection in the large mirror on the flower shop's workroom wall in front of them. She wasn't narcissistic, but she did like seeing how her floral arrangements looked from all angles. The mirror helped accomplish that.

Today it helped reassure her that her short dark hair hadn't turned white yet, despite the wild antics of this week's batch of Bridezillas. Her high cheekbones and green eyes were her best features, while her pointy chin didn't please her at all.

Frowning, she leaned closer. Was that a smudge on her forehead? Or a wrinkle?

"So, like, did you two have a secret baby together or something?" Jessica asked. "They're always doing that on the daytime show I watch. That or switching babies or stealing them."

"Mmm-hmm." Pam was no longer really listening. Instead she was focused on wiping the smudge off with a damp paper towel. If it was a wrinkle, it was a water-soluble one, thank heavens.

"And then those babies turn into teenagers overnight with some hunky young actor taking the role. Yummy." Jessica smacked her lips.

"Sorry to disappoint you, but Michael and I did not have a secret baby." They did share a secret, though. At least *she'd* kept it a secret. He better have, too, if he wanted to live to see that wedding this weekend.

Jessica took a sip of her Diet Coke before asking, "So were you a cheerleader and he was, like, the football hero or something?"

"How did you know I was a cheerleader?"

"Because you've got that totally perky thing going on."

"Hey, I can be crabby."

"Only if someone calls you elfin. They warned me about that before I took this job."

"Who did?"

"Everyone in Serenity Falls."

"Well, that sure narrows it down," Pam noted drily.

"So tell me about you and this Michael."

"Yeah, go ahead and tell her about us," a male voice drawled from the doorway.

Pam's heart sank faster than stocks in Enron.

She took her time turning to look at him. Even so, his appearance reminded her why she'd made the stupid mistakes with him that she had. Tousled brown hair that he was even now shoving out of his storm-cloud gray eyes. He'd once claimed they were just blue, but she knew better. They could go dark with passion or light up with humor.

The slight bump just below the bridge of his nose was caused by her throwing a football at him and breaking his nose when they were in high school. It was how she'd first gotten his attention, not that she'd planned on doing him bodily harm. At least not at that point in their relationship.

She'd tearfully apologized as only a fifteen-year-old girl could. He'd manfully accepted as only a sixteen-year-old could.

Two weeks later they were going steady.

Two years later, they were going at it hot and heavy in the backseat of his black Camaro, where she gave him her virginity.

"Uh . . . I'll, like, leave you two alone," Jessica said.

"Your assistant seems a little nervous," Michael noted after she'd departed. "Why is that?"

Pam shrugged. This gave her more time to compose her voice

into something resembling indifference. She wasn't there yet, so she wasn't prepared to actually speak.

"Are you nervous, too?"

She shook her head, trying her best to do so with a scoffing expression on her face. A quick glance in the mirror told her she'd done a pretty good job of it. Then she remembered that the last time they'd gotten together he'd told her that what he referred to as her "surely-you-jest" look turned him on immensely.

The last time they'd gotten together . . .

It wasn't that long ago, actually. Only the four weeks since their ten-year high school reunion—when she'd once again fallen into his arms and had sex with him.

Granted, it wasn't in the backseat of his car this time. They'd done the deed, several times, in the king-size bed in the hotel room he'd rented clear over in Redmond because all the local places were full. But still . . .

She wasn't the kind of woman who was into one-night stands. Even if they were with her first love.

"So I've merely left you speechless, is that it?" Michael asked, swirling his index finger around her ear.

"Yeah, right," she mocked him before quickly moving several steps away. No way was he seducing her with that finger swirl thing again. That's how things had gotten started last time.

"Hey, you want to dance?" he'd asked her at the reunion.

She'd been prepared to say no. Then he'd circled the sensitive curve of her ear in an endearingly sweet caress that had her nodding and going into his arms.

Not gonna happen this time, she firmly reminded herself.

Been there, done that.

And yes, it had been an awesome night. The sex had been breathtaking. But the morning after had stunk.

She'd opened her eyes to find the bed beside her empty. Ditto for the room. Her first love had taken off . . . again.

Fool me once, shame on you. Fool me twice, shame on me. Fool me three times, and I'll have to shoot you.

Not that Pam was normally a violent person. On the contrary. Ask anyone in Serenity Falls and they'd tell you that Pam Greenley, aka the Flower Girl, was cheerful and easygoing. That nothing got her down.

That last one was a lie, of course. But she'd worked hard to present a positive outlook to the public.

"Cat got your tongue?" Michael moved closer to touch her again. She slapped his hand away. "What do you want?"

"Now that's a loaded question."

Pam narrowed her eyes at him. Along with her perky disposition went a normally well-restrained Irish temper that could get intense if she allowed it to.

"Why are you here?" she demanded.

He blinked those gorgeous gray eyes at her with assumed male innocence. "I came for Pete's wedding."

"You hate weddings." He'd told her that much a month ago when she'd said that she'd branched out from the family nursery business into her own wedding floral shop. She'd shared her business dreams right before he'd removed her bra and kissed her left breast in his hotel room. After that, she'd shared other fantasies instead . . .

"I do hate weddings and I'd hoped to avoid this one, but . . ." He shrugged.

"And you know all about avoidance," she muttered, angrily booting the seductive image of him in that hotel room out of her mind.

"What's that supposed to mean?"

"Nothing."

"You're as good at avoidance as I am," Michael said.

"Not even close."

"You're too modest. You totally avoided my phone calls."

"What phone calls?"

"The ones I made to you here."

"I never received any phone call from you."

"Your assistant said you were unavailable. She sounded like she was ninety and had a smoker's voice."

Phoebe. Pam's assistant before Jessica. Phoebe, who'd run off with the county coroner, nicknamed "Tiny" despite the fact that he resembled an ancient sumo wrestler. "She was not ninety."

"No? How old was she?"

"Only eighty."

"Did she give you my message?"

"What was your message?" she countered.

"That you should give me a call sometime."

"Sometime? As in, before you die?"

"That would be helpful, yes."

"How many times did you call?" Pam demanded.

"I don't know. Once or twice."

"Once or twice?" Her voice reflected the outrage she felt. She was worth more effort than that. *Much* more.

"Now what's wrong?" He said it in that tone of voice that men use when they were dealing with a totally unreasonable woman. She recognized it. Her brothers used it on her often enough.

"Nothing." She regained her control. "So how long are you in town?"

"Just a few days."

"That's good."

"It is?"

"I mean you've got a busy life back in Chicago, right?"

"Right."

"With a busy *social* life, right?"

He raised a dark eyebrow. "Define busy?"

"Never mind. I'm really busy myself." She waved her hand around the cluttered workroom area. "I've got five weddings this weekend."

"Is that a lot?"

She was tempted to dump a nearby batch of Shasta daisies—water and all—on his head. Which wasn't like her. Was the Bridezilla syndrome contagious?

"Yes, it's a lot," she replied between clenched teeth.

"Doesn't seem like a lot to me," he drawled.

Did the man have a death wish?

Michael watched the color rise in Pam's face. He was deliberately goading her because he hated the way she could just tune him out, as if he were a radio station she didn't like.

She must have learned that trick from her two brothers, because he'd never met another woman who could do that the way she did.

But then Pam did a lot of things that no other woman had ever done. To him. To his mind.

And that freaked him.

And because he was freaked, he'd loved her and left her. Not once but twice.

He hadn't planned on coming back this time. Sure, he'd called her once, maybe twice. But he'd been relieved when her assistant had said she was busy. At first, it had reassured him that she wasn't breaking her heart over him or anything.

Then it bothered him.

Which freaked him even more.

Michael prided himself on being logical. That was one of the reasons why he was such a highly sought after corporate trou-bleshooter. Because of his logic.

It was logical for his parents to move from the cold climate here in Pennsylvania to the more appropriate climate in Arizona ten years ago. It was logical for Michael to get his undergrad and business degrees from Northwestern University in Chicago because it was one of the top-rated schools in the country. It was logical that a long-distance relationship with high school sweetheart Pam wouldn't work out—they never did.

So he'd made a clean break of it.

Pam had not taken it well at the time. She'd almost broken his nose again with the top of her head when she'd sat up in the backseat of his Camaro to yank her bra back on.

Michael had continued to calmly list all the reasons it would be best for them both to start this new chapter in their life, the university years, with a clean slate.

"You're right!" she'd shouted at him. "A clean slate! To see other people! In fact, I plan on going to UPenn and having sex with as many guys as possible! It's been at the top of my lifelong goals list. That and seeing the Eiffel Tower."

Looking at her now, he wondered if she had ever gotten to Paris. He didn't want to know how many guys she'd seduced on campus. He'd often told himself that she was too sweet to really do what she'd threatened, but knew she had a stubborn streak a mile wide. Not that it came out that often . . . but when it did, you were in deep shit.

Like right now.

Michael couldn't remember what they'd been talking about. He'd gotten distracted by how good she looked in her Bloomers T-shirt and khaki shorts. She'd been cute enough in high school but now . . . she was even better.

Men were visual creatures and he was certainly no exception. And he liked what he saw when he looked at her. Short dark hair, soft to the touch. Creamy skin, soft to the touch. A full mouth, soft to the touch.

He was definitely seeing a pattern here. She still got to him.

"Go away," she told him.

"Why would I want to do that?"

"Because I asked you to. No, wait. Silly me. Since when do you do what I ask you to?"

"Since now. If you want me to leave I will."

"Good."

"I'm going." He reached out and caressed her mouth with his thumb.

He was gone before she could bite him.

Then he was right back again. "There's just one more thing . . ."

CHAPTER TWO

"Now what?" Pam didn't have time for this. She had tons of work to get done. She didn't have a minute to breathe let alone to shoot the breeze with an ex-lover who had the manners of a hyena.

"You're not mad, are you?" Michael had the nerve to ask. "Because you seem mad."

"Mad?" she repeated. "About what?"

"How should I know?"

"I think *you're* the one who's mad, as in a few pancakes short of a stack. Several seats short of a minivan. Go away!" She placed her hands on his chest and shoved. If she'd been thinking clearly, she'd have realized it was a pointless endeavor with about as much chance of success as moving the tall columns in front of the courthouse. "Go! *Vamanos. Au revoir.*"

He pounced on her French. "Aha, so you did go to Paris. You said you'd get there someday."

"What's going on here? Is there a problem?" her older brother Harry demanded in his booming voice. With their parents on a two-week Mediterranean cruise celebrating their thirty-fifth anniversary, Harry was promoted from assistant manager of the nursery to head honcho of all he surveyed.

At six-foot-six, Harry loomed over most people—including six-foot Michael.

"No problem," Michael replied. "Your sister and I were just talking."

Harry eyed him suspiciously. "And you are?"

"Michael Denton. Pam and I went to high school together."

Harry nodded and relaxed his stance a bit. "Right. I heard you were stepping in at the last minute for a wedding this weekend."

"That's right. Weddings aren't really my thing. I try to avoid them as much as possible," Michael confessed man-to-man.

Harry nodded again. "I hear you."

And bingo, her brother went from protective mode to buddy mode. That fast. Pam was amazed at the speed of the transformation and at Michael's skill in orchestrating it all.

The look she blasted his way indicated that she knew damn well what he was up to and that she wasn't buying anything he was selling.

"My brother is happily married," Pam informed Michael.

"Yeah, but we eloped," Harry said.

She frowned. "What does that have to do with anything?"

"It means he avoided the dog-and-pony show," Michael explained. "But not the ball and chain."

Pam waited for her brother to defend himself, but instead the moron just laughed and slapped Michael on the back as if they were long-lost friends suddenly reunited.

"I find that comment offensive," Pam said on behalf of all womankind.

Both men rolled their eyes at her.

She narrowed hers at them and pointed to the exit. "Out! Both of you!"

They turned and left. But not before Michael gave her one more departing grin. "I'll be back."

"Don't bother!"

Hardly a brilliant parting comment on her part. In fact, Pam spent the next hour trying to think of any number of things she could have said. Something brilliant, something dripping with sarcasm, something guaranteed to shoot his ego down in flames.

Unfortunately nothing came to mind. Except the memory of him, naked, in bed with her, licking his way from her throat all the way down to her thighs.

• • •

"Adele, when are you going to dump this place and run away with me to Chicago?" Michael demanded before kissing her hand.

"Oh stop, you!" The talented cook at Maguire's Pub giggled, displaying her slightly crooked front tooth. Affection gleamed in her warm brown eyes. She was his mom's friend and he'd known her since he was a kid. "You're just after my sweet potato fries, like all the other men."

"Other men?" Michael repeated with horror, placing his hand on his chest as if deeply wounded. Hey, he hadn't been in Drama Club in high school for nothing. "I thought you only made these for me!"

"You and a few thousand others. Did I tell you they're on the menu permanently now?"

"Yes. Tell me, how does it feel to own Maguire's?"

"I'm only *one* of the owners. Along with Luke and Tyler."

Michael was familiar with Luke Maguire, a tough kid who'd left Serenity Falls the instant he'd gotten his high school diploma. He'd heard that Luke had returned to temporarily take over the pub after his father's death, before taking off again. But Tyler was a new name for him. "Who's this Tyler guy?"

"He's real nice."

"He from around here?"

"No."

He waited for more, but she didn't add any additional information. Instead she said, "I heard you were over at the flower shop to see Pam."

"Who told you that?"

"Mabel. And as the town gossip, I figured she had the story right. Didn't she?"

"This is why I moved to the big city. To avoid small-town gossip."

"Oh please." She rolled her eyes. "You moved to make big bucks. Which I hear you've done. Your mother tells me that you're very successful."

He shrugged. "You know how moms are."

"I certainly do. She asked me to keep an eye on you while you're in town."

"She what?" Michael almost spewed his beer all over the table.

Adele calmly handed him a napkin. "You heard me."

"Since when do I need a keeper?"

Adele shrugged. "She's your mother. She's way out in Arizona and she worries."

"Come on," he scoffed. "What's there to be afraid of here in Serenity Falls?"

No sooner had Michael asked the mocking question than he heard the answer blaring inside his head. Not a what. A who—Pam. Ball-and-chain temptation. That was what there was to be afraid of here. Very afraid. More terrifying than anything Wes Craven could come up with.

Not because of Pam, but because of Michael.

He had a plan, and it didn't involve settling down until he was thirty-five and owned a penthouse condo on Lake Shore Drive and had a twenty-two-foot sailboat docked in Monroe Harbor.

That was when he'd consider getting married.

Maybe.

● ● ●

"Why did I think I wanted to get married?" Annie Weiss demanded, grabbing hold of Pam's right arm and yanking her down into the chair beside her. "Tell me, what was I thinking?!"

"That you love your fiancé." Wincing, Pam released herself from the bride-to-be's desperate grip. They were seated in the gazebo area of the store, amid silk floral displays and albums filled with photos of various arrangements of fresh flowers. Pam usually scheduled three or four meetings with her clients in the months leading up to their big day and used e-mail or phone calls to confirm any last-minute things.

Annie, a high school classmate of Pam's though not a buddy, had just come barreling in without any warning—but with a wild gleam in her eyes. "We could just live together. Lots of people do. We don't have to get married."

Pam wasn't expecting the usually calm Annie to go this ballistic.

"Are you saying you want to cancel your wedding two days before the event?"

"I don't know what I'm saying!" Annie moaned, shoving her gorgeous long hair away from her face.

Pam didn't envy Annie her perfect blonde hair or the fact that she'd won the class president election their senior year instead of her . . . by a mere ten votes. But Annie was willowy and tall and Pam did have a hard time forgiving her for that. Still, this was business.

So she tried to be reassuring. "You know, it is normal to be nervous. I mean, this is a big day."

"Everyone will look at me." Annie placed a hand to her forehead à la Scarlett O'Hara. "It's freaking me out!"

Yeah, so? You're a perfect size eight. And tall. So everyone looks. Get over it! I have no pity for you!

Before Pam could formulate a more politically correct answer, bridal diva Joy Lewin marched in. "You've got to do something!" she wailed.

Only able to handle one meltdown at a time, Pam said, "I'll be with you in just a moment—"

"No!" Joy actually stomped her feet, drawing Pam's attention to the really cute pair of raspberry kitten-heel mules the twenty-three-year-old was wearing. Hadn't Pam seen those on the Nordstrom website and lusted after them? "Not in a minute. Now!"

"She's talking to *me* now," Annie declared, two spots of angry color marking her cheeks as she stood up.

Joy refused to back down. "Not about anything important."

"About my wedding," Annie said.

Joy waved her words away. "That can wait. My wedding is bigger than yours, so that gives me top priority."

Two outraged Bridezillas. One tall. One short. Both overwrought. A recipe for disaster.

Joy pushed. Annie pushed back. The petite Joy landed on her butt with her capri-clad legs draped over the silk blue hydrangea display that she'd knocked over. A white wicker side table and small plant stand were victims of the ensuing domino effect, creating instant havoc.

"You assaulted me! Call the police!" Joy hysterically ordered Pam. "I want her arrested!"

Remind me again why you thought five weddings in one weekend was a good idea? the inner Pam demanded.

"Shut up," she muttered to herself.

"What?" Joy's outrage was now aimed at Pam, too.

"I said, I'm sure we can work something out . . ."

But Joy was already dialing 911 on her cell phone. Three minutes later, Sheriff Norton strolled in. "So, girls, what's going on here?"

"It's all just a big misunderstanding," Pam began.

Joy pointed a finger at Annie and yelled, "She attacked me!"

Annie pointed and yelled right back. "She attacked me first!"

"Why is there a police car out front?" Harry demanded over the shouting match. "It looks bad for business."

"Forget business," Michael said from right behind him. His stormy-gray-not-blue-like-he-said eyes sought out Pam. "Are you okay?"

No. She wasn't okay. How could she be, with two brides-to-be fighting in her gazebo? She'd been a stunned witness to the battle of the bizzaro brides.

"Quiet!" Sheriff Norton bellowed over the increasing din.

Pam shot him a grateful look. That gratitude didn't last long when he added, "You've got some explaining to do."

It took her a second to realize he was speaking to her, not the two combatants.

She pointed to her chest as if to say "Who me?"

The sheriff nodded, as if silently confirming, *Yes, you, missy. The idiot who overbooked this weekend and had hot sex with Michael Denton at your high school reunion last month.*

"I . . . I, uh, don't know what to say," she mumbled.

He opened an official-looking notebook. "Just tell me the facts."

"Well, Annie was talking to me about some last-minute concerns regarding her wedding."

"What kind of concerns?"

Pam exchanged a look with Annie, whose visual message was *Mention my cold feet and I will come after you with a very sharp object.*

"Uh"—Pam groped for words—"concerns about the uh . . . the groom's . . . his, uh, boutonniere."

"Is Pete having trouble getting his *boutonniere* fired up?" Mabel Bamas, the town gossip, stepped out from behind a stand filled with African violets. She had a record of showing up in the middle of things. "Tell him to get some Viagra. He's a doctor, he should know these things."

"Pete is not having trouble getting anything up," Annie quickly assured the assembled group. "Or keeping it up."

Sheriff Norton sighed. "Ladies, if we could leave the subject of Pete's erectile function and return to the incident here."

"Right," Pam eagerly agreed. "So Annie and I were speaking—"

"Where?" the lawman interrupted her to ask.

"Here in the gazebo." Which now looked like a herd of hippos had trampled through it.

"Then what happened?"

"Joy came in, demanding to speak to me. I told her I'd be with her in a minute—"

"Where's my daughter?!" Enter Joy's overindulgent mother, Louise. "What's going on here?! Baby, are you okay?" She grabbed Joy and fiercely hugged her.

"That lunatic attacked me," Joy tearfully said.

Annie hurriedly stepped behind the sheriff. Pam couldn't blame her. No one wanted to clash with Louise Lewin. Local legend had it that a few years ago she'd taken off her shoes and smacked her sister with them right in the middle of Main Street. Luckily they weren't stilettos and there hadn't been much traffic at the time.

"Hold on there," the sheriff warned Louise as she leaned down to remove her shoe. Apparently he'd heard the stories about her footwear weaponry as well. "It appears to me that both these females are equally to blame for this incident. Is that right?" he asked Pam.

"I, uh . . ." *What, you want me to upset both clients and have them both stiff me with a roomful of unpaid flowers? Thanks a lot, Sheriff.*

Luckily, he didn't wait for her reply but made his own observations. "Seems to me that both of you females need to go on home now and settle down. Any more trouble from either of you and you'll spend your wedding day in a jail cell. Is that clear?"

Annie and Joy nodded, although Louise looked like she wanted to argue . . . and remove at least one shoe to emphasize her point. But in the end she did neither.

When everyone finally cleared out, Michael remained. "I had no idea the flower business could be so . . . exciting. It's even better than professional wrestling on pay-per-view."

CHAPTER THREE

Pam had the strangest urge to kiss Michael. Which clearly meant she was losing her mind. She didn't even register what he'd said.

She had to be in shock from the aftereffects of the battle of the ballistic brides. That had to be why she kept staring at his mouth as if mesmerized.

She remembered the way he'd tasted a month ago, the feel of his lips on hers, his tongue doing a seductive tango with hers.

Was he dying to kiss her, too?

He moved closer.

She swayed toward him.

Her eyes fluttered shut in preparation for THE KISS, which had gained capital-letter proportion in her mind now. The anticipation was *huge*.

Now? Now? Yes . . . his hand was on her shoulder . . .

Instead of tenderly embracing her, he abruptly shoved her in a chair and pushed her head down between her knees. "Do not faint! Take deep breaths."

Dazed by this sudden turn of events, Pam stared at her legs. This close up, she could see a bit of stubble. She needed to shave them. Maybe that was why he wasn't on the same romantic wavelength with her. Maybe if she'd shaved her legs, he'd have been as turned on as she was. He'd have been overcome with the desire to kiss her.

His hand was on the back of her head like a giant paperweight. She could feel his fingertips against her scalp, moving through her hair. She closed her eyes as memories washed over her . . .

"Are you fainting?" Michael impatiently demanded from somewhere directly over her head. "Do *not* faint! I *told* you not to do that! Stop it right now! *No* fainting!"

She sighed. He was totally ruining her fantasy.

Reality often had a way of doing that.

A second later, a trickle of cold water running down the back of her neck had her jerking upright with startled outrage. "What are you doing?"

Michael stood there with a vase full of water in his hands. "Preventing you from fainting."

"By pouring water down my back?"

"Hey, I'm not a doctor like my cousin, okay? I'm not an expert at first-aid stuff."

"No kidding. Give me that." She yanked the vase away from him, ending up sloshing water on them both.

Michael seemed particularly intent on her all of a sudden. Looking down at the wet T-shirt plastered against her breasts, she could see why. Her nipples were like two beacons eagerly signaling "Here I am, big boy, come get me!"

She quickly folded her arms across her chest.

His Adam's apple bobbed and his eyes glazed.

Now what? She looked down and realized she hadn't placed her arms correctly. Instead of covering the affected area, she'd lifted her breasts higher as if to bring them even more to his attention, the same way those sexy corsets in the Victoria's Secret catalogs did.

Not that Pam had that kind of a figure. Those models were tall and thin and looked "smokin' in a swimsuit," according to her brothers. She'd never been described as *smokin'* in her entire life.

She was short and squat. Models were willowy. They were dainty roses. She was a shrub. A shrub with nipples. Beacon nipples.

She covered them and glared at Michael. "I think you've done enough damage here for one day."

"Me? I'm not the one who participated in the wedding wars."

"Is this a bad time?" a woman asked from a few feet away, staring at them both as if they were alien life-forms on a first-name basis with E.T. or Yoda.

"Depends who you ask," Michael drawled.

"I'm asking Pam Greenley," the newcomer stated.

"That's me." Pam kept her arms plastered across her damp chest.

"Good. I'm Arielle Chesney with *Bridal Magazine*. I called you a few weeks ago about doing a story on your shop."

She'd called, but she'd never said she was coming today!

Just shoot me now. And not with a camera.

Pam would have closed her eyes in horror, but was afraid doing so would make Michael shove her head between her knees again.

"I was hoping you might have some time now to talk to me," Arielle continued.

"She's really busy—" Michael began. Pam shoved the vase at him with enough force to make him take a few steps backward.

"Of course I have time." Pam stepped away from the mayhem

in the gazebo. "If you'll just step into my office, I'll go put on a clean T-shirt."

"I saw a police car pulling away as I arrived," Arielle noted.

Pam flashed her a confident smile. "Yes, that was our town sheriff. Buying some flowers for his wife. And it's not even her birthday or their anniversary. Wasn't that sweet of him? But he's a bit of a bull in a china shop, so I hope you'll excuse the slight disorder." By now Pam had steered Arielle into her office. Only then did she recall that she had papers piled on the chair designated for visitors. She quickly dumped them on the floor, where they slid drunkenly to one side. "I'll just have my assistant bring you some tea and I'll be right back." *Unless I run screaming out of town, never to return.*

"Jessica." Pam grabbed the nineteen-year-old out in the workroom as if she were a life preserver on the *Titanic*. "Please get some tea for our guest. She's with *Bridal Magazine* and she's here to talk about doing a story about Bloomers. So we have to be on our best behavior."

"Best behavior?" Jessica popped her bubble gum. "What's that supposed to mean?"

"Yeah. What's that supposed to mean?" Michael asked from right behind Pam.

"Why . . . are . . . you . . . still . . . here?" Pam bit out each word as if it were a giant boulder.

"I just wanted to make sure you weren't going to faint again."

"I never fainted in the first place."

"Only because I stepped in and saved the day."

"No, because I was *never* in any danger of fainting."

"You were standing there swaying and then your eyes did that fluttery thing and closed."

"I was thinking." *About kissing you, but I'm totally over that now.* "Listen, I don't have time to argue with you. I've got to go change." She grabbed the only remaining T-shirt from the cabinet for employee use and rushed to the tiny bathroom at the back of her workroom.

Again, memory came too late as she realized that the new order of Bloomers T-shirts hadn't come in yet and the one she was now wearing was extra small . . . which made her breasts look extra big.

Thankfully, she found a smock hanging from the back of the door, which made her look more like a lab technician and less like a Hooters girl in a nursing bra.

Good. Fine. Breathe. You can do this.

She returned to her office to find that Michael was sitting on the edge of her cluttered desk, his denim-covered butt dangerously close to her ceramic Hershey's Kiss paper-clip holder, chatting away with Arielle.

What kind of name was that anyway? Arielle. Sure, it was okay for the Little Mermaid, who her nieces loved. But not for an adult.

Not that Arielle was acting like an adult. She was gazing up at Michael with admiration and that female hunter look that said she was on the prowl and he was fair game.

Okay, calm down. Having hostile feelings for the person who might be doing a story about her store in one of the nation's leading bridal publications was not a good thing.

Priority number one: get rid of Michael. "Thanks for stopping by, but I know you've got to go now."

"But she just got here," Michael said with a killer smile aimed at Arielle.

Pam clenched her fists before reminding herself to remain calm. "I wasn't talking about *her*, I was talking about you."

"Well, then, relax, because I don't have to leave now."

"Yes, you do."

"No, I don't. Look, your assistant brought me tea." He held up the mug for her appraisal.

"She was supposed to bring it for Arielle."

"She has some, too." He nodded in the reporter's direction.

"If you don't mind, I'd like to get started," Arielle said.

"I don't mind at all. Good-bye, Michael." The look Pam gave him promised him severe bodily harm if he didn't vacate the premises immediately.

"He can stay," Arielle purred.

"He doesn't have anything to do with the business," Pam quickly pointed out.

"I realize that. He told me he's a corporate troubleshooter from Chicago who's in town for his cousin's wedding."

And did he tell you that he sleeps with women and then takes off without a word? I'll bet he didn't brag about that *character trait of his, did he?*

"I couldn't help noticing that you've got the book *How to Hook Your Guy* on your desk," Arielle said. "Are you a fan?"

Pam played dumb. "Of what?"

"The book."

"I haven't even glanced at it," Pam flat-out lied. She'd read enough to deem the book a total wall-banger. "A client gave it to me as a joke." A *bad* joke.

"I've heard of it," Michael volunteered.

The look she sent him said, "Who cares . . . go away before I hurt you."

"There's a lot of buzz building around it," Arielle said. "I hear the author tells it like it is, giving women insights into the way men think."

Men don't think. They react. Pam had to bite her tongue to refrain from telling Arielle that. Let the mermaid-woman discover the sad fact for herself. Just not with Michael.

Arielle switched on a mini recorder. "So, Pam, tell me about your business. What made you decide to open a bridal floral shop?"

"My family was already in the nursery business. Greenley's Garden Center was actually started by my grandfather over forty years ago. I've always loved flower arranging." No point confessing that she didn't have a green thumb and couldn't grow a thing. She'd accidentally killed more houseplants than she could count. Schefflera shuddered in terror when she walked by. Philodendron shriveled up at the mere sight of her. "So I decided to branch out into my own specialty store."

"Why bridal arrangements? Is she a romantic?" Arielle directed the second question to Michael.

Taking a page out of a guy's playbook, Pam reacted without thinking. Michael had to go. Bumping his elbow resulted in his tea spilling onto his crotch.

She hadn't chosen the location of the spill, just the mishap.

"Oh, I'm so sorry about that." The only reason she dabbed her paper napkin on his crotch was because she saw Arielle leaning forward about to do the same thing. "You better go change."

Michael's look told her that he knew this had been no accident and that while she might have won this round, the battle between them wasn't over. It was just beginning. And it was going to get messy.

• • •

Pam walked into her kitchen to find a mess on the floor. There was nothing like dog poop to bring you back to earth in a hurry. "I was only five minutes late. Okay, twenty minutes. Maybe thirty. Forty tops. You couldn't wait?"

Rosebud, the award-winning dachshund in the Little Wieners category in the Serenity Falls Wiener Dog Race last November, merely looked at Pam and gave her rottweiler-strength bark—the one that had sent the cable guy running from the house in terror a few weeks back.

It didn't have the same effect on Pam. "Don't give me that. I am *not* buying that excuse for one minute." She reached for the paper towels. "This is payback, isn't it? Because I wouldn't let you maul my only pair of designer shoes. They were Jimmy Choos. Do you understand? Not Jimmy C-h-e-w-s," she spelled out.

Rosebud wagged her tail.

"Dogs are supposed to be supportive of their owners," Pam continued as she cleaned. "Loving and blindly loyal. That's why I didn't get a cat."

Rosebud growled at the sound of the word *cat*. The dachshund had had a thing about them ever since the big orange tom next door had refused to back down when Rosebud had raced over to scare the feline. Instead the doxie had freaked at seeing the huge cat and ended up running back home while the aptly named Moose sat and washed his face and whiskers with insulting indifference.

At the time, Pam had read the cat's mind. "Dog? You call that little sausage a dog? Hah! Puh-lease. I make larger deposits in my litter box."

"Hey, I was supportive of you when you came back with your tail between your short little legs," Pam reminded her doxie. "You're not tall and willowy in the dog world. You're short and stubby like me. That's why we girls need to stick together and not create stress. I don't need any more stress right now. Did I tell you that Michael is back in town? Or that I'm now so far gone that I'm actually confiding in my dog?"

When Pam's phone rang, she stared at it with some trepidation before checking the caller ID window. When she saw who it was, she grabbed for it. "Julia, thank God!"

"What's wrong?" Julia Wright asked her.

Julia was one of Pam's closest friends, a librarian at the local library. She'd taken off with town bad boy Luke Maguire a little over a month ago, riding off into the sunset on the back of his big, bad Harley.

Okay, so it hadn't actually been sunset, but still . . .

Thank God for cell phones! And unlimited long-distance with no roaming charges. After Pam had made an idiot of herself by falling into bed with Michael at the high school reunion a month ago, she'd immediately called Julia, who'd been in Montana or Wyoming or Colorado . . . one of those western states.

Despite the miles between them, Julia had calmed Pam down.

"What's wrong?" Pam repeated, tossing the paper towel–wrapped dog poo into the garbage and leaving the kitchen. She'd have to wash the floor before she went to bed tonight, but she couldn't cope with that chore right now. "Michael's back in town."

"Oh no."

"That's putting it mildly."

"Why is he there?"

"Not because of me, that's for sure. He came because he had to act as a last-minute stand-in as best man at his cousin's wedding."

"Have you seen him?"

"Seen him and had him throw water on me. He said he did it so I wouldn't faint."

"Faint? You never faint. You're not the fainting kind."

"Thank you. My point exactly." Pam sank onto a floral slipcov-ered chair and slung her legs over the ruffled arm. "He's an idiot."

"Yes, he is. So do you still lust after him?"

"Yes."

"Bummer."

"You'd think I'd have learned my lesson by now. I mean, the man is only looking for a one-night stand. He claims he called me—"

"Wait, he said he called you?"

"Only once."

"That doesn't count."

"Exactly. Where are you?"

"Idaho. The Sawtooth Mountains."

"I guess that's too far away for you to come over tonight, huh? Even for Pop-Tarts?" They were Julia's favorite food—morning, noon, or night.

"A little far, yes."

"I miss you."

Julia's voice softened. "I miss you, too."

"Is Luke treating you right?" Pam demanded. "Because if he's not, he's going to have to answer to me and to Rosebud."

Julia laughed. "Luke has already figured out that you're a softie, but he knows that Rosebud has the heart of a rottweiler. He wouldn't do anything that would set her off."

"Thanks for that dog toy you sent her, by the way. And your mom was doing fine the last time I checked on her. I've got five weddings this weekend, so I'm feeling totally overwhelmed at the moment. I actually had two of the brides-to-be fighting in my gazebo today. The sheriff came. And did I tell you that *Bridal Magazine* may be doing a story on me?"

"You said someone had called you, but no details."

"She showed up this afternoon out of the blue."

"When the brides were fighting?"

"Luckily, no. But when Michael was still there."

"What was he doing there?"

"Aggravating me."

"Sounds like he succeeded," Julia said wryly.

"I'm tired of letting him call the shots. He's only been in town since this morning and he's already disrupted my work twice. I need to do something about that."

"Uh, Pam, I know that tone of voice. Don't do anything you'll regret," Julia warned.

"Like have sex with him again? Don't worry about that. My pants are staying on. And so are his. Well, I guess I can't control that . . . his pants, I mean. But even if his come off, *mine* are staying on."

"Ooo-kay then."

Pam looked over to see that Rosebud had taken Pam's new straw purse in her mouth and was now happily dragging it to her. "I'm not taking you for a drive tonight. I need to go see Michael by myself," she told her doxie.

Rosebud dropped the purse at her feet, ran back down the hall and returned with her leash in her mouth, reminding her owner that she still owed her a walk. "Hold on a sec, Julia, I just have to put the dog's leash on."

Pam continued her conversation as she took her dog out, with the leash in one hand and her cell phone in the other.

"I'm outside now, so I have to watch what I say," she told Julia in an undertone.

"I understand. Serenity Falls does have a way of finding out things."

"Not everything."

"So tell me more about this reporter from the magazine."

"She has the hots for a certain person . . ."

"Michael?"

"Bingo. She just met him this afternoon, but he seems to have that effect on females."

"Him dating the reporter could make things complicated."

"No kidding. That's why I'm going to warn him away."

"Will that work?"

"Probably not, but I have to try. Then I have to figure out how I'm going to be in two places at once tomorrow morning—at the shop completing the revised centerpieces for a reception and meeting the *Bridal Magazine* reporter for breakfast."

"Two places at one time . . . if you get that trick done, let me know."

"Any last-minute advice?"

"Not really. You're speaking to the woman who threw stones at Luke's window to get his attention."

"Hey, I might use that . . ."

By the time Pam got Rosebud back home, quickly washed the kitchen floor, answered a dozen phone calls from frazzled brides and completed notes on the revisions to the various floral arrangements, it was a little after ten.

Michael was probably back at the town's only bed-and-breakfast by now. Mabel had told her that he was staying at the Granite Inn, so named because of the building's construction, and not at the Tip Top Motel.

Mrs. Zoranski ran the Granite Inn with skill and lots of cleaning products. The place was immaculate enough to perform surgery on the hardwood floors. And the inn had nice four-poster beds . . .

Forget the furnishings. What if mermaid-woman Arielle was in there with him? On one of the four-poster beds? How could Pam find out?

He had a ground-floor room. Mabel said so. Which meant Pam could go by and happen to glance in his window, if the drapes were open. If they weren't . . . well, she'd cross that bridge when she got there.

Rosebud was not pleased at being left behind when Pam tried to sneak out the back door.

Wait, maybe that would be a better cover, to take her dog out for another walk. What could be more normal than that?

Ten minutes later, she'd walked to the Granite Inn. Thankfully, there was only one guest room located on the main floor. The drapes were open. The light was on. Pam and her dog moved closer until she was standing beside the large rhododendron bush. Where was Michael?

A pair of men's jeans were tossed onto the bed. Was he in the shower?

The bathroom door opened and a man emerged . . .

Eeew, yuck! It was Mr. DiFranco, Joy's soon-to-be father-in-law. An ape-like pest exterminator with a flabby beer belly and an apparent aversion to using towels to cover any part of his hairy anatomy.

Putting her free hand to her eyes, Pam stumbled backward, away from the terrible ugly-naked-guy image that threatened to give her nightmares for all eternity.

A second later, she squealed as a hand grabbed hold of her butt.

"What are you doing peering into strange men's windows at this time of night?" Michael asked her, his breath warm in her ear.

CHAPTER FOUR

"Take your hands off me or I'll sic my vicious dog on you!" Pam's voice was fierce.

"What vicious dog? The one rolling on her back at my feet?"

Sure enough, there was Rosebud: her tummy in the air, begging for attention. The traitor. Another female instantly overwhelmed by Michael's spell.

"What's going on out there?" The demand came from Mr. DiFranco, who'd opened the window to his room and stuck the top half of his naked body out of it.

Pam instantly closed her eyes. "I am not fainting," she warned Michael in case he got any ideas of shoving her head between her legs again. "I just can't look at him," she muttered. "Not again."

"Everything is fine, sir," Michael called out.

"Well, keep it down out there," Mr. DiFranco grumbled.

The window closed with a *thwack*. The kind of *thwack* Pam wanted to give Michael. "I told you to get your hands off me!"

Pam turned to shove him, but instead tripped over the dog's leash and tumbled forward. She instinctively put her hands out to stop her fall. Her palms met Michael's abdomen and she took him down with her, landing on top of him with enough force to make the air whoosh from her lungs.

But not his. "If you wanted a roll in the hay with me, all you had to do was ask."

She ignored the laughter in his voice because she had other things to be concerned about. Like getting oxygen.

When she did draw in a breath she wished she hadn't. "This isn't hay, it's manure! Mrs. Zoranski uses it as fertilizer." She tried to prop herself up to get a better view of the horticultural damage she'd wrecked. "Oh no, we've flattened her iris!"

"Uh, you want to watch where you're putting those fingers of yours?" Michael drawled. "Before you flatten something else that's quickly rising to the occasion?"

Her hand was on his thigh, her thumb dangerously close to the fly of his jeans.

If they weren't resting in stinking fertilizer, she might have been much more tempted to be wicked. As it was, she scrambled to her feet.

Standing there, she looked down at him accusingly. "You make me do stupid things!"

Michael quickly got to his feet as well. "How do you figure any of this was my fault?"

"I don't know why I even bother speaking to you."

"I don't know, either. Especially when you'd much rather be kissing me."

"That is such a lie—" The last word was muffled as his mouth closed over hers.

They both smelled of manure. Not exactly conducive to an ideal romantic moment. In addition, Rosebud was racing around them, binding them together with her leash. Pam noticed all these things, but only distantly.

Her main focus was on Michael's tongue teasing her lips until they parted for him. The man could kiss. They'd spent plenty of time in high school making out, just kissing for hours. Oh, yeah, he was a totally primo kisser using just the right amount of tongue thrust—not too much, just enough to make her furious with herself for wanting him after what he'd done to her.

She wasn't falling for him. This time, she was the one in control. She broke off the kiss to give him hell.

"I came here to tell you to leave me alone." She slid her hand behind his head and pulled him close to kiss him. "I mean it!" She kissed him again. "Do not think I'm falling into bed with you!" She French-kissed him this time, full frontal tongue. "It won't happen! Got that?" She glared at him before freeing herself and walking away like a queen departing court.

Michael stared after her—stunned, aroused, and impressed.

Be afraid, buddy, his inner bachelor warned him. *Be very afraid*.

•　•　•

A new day. A new Pam. One who wasn't going to get distracted by Michael or rabid brides frothing at the mouth. She was here at the Serenity Falls Cafe ten minutes early, dressed in a power outfit—a black Ann Taylor suit and a stunning turquoise nugget necklace that always gave her confidence.

Pam looked like what she was—a successful businesswoman

about to be interviewed by one of the premier magazines in her industry.

Pam carefully sipped the coffee she'd ordered while she waited for Arielle to show up. There was no sign of Michael, for which she was grateful. She did not appreciate Mayor Walt Whitman and his ever-present clipboard sliding into the booth across from her, however.

"I'm expecting someone," she told him.

"I know you are. Arielle Chesney with *Bridal Magazine*. I hope you plan on telling her that Serenity Falls is a pocket of beauty and culture here in Pennsylvania. And of course you'll want to inform her that we're on the top-ten list of Best Small Towns in America."

The top-ten announcement had been made the same day that Julia and Luke had left town. Not that there was any connection between the two events, but Pam had them irrevocably linked in her mind.

Then his words really hit her. "Wait a minute! How did you know about Arielle?"

"From Jessica's blog."

Pam almost spit out her coffee. "Her what?"

"Blog. It's a sort of online diary on the Internet."

"I know what a blog is. I didn't know that Jessica has one."

"Sure. Most people do these days. If you really want details, you should check out Mabel's blog. She's always plugged into the latest news."

"Gossip, you mean."

"But Jessica really scooped her on this story."

"I don't believe this."

"You really should be more Internet savvy." Walt flagged down a waitress and ordered a coffee for himself. "I've been meaning to tell you that your website could use some updating. As a member of our business community, you do have a responsibility. After all, we have a certain image to maintain now that we're one of America's Best Small Towns. Even the cafe here is online."

"Why?"

"Because they're selling their pies via the Internet. And doing a great job of it. Which is why they're already out of cherry pie even though it's barely eight in the morning. They've been getting orders for it from as far away as California. Can you imagine, our Serenity Cafe pies going all the way to the West Coast! And of course, the town itself has a wonderful website."

"Well, I don't want to keep you," Pam said in an attempt to get rid of him.

"Nonsense. As mayor, I should personally welcome this reporter to our town."

"No, that's not necessary at all."

Salvation came in the form of Angel, Julia's New Age entrepreneur mom. "Walt, Tyler wants to speak to you about the new outdoor mural he's planning on painting over at Cosmic Comics."

"That's not allowed!" Walt launched himself out of the booth, grabbing his clipboard before making a quick exit.

"Thanks," Pam told Angel. "Is Tyler really planning on doing another mural?" He'd already done one inside Maguire's that had created quite a stir.

Angel shrugged. "I have no idea. But I saw the frantic look on your face and said the first thing I could think of to send Walt elsewhere."

"I appreciate it."

"I was glad to help. You talked to Julia last night, right?"

Julia's mom had a way of knowing things, without using customary means. Pam couldn't keep up with all the metaphysical things Angel talked about—auras, tarots and runes, oh my.

"Yes, I spoke to Julia."

"She's doing well." Angel quickly changed the subject. "Is it true that you're meeting with someone from *Bridal Magazine* this morning? I saw it on Jessica's blog."

Pam was going to have to kill her assistant. But not until after this weekend. She needed Jessica's help for these five weddings. She'd do her bodily harm later.

"I can see from the look on your face that it's true," Angel continued. Her gauzy azure top and skirt flowed around her as she hurriedly took the seat that Walt had just vacated. The amethyst crystal she always wore around her neck caught a ray of sunlight peering in through the cafe's front window and gave it an eerie purplish glow. "I hope you plan on discussing the fact that magazines such as this create unfair pressure on young women to marry and conform."

"Sure, I'll tell her your concerns," Pam fibbed. Anything to get rid of Angel.

"Maybe I should stay and speak to her myself."

"No!" The other diners in the cafe turned to stare at Pam. "No," she said in a quieter and less hysterical tone of voice. "She only has time to speak to me. If she sees others, she'll leave."

Great, that made the reporter sound like a drug pusher who would get antsy if a buyer showed up with an escort. That didn't stop Pam from continuing. "'Come alone,' she told me. I've got to honor that, or she'll flee."

Angel nodded. "I understand. I'll leave the matter in your hands." She took one of them in hers. "You've got a long life line."

"But a tight schedule."

"Right. We don't want to spook our prey. You really should switch from coffee to green tea," Angel added before getting up. "Much better for you."

Pam was thinking that she should have had the reporter come to her home, where they wouldn't be interrupted by mayors or aura-avid New Agers, when Arielle arrived. She wore black, like Pam, but she did so with a New Yorker's innate sense of style.

Arielle ordered a bagel, no butter, and a double latte.

"They only do regular or decaf coffee here," Pam said apologetically.

"Maybe we should have met at Starbucks."

"We don't have one here."

"Must be one of the few places that doesn't," Arielle grumbled. "And no smoking?" She raised an eyebrow.

Pam could only nod apologetically.

She shoved her pack of cigarettes back into her Prada purse and removed an ultrathin laptop. "Okay, then, let's get started. You told me yesterday how you got into the business. Tell me, what makes your designs unique?"

"I try to listen to my clients and give them the image they've fantasized about and are looking for. I get information on their dresses, on possible themes they want, their color schemes, that sort of thing."

"And what themes are you seeing right now?"

"A variety. From fairy-tale weddings with glass-slipper centerpieces to Asian influences in more minimalist designs to floral Victorian motifs."

"What challenges are you facing working in a small town like this?"

"Serenity Falls was recently selected as one of America's Best Small Towns," Pam dutifully told her.

"Has that helped your business any?"

"It hasn't hurt it," Pam diplomatically replied, since she had no idea of the answer.

"So what challenges do you face working in a small town? Even if it's one of the country's best, it's still small. How is it different compared to working in a larger market?"

"I think I get to know my clients better." *Except when I have five of them on one weekend and they try to do me bodily harm.* "Word of mouth is one of my most powerful marketing tools. I get recommendations from other clients or they see photographs at the local photographer's studio from some of the weddings I've done recently."

"So you work with other local vendors?"

Pam nodded.

"I got those photos of your designs you e-mailed me last night." Arielle tapped her laptop. "I have to run them by the editor to see if we want to use them or take photos of our own. If so, we'll send a photographer out. We'll let you know." Arielle looked out the cafe window at the village hall tower. "Is that the correct time?"

"No, it's five minutes fast," Pam replied. "It's been like that since the day Pearl Harbor was attacked, when lightning hit it during a freak storm in December."

But Arielle was no longer listening. "I've got to run. Thanks for your time. I think I've got enough information for now." She slid her laptop back into its case.

"If you need anything more, just call me. You've got all my numbers, right?" Pam said.

"Right. Speaking of numbers, do you have Michael's?"

Yeah, she had his number. He was in town to make trouble and she refused to allow that to happen.

"His phone number?" Arielle pressed.

"No, I don't. But you do know he's gay, right?" Pam couldn't help it. The words were out before she could stop them.

Arielle's face reflected her disappointment. "Really? He totally flew under my gaydar. Usually I'm pretty good at picking up on that vibe."

Pam just smiled and shrugged. Michael had certainly brought out the liar in her. And the vixen.

• • •

"When were you planning on telling your mother?" Adele demanded as she plopped a plate of crisp fish and chips on the table before Michael at Maguire's Pub.

"Shouldn't you be letting the servers bring out the food for the lunch crowd while you cook and manage the place?" the businessman in Michael couldn't help asking. "You've got a busy establishment here."

"Don't try and dodge the question." Adele stood as if planted in place, her hands on her hips. "When were you planning on telling your mother?"

"Telling her what?"

She moved closer, leaning over the table to speak to him confidingly. "Look, I can understand your reluctance to tell your father. The man makes Rush Limbaugh look like a flaming liberal. He's not exactly the kind to spill your guts to. But your mom . . . she'd stand by you, no matter what."

This had to be about the secret he'd been keeping. One of the secrets. He was juggling several at the moment. "How did you find out?"

Adele sat across the table from him. "That doesn't matter right now. Does your mother know?"

He shook his head.

"When did you plan on telling her?"

"I was going to tell her last month, but I wasn't sure how she'd take it," he said.

"You know she'd support you, no matter what. You need to tell her right away. Today."

"I'll send her a copy of the book."

"What book?"

"The book I wrote." He spoke in an undertone. *"How to Hook Your Guy."*

"You wrote a book telling men how to date other men?"

"No, of course not!" Aware of the sudden stares from those seated nearby, he quickly lowered his voice. "The book is written for women, telling them how to hook the man of their dreams."

"I see. Well, I guess gay guys are good at giving advice like that. I mean, they even made a TV show about it. *Queer Eye for the Straight Guy*, right?"

"What are you talking about?"

"The fact that you're gay."

Michael's eyes popped open and his jaw dropped. "I am *not*!"

"It's too late." She patted his hand reassuringly. "You've been outed."

"I'm telling you, I'm not gay!" He had to keep his voice quiet so the other diners wouldn't hear him. While his volume was low, his vehement intensity was not. *"No way!"*

"But you just said you hadn't told your mom yet."

"That I'd written a book using a pen name. Not that I prefer men to women."

"It's on Mabel's blog today. She got the information from a very reliable source."

"That I wrote a book?"

"No, that you're gay."

"Who is Mabel's reliable source?"

"I don't know. Mabel didn't say. Wait a second." This as Michael abruptly stood and shoved his chair back. "Where are you going?"

"To have a little talk with Mabel," he growled.

"What about your lunch?"

"Wrap it up for me. I'll be back for it later. Oh, and do me a favor, would you? Don't tell my mom about the book thing until I talk to her. In fact, don't tell anyone."

"I won't. But don't you do anything you'll regret later."

"I won't." He *would* make Mabel regret she'd ever put him in her blog, however.

Michael had no trouble finding town gossip Mabel Bamas at the video store where she worked. She had the same tightly curled, bubblegum pink hair she'd had when he was in high school.

She flashed him an Efferdent smile. "Do you need help?"

"Yes, I do. You see, I just discovered that someone has been spreading false rumors about me."

She picked up a pair of glasses beside the cash register and studied him. "You're that gay guy. Michael Denton."

"I am not gay." Since his teeth were clenched the words came out slightly strangled.

She was clearly skeptical. "I heard from a very reliable source that you are."

"They lied. And I want to know who that source is."

Mabel raised her chin and gave him a haughty look that would have done Barbara Walters proud. "A reporter never reveals their source. I saw that movie *All the President's Men*. Robert Redford looked mighty fine in that one, I can tell you. I don't think he's gay, do you? A lot of those handsome actors are, you know."

"Do you realize that you can get in legal trouble for saying something about me that isn't true?"

"I said that I heard a reliable source saying you're gay. And that's the truth."

"Who? Who did you hear saying I'm gay?"

"I can't tell you her name."

"So it was a woman?"

"Maybe. I can't answer that on the grounds that I might incriminate myself. Now what movie did I see that in? Was it *Legal Eagles*? Wasn't Redford in that one, too? Anyway, did you see *The Birdcage*? Didn't you think Robin Williams was great in that?"

Michael's jaw was clenched so tightly he couldn't speak.

Mabel frowned. "You weren't offended by that movie, were you? I heard that some of you people weren't happy with it."

"Listen carefully. I . . . am . . . not . . . gay." He paused between each word as if speaking to a toddler.

"I understand." She patted his hand like Adele had. "You probably haven't told your parents yet, so it's awkward for you."

Michael tried to control his aggravation and anger and instead use his logic to break this mystery. A reliable source, a woman, had said he was gay. Who would do such a thing?

Only one name came to mind.

He deliberately changed his voice to a more calm tone. "So where did you hear Pam tell someone that I was gay?"

"At the Serenity Cafe," Mabel replied without thinking.

Michael smacked his hand on the counter. "I knew it!"

Mabel jumped. "If you knew it, then why did you come in here?"

"It's *not* true. Put that in your blog. And while you're at it, add that a reliable source told you that Mrs. Zoranski's iris weren't flattened by the Great Dane next door but by a certain flower store owner and her first love."

"You mean you and always-a-flower-girl-never-a-bride Pam?"

"Remember, reporters never reveal their sources," Michael reminded Mabel before leaving.

• • •

Only noon and already Pam had taken three extra-strength Excedrin, consumed a really huge bowl of seedless red grapes and guzzled three bottles of AriZona Green Tea with Ginseng and Honey. And that was just in the past thirty minutes.

She glanced up at the Howard Miller Garden Italiana antique-style clock with its large, elaborately rendered numbers and hand-painted flowers in the center. She had similar flowers painted on the sign hanging outside her store, and the same style was used on the word BLOOMERS.

She'd restored the wedding gazebo to its prefight order and was now focused on the flowers for Brittany's wedding at ten tomorrow morning. Brittany, who wanted a honker-size bouquet. Because in her world, size mattered.

Pam's workroom was filled with the mellow sound of Norah Jones as she coaxed a cluster of pink roses and white freesias into place for the dramatic cascade bouquet she was creating. This was her favorite time—working with the flowers, making the image she saw in her head a reality before her.

Her concentration was broken by male hands on her waist and a husky voice in her ear whispering, "So I'm gay, am I?"

CHAPTER FIVE

Pam decided her best offense was a good defense. "I have no idea what you're talking about."

"Whispering." Michael's warm breath on her ear gave her goose bumps and made her knees go a little wobbly. Or maybe that was caused by the two Red Bulls she'd consumed for breakfast. "Not talking, whispering."

"Right. Stop it. Right now." Taking several steps back, she waved green floral foam at him, not exactly a weapon of choice by most self-defense experts.

"I know everything." He looked smug. Sexy and smug in jeans and a Cubs baseball shirt. "Mabel caved in to my superior interrogation techniques."

"What did you do to the poor woman? Tie her to a chair and shine a bright light at her?"

"It wasn't necessary. She told me that she overheard you telling someone at the Serenity Cafe that I was gay."

Pam refused to be intimidated. "Mabel's hearing isn't the best."

"She put it on her blog today."

"Really? She finally admitted on her blog to having a hearing problem?"

"You know what I'm talking about. What I want to know is why did you do it?"

"Do what?"

"Start a rumor that I'm gay when you know I'm not."

"Have I mentioned to you that I have five weddings to prepare floral arrangements for this weekend? And that three of them are tomorrow? Do you realize that the wedding business is a forty-five-million-dollar industry? As a number-crunching problem-solver, you should find that exciting."

"You know what really turns me on?"

I don't know and I don't care. That was what she should say. But for some reason the words wouldn't come out of her mouth. Instead she feebly muttered, "I really do *not* have time for this right now."

"Just answer the question. Who were you talking to? Who did you tell?"

"No one."

"You just stood in the middle of the cafe and announced to everyone there that I'm gay?"

"Of course not!"

"Then who did you tell?"

"I didn't say that I told anyone."

"*I'm* saying you did. *Mabel* says you did. Wait a minute, weren't you meeting that reporter for breakfast at the cafe? Did you tell her? Did you tell her that I'm gay?"

Pam refused to answer him.

His expression turned thoughtful. "Now why would you do that? Why make her think I didn't like having sex with women?"

"I was doing her a favor."

"Really. How do you figure that?"

"My lips are sealed."

"Yeah? Well, I can fix that." He kissed her.

Instant fire. Immediate passion. The feel of his mouth on hers carried enough voltage to light up the entire Eastern Seaboard and then some. Her lips parted. His tongue stroked hers with sultry hunger as he scooped her up and set her on the worktable.

Wrapping her legs around his hips, she tugged him closer, moaning with delight as he did that nibbling caress she loved so much. Her breasts were crushed against his chest, her feminine mound pressed directly against his arousal. His hands clenched against her bottom as he tilted her back, increasing the angle of intimacy in their sizzling embrace.

Everything about him communicated manly stuff like strength and power and sex that made her inner female howl for release. The hard ridge beneath the placket of his jeans throbbed a feed-the-need message that her body instantly recognized and responded to. Primitive jungle drums of desire pulsed through her, erasing any thought of restraint.

No one made her feel the way he did.

She shoved her hands through his hair, loving the feel of the surprisingly silky strands between her fingers. Michael shifted his hands, moving them under her T-shirt and focusing on unfastening her bra. He'd almost completed that task when Jessica walked in.

Pam would have been oblivious to the newcomer were it not for Jessica's startled gasp.

Pam's eyes shot open as her assistant stood there speechless for a minute.

"I suppose I can't, like, put this in my blog either," Jessica noted with regret.

Pam quickly unwrapped her legs from around Michael's waist and hopped off the table. Her wobbly knees wouldn't quite support her so she had to hang on to the table edge for support. "You suppose correctly."

"So he's, like, not gay?" Jessica asked. "Never mind," she quickly added after seeing Pam's glare. "I'll leave you two alone then."

"Good idea," Michael said.

"Bad idea," Pam said, shaking her head so fiercely she got a little dizzy. Or maybe that was due to the lack of oxygen caused by their wild kiss. "Stay here, Jessica. We have work to do."

Michael just smiled, as if he knew that she needed reinforcements to keep her from surrendering to him. Or jumping his bones.

And the knowledge was enough to let him know that he'd won this round. So he left, the look in his gray eyes a promise that this battle was just beginning to heat up.

●   ●   ●

"So what wedding is all this stuff for again?" Algee Washington asked her early the next morning. People said that he resembled Michael Clarke Duncan, that actor in *The Green Mile*. With his tough, tank-like body and gleaming shaved head, Algee was an imposing figure. But Pam knew he was actually a marshmallow at heart.

Algee had offered her the use of his brawn and his van to help transport the flowers to the church for the setting up. She already had the Bloomers van filled to capacity and had needed more help.

As a fellow business owner, Algee could relate. His Cosmic Comics store was down the street from Maguire's.

He was a great buddy to have—generous and funny. And fond

of matching up surnames for outlandish nuptials. "Is it the Hardy-Butz wedding?" Algee asked. "Or the Small-Fry wedding?"

"Neither."

"No?" He easily transported another load to the van. "Then it must be the Baird-Bottoms wedding."

She grinned and shook her head.

Algee tried again. "How about the Weiss-Guy wedding? The Knott-Reddy wedding?"

That last one described Ann's cold feet. Pam only hoped that she'd gotten over that by now. Her ceremony wasn't until tomorrow afternoon at the Serenity Falls Country Club.

Pam had four nuptials to get through before that. Three of them today.

She shot Algee a grateful look. "Have I thanked you for being such a pal and helping me out?"

Algee nodded. "Yeah. Several times. But don't let me stop you from doing it again."

She gave Algee a hug almost as huge as he was. "You're such a great guy. Why hasn't some girl snatched you up yet?"

"Because she hasn't read this book." He pulled *How to Hook Your Guy* out of the garbage, where she'd tossed it earlier that morning.

"That book?" Pam grimaced. "It's awful."

"It might not be politically correct, but that doesn't mean it's not the truth."

"The guy who wrote it isn't even married. So where does he get off telling women how to get the man they love to propose to them?"

"Stephen King didn't have to kill anybody to write about it."

"The entire concept of pretending to be someone you're not in order to *hook*"—she used air quotes—"a man is revolting. Whoever wrote this book is a self-centered, heartless and emotionally void robot. All he does is talk about what men want. Men want sex. Men will ask for your phone number and then never call you. Men will watch sports. Men want you to fulfill their needs without having to fulfill any of yours."

"Are we dissing men?" Julia's younger sister Skye—the wild one—asked as she strolled in. "Algee told me you could use some help today, so here I am. Sounds like I arrived just in time."

Pam eyed her cautiously. Today Skye was dressed fairly normally, in jeans and a GOT BRAINS? T-shirt. Even her short spiky hair wasn't the neon red it had been a few weeks ago, but a more normal auburn color.

Pam knew from past experience and from what Julia had told her that Skye was a free spirit who didn't like being told what to do. She was also the single mom of a four-year-old toddler nicknamed Toni the Biter.

"Where's Toni?" Pam asked.

"Angel is watching her," Skye replied.

Pam still couldn't get used to referring to your mom by her first name, but then the Wright family was not your run-of-the-mill sort.

"You can stop looking at me as if I'm going to demolish something," Skye drawled. "I can behave for short periods of time."

Mary Delaney, the part-time assistant that Pam would normally have used, had called very early to say she had food poisoning and couldn't even leave the bathroom let alone her home. Pam had made a few phone calls, but no one else was available on such short notice.

"Thanks. It's nice of you to volunteer to help me out like this," Pam told Skye.

"Tell her how nice I am, Algee." Skye bumped her hip against his.

"She's hell on wheels, but I think she'll be okay for today," Algee replied.

"Some friend you are," Skye muttered. "So why are we dissing men?"

"It's all about this book." Algee held it up for her.

"Hey, I've heard about that. How to hook a guy, huh? What are they? Dumb fish? Smart sharks?" She thumbed through the pages. "Hey, listen to this. It says here that men quickly categorize women as lifetime mate potential or just good-for-now girls."

Was that how Michael had viewed her? Pam thought. As a good-for-now girl? Good for a one-night stand but nothing more? And since he was now back in town, why not kiss her again to try and get her back in bed one more time?

Michael had said he'd heard of the book. Did that mean he'd read it? Agreed with what was in it?

He didn't even have to be present to mess up her thoughts.

As if reading her mind, Algee said, "Yo, did you know that Mabel put you in her blog today? Said that you and Michael were rolling around in the garden over at the Granite Inn in the middle of the night."

Pam almost said that it hadn't been the middle of the night, before stopping herself from inadvertently revealing that Mabel's story was true. "What are you doing reading that stuff?"

Algee shrugged. "As a temporary member of the town council, it's my duty to keep on top of local news."

"Now you sound like Walt," Pam noted.

Algee's expression was an outraged/insulted combo platter. "Hey, if you're gonna insult me, I'm outta here."

Skye just rolled her eyes. "Men are *sooo* sensitive."

"Look, we only have a limited time to set everything up at the First Baptist Church, so we need to get moving," Pam said.

At the church, Skye was surprisingly good at following directions and fastening the fuchsia tulle pew bows along the aisle.

"Tell me again what fuchsia is?" Algee asked as he easily hefted a large floral display and set it behind the altar.

"It's a flower and a shade of pink," Pam replied as she eyed the area to make sure it matched her plans.

Algee shook his head. "Never heard of it."

"We need another box of pew bows," Pam told Jessica, who had met them at the church. "They're in Algee's van. I've got to speak to the groom about some special arrangements."

"The homing pigeons," Jessica told Algee and Skye on her way out.

Algee blinked. "The what?"

"Homing pigeons." Pam shoved her hair out of her gritty eyes. She hadn't gotten enough sleep last night and was guzzling Diet Coke like an addict to get the caffeine fix. She'd used up all the Red Bull energy drinks in town. Cleaned the place out. "Instead of a dozen doves, Brittany's fiancé Clay wants to release his pet homing pigeons as the couple walks out of the church. They'll circle overhead—"

"And shit on the crowd below," Skye noted.

"And head home," Pam calmly continued. "Don't give me that look. It's not my wedding, it's theirs, and my job as the floral designer is to help them fulfill their idea of a dream wedding. Clay and Brittany are a young couple very much in love." And not very smart, but who was she to judge?

"So now you're bird wrangler as well as wedding floral designer." Skye applauded her. "I'm impressed."

"Clay takes care of the birds. Well, his dad does. I just figure it into the overall event."

Jessica came rushing in with the box of bows and a frantic look on her face. "I just heard the birds are gone!"

"What?"

"Clay can't find his birds."

The next half hour was frenzied: Pam had to keep focused on making sure that the bouquets didn't get lost, that the flower girl didn't eat the rose petals lining the aisle, and that Clay didn't leave to go find his pet pigeons.

The guests were arriving as Skye and Jessica slipped out the back, having put the last flower in place seconds before.

Pam, dressed in dark pants and a Bloomers T-shirt, was pleased to see everything coming together as she'd planned. Except for the birds.

"I found 'em sitting outside on the railing," Clay's dad burst through the church's front door to announce.

"Good luck," Pam said as she quickly departed.

She had to race back to the van to get the centerpieces for the reception, which was being held in the church basement.

The tables and chairs were already set up as she and her helpers put the arrangements in place. Pink chiffon had been draped over the tablecloths to pick up the color of the centerpieces of tightly packed squares of pink roses. Tall white glass vases filled with white lilies decorated the reception tables.

The caterer brought in the wedding cake, which Pam helped highlight with an eye-catching circle of tiny shocking pink roses.

One wedding down, four to go.

Next up at noon was Leah's the-bouquet-makes-my-nose-look-big wedding. Leah was a paralegal from Pittsburgh who'd brought her fiancé to her hometown for a small stylish wedding with an Asian theme. Since there were only forty people attending the reception, redoing some elements wasn't as difficult as it would have been for a larger event. Pam tweaked the shape of the nosegay bouquet, adding a few more oriental lilies and a bit more Ming fern.

The wedding took place at the All Saints Episcopal Church, with its beautifully elegant steeple rising up toward the intensely blue sky. The reception was right across the street, on the manicured grounds of the public library. The pond with its koi fish provided the backdrop for the tented reception area, where Pam had done simple yet elegant centerpieces of bold orange lilies and Ming fern in ceramic Chinese bowls provided by the bride.

The day ended with Chloe the perfectionist micromanager's wedding. Her fiancé, Glen, had fallen off the couch last night while having a nightmare about spiders. He'd ended up in the emergency room after landing on and smashing a glass coffee table to get away from those dream-induced arachnids. And he hadn't even had a single drink.

It was a good thing Glen wasn't engaged to Joy, because her mother would have knocked him senseless with five-inch stilettos for ruining her baby girl's big day with a face that looked as if he'd gone a few rounds with Mike Tyson.

Chloe's mother was just glad Glen showed up at all; Chloe herself was relieved he wasn't badly injured and believed the guy when he kept saying he looked worse than he felt.

Pam had the opposite problem. She felt worse than she looked. And she didn't look all that hot after twelve hours on the job.

At least the flowers looked great, as did Chloe's fragrant all-white bouquet of stephanotis and roses adorned with ivory satin ribbon. The wedding and reception were held at the Serenity Falls Country Club, where Chloe had chosen to make a statement with the violet-and-blue centerpieces that matched her bridesmaids' nosegays of blue delphinium and hydrangea and purple lisianthus.

There were plenty of jokes that the colors should have been black and blue, given Glen's appearance.

Pam was just preparing to leave when she ran into Michael, who came strolling out of one of the other private rooms at the country club.

She was vaguely aware that he looked great in gray linen trousers and a crisp white shirt, but was too tired to really get excited about it. She didn't even protest when he gently turned her around and began giving her a backrub to die for.

"You're looking a little tense," was his understatement of the year.

"Why are you being nice to me?" she muttered suspiciously even as she tilted her head to give him better access.

"Because I like you. I've never stopped liking you." He stopped the massage for a moment, as if surprised by his own words.

Being busy all day had kept her from thinking about the incident with Michael in her workroom yesterday afternoon, when she'd twined her legs around his hips like two yards of wired pink taffeta ribbon wrapped around a bridal bouquet.

But now that his hands were on her body again, those earlier rushes of chemistry came streaking back. But so did an unfamiliar warmth in her heart—because he wasn't trying to seduce her with his touch, but rather to heal her, and she could feel the difference.

"There." He gently kissed the back of her head. Such a gentle touch compared to the wild intensity of their embrace yesterday. "Go home and get some sleep."

She did, thanks to his healing massage, only to wake up several hours later to the sound of someone banging on her front door. Rosebud was barking, doing her rotweiller guard dog impersonation.

Peering out her bedroom window on the second floor, Pam discovered Louise Lewin on her front steps yelling, "It's all your fault!"

At the sound of Louise's screeching voice, Rosebud dove beneath Pam's bed. Pam wished she could follow her pooch.

"It's your fault that she's run away!" Louise continued when Pam reluctantly went down and opened the front door.

"Who has?"

"My baby girl! She's disappeared!"

"Did you call the police?"

"They don't care."

Pam grabbed her cell phone from the foyer table and dialed 911. "This is Pam Greenley. Did you know that Joy Lewin is missing?"

"So's her mom."

"No, her mom is here. At my house. Banging on my door."

"Hold on." The dispatcher was back in a second. "The sheriff wants to know what kind of shoes she's wearing."

"You tell him it's his job to protect and defend no matter what footwear she's got on," Pam growled.

Sheriff Norton showed up a few minutes later, lights flashing but siren turned off on his police car.

"It's all her fault!" Louise sobbed against the sheriff's broad chest while pointing an acrylic-nailed finger at Pam. "She didn't take my baby girl's floral concerns seriously."

"She kept vacillating between the different kinds of roses," Pam explained to the bemused sheriff.

"The pressure was just too much for my Joy to handle!" Louise sniffed.

"Did you call her fiancé, Jay, and see if he's heard from her?" the sheriff asked Louise.

The distraught woman nodded. "I left tons of messages on his cell phone voice mail but got no answer."

"Maybe the two of them are together. Did you consider that?"

"On the night before their wedding?" Louise was outraged by the sheriff's question. "What are you suggesting? That they're off somewhere having s-e-x?" She spelled out the word. "My baby girl is a virgin!"

"Maybe she's out with her friends, at some kind of bachelorette party," said Pam.

"Never! She'd never associate with male strippers!"

"Calm down now." The sheriff tried to listen to news coming over his shoulder radio. "What? Where are they? Okay, thanks.

"We found your daughter," he told Louise.

"Thank heavens! Where was she?"

"Uh . . . with her fiancé."

"I'm going to kill him!" Louise leaned down to remove her shoe and wave it in the air, but the fuzzy slipper lacked any real intimidation power. "They couldn't wait twenty-four hours?"

Pam and the sheriff just stood back and let her rant.

"Weddings don't always bring out the best in people," Pam had to admit.

CHAPTER SIX

Another night with little sleep. Pam kept having nightmares featuring Louise as a giant mutant spider stalking her while wearing eight shoes—all of them sharp Marc Jacob stilettos.

Pam had to turn on the TV after that and watch infomercials, since nothing else was on at four A.M. She'd almost ordered a food dehydrator with two sets of free knives before coming to her senses and heading downstairs for some coffee.

Three weddings down, two to go. Including Joy's elaborate fairy-tale extravaganza today. Unless she'd eloped in the middle of the night.

No such luck. Diva Bridezilla Joy called Pam at five in the morning. "Are you sure that the flowers match the bridesmaids' dresses?" Joy demanded. "I have four of them, you know. Bridesmaids. And two hundred and fifty guests. Everyone who's anyone will be there."

"Right. And yes, I am sure the flowers match the dresses. We compared them to the sample dress."

"Which one?"

"The most recent."

"Because I changed the bridesmaids' colors."

"Yes, I know."

"Several times."

"Yes, I know."

"The first red was too yellowy and the second was too glaring. The third was just right."

"You and Goldilocks," Pam muttered.

"Huh?"

"Never mind. You should get some sleep."

"My mom told me she was over there earlier."

"Yes."

"She wasn't real happy about the fact that Jay and I were together."

"I gathered that."

"She's old-fashioned that way."

"Uh-huh." Pam's eyelids started to droop . . . then to close.

"Hey, are you listening to me?"

Pam jerked awake at the nails-on-chalkboard sound of Joy's high-pitched, demanding voice.

"You've got a path of red rose petals along the aisle in the church, right?" Joy continued. "The latest red, not the yellowy one."

Even Chloe the perfectionist micromanager hadn't been this bad. "Everything is under control," Pam assured Joy. "There's nothing to worry about."

"My mother believes that saying brings bad luck."

"Then I'll knock on wood, how's that?" Pam rapped her

knuckles on her nineteenth-century pine dining table and ended up ripping a nail in the process.

"I'm wearing a tiara, you know."

"Yes, I know." Pam waved her bleeding finger in the air, which made Rosie jump up and down, ready for playtime. "The strand of Swarovski crystals in your bouquet will add the perfect touch of sparkle to go with your tiara."

"I've been dreaming about my wedding since I was five. I want to look like a princess."

And I want some more sleep, Pam thought.

The bottom line was that Joy had more chance of her royal princess dream coming true than Pam did of grabbing a few more Z's.

After talking to Joy for another twenty minutes, there was only enough time for Pam to grab a quick shower and let Rosebud out into the backyard for a quick potty break.

Breakfast was an energy bar stuffed in her purse for later. A quick glance in the gilded antique mirror by the front door alerted Pam to the fact that she had her yellow Bloomers polo shirt on inside out. Muttering under her breath, she rectified the fashion faux pas before verifying that her khaki pants weren't suffering from the same mistake.

Outside, Pam was stopped on her way to her red PT Cruiser by Mrs. Selznick, who was walking her anxiety-ridden, afraid-of-his-own-shadow Chihuahua named Terminator.

"I should warn you that I may be giving you a run for your money," Mrs. Selznick told her.

Pam's fuzzy, buzzing brain couldn't make sense of her words. "What do you mean? Are you going to stop taking Rosebud out for her walks with you and Terminator?" She panicked at the possibility.

"Of course I'll still take Rosie. I meant that I've signed up to take a home course in what you do."

"What I do?" *Like having sizzling sex with my high school boyfriend? And then tackling him in a bed of manure? Or do you mean the way I wrapped myself around him like a lap dancer at work?*

"Wedding floral design," Mrs. Selznick explained. "I registered for it on the Internet."

Mrs. S, as everyone who knew her called her, loved taking classes. She'd already taken tons of them, from clog dancing to scrapbooking.

"So you'd better watch out," Mrs. S cheerfully informed her.

"I'll do that." No sooner had Pam said the words than she stumbled over her own two feet.

"I told you to watch out." Mrs. S shook her head. "Young people these days, they just don't listen."

Pam was tired of listening. She just wanted this weekend to be over. The sooner, the better.

•   •   •

Serenity Falls' Wedding of the Century, as diva bride Joy liked to bill it, was taking place at St. Mary's, with the reception being held afterward beneath a huge white tent set up on the oak tree–studded grounds.

Pam had gotten there early because she knew this would be a difficult event. She was right.

She'd barely gotten out of the Bloomers van when she was accosted by Louise, who was wearing a very expensive pair of Manolo Blahnik shoes that she'd been bragging about for months.

"The bridal bouquet is missing!" the mother of the bride dramatically declared.

"I have it right here," Pam reassured her.

Louise glared. "Why didn't you say so?"

"I told Joy I'd bring it with me—"

"Never mind. We've got another crisis. Terry has broken out in hives. She's one of the bridesmaids."

"Have you contacted a doctor?"

"It's your fault."

Pam was getting tired of hearing that accusation from Louise. "How do you figure that?"

"She's allergic to something in her bridesmaid's bouquet."

"I asked about any allergies months ago, when we first started planning the floral arrangements!"

"She's my husband's cousin-in-law's daughter. How am I supposed to know her allergies?" Louise retorted. "Now I can't understand a word she's saying because her face is swollen. Maybe you can decipher her gibberish."

"I ad amegency woot canal," Terry muttered thickly. "Flowas made swaying woose."

"Swaying? Oh, swelling. You had an emergency root canal and your face was already swollen, but your reaction to the flowers made the swelling worse. I get it. Do you know what you're allergic to in the bouquet?"

"Ucawupus."

Okay, that one was harder to translate, but Pam figured it out after a moment or two. "Eucalyptus. Right. Okay, I'll remove that from all the bridesmaids' bouquets. Meanwhile, you check with your doctor to see if you can take some Benadryl or something to help your allergic reaction."

Pam hurriedly gathered up all the bridesmaids' bouquets and set to work on them, removing the offending greenery.

"Are you Pam Greenley?" someone asked.

"Yeah," she muttered, her focus still on the final bouquet she was adjusting.

"Hi, I'm Roxie Smith." A woman's hand was thrust into Pam's line of vision. "I tried calling your cell but only got your voice mail."

Because Pam had forgotten to recharge her phone last night, distracted as she'd been by Louise's middle-of-the-night visit. The 911 call Pam had made at that time had been the battery's last gasp.

"Your brother told me I could find you here," Roxie cheerfully continued. "I'm a photographer with *Bridal Magazine*. We'd like to get a few shots of you in action today."

Pam froze. "Today?"

"Yes. Is there a problem with that?"

Yes. Big-time problem. As in I'm not ready for my close-up, Ms. DeMille.

What was it with this magazine anyway? First the reporter showed up without advance warning and now the photographer, who had at least tried to call first but not enough ahead of time.

Really, people, was twenty-four hours' notice too much to ask for? Pam really didn't think so. Inside she was working up a good head of steam that sputtered as she muttered, "Well, I . . . I don't know if the bride would approve."

"If she doesn't, we won't proceed. Why don't you check with her?"

"*Bridal Magazine!*" Joy shrieked a few minutes later. "Everyone across the entire country will see my wedding and me in my tiara! Of course it's okay with me. Are you crazy?"

Pam returned to give the news to Roxie, who was sitting on a bench in front of the church reading a book. Not just any book. *How to Hook Your Guy.*

Noticing her interest, Roxie said, "Everyone in the office is talking about this book. They either love it or hate it."

"I can understand why."

"You've read it?"

Pam shrugged. "Part of it."

"I finished it a week ago. Gave me the courage to dump my boyfriend. I was just rereading a bit." Roxie closed the book and returned it to her large tote. "So what did the bride say?"

"I don't think she's read the book."

"I meant about the photography shoot."

"Right." Pam felt like an idiot. "She was fine with it." In fact, Joy had almost tripped over herself to sign the release form that Pam returned to the photographer.

"I'm here to focus on your work," Roxie reminded Pam.

"My designs, not me, right?" Pam had seen a brief glimpse of herself in one of the many mirrors in the large anteroom where Joy was holding court. It hadn't been a pretty picture. Pam's dark hair was turning frizzy in the June humidity. Her face was already flushed and sweaty. The stress that had caused her insomnia last night had created a zit on her chin today. No, definitely not a pretty picture.

"We want to include you at work."

"How about some shots of me at my shop tomorrow?" Pam suggested. By then she could slather on enough foundation to hide a zit the size of Mount Everest.

Roxie shook her head. "Sorry, I'm only in town for today."

"She'll be ready in a sec," Jessica declared, showing up out of no place to take Pam by the arm, leading her back inside the church to the ladies' room. "My mom's an Avon lady so I've got, like, lots of stuff to make you look good," Jessica reassured her, already applying a coating of shimmery powder to Pam's face.

Pam grabbed her arm. "Don't make me look weird."

Jessica rolled her eyes. "You should learn to, like, trust me. I mean, I didn't put anything in my blog about you and that hottie Michael making out in the back room."

Pam groaned. "Don't remind me."

"Stop talking." Jessica waved a lipstick at her. She was a magician, pulling cosmetics from her huge bag like rabbits out of a black hat. "I'm an artist at work here and I need to concentrate."

Pam was afraid that no amount of concentration could make her look good for this photo shoot, or make her truly forget about Michael.

•   •   •

"Why are you calling me on a Sunday?" Michael asked his editor and former college roommate Tommy Ito. "Don't those New York publishers give you any time off?"

"I've got good news to share. Since your book hit the bestsellers lists, it's going back for a second printing."

"You're kidding, right?"

"No, I'm totally serious. I told you it would be big." Michael and Tommy had often talked about women, and what the female sex wanted from men. Michael had logically expressed his views, not caring if they were politically correct. His long-time buddy just so happened to think that it would make a great book. So Tommy had convinced Michael to write his views down, just as he'd voiced them.

How to Hook Your Guy was the result. Michael had only broken the news that he'd written a book to his mom about an hour ago. Surprisingly, she hadn't sounded very surprised.

"You did get that writing award," she'd reminded him.

"That was in the third grade, Mom."

Tommy's voice brought him back to the present. "So when are you going to give me the next installment?"

Michael frowned. "What next installment?"

"I don't know. Think of something. Maybe *How to Keep Your Guy Hooked*. Get me some preliminary pages ASAP. Gotta go."

Michael had taken the call on the grounds of the Granite Inn, not realizing he wasn't alone until he looked down to find a dog at his feet. Not just any dog, but a dachshund that looked familiar to him. A giant Tootsie Roll with legs.

"Rosie! Come back here!"

Michael didn't recognize the woman's voice frantically calling for the dog, but he knew it didn't belong to Pam.

"Rosie!"

The dog just looked up at Michael with big brown eyes and then plopped over and showed him her belly, indicating he should rub it.

That was when it hit him. He'd been conning himself. Trying to make himself believe what he'd written in his book.

But Pam hadn't followed any of his suggestions to hook him.

Yet that's exactly what she'd done. Hooked him good. Embedded herself deep in his heart with lightning speed.

It wasn't logical, but it was true.

Shouldn't he have been looking into Pam's eyes when he got this epiphany? Not staring down at her dog.

What was wrong with him? He bent down to pet the animal, hoping that simple gesture would help get his tangled thoughts in order.

"There you are!" An older woman approached. "You naughty thing, you."

Was she talking to him, or the dog?

"Running out like that."

The accusation could apply to him as well as the dog. He'd run out on Pam a month ago.

But he'd come back. The wedding was just an excuse. He was good at making those. He'd really come back because of Pam. He was realizing that now. Or maybe he was just willing to finally admit it now.

"Shame on you," the woman continued.

Right.

"You should know better," she added.

Absolutely.

"Now tell this nice man you're sorry."

Huh?

Rosie the dog had her eyes closed in ecstasy as he absently continued petting her tummy.

"I'm so sorry," the older woman apologized. "Rosie got away from me when Terminator and I went for a walk." She held a shivering Chihuahua in her arms. "She seems to like you."

"Yeah," he said gruffly.

"You're Michael Denton, aren't you? I'm Mrs. Selznick. You lived a few blocks away from me when you were growing up."

Michael nodded absently, his mind still consumed with the giant *aha* moment he'd just experienced regarding his feelings for Pam.

He gave the terrified Terminator a look of empathy. He could definitely relate. Getting swept off your feet by a female was a very, *very* scary thing.

•   •   •

"Tell me that wasn't thunder," Pam ordered Jessica.

"You want me to lie?"

A flash filled the darkening sky and a sudden burst of wind

flapped the edges of the tent where the reception was about to be held. At least they'd gotten the tent with side walls to keep out bad weather.

"It's not the rain, but the hail you have to worry about," Mabel said, magically appearing at their side.

"What are you doing here?" Pam demanded, still peeved that Mabel had leaked her name to Michael.

"I'm covering this event for the *Serenity News* and my blog. Which reminds me, do you have any comment regarding the story that you and Michael were rolling around in Mrs. Zoranski's garden the other night?"

"Since when is that something the newspaper would cover?" Pam demanded.

"It's for my blog."

Pam rolled her eyes. "I don't believe this."

"I don't either. This wedding has been full of news. First the bridesmaid almost dies—"

"She didn't almost die," Pam corrected her. "She just had an allergic reaction."

"To being beaten up by the bride's mother. That's why the poor girl's face was so swollen. Because Louise beat her up. With those expensive shoes of hers."

"That's not true. She had an emergency root canal."

"Is that what made Louise so crabby?"

"The bridesmaid had the root canal." *Louise was born crabby*, Pam silently continued. Or so she imagined.

"And then there was a Peeping Tomasina taking photos. Milt from Milt's Photography was hired to take photos and he wasn't happy about having competition."

"That was the photographer from *Bridal Magazine*," Jessica inserted before Pam could stop her.

"So they heard about the wedding of the century and came to take photos for their magazine?" Mabel hurriedly scribbled in her lime green Rock the Vote notebook. "What caught their attention? Was it the tiara? Or the carriage that took the bride and groom away from the church and is supposed to bring them back again? I bet it was the carriage, right? Those white horses were a nice touch."

"It wasn't the carriage," Jessica said. "It was Pam's glass slipper centerpiece with red roses."

Mabel frowned. "What are you talking about?"

"The magazine photographer was here to cover Pam, not Joy."

Mabel frantically scribbled some more. "So, Pam, does this mean that you and Michael are getting married?"

"No, it means the magazine is doing a story about my floral designs, not my private life."

Mabel raised an elaborately penciled eyebrow. "Maybe they don't know how exciting your private life has been lately. You accuse Michael of being gay, when the night before you'd been cavorting with him on the grounds of the Granite Inn. Which reminds me, why pick that location? I mean, come on, get a room. He has a room there, in fact. So why not take it inside, instead of ruining Mrs. Zoranski's prized iris?"

"I'm not here to gossip, but to work," Pam told Mabel. "We've still got arrangements to set up, so you'll have to leave now. This area isn't open to the public yet."

Mabel sniffed but did depart, perhaps because Joy's father-in-law showed up and glared at her.

Pam had to turn away. She still hadn't recovered from seeing the guy naked through the window at the Granite Inn the other night. And she hadn't recovered from kissing Michael. She was beginning to wonder if she ever would . . .

CHAPTER SEVEN

Pam congratulated herself on surviving Joy's wedding and the Silly String extravaganza that kicked off the actual reception. No hail. Lots of rain. Her job there was done.

Four weddings down, one to go.

Pam and Jessica arrived at the Serenity Falls Country Club and dodged the few remaining raindrops as they unloaded and headed inside. After finishing setting up the area where the ceremony was to take place, they next focused on the ballroom, where the reception was to be held.

Pam was focused on visualizing the final floral impression when she was suddenly stopped in her tracks by Annie Weiss' stranglehold on her arm. "What size are you?" Annie frantically demanded.

Pam stumbled forward as the wheeled cart filled with the centerpieces for the ballroom tables smacked right into her butt.

"Sorry about that." Jessica sent her an apologetic look from close behind her. "I wasn't, like, expecting you to stop."

"I wasn't expecting it either." Pam rubbed her sore derriere.

"What size are you?" Annie repeated, even more hysterically this time.

"Calm down," Pam said, remembering that the last time Annie had gotten upset, her shop had gotten trashed and the police had been called in. "I have no idea what you're talking about."

"Never mind." Annie started hauling Pam after her, yanking her down the hallway away from the ballroom area. "The dress will fit. We'll make it fit."

"What dress?"

"My maid of honor's dress. She's got food poisoning and is a no-show. So you're taking her place."

"Oh no." Pam emphatically shook her head. "Not me."

"Yes, you." Annie continued tugging her down the hallway.

"I'm just the floral designer. There must be someone else who can do it."

"Do you think I'd ask you if there was anyone else?" Annie opened a door and shoved Pam inside. "Here she is," she told the assembled group of older women who descended on Pam en masse and started removing her clothes.

"Hey!" Pam batted their age-spotted hands away. "Stop that!"

"Relax," Annie said. "These are my grandmas and great-aunts. They'll take care of you. Get you into the dress."

"No, wait. I—" Pam unsuccessfully tried to hang on to her khaki pants, but they were yanked down around her ankles. A bunch of bullies had done the same thing to her in the second grade. But these weren't bullies, these were kind-faced, white-haired old ladies armed with straight pins.

"Stand still." One of them rapped Pam's knuckles. "We don't have time for any nonsense."

"Hey," Pam protested. "No hitting! Any more hitting and I am so out of here," she warned the group with a narrowed glare.

"You have such bags under your eyes," another said. Since the speaker wore enough makeup to cover all the faces on Mount Rushmore, Pam wasn't too insulted. Clearly this woman was no beauty expert with *In Style* magazine. "You must not be getting much sleep."

"That's because she's been too busy rolling around in the garden with that Denton boy. I read all about it in Mabel's blog."

"What's a blog?" another asked, since Pam was too stunned to say a word.

"You really do have to get hooked up to the Internet, Betsy. Get connected."

"I don't want to get connected. I went out with that gigolo Ernie Marciano just last week and he was trying to connect his hands with my breasts. The man was an octopus, I tell you. Stand still," Betsy added for Pam's benefit.

"This is not in my contract," Pam muttered.

"Yeah, yeah." They yanked a dress over her head. It was green. Pam knew because she'd been sent a sample of the maid of honor's dress to help her come up with the floral designs. She also remembered that it was one of the few shades of green that looked absolutely stinking barf-awful on her.

Apparently the gang of grannies noticed this, too.

"Betsy, we need makeup over here quick!"

Pam knew she should have gotten more sleep last night, instead of yearning for a food dehydrator from the TV infomercial. Maybe if she'd had more rest, she'd be able to fight back the unruly Medicare-eligible mob. Maybe not, but she liked to think so. Although it was tough battling a bunch of old ladies.

Five minutes later, Pam stared at the mirror in horror. "No more hairspray," she growled at Betsy, who wisely stepped away.

The brilliant green, glittery eye shadow and layers of mascara made Pam look like a Las Vegas hooker. And not a very high-priced one. She reached for a Kleenex.

"What are you doing?" Betsy demanded.

"Wiping some of this off."

"No time!" They grabbed her and whisked her off. "You're up." With a little shove, they stuck a bouquet in her hands and sent her stumbling down the aisle.

The only good thing about the dress from hell was that it was long enough to hide the fact that Pam was still wearing her Nike footwear.

One of the many bad things was the fact that the dress had clearly been designed for someone with smaller breasts than Pam's. The amount of cleavage she was showing went right along with that Vegas hooker motif that she had going with her excessive makeup.

If Pam stood up too straight, her breasts almost tumbled out of the sweetheart bodice. If she bent over, her butt looked huge beneath the bow-festooned back.

Feeling everyone's eyes on her, Pam tried to act as if she were a confident model wearing something utterly ravishing on some designer's runway in Milan. A big stretch for her, but worth a try. All the while she was thinking that the maid of honor whose place she was taking had probably faked an illness just to get out of wearing this ridiculous outfit.

And then she saw him. Michael. Standing at the end of the aisle. Looking at her.

Not with passionate hunger in those gray eyes of his. No, sirree. He was staring at her with stunned disbelief.

Pam supposed she couldn't blame him. She'd looked at herself in the mirror the same way a few moments ago. Half the audience was probably watching her with similar horrified expressions.

She wanted to stop the ceremony right then and there to tell the assembled group that this wasn't her idea and that yes, she did know this puke green color made her look anemic. And to tell them all that she'd always suspected that Annie had somehow manipulated the ballot count back in high school so that she'd won that election. Stolen it. By a mere ten votes.

But it was too late now. All Pam could do was make the best of a sticky situation and pray that Jessica had finished setting up the centerpieces in the ballroom.

Pam winced when a pin from the dress's hem jabbed her ankle as she turned to go into what she assumed was her final position. She'd certainly been to enough weddings to know the drill.

Now she was staring directly at Michael. He, of course, looked James Bond handsome in a classic black tuxedo with a white formal shirt. No trendy pink ruffled shirts or garish cummerbunds. His cousin Pete, the groom, was looking a little green around the gills but soon perked up when Annie came down the aisle, looking all calm and gorgeous. And tall.

Pam wanted to kick her right then and there, but restrained herself.

Clearly, being exposed to so many Bridezillas over the past few days had brought out Pam's inner warrior. Not enough to fight her way out of this situation, however.

Annie had probably known Pam wouldn't be able to battle a

bunch of old ladies. That had really been a cheap shot, but an effective one.

Thankfully the ceremony was a relatively short one.

Pam's thoughts kept wandering to her centerpiece arrangements for the ballroom tables, hoping they looked good. The one silver lining was that Roxie, the photographer from *Bridal Magazine*, wasn't here to capture Pam in this garish getup.

Michael was beside her during the processional afterward.

"Where do you think you're going?" He grabbed hold of her arm as she tried to take off.

Pam was getting tired of people grabbing her. First Louise this morning, then Annie, then the grannies, now Michael. Something about her expression must have warned him that she was about to blow.

So what did the man do? Release her and set her free? No, he leaned down and had the nerve to say, "Are you okay? You look funny."

"Really?" She propped one hand on her hip. "You don't like the Vegas hooker thing I have going on here?"

He raised a dark eyebrow. "Was that the look you were aiming for?"

"I wasn't supposed to be here at all, as you damn well know! Annie hauled me in at the last minute because her maid of honor got sick. It was probably this dress that did it to her. It's enough to make anyone ill."

Pam didn't even realize that her bosom was heaving until she saw the glazed look in Michael's eyes. He was staring at her chest as if mesmerized. "They're breasts," she growled at him. "Get over it."

"We've got to go pose for the photographer." This time he looked her in the eyes.

"Not in a million years. There isn't enough money in all of Serenity Falls for me to agree to memorialize this fashion atrocity on film."

"Actually it's digital . . . and you can't refuse. You don't want to ruin Annie's wedding day, do you?"

"No, I don't want to ruin her day. I just want to beat her up."

Michael brushed his fingers over Pam's arm in a move that was meant to be soothing. Or maybe he was trying to turn her on. If so, he was succeeding. "What can I do to make you feel better?"

Take me to bed and do that swirly thing you do with your tongue . . .

"There you two are," the groom interrupted them. "Hurry up, they're taking pictures now."

"Come on," Michael urged her.

"You weren't even planning on coming to this wedding," she reminded him. "He's your cousin and you weren't even coming."

"We were never all that close," Michael said even as he maneuvered her outside to the gathering waiting for them.

"One picture," Pam growled. "Then I'm out of this dress."

Michael grinned. "If you want to take the rest of the shots in the nude, that's fine by me."

"Pervert."

"Prude."

"Smile," the photographer said.

In the end, Pam had to sit through the reception and various champagne toasts. By her second glass, the world seemed a happier place. By her fourth glass, she was out on the dance floor, barefoot and boogying to "It's Raining Men."

She didn't lack for male dance partners. Apparently the Vegas stripper look went over well with the male half of the population.

Hours later, Michael found Pam curled up and asleep in a wing-back chair in one of the country club's few quiet alcoves.

"Come on, Cinderella." He gently tugged her to her feet. "The clock is about to strike midnight and your coach might turn into a pumpkin."

She swayed and blinked at him. "I shouldn't drive."

"I agree." He deftly guided her to his rental car. She was asleep in the passenger seat by the time he put the key in the ignition.

Half carrying her upstairs to her bed was torture for him. Not because she was heavy, but because she was temptation personified. Her breasts threatened to tumble out of her dress at any second.

She bounced up off the bed the moment he placed her on it and started stripping off the dress. "Bad dress," she kept muttering. "Bad, bad, bad . . . where's my bra?"

He gulped at the sight of her standing there wearing nothing but a confused frown and a silky pair of yellow bikini panties.

"Where are you going?" he croaked when she took a few weaving steps toward the door.

"Rosie needs to go out."

Right. The Tootsie Roll with legs. "I'll do it."

Michael returned a while later to find that Pam had crawled beneath the covers, leaving her backside exposed. Michael rearranged the covers, tucked her in, then sat on the bed a moment to get his bearings.

Staring down at her, he wondered what it was about this woman that got to him. She'd knocked him flat the first time he'd seen her, when she'd thrown that football at him in high school to get his attention.

She'd gotten his attention all right. And then some.

Now, ten years later, he was still fascinated. And she hadn't done anything to get his attention this time around. Well, she had had sex with him after the reunion. Why? And why did he care what her reasons were?

Because she was more than just a one-night stand. Which was why, when she sleepily reached out for his hand and whispered, "Stay," he did.

• • •

The first seductive nibble was on her ear. Then her nipple . . . her navel . . . her thigh. Her legs languidly opened for Michael, who courted her passion-drenched silken folds with erotic creativity. A tongue-touch here, a nibble there.

He built her pleasure from one plateau to another, increasing the tension and the need until she thought she'd die from the need for completion.

Her eyes flew open. A dream. It had all been a dream.

Wait a second. She blearily blinked at the male arm around her waist. That was real.

A quick glance over her shoulder confirmed that Michael was sleeping in her bed. But he was on top of her covers, a light throw over him.

She could tell by the pale light in the room that it was barely dawn.

Her mind returned to the erotic dream. Had it been a dream or a reenactment of what had happened in the middle of the night? Surely she hadn't consumed enough champagne to not know if he'd made love to her?

Carefully sliding out from beneath his embracing arm, she gingerly sat up. She definitely had a headache. The rest of her body ached, too, with unfulfilled desire.

Which meant that the darkly seductive moves he'd made on her were all in her head. Not real.

She stood, almost tripping on the barfy green maid of honor dress still pooled on the floor.

A shower. She needed a shower. And aspirin. She headed for the bathroom, stepping over a still-snoozing Rosebud.

Minutes later, she felt much better with hot water streaming over her head. Now she could start thinking coherently. If they hadn't had sex last night, then what was Michael doing in her bed?

And then memory returned. Her removing the awful dress. Him taking out her dog for a walk. Her asking him to stay.

The Laura Ashley shower curtain was carefully moved aside. "You okay?"

Pam stared at Michael, who was wearing a deliciously sexy rumpled look and a killer pair of black silk boxers. She didn't need to think twice. She simply acted.

Sliding her fingers into the elastic waistband, she tugged him into the shower with her.

He came willingly, eagerly, kissing her before she could have any regrets. Holding both her wrists in one hand, he raised her arms over her head so that he could caress her bare breasts with his other hand. He brushed his thumb over her nipples while seductively nibbling on her lower lip. His kisses trailed down her throat to her right breast, where he took her into his mouth, his teeth tenderly grazing her sensitive skin.

A wave of passion threatened to overcome her. She'd already been primed by that erotic dream and now the reality was enough to send her spiraling out of control. When his fingers slid lower to seek out her clitoris and fondle it, she almost screamed with pleasure. She went weak at the knees as he pressed her against the ceramic tile wall and continued his sensual moves.

"Now," she whispered, freeing her hands so she could reach for him. Somehow his boxers were gone and he was all male flesh, silky and hard in her hand. "I want you in me now."

"No condom," he growled.

"Bathroom drawer," she gasped.

With record speed, he whisked her out of the shower, and set her on the granite countertop. The steamy mirror showed their blurry reflections as Michael tore open a packet. Seconds later he stood before her, sheathed in the condom and positioned between her legs.

He kissed her with hungry passion, instantly reigniting her entire body. His hands moved down her back to grab her bottom as he pulled her closer to him. She guided him in and then held on for dear life as he thrust deep within her. Wrapping her ankles around his waist, she gloried in the intimate contact, the friction, the elation. In, out. In, out. Slow and sweet. Fast and hard. Her orgasm came with clenching bliss, her shout of satisfaction followed by his.

Ten minutes later she still felt boneless in his arms as he carried her back to bed, where they made love again before drifting off to sleep.

* * *

Pam bounced awake, smacking the alarm before realizing the noise came from the phone. It was Monday. Bloomers was closed. She always slept in on Monday. "Hello?"

"Did you know that Michael Denton is the guy?" Mabel said.

Yeah, Pam was starting to realize he really was the guy. The guy for her. She could hear him in the bathroom and couldn't wait for him to return to her side.

"He wrote the book," Mabel continued. "I Googled him and his name came up on a site listing pen names and real names. At first I thought it had to be some other Michael Denton. But I checked some more, and it's him, all right."

Yeah, it's him, Pam thought dreamily.

"He's the one," Mabel said.

Yeah, he is.

"The one who wrote *How to Hook Your Guy.*"

CHAPTER EIGHT

Pam fell out of bed, narrowly missing Rosebud, who yelped and dove under the bed.

"Hey, are you okay?" Michael asked from the threshold to the bathroom. He rushed to her side.

The man who'd given her multiple orgasms last night.

The man who'd written the book.

The book that said give him space.

The book that declared men wanted one more inch in their pants.

The book that advised women never to admit to having more than ten lovers. Okay, not a problem for her, but still . . .

Michael wrote the book. The wall-banger book. The banger book.

"Hello, hello?" Mabel shouted into the phone.

Pam hung up. She couldn't deal with the town gossip right now.

"Are you okay?" Michael repeated as he helped her to her feet.

She sat on the edge of the bed and pulled the sheet over her naked body. Suddenly, she felt chilled to the bone. "Is it true?"

"Is what true?"

"Did you do it?"

His grin was wicked. "We both did it. A number of times this morning."

"I'm not talking about sex. Well, I am . . . but not between the two of us."

"Huh?" He put his hand on her forehead. "Did you bump your head when you fell?"

She pulled away. "You. Did you write that book?"

"What book?"

"Don't play dumb with me. You know damn well what book. *How to Hook Your Guy*."

His hand fell to his side. "Where did you hear that?"

"From Mabel. Are you saying she's wrong?"

The guilty look on his face was answer enough.

"So what was this?" She waved her hand at the bed. "Research for a sequel?"

"No!"

"What, then? I can't believe you're the idiot who wrote that book."

Clearly stung by her disdain, he said, "It's on the bestseller lists."

"I don't care if it sells more copies than *The Da Vinci Code*, it's still an insult to women."

"It was never intended that way."

"If you're so proud of writing it, why didn't you tell me you were the author?" she retorted.

"Because I knew you wouldn't take it well."

"You mean I wouldn't have sex with you if I knew you'd written that book." Pam was smart enough to realize the book was an excuse. All her earlier doubts about him had returned tenfold. What he saw in her. Why he'd left her. Those were huge unknowns. "And since you were only going to be in town for a few days, you didn't want to ruin your chances of getting some. Smart move."

"You've got it all wrong!"

The sound of their raised voices propelled Rosebud into guard-dog mode. The little dachshund shot out from beneath the bed ruffle as if from a cannon. She growled at Michael.

Pam yanked on a tank top and shorts from the dresser beside her bed. "You've already walked out on me twice," Pam told Michael. "There won't be a third time." Bending down, she scooped Rosebud into her arms, the same arms that had wrapped around him only a few hours before. "I'm taking Rosebud for a walk. I want you gone by the time I get back."

"Pam, you've got to listen to me . . ."

But she was already gone.

●　　●　　●

Michael got it. He understood that Pam had left him before he could leave her yet again. He got that. But he didn't know how to make things right.

So he called in reinforcements. Maguire's was closed on Mondays, so Adele had offered the pub as a meeting place.

"I've asked you here because I need your help."

Adele smiled at him reassuringly. "Whatever I can do to help, you know I'll do."

"I don't even know why I'm here. Not that I'm complaining," Mabel quickly added.

"I screwed up," Michael admitted. "Big-time."

"You're a man. You can't help screwing up," Mabel said. "Trust me. I've been married three times. Men screw up all the time. No news there."

Maybe calling in Mabel hadn't been one of his better ideas, but he was desperate here. "I hurt Pam and I need to do something to make it up to her."

"Did you try talking to her?" Adele asked.

"She won't listen to me," Michael replied.

"Why not?"

"Use the dog," Mabel said. "That always gets to a woman, when a man is kind to her pet."

"Have you tried Googling romantic apologies?" Adele asked.

Michael blinked at her.

Adele shrugged. "What? You don't think I'm connected to the Internet? Half the people in this town are blogging."

"Yeah, I noticed that."

"Didn't they teach you anything in that big city of yours?" Mabel said.

Michael rubbed his forehead wearily. "Apparently not."

"Let's get back to why she's angry with you," Adele said before pouring him another cup of coffee. "How exactly did you screw up?"

"I didn't tell her that I wrote *How to Hook Your Guy*. She only found out this morning—"

"Oops. I told her," Mabel confessed.

"So this is all *your* fault." Adele's concern for Michael turned into aggravation with the town gossip.

"Hey, don't try to pin the blame on me," Mabel retorted. "He should have told her himself."

"She does have a point," Adele had to admit, returning her attention to Michael. "So how can we help you?"

He had no idea. What had he been thinking, asking these two older women to give him advice? Both women knew Pam, but were hardly her best friends or anything. He'd heard her closest friend, Julia the librarian, had left town with Luke Maguire, so he couldn't ask for her advice. "Maybe I should try calling her friend Julia. Do you have a number where I could reach her?"

"I have Luke's cell number," Adele said. "But I don't think talking to Julia would help. She'd just kick your butt for hurting her best friend."

Mabel nodded her agreement. "She used to be quiet but now she's a kick-butt kind of librarian."

"Anyone else I should consult about Pam?" Michael asked.

Adele's expression turned thoughtful. "Well, her parents are out of town on that cruise. Her brother Harry is still here. But I'm not sure that discussing this with her family would be a wise move."

"Yeah," Michael knew he sounded discouraged. He didn't care. "Probably not."

"I asked Pam at Joy's wedding yesterday if you two were going to get married," Mabel stunned him by abruptly announcing.

His heart raced. "And she said?"

"You know, it occurs to me that she never actually denied it. So are you two getting hitched?"

Michael tugged at the tightening collar of his shirt. He couldn't breathe.

"You see?" Mabel's voiced faded in and out of his consciousness. "He's not denying it, either."

Michael saw spots in front of his eyes.

Suddenly his head was shoved down between his knees. "Do not faint!" Pam growled in his ear.

"What's going on here?" she demanded of the other two women.

"Oh, for heaven's sake," Mabel said impatiently. "Can't you see the poor guy is crazy in love with you?"

Pam started seeing black spots in front of her eyes.

Mabel pushed Pam onto the seat beside Michael and shoved her head onto her knees. She turned her head at the last minute. Bad move. Now she was facing Michael.

"I don't faint," Pam growled.

"Me neither," Michael growled back.

Still she remained where she was, her cheek against her knees, her eyes fixed on his, her voice uncertain. "You're not *really* crazy in love with me, are you?"

"Yeah . . . yeah, I am," he huskily admitted. "What about you? Any chance you're crazy in love with me, too?"

Here was the moment. The question. She'd been walking around Serenity Falls all morning searching for the right answer.

What were her feelings for Michael? Was it just sexual attraction? Nostalgia for her first love? Or was there more?

He'd just admitted he was crazy in love with her. In front of witnesses. And not just any witnesses. In front of Mabel, who'd spread the news from one end of Serenity Falls to the other.

Which meant he loved her. Maybe he was as mixed-up as she was. Maybe he hadn't seen this coming any more than she had. Maybe he'd run scared and that was why he'd left before.

Maybe it was time she just laid her feelings on the line. "Yeah." She cleared her throat and wiped away a tear. "Yeah, I am crazy in love with you."

A second later, Michael was on his feet and had her in his arms.

"I'm not sure it's wise to be kissing like that when you both almost fainted," Mabel said with obvious disapproval.

Pam ignored her and spoke to Michael, her hands cupping his

face. "You live in Chicago. I live here. You told me long-distance relationships don't work."

"He was young and dumb," Mabel stated. "Ouch! Why'd you hit me, Adele?"

"You be quiet now," Adele advised. "Michael is a problem solver—"

"He's a troubleshooter," Pam corrected her even as she spread a string of kisses across his face.

"Same thing," Adele said. "He'll come up with something."

"Feels like you're coming up with something right now," Pam wickedly whispered in Michael's ear as she rubbed against him.

"Excuse us, ladies," Michael said as he swept Pam out of Maguire's. "We've got a few details to work on in private."

Fifteen minutes later, Pam and Michael were naked on her bed, where he was rolling a condom on with her sultry assistance.

"I thought we were going to work on details," she murmured. "This doesn't feel like a detail to me." She held him in her hand. "This feels like something major."

"It is something major. Major Mike standing at attention, ready and reporting for duty."

"Mmmm. I can tell you're ready." She perched atop his thighs and grinned down at him. "I'm ready, too."

"You think so?"

"You don't?"

"I think I should check to be sure." He tugged her up to his chest and leaned her back against his upright knees. Then he parted her legs wide.

Her feet were braced on either side of his head. "What are you doing . . . Oh!" She gasped at the intense jolt of sizzling bliss that shot through her at the darkly erotic touch of his curled tongue.

He made a meal of her—devouring her, feeding her hunger, satisfying her while making her want more.

"Now I think you're ready." He breathed the words against her thigh before repositioning her so she could ride him.

She sank down onto his throbbing hard length. "Are you sure *you're* ready?" Her sultry smile belonged to a woman who knew she was loved.

"Oh, yeah." His wicked grin belonged to a man looking at the woman he loved. "Bring it on."

Heaven Can't Wait

PAMELA CLARE

"Do you, Lissy Charteris, take me, Will Fraser?" He looked down at her, his dark hair damp with sweat, a half-grin on his face, and nudged the thick, hard tip of his cock inside her.

Lissy could wait no longer. Her legs caught above his shoulders, she lifted her hips, reaching for fulfillment. "Yes! Yes! Oh, now! Yes!"

An amused gleam in his blue eyes, he withdrew, his thumb drawing lazy circles over her swollen, aching clitoris. "Uh-uh. You're supposed to say, 'I do.'"

She moaned in frustration, clutching fistfuls of linen tablecloth, her body about to combust. "I do! I do! God, I do, Will!"

"That's better." His gaze locked with hers, and his big hands seized her hips.

Then with one slow thrust he filled her.

"Oh! Oh, God, Will!" His name was the last coherent word she spoke, her voice unraveling into a long, throaty moan as he pushed himself in and out of her, thick and hard.

It felt so good. It felt better than good. Having him inside her was both bliss and torture.

He groaned. "Damn, Lissy! You drive me insane!"

But she was the one going crazy, the sweet, slippery friction of his thrusts fueling the raw ache inside her, forcing her to the jagged brink.

She would never, could never get enough of him. She wanted to touch him, frantic to feel the rasp of his chest hair, the iron ridges of his muscles, the velvety softness of his skin. But he was just beyond her reach.

He took her ankles in his hands, spread her legs further apart and forced her knees to bend, opening her completely, exposing every bit of her to his view. He was watching—watching where his body slid into hers, hot and slick and demanding.

"Jesus, Lissy, sweetheart!" He drove into her deep and hard and fast, penetrating her to her core.

In a heartbeat, she hovered on the radiant edge of an orgasm, the shimmering ache inside her now a tight, pulsing knot.

"Look at me, Lissy!" he growled. "I want to see your eyes when you come!"

She did as he asked, found herself staring into eyes dark with lust, with hunger, with love.

And then, even as his gaze held hers, it took her—blinding-bright and shattering.

Orgasm surged through every inch of her, a merciless rush of white-hot ecstasy, ripping a cry from her throat, her muscles clenching greedily around him as he kept up a relentless rhythm, prolonging her pleasure with forceful strokes.

Then she saw his pupils dilate with the shock of his own climax, his forehead furrowed as if he were in pain. He groaned, arched his back, his body shuddering with the force of release as he drove himself hard into her once, twice, three times, coming deep inside her.

Lissy had no idea how long she lay there on the dining room table, floating in the musky scent of sex, listening to the sound of their mingled breathing, feeling him pulse inside her. She probably could have stayed that way forever, body and heart and mind utterly satisfied.

She felt him press kisses against her moist skin, paying special tribute to her now ultrasensitive nipples. Then he wrapped her legs around his waist and drew her into a sitting position so that she was pressed against his bare chest, his arms around her, her bottom resting on the edge of the table, his erection still hard enough to stay inside her.

He kissed her hair. "God, woman, I can't get enough of you!"

She rubbed her cheek against the damp curls on his chest, let her hands explore the smooth muscles of his back. "That's good to hear, because two weeks from tomorrow you'll be Mr. Lissy Charteris, and you'll be stuck with me."

He chuckled, a warm sound that vibrated deep in his chest, then held her closer, his lips still pressed against her hair. "Please tell me you don't have any damned shows or gallery openings tonight."

"Not a one." She snuggled more closely against him, savored the hard feel of his body against hers. With the demands of her job as fashion editor and his as a sports columnist and football commentator, it was rare for them to have a Friday night at home together.

"Good, because I intend to keep you naked . . . all . . . night . . . long." He punctuated his words with kisses, then nipped her lower lip.

She nipped him back, then smiled. "So I guess if I'm naked, you're picking up the takeout, right?"

They'd ordered some Thai from the place down on Colfax—the best Thai restaurant in Denver—but had gotten distracted before either one of them had gone to pick it up. Clothes lay scattered in the hallway beside shoes, briefcases and cell phones.

With a frustrated groan, he withdrew from her, lowered her to her feet. "I guess so. But you have to stay naked—no bathrobe, no towel, nothing but your gorgeous hair and a smile. Got it?"

"Got it."

She watched him gather up his clothes and dress, enjoying the sight of him naked, his back to her—his broad shoulders, the bulge of his triceps, the powerful V of his back as it tapered to his waist, the tight mounds of his bare ass, the hint of testicles any time he bent over.

There were definite advantages to being the fiancée of a former football star.

When he turned to face her, his trousers were already up to his hips, so she caught only a glimpse of his wonderful cock. But his chest, with its dark curls and flat brown nipples, was still bare. She let her gaze follow the groove between his pecs down past the ridges of his belly to where it disappeared in a trail of curls beneath the waistband of his pants—and nearly moaned when the white fabric of his shirt ruined her view.

He grinned, revealing his dimples. "Hold that thought. And stay naked."

Then he grabbed his wallet and keys and was gone.

•　　•　　•

Lissy quickly picked up her clothes and sorted them into piles headed for the dry cleaner's or her own washing machine. Then she went into the bathroom, sat on the edge of the tub and began to rinse between her thighs.

How had she gotten so lucky? And it had to be luck—or divine intervention.

She hadn't liked Will when she'd first met him years ago. They'd been introduced when he first joined the staff of the paper as its new celebrity sports columnist and she was assistant features editor. Instantly repulsed by his hotter-than-hot looks and the knowledge he'd once been a college football hero of some kind, she'd turned up her nose at him, regarding him as a brainless jock with little going for him beyond a perfect body, thick dark hair, gorgeous blue eyes and a devastatingly handsome face.

How wrong she'd been.

She stood, patted between her legs with a fluffy towel, then took up her comb and began to work the tangles from her hair.

It hadn't been until that Saturday morning she'd gone jogging in City Park and stepped into a sprinkler hole that she'd gotten to know him. She'd wrenched her ankle badly and was sitting on the ground, in pain, calling herself names for not bringing her cell phone, when he'd emerged from a group of little boys who were playing football on the other side of the park.

Dressed in faded jeans that accentuated the perfection of his ass and a black T-shirt that seemed stretched across the muscles of his chest, he'd knelt down, carefully removed her running shoe, and gently peeled her sock away to reveal an ankle that was purple and swelling.

"You don't need a ride home," he'd said. "You need a ride to the hospital. If you can wait a few minutes, we're almost done for the day. Otherwise, I can call a cab."

Thank God she hadn't asked him to call a cab.

He'd carried her to his beat-up Chevy pickup—weren't football stars supposed to drive flashy sports cars?—and driven her to the

ER. Then he'd waited with her while the doctor examined her ankle, took X-rays and pronounced it broken.

"I'm so sorry about what happened. Not much you can do to come back from an injury like that," the doctor had said to Will, seemingly out of the blue. "Can I have your autograph? What did you think of the TV movie version? Made my wife cry. It must have been weird to watch your own life on the screen."

"I didn't watch it," Will had answered, graciously signing his name in black felt marker on the doctor's blue scrubs.

TV movie version?

Lissy had gone online that night, done a little research and discovered there was much more to Will Fraser than she could possibly have imagined. According to archived newspaper articles, he'd been raised by a single mother who'd worked as a waitress in Aspen, where he'd grown up in poverty amid wealth. He'd excelled both in academics and in sports in high school and had gotten a full scholarship to the University of Colorado at Boulder, where he'd been their starting wide receiver—which, Lissy'd later learned, had to do with catching the ball.

He'd been on his way to a lucrative professional career, when his knee had been shattered in the second-to-last game of his college career. He'd been in the second of four surgeries when CU had won the Orange Bowl that year. His football career abruptly over, he'd graduated magna cum laude with a degree in history, only to learn that his mother was dying of lung cancer. Though he'd spent every dime he'd earned by selling the rights to his story on the latest medical treatments for her, he buried her less than a year after he'd buried his dreams of playing professional football.

For several years, he'd worked for CU as a receivers coach. Then he'd joined the staff of the *Denver Independent*, covering football, commentating for the local ABC affiliate and coaching inner-city kids in his free time.

And Lissy had thought him a mindless jock.

On her first day back at work, she'd hobbled over to his desk on her crutches to thank him for his help and had asked him if she could repay him with dinner at his favorite restaurant. He'd accepted, and the two of them had ended up on her floor rutting like wild animals until dawn, as he'd helped her find creative ways of keeping her ankle elevated.

A month later they'd given up on pretense and moved in together.

Eight months after that, he'd proposed, getting down on his bad knee and offering her the most beautiful engagement ring she'd ever seen—a two-carat antique oval diamond set in filigreed white gold. She'd barely been able to speak, but somehow she'd said yes.

She set her comb aside and glanced in the mirror, smoothing her hands over her auburn hair and down her naked body, mostly content with what she saw and even more pleased by the way she felt—warm, languid, sexy.

She reached for her bottle of Chanel, then stopped.

He'd said naked—nothing but her hair and a smile.

She walked around the condo, lighting candles, her pulse quickening in anticipation of the pleasure to come. Sex with Will was . . . indescribable. No man had ever made her feel the way he made her feel—as if life began and ended in his arms.

She loved him more than she'd ever thought she could love anyone.

She had just turned down the covers on their bed, when the phone rang. Knowing Will would be back in a few minutes, she was tempted to let it ring through to voice mail. Then she saw the number on caller ID.

Lead in her stomach, she picked up the receiver. "Hello, Mother."

·   ·   ·

Will stepped around the orange cones that blocked the sidewalk in front of their condo complex. Lord knew how much longer this construction project—which seemed to eat more of the street and sidewalk every day—would take the city to complete. He couldn't wait until they moved out of this place and into the old Victorian they'd bought a few blocks away on Capitol Hill. He'd finished fixing it up last week, and they'd started moving their belongings one pickup truck–load at a time. When they got back from their honeymoon in France, they'd rent a U-Haul, and Will and his friends would make short work of the rest of it—furniture, clothes, dishes, the new plasma TV.

He took the front steps to their condo two at a time, oblivious to the pain in his knee, the spicy-sweet scent of chicken pad thai wafting from the plastic bag in his hand. He was ravenous—in more ways than one. The thought of Lissy waiting for him, warm and willing and naked, was making him intensely horny.

He slipped the key into the door, pushed it open and saw a handful of candles lit on the coffee table. He smiled. "Honey, I'm home."

Saying it amused him, pleased him. Perhaps it was the suburban normalcy of it. Or perhaps it was the fact that at age thirty-two he'd almost given up on the idea of having a honey to come home to. Not that there hadn't been lots of women in his life, but most of them had been more interested in fucking his name than in having a relationship with him. Once they'd discovered he wasn't rich and realized how mundane the life of a sports journalist was, they'd moved on to the next bit of beef in a jockstrap.

But not his Lissy. The very things that attracted other women to him had left her cold—perhaps because she knew how little money could buy.

That and she'd had a pathological loathing for sports.

He found her in the dining room, setting china plates, silverware and water glasses on the table they'd so recently sanctified, her long coppery hair swaying as she moved, her luscious round ass bare. She looked over her shoulder at him, her lips curving in a smile that made his blood run hot.

Then he saw the look in her green eyes.

He set the plastic bag on the sideboard. "What's wrong?"

She turned toward him, hair spilling over one soft shoulder, and walked into his arms. "Nothing really. My mother called."

He ought to have known. He pulled her closer, felt the tension in her body, reined in his own temper. "What was it this time? 'He's marrying you for the money,' or 'He's marrying you for sex'?"

"Both. Maybe we should just elope so she'll give up."

"Since I'm after your money *and* your body, I'll do whatever you want to do."

She laughed. "What I want to do is eat! I'm starving."

●　　●　　●

It wasn't until hours later, when the pad thai was long gone and other appetites had been temporarily satisfied, that Will got an idea as to what her mother must have said to upset her.

She sat before him in the tub, her back against his chest, her head resting limply against his shoulder, her damp hair clinging to his skin, while he lazily fondled a lush breast.

"Do you think it's possible for a couple to have too good a sex life?"

He managed not to laugh out loud. "Hell, no. Are you kidding?"

"What I mean is could a couple get together and end up getting married just because they had a great sex life? Could they mistake hot sex for love?"

She wasn't kidding.

There were times Will wished he could rip the phone line out so Lissy's mother could never call again. The woman had all the misery her late husband's money could buy, and she seemed to be doing her best to make sure her only child was miserable, too. Thank God she hated snow and lived in San Diego!

A wealthy attorney and his useless trophy wife, John and Christa Charteris had led a cold life, not a shred of affection between the two of them, as far as Will could tell from the stories he'd heard. John had wanted Christa for sex and looks, and Christa had hooked onto him for money and prestige. Their marriage had generated very little love in which to nurture a child.

Lissy's relationship with her father, never warm, had soured after she'd left the pre-law program at Cornell to double major in art and English. Her father had cut her off, both financially and emotionally. Though he'd eventually resumed paying her tuition, he'd died of a heart attack without making amends. Her relationship with her mother, a calculating woman who clearly did not approve of her daughter's independent streak or her choice of man, wasn't much better.

Lissy Charteris. Poor little rich girl.

Growing up, Will wouldn't have thought it possible to be wealthy and unhappy. He'd watched his mother literally work herself to death to feed him and keep the overpriced roof over their heads and had thought having money must be the solution to everything. He'd planned to earn millions through football, only to have that ripped away from him. It was his mother's illness and death that made him see money for what it was—a convenience, but no substitute for health or life or love. Eventually he'd come to disdain those who'd had the way paved for them, preferring to spend time with people who'd earned their way through life.

Lissy was both. Born to privilege, she'd turned her back on it in order to live the life she wanted. It was just one of the things Will cherished about her.

Feeling the frustration he always felt when he thought of how her mother treated her, he said the first thing that came to mind. "Hot sex is a better reason than most to get married. Look at all the people who marry for money or power or property."

Like your parents.

He felt her stiffen, knew he'd somehow said the wrong thing, so he hastily added, "Of course, when it comes time for me to walk down the aisle, it will be for the right reason, the only reason that matters—my bride's cooking."

Her snort, followed by giggles, told him he'd been reprieved.

• • •

Lissy lay with her head against Will's sweat-slick chest, running her fingers absentmindedly through his chest hair, her body limp and glowing from their most recent round of crazed sex. She loved these nights when she had him to herself.

An unpleasant flutter in her stomach drew her mind back to what she'd spent all evening trying to forget—her mother's call. She was still trying to get Lissy to postpone the wedding until Will signed a prenup, dangling cash in her face as if she could be bought. Hadn't she proved long ago that she didn't give a damn about her parents' money?

But it wasn't the usual discussion about divorce and assets that had bothered her; it was her mother's comment about sex and love. She had quoted some study showing that couples who'd lived together before getting married had a higher divorce rate than those who waited to have sex until after marriage.

Lissy had argued that the study, like most, was skewed from the beginning, as people who waited until after marriage to have sex tended to be people who also opposed divorce. Statistics never told the whole story. Any good journalist knew that.

You wouldn't be the first woman to confuse a man's sexual attention with love, Melisande. Just wait till he gets his fill of you and the hormones wear off. Men like him marry for two things: sex and money.

Not her Will. No way.

"Do you realize that a hundred or even fifty years ago, we'd both be virgins?" She didn't know she'd spoken until she heard her own voice.

His fingers stroked the hollow above her hip. "Good thing it's not a hundred or even fifty years ago. My balls would have burst by now."

"But don't you think things were more romantic then? Sex would have been a great mystery for us."

"I doubt it would have been that much of a mystery. We'd probably both have grown up in the country and seen our share of farm-animal lovin'."

"The point I'm trying to make is that neither of us would have any personal experience with sex until our wedding night."

"That's assuming that I hadn't already charmed my way into your bloomers or found some 'loose woman' willing to let me defile her." His voice dropped to a dark, velvet purr. "I can be *very* persuasive."

Lissy sat up, trying not to laugh, and glared at him. "You're ruining my fantasy."

He grinned, stretched and folded his muscular arms behind his head. "Oh. Sorry. Go on. I'm listening."

"After the reception, we'd go to the bridal chamber, where everything would be roses and candles. There'd be a fire in the hearth—"

"—if it were winter."

She ignored him. "You'd undress me first and then yourself. I'd probably never have seen a naked man before, so I'd be shy and afraid—"

"Oh, Will, it's soooo big! Please, don't hurt me!"

"—but you would soothe me and assure me that everything was going to be fine. Then you'd undress yourself, carry me to the bed and make passionate love to me."

He reached out, ran his fingers down her hair. "Are you sure that's how it would go? I think you've read too many novels. If it were a hundred years ago and we were both virgins, I think it would go more like this."

"Do tell."

"We'd have been raised to see nudity as shameful, so the room would be dark, and you would have changed from your wedding gown to a proper white nightgown and gotten into bed before I entered the room. I'd come in, wearing my nightshirt, and crawl into bed with you. You'd be worried that it was going to hurt, and I'd be worried that my dick might not work. I'd lift your gown up to your hips, spread your legs, and it would be over in a minute. You'd hate it, *and* you'd get pregnant—with the first of my twelve children."

She fought back a giggle. "Thank you for that enchanting vision of romance."

"You're welcome." His knuckles grazed a nipple, sent heat skittering into her belly.

She batted his hand away. "You're just afraid you can't do it."

He frowned. "Do what?"

"Wait."

He raised a dark eyebrow, raked her with his gaze. "It's a bit too late for that, isn't it?"

And then it came to her. "Not if we start over."

"Start over?"

"You know—wait until our wedding night to have sex again."

The look on his handsome face almost made her laugh out loud, but there was something about this that felt important to her.

Then he sat up and brushed a strand of hair from her cheek, the humor gone from his eyes. "This is about something your mother said, isn't it?"

She hated that he was able to see through her so clearly. "I just think it would add to the romance if we held back a little bit, made ourselves wait. It's only two weeks. Unless you don't think you can hack it."

Will was tempted to end this conversation by pulling her beneath him and showing her just what she'd be giving up, but something told him saying the wrong thing just now would be a bad idea. Besides, he wasn't one to turn down a challenge.

"If you want to wait until after the wedding to have sex again, that's fine."

The surprise on her face mirrored the astonishment he felt.

What the hell did you just say, Fraser? Are you an idiot?

Her eyes narrowed. "You really think you can do it?"

Her long hair hung about her heart-shaped face, tangled from a night of repeated lovemaking. Her nipples peeked out from between the strands, just begging to be licked and sucked. Her lips were swollen from kissing, and her cheeks were still rosy from her last orgasm, when she'd ridden him to within an inch of his life.

Her green eyes shone with a mix of intelligence and feminine allure. And he was agreeing *not* to fuck her?

"Of course I can do it. I'm not some eighteen-year-old college student."

She sat up on her heels. "Then how about we make a bet?"

He leaned back on his elbows, suddenly feeling competitive. "You name it."

"Okay. We agree not to have sex again until our wedding night, and whoever gives in and asks for it first loses."

That sounded easy enough—two weeks, no sex. "Fine. It's a deal."

"But there has to be some penalty." She hopped out of bed, walked the length of the room, forcing him to stare first at the bare curves of her scrumptious ass, and then at the auburn curls of her muff. "If you lose, you and your groomsmen have to wear the mauve cummerbunds I wanted."

He gave a snort, lifted his gaze to her face. "In that case, there is no way I'm going to lose. I'm not wearing pink."

"Mauve."

"Whatever."

She crawled back into bed, smiling. "We'll see."

"And what about you, Miss Lissy? What price will you pay if you come begging for it?" And then he had it. "I know. You'll have to promise to love, honor and *obey* me."

Her mouth fell open in outrage. "No way! Absolutely not!"

He couldn't help but chuckle. "Okay, then. How about this? If you lose, you have to wear the slutty gown."

"The Oleg Cassini?"

He had no idea what the designer's name was, but he'd loved the way she'd looked in that dress—ultrafeminine and sexy as hell—and had been disappointed when she'd decided to go with something else. "The one that's skintight and has the crystals on the straps."

She gaped at him. "The Badgley Mischka! I'm fashion editor of the paper, Will. I can't walk down the aisle half-naked!"

"Then I guess the bet is off." A part of him—the part located about six inches below his navel—heaved a sigh of relief. He reached over and turned off the bedside lamp.

Then out of the darkness, she spoke. "You're on."

• • •

Lissy's first inkling that their bet might not be as easy to honor as she'd imagined came the next morning when she awoke to find herself rubbing her bare derriere against something delicious and hard. Still half-asleep, she was already wet and more than a little turned on.

With a surprised gasp, she scooted away from him only to discover he was asleep—and sporting a glorious, thick, full erection.

She rose, pulled on her white silk bathrobe and headed off to the shower, drowsily pondering the strangeness of penile hydraulics and wondering how she was going to make it two weeks when her body seemed inclined to betray her even while she slept. Clearly, she had to do something to protect herself.

She brought it up as she sliced a grapefruit in half for their breakfast. "I'm moving into the guest room until after the wedding."

Will, who had just shuffled out of the bedroom wearing nothing but boxers and a serious case of bedhead, looked at her as if she'd just suggested a vacation on Mars. He poured himself a cup of coffee, leaned back against the counter and sipped with the reverence of a man at prayer.

Some people needed their coffee in the morning. Will was one of those people.

After five minutes had passed and he'd moved on to his second cup, he spoke. "Okay. But isn't that taking things a bit too far?"

Not willing to admit that she'd nearly lost the bet before she'd even opened her eyes this morning, she shrugged. "It just seems that if we're not having sex, we shouldn't be sleeping together either. It's more romantic that way, don't you think?"

She plopped the grapefruit halves on lunch plates, plucked two slices of fresh, hot toast out of the toaster, and carried the plates over to the kitchen table.

"Okay," he said, echoing himself and looking completely confused. "I'll move the boxes out for you, make some room."

Then he set his coffee down on the table and went off to fetch the morning papers. He returned with an armful, and the two of them quickly sorted through the plastic bags and newsprint. He got all the sports sections. She got all the fashion, arts and lifestyle sections. Whoever finished fastest got first dibs on the news sections.

Neither of them spoke as they nibbled their breakfasts and perused the pages. Reading newspapers was serious work, offering the conscientious editor a chance to spot every typo he or she had missed the day before, as well as the opportunity to compare the contents of one's own paper to that of the competition. As Tom Trent, the paper's rather caustic editor in chief was fond of saying, being a journalist meant starting every day with your bare ass hanging out the window, waiting for passersby to come along and smack it.

In the world of newspapers, mistakes were very public.

A half hour later their gazes met over the serrated edges of newsprint.

"Anything?" He reached for his coffee.

"I think the *Post* completely overplayed that feature on customized drapes. I mean, how exciting are drapes?"

He rubbed his foot against hers beneath the table and grinned. "Pretty damned exciting—if you're a window."

The contact was reassuring, comforting—arousing. "Do you know that a hundred or even fifty years ago you'd have ruined me?"

His grin grew wider. "Not me, sugar. You were ruined when I met you."

"No, I mean by moving in with me. You'd have ruined my reputation for all time."

He got a disgusted look on his face. "What did people do before television—sit around discussing their neighbors' sex lives? 'Verily, Myrtle, methinks he hath boffed her silly.' If you ask me, whatever we've lost in romance, we've more than made up for in the people-minding-their-own-business department."

She glanced at the microwave clock, stood and gave him a chaste kiss on the cheek. "I've got to get dressed. I'm meeting my bridesmaids for our final fittings this morning, and then we're going to lunch."

He grabbed her around the waist, pulled her into his lap and planted a kiss on her mouth. "Don't forget to put the slutty dress on hold. You might need it."

•   •   •

At first, the fittings had seemed to drag on forever. The seamstress kept talking on her cell phone, which made her lose her concentration to the point where Lissy had become truly irritated. But then she'd slipped into her gown and looked in the mirror.

She'd looked like . . . a bride.

She'd found herself staring, transfixed, at her own reflection, tears streaming down her cheeks, her heartbeat fluttering.

"I'm getting married," she'd said, as the seamstress had handed her tissues.

The gown she'd chosen was an empire-waist Vera Wang sheath of white silk with delicate cap sleeves. At five-foot-four she couldn't pull off the poufy princess look, and she'd loved the way the empire waistline emphasized her breasts.

Holly, her maid of honor, and Tessa, Sophie and Kara, her bridesmaids, were wearing mauve empire-waist gowns with white silk sashes. The look worked as well for Holly, who was model-thin and would look stylish in burlap, as it did for Kara, who'd had a baby not quite a year ago and was still nursing.

They'd ordered salads and waters all around—not the most exciting lunch, but appropriate when only two weeks away from a day they all wanted to look sleek and slender.

At first they'd talked about the newspaper—a hard thing not to do when they were all journalists. Holly worked as an entertainment writer, while Tessa and Sophie were part of the paper's elite Investigative Team, or I-Team. Kara had been part of the I-Team but had quit to work freelance when she'd gotten married. Members of the I-Team did hard-core journalism, the stuff that made headlines, stuff Lissy had no desire to do.

It wasn't until they were almost through their meal that Lissy told them about the bet.

"I think it's really romantic," said Tessa in her soft Georgia accent, pushing her empty plate aside. With her long blond curls and big blue eyes, she looked like Goldilocks, but Lissy pitied anyone who misjudged Tessa. "But then I've always told you Will is a real gentleman. He'd do anything for you."

"Except wear mauve cummerbunds." Kara, who was married to a state senator, dabbed her lips with her napkin and smiled. Her long dark hair hung in a braid over her shoulder. "I don't think Reece would have done that either."

"If you stick to it, you'll have the most amazing wedding night.

You'll both be ready to rip each other's clothes off." Holly squeezed lemon into her fizzy water. With short platinum blond hair and huge brown eyes, she reminded Lissy of an elf. "But if you lose— and with a stud like Will, losing would feel like winning—you'll look gorgeous in the Badgley Mischka."

The others nodded in agreement.

"You do look lovely in that gown," Tessa said. "The way I see it, if you've got it—"

"—flaunt it," they all said in unison before erupting in laughter.

Holly shrugged her slender shoulder. "I just don't know how you're going to make it for two weeks living with Will without mauling him."

Sophie leaned in, a smile on her freckled face, her sleek strawberry-blond hair sliding over her shoulder. "Batteries."

Lissy felt her cheeks turn pink. But why should she be embarrassed? They were all women. They'd surely all had a battery-operated boyfriend at one point or another. "I retired that particular device after my first date with Will. Besides, two weeks isn't all that long."

•   •   •

Will's best man stared at him as if he were insane.

"That has got to be the most lame-ass thing I've ever heard."

A former CU linebacker, Devon King bore a strong resemblance to Montel Williams—but with hair. He'd been one of Will's closest friends through college and had stood by Will when his life had come crashing down around him. Of all his teammates, Devon had been the only one to attend Will's mother's funeral. Unable to bank on a pro career, Devon had gone to law school after graduation and was now a defense attorney. The two of them coached kids' football on the weekends during the summer. This year, they had a team of eight-year-olds sporting little Steelers uniforms.

"Lissy thinks it's romantic." Will grabbed a duffel bag crammed with gear out of the back of his pickup and swung it over his shoulder.

But Devon was still staring at him, openmouthed and unmoving.

"Oh, come on, man! What was I supposed to say? 'No, Lissy, darling, you've got me by the gonads, and I can't last two days, let alone two weeks'?"

"That would have been better than 'yes.'" Devon gave a disgusted snort. "Let me get this straight. You agreed not to have sex with your extremely fine fiancée because she thinks *not* having sex is somehow romantic?"

"It's more than that. I think it has to do with something her mother said to her. Lissy asked me if it was possible for a couple to get married because they mistook great sex for love."

"Like that's a bad thing." Devon grinned. "So you went along with it to prove there's more to your relationship than sex?"

Will knew he had to tell Devon the whole truth. "That's part of it. Also, she bet me."

Devon shook his head. "You never could turn down a dare. What happens if you lose?"

This was the hard part. Will tried to say it casually, as if it didn't matter. "We have to wear those pink cummerbunds."

"Hell!" Devon jerked as if he'd been struck. "Man, I will personally come to your place at two A.M. to dump ice on your crotch. I am not walking down the aisle wearing pink!"

The horror on his friend's face made Will laugh. "Don't worry. I have no intention of caving. It's only two weeks. Let's get set up. I see a few mini Steelers waiting for us."

Still frowning, Devon grabbed a bag of balls and they started toward the field.

• • •

Will got home, sweaty and thirsty, to find Lissy on the phone with their wedding planner, working out minuscule details of the rehearsal dinner, the ceremony and the reception. Rose petals instead of rice. Silk organza ribbons on the banisters, white not mauve, which would just be too much. Fourteen people requesting vegetarian entrees at the reception. Add a fourth layer to the chocolate truffle cake.

Thank God he was the groom and didn't have to deal with that stuff. It would have made his brain bleed.

He tossed his sweaty clothes into the laundry and stepped into the shower. By the time Lissy was off the phone he was covered with soap.

She stuck her head in through the bathroom door. "Do you realize this is our last two days of peace and quiet before the wedding? This week is crazy-busy for both of us at the paper. Next weekend is the bridal shower and the bachelor and bachelorette parties. Then the week after we have wedding stuff almost every day."

They did? All he could remember was the rehearsal and the wedding itself. He made a mental note to check his planner against hers. But what he said was, "Mm-hmm."

He turned his back to the spray and let the water spill over his shoulders to rinse the soap away. He saw her look at his bare chest, then his abdomen, then lower still, and watched her pupils dilate. Her reaction sent a rush of blood to his groin, and he felt himself start to swell. He turned away, trying to hide his growing erection, and rubbed slick soap over his ass.

When she spoke, her voice was unnaturally light and casual. "Well, what would you like to do tonight?"

He'd like to have a repeat of last night. He'd like to bury his cock deep inside her and fuck her in a half-dozen positions, a half-dozen different places. But he couldn't say that—not without seriously pissing off Devon and the rest of his groomsmen. "What did people do a hundred years ago?"

• • •

They had an early dinner, then caught a new French art film that Holly had recommended at Chez Artiste, leaving the theater two hours later confused.

"Did that make any sense to you?" Lissy tried to piece the images and subtitles together.

Will unlocked the passenger door of his pickup and opened it for her. "I liked the part where she ate her lipstick. And all the bare breasts—I liked those, too."

Lissy waited until he'd climbed into the driver's seat to continue the conversation. "What is it with French art films anyway? They portray women as if we're all just dying to get into bed with one another."

Will turned to her, his disappointed frown visible even in the dim yellow light of the street lamp. "You mean you aren't?"

"Of course not!" She answered before she realized he was joking.

"Damn, Lissy! Way to ruin my fantasies. And I suppose next you're going to tell me there's no Santa Claus."

His sulky tone made her laugh. "Just drive."

The night was warm, one of those not-too-hot, not-too-cool early June nights when the Colorado sky was so clear the snow-capped peaks of the Rockies were visible even in the starlight. They went to their favorite coffee shop, where they tried to decipher the film's deeper meaning over frothy cappuccinos, and then took a stroll on the 16th Street Mall, its rows of trees lit up by tiny white lights. They passed street vendors, a few Bob Dylan wannabes, an amazing sax player, a guy making funny animals out of balloons, and a fit-looking woman with dreadlocks performing on a unicycle.

Lissy didn't know if it was just her imagination, but the Mall seemed to be crawling with lovers. A young couple dressed in black, their faces full of metal piercings, their eyes locked on each other. An old man and woman walking hand in hand, their skinny, pale legs sticking out of matching Bermuda shorts. A couple in their early thirties walking slowly along the red bricks, the woman's belly big and round with their baby.

It had been a pregnancy scare that had gotten the whole marriage ball rolling. Lissy had missed a few pills, and then she'd been late. Only when the test had come up negative had they realized they were more disappointed she *wasn't* pregnant than they had been afraid that she was. Will had proposed a month later.

Lissy watched the woman's round tummy as she passed, felt the warmth of Will's big hand surrounding hers and tried to inhale the sweetness of the moment. "I felt like a bride today."

Will looked down at her, saw the dreamy look on her face. He could only imagine what she was talking about. No little boy sat around at the age of six planning what kind of tux he'd wear on his wedding day. Guys just didn't dream about being grooms the way women dreamed about being brides. But guys did dream of being husbands and fathers. Perhaps what she'd felt was similar to the feeling he got when he saw her asleep at night, safe and sound—a warmth beyond contentment that told him all was right with the world.

He gave her hand a squeeze. "Have I ever told you I love you, Lissy Charteris?"

She smiled up at him. "Once or twice."

He spotted a vendor selling flowers off to his right. He stepped away from her, pulled out his wallet and handed the man a twenty in exchange for a dozen pink roses. Then he turned to her, held out the roses and spoke in his loudest, most dramatic voice. "I love you, Lissy!"

People around them stopped, watched, laughed.

"You're a lunatic, Will Fraser!" Lissy's sweet face lit up with a smile, and she ducked her head the cute way she did any time she felt embarrassed, long hair spilling over her cheek. Then she looked into his eyes. "But a very handsome lunatic. I love you, too."

•   •   •

They said good night outside the guest room, with slow lingering kisses that made Will's blood burn—and turned his cock to concrete.

"I had a wonderful time tonight." She leaned against him wearing one of his old T-shirts, her breasts pressing into his ribs, her arms locked at the back of his neck. "It was almost like we were dating again—and very romantic. Thank you for the roses."

"I had a good time, too." A voice in his head told him to quit kissing her, to let go and step away. But he loved the taste of her mouth. He took her lips with his, let his tongue toy with hers, felt her melt against him—then felt her stiffen. And he knew.

She'd discovered wood.

She stepped back from him, rested her hands on his chest, glanced down at the bulge in his boxer briefs. "I guess we shouldn't be doing this—or not too much of it, anyway."

Will felt his mouth move, heard his own voice. "I guess not."

*What do you mean, you frigging idiot! It's exactly what you
should be doing!*

A part of him wondered what she would do if he kissed her
again. He could tell from the sharp points her nipples made
through his T-shirt she was turned on, too. But some part of him—
some really stupid, overly chivalrous part of him—thought that
might be cheating.

She smiled, looking insufferably sexy and sweet. Then she
kissed him—on the cheek. "Good night, Will. I love you."

"Good night, sugar. Sweet dreams."

• • •

Lissy lay in the small twin bed, her body pleasantly aroused. It
really had been a wonderful evening. She loved Will's sense of humor and his whip-smart mind and had enjoyed discussing the film
with him, even if neither of them had understood it or liked it. She
felt she could talk to him about anything and never grow tired of
hearing what he had to say. And even though they'd been together
for a year and a half now, he still surprised her, as he'd done
tonight by bellowing, "I love you!" on the Mall.

All in all, their first day of no sex had been well worth it. Not
that it had been easy. Seeing him in the shower today had brought
her to the edge of a meltdown. The sight of soap bubbles sliding
over the muscles of his chest and abdomen, his dark body hair
slicked against his wet skin, bubbles gathered in the wet hair that
covered his testicles, had left her sopping in an instant. Clearly, unless she wanted to walk down the aisle in a barely there Badgley
Mischka, she was going to have to be more careful.

No, it hadn't been easy. Not then, and not when she'd been
tempted to follow him to their bed so he could rock her world with
that hard cock of his. Still, today had proved they didn't have to

have sex to cherish being with one another. Maybe going without sex for a while would deepen their relationship.

She rolled over, ignored the tingle between her legs and was soon fast asleep.

．　．　．

Will fell asleep, too, but a few hours later and only after he'd wrapped his mind around Lissy—and his hand around himself.

．　．　．

Lissy woke early the next morning when she tried to snuggle against Will and found herself pressing into a rough, cold wall. Unable to fall back asleep, she took a shower, brushed her teeth and started a pot of coffee.

They spent the morning doing chores. Lissy did laundry and went shopping for groceries, while Will packed their books, photo albums and his collection of vinyl LPs, carried them through the "Cone Zone" to his truck, and moved them to the new house. They were halfway through the grilled salmon salads Lissy had picked up for lunch when Devon called and asked if Will was in the mood for a little game of touch.

And so Lissy found herself sitting next to a cooler full of Fat Tire in the park down the street from their condo watching Will toss around a football with his groomsmen. There were a thousand other things she could have been doing, but she loved to watch Will play, partly because he enjoyed it so much and partly because—okay, she could be honest with herself—there was something about six-foot-plus of sweaty man in battle against sweaty man that made the secret girly part of her squeal.

She certainly knew more about football than she had when she'd met him, and she knew talent when she saw it. Will had more than his fair share, his movements powerful, focused and graceful. Even with his knee injury, he ran like the wind, though he limped slightly between plays. With hands that had been described as "magic" by sports commentators—and Lissy knew they *were* magic, only not in the way sports commentators thought—he seemed to lure the ball out of the air and against his chest.

And he looked damned sexy doing it.

Although it was hazardous to her libido—how could she watch him jump and grunt and run and sweat and not get turned on?—she couldn't make herself walk the hundred steps home.

At least he was having a good time. That was what mattered.

Will caught another pass and ran it out of bounds, enjoying the exertion.

Then Devon called a time-out and pulled everyone, including the three members of the opposing team, into a huddle. "Is she watching? Good. Will, take your shirt off. The way we see it, you need to play some offense here. As long as you're just playing D, you're going to lose."

Nods all around.

"You told everyone?" Will glared at his best friend.

Devon shrugged. "You give in, and we wear pink. It's our asses on the line."

More nods.

"Except mine, of course, because I'm only an usher," Chris grumbled.

"Let's face it, man. You don't stand a chance. Lissy is . . . well, Lissy is one fine female."

"Extremely hot," Chris added.

"She's . . . whoa, yeah . . . hot," stammered Robert.

"A total babe," Scott agreed.

"I'd do her," Nick said, acting surprised when Will glared at him. "What?"

"What are you guys suggesting? You want me to cheat?"

"Not cheat," Devon said, smiling from behind his mirrored sunglasses. "Just turn up the heat on your woman. Play to win."

The idea had its appeal. Will wasn't looking forward to two weeks of sleeping alone and solo sex. He glanced at Lissy, caught her smile, then shook his head. "I don't think so. I agreed to this, and I'm just going to have to ride it out."

"Just take off your shirt, man, then go fetch a beer."

Nods.

Hadn't he had the same thought last night?

Play to win.

"Do you know how weird it feels to hear you say that, Devon? 'Take off your shirt.' " Despite the niggling of his conscience, Will yanked the sweaty T-shirt over his head. "If I catch you eyeing me, dude, I'll kick your ass."

He sauntered over to where Lissy sat in the shade, tossed the T-shirt on the ground and reached into the cooler for a cold one. "How you doing, sugar? Hot day."

"Yeah." Her gaze was fixed on his pecs.

●　　●　　●

Lissy dropped the chicken strips into the wok and stirred them, her blood sizzling hotter than the pungent sesame oil. Watching him play a hard game of football, all those delicious muscles shifting and bunching beneath his sweat-slick skin, had left her wishing she'd never suggested this stupid bet. She'd be in the shower with him right now, running her hands over those luscious muscles, washing that spicy man-sweat away, instead of stewing in her own pheromones in the kitchen.

Why had she gotten herself into this?

You wouldn't be the first woman to confuse a man's sexual attention with love, Melisande. Just wait till he gets his fill of you and the hormones wear off.

Is that what had happened to her mother? Had she married her father in the afterglow of an orgasm only to regret it later? Lissy had always known her parents' marriage was an unhappy one, but she'd never understood how unhappy it was until she'd left home, watched other couples and seen her parents from the outside. They were angry, bitter, worn.

Even when she'd been a little girl they'd slept in separate bedrooms, lived separate lives, coming together only when occasion demanded. She knew her father had fooled around with other women, his unfaithfulness seeming to rob her mother of what remained of her youth. No amount of money had been able to fill the void between them.

But Lissy's relationship with Will was nothing like theirs. She and Will truly loved each other, loved spending time with each other. They earned about the same amount of money, held similar jobs, had similar interests. She would not wake up one morning to find herself in her mother's shoes.

Still, a bet was a bet. She had agreed to it. Worse, it had been her idea. And now she was stuck with it.

She dropped chopped veggies into the wok and watched them fry.

• • •

"No, sugar, I'll do it. You made supper. It's my turn to do dishes." Will stood, winced.

She looked up at him, concern in her pretty eyes. "Your knee?"

"Yeah." He picked up their plates and silverware, took another step, allowed a hiss of breath to pass his teeth. His knee *did* hurt. Not much. But it *did* hurt. "Damn!"

She stood, took the plates from his hands. "Sit, hon. I'll get an ice pack."

"No, let me handle this. It's not bad." He was telling the truth.

She gave him a worried frown. "Liar. Sit and elevate it. I'll be right back."

He sat and lifted his leg onto a chair, suppressing a satisfied grin. She'd been distracted and grumpy during dinner, and he thought he knew why. He'd followed the football game with a shower and had come to dinner wearing a pair of old jeans and a Calvin Klein shirt—which he'd left unbuttoned. She'd spent the better part of their meal trying *not* to look at him.

Devon was a genius. Will could win the bet *and* get Lissy back into his bed, protecting his groomsmen from the Curse of the Pink Cummerbunds while preventing himself from becoming the first man in history to die from a case of blue balls.

He soothed his conscience by telling himself it wasn't cheating. Nothing in the conditions of their wager prevented them from trying covertly to seduce the other person. And when Lissy gave in to her lust, he'd not only make certain she enjoyed it, but he'd also prove what a great guy he was by letting her wear the Very Wang or whatever gown it was that she liked so much.

When Lissy returned, she had a pillow, a tea towel and an ice pack in her hands. She looked down at his knee. "Oh!"

He pretended not to understand the problem.

"You're going to have to take off your jeans."

He nodded, stood, unbuttoned his fly. Then he slipped the worn denim down his hips, letting his cock hang free, and watched her eyes widen. "Sorry, Lissy. You said dinner was ready, so I hurried."

*   *   *

Lissy drew an *I* and Will a *P*, so Lissy went first. Will watched as she calculated the value of her letters, then set five tiles on the board: N-I-G-H-T.

"Double letter score on the *T* for ten points." She scribbled her points on paper and drew five more tiles.

It had been decades since Will had played Scrabble. With sex out of the question and nothing decent on television, he'd figured they'd rent a DVD. But Lissy had found the old board game last week while packing the contents of the guest room closet and had wanted to play.

"You can keep your leg elevated, and we can still have some fun," she'd said, dropping a pair of gym shorts in his naked lap.

He adjusted the ice pack on his knee, looked at the letters on his tray, then bit back a smile and set down his tiles, taking advantage of her *T*: B-R-E-A-S-T-S.

"Double points for the *R* for a total of ten. We're tied." He pulled six new tiles and sat back to see how she'd react.

"The game has just started." Her green eyes held defiance. Using the second *S* from BREASTS, she spelled out S-E-X for eleven points.

Will studied the board and pulled three tiles from his tray; using the *B* in BREASTS, he spelled B-L-O-W for ten with a double score for the *L*.

She smiled sweetly, picked up a tile and dropped an *N* above his *O*, spelling NO. Four points. "Your turn."

Will was glad they weren't playing poker, because once he'd looked the board over and considered his tiles, he was unable to keep himself from smiling. He pulled five tiles from his tray and set them down one by one, using the *R* from BREASTS: P-E-C-K-E-R.

"Double word score for a hot twenty-eight points. Top that, sugar."

Lissy squirmed in her seat, considered her options. She would put him in his place. She picked up three tiles, and going down from the *P* he'd just placed added U-N-Y to spell PUNY. It was only eight points, but sometimes it wasn't the score that mattered.

She looked up at him, ready to gloat—only to find him watching her through intense blue eyes that told her *he knew* she knew better. There was nothing puny about Will.

She swallowed, watched him set out his next word for twelve points: L-I-P-S.

She rolled her eyes, used his *L* to spell L-I-M-P. Eight points.

He gave her a lopsided grin and shook his head, drawing her gaze down to the telltale bulge in his shorts. Then he used the *E* in SEX to spell E-N-T-E-R. Seven points.

She lifted her chin, used his *N* and spelled out N-E-V-E-R for ten points.

He narrowed his eyes at her, bit his lower lip. Then a slow smile spread across his face as he moved back up the board and used the *A* in BREASTS to end the word V-A-G-I-N-A. Twelve points.

And so it went, crossword warfare, neither of them speaking, Lissy barely breathing, until Will passed two hundred points with the fifteen-point word Q-U-I-M.

Lissy stood, glared at him and began tossing the wooden tiles back into the little velvet bag. "So long as you understand, Will Fraser, those four letters are as close as you're getting to the real thing until you say 'I do.'"

• • •

This time, Lissy said good night to Will while he was in the bathroom brushing his teeth, then fled to the safe haven of the guest room.

. . .

Will heard Lissy open the bedroom door. He opened one eye and glanced at the clock—twelve-oh-five. He pretended to be asleep, certain she was about to crawl beneath the sheets and wake him for a bit of midnight madness. Instead he heard the drawer of her nightstand slide open, then close. And then she was gone.

A few minutes later, he heard a faint buzzing sound.

And then it hit him.

She was having sex with herself! Without him!

He sat up, intensely aroused and irritated. He'd spent the better part of the day trying to get under her skin, and she was taking it out on a sex toy?

He'd set one foot on the floor on his way to replace the stupid bit of vibrating plastic with something real when he caught himself. He forced himself back into bed, flipped onto his side and punched a pillow. And listened.

By the time the buzzing stopped ten minutes later, he was hard as steel. He'd take care of the steel tonight. The vibrator he'd take care of tomorrow.

She wasn't getting off that easily.

. . .

The wall woke Lissy again early Monday morning. She took a shower, slid into her bathrobe and had breakfast ready and coffee brewing when Will emerged from the bedroom, looking tired and surly. She poured him a cup, handed it to him, then kissed him on the stubbly roughness of his cheek. "Morning, babe. How's your knee?"

He sipped, frowned. "My knee? Oh. Better. Thanks."

"Should we ride together?"

He looked into his coffee, shook his head. "Take your car. I'll be at Broncos team camp most of the day. We're doing a couple of live feeds."

"A late night?"

He nodded. "How about you?"

"A day of boring meetings. We've got to pin down the concept for our fall fashion preview, and I need to finish interviews for the staff writer position. We can't head into the rest of the summer understaffed."

He set his coffee down, pulled her into his arms and kissed her forehead. "I miss you, Lissy. I miss having you in our bed. Sex or no sex, it's not the same without you."

She pressed her cheek into his chest, sank into the haven of his body. "I miss you, too. But it's only—"

"—thirteen more days."

Thirteen more days.

Somehow that had begun to sound like a long time.

That was what she thought, but that was not what she said. "Don't tell me you're ready to cave so soon."

"Who said anything about giving up? I was simply stating a fact." Then he kissed her on the nose. "Have a great day."

"You, too." Lissy watched him head back up the hallway toward the shower and wished he'd had the good grace to give up. Although sex with her vibrator relieved some of the tension and helped her sleep, it didn't come close to the pleasure of sex with Will.

She hurried to the bedroom, got dressed, then grabbed her briefcase and purse and drove through early morning traffic to the five-story office building that housed the *Denver Independent*. As a senior editor, she got one of the coveted parking places beneath the building—a luxury that saved her countless hours searching for a spot on the streets of downtown Denver, where parking was a blood sport.

She had a meeting with her assistant editors, interviewed two candidates for the staff writer position and then shot down three design concepts for the fall fashion cover. By ten, she was beginning to feel in control again. Not even her mother, who called to demand once again that Will sign a prenup if she wanted her to attend the wedding, ruined her morning.

Because Will was in Englewood watching the Donkeys—she only called them that because it irritated him—she had lunch with Holly. Over a salad so wilted it looked like it had been fished out of the alley garbage can, she found herself telling Holly about the weekend: how she'd woken up ready to jump Will's bones and had moved into the guest room, how the sight of Will in the shower had driven her out of her mind, how she'd nearly melted watching Will play football without his shirt, how he'd toyed with her over a game of Sex Scrabble.

"Thirteen days sounds like forever!" She leaned forward and whispered, "And there's not a vibrator in the world that comes anywhere close to him."

For a moment Holly said nothing but nibbled at her fruit plate. Then she smiled. "He's doing it on purpose, you know."

"Doing what on purpose?"

"Trying to turn you on. Trying to make you so desperate you'll give in first."

"Oh, no! No, no, no! Will wouldn't do that." When Holly gave her an exasperated how-can-you-be-so-stupid look, Lissy tried to explain. "Scrabble was my idea, and I'm the one who walked in on him when he was in the shower. He didn't ask me to come in. And he's played football without his shirt before. No, it's me. I'm just—"

"—head-over-heels in love with a very sexy man," Holly finished for her, then continued, "who knows perfectly well how he affects you and is doing everything he can to make you lose the bet before he does."

Lissy shook her head and stood, cafeteria tray in hand. "I just don't think he would do that."

Holly followed her to the trash. "Lissy, dear, Will is special, but he's still a man."

•   •   •

"The Broncos have a young receiver corps this year, heavy on strength and speed but light on experience." Will spoke into the mic on his headset, almost finished with their second live broadcast of the day. The hot June sun beat down on him, made him sweat beneath the sport coat the station insisted he wear. "Receivers Coach Tony D'Angio put them through their paces today running cross patterns and focusing on technique—footwork and hand position."

From the station downtown, helmet-haired sports anchor Don Philips was interviewing him, his voice buzzing in Will's earpiece. "Darius Williams was taken out with a pulled hamstring. Any word yet as to how serious it is?"

"No, Don, though it's unlikely he'll return to the field this week. The coaching staff is working hard to prevent preseason injuries in hopes of avoiding an early season like the one they had last year. They've added extra stretching and conditioning workouts, which are also helping the newest members of the team adjust to playing at altitude."

"If anyone knows what injuries can do to a player's career, it's you, Will. It was a devastating knee injury that ended your career, taking you from Big 12 star to former college legend overnight."

Will hated it when Don brought up his past, but Don seemed to love rubbing it in. "That's right, Don. Neither the coaches nor the players want to see that scenario unfold here at team camp, so, while they're training hard, they're also holding back a bit, waiting for their conditioning to peak before they push forward into the more strenuous workouts."

"Checking in with Will Fraser at Broncos team camp in Englewood. We'll continue to follow events as the week unfolds. Tonight, the Red Sox—"

Will waited until the red light on the camera went out, then ripped off his headset. "Stupid dick."

"Don't listen to him, Will." Merrill, the cameraman, began breaking down the equipment. "The asshole can't catch a clue, much less a football. Spends his days worrying about his hair."

"Thanks, Merrill. Go find yourself something cold to drink and some AC."

Will had assumed he'd be over it by now. It had been eleven years since his dreams of playing pro football had ended in one moment of shattering pain. Although he'd never played a single pro game, he had turned professional football into a solid career for himself, using his name and his knowledge to earn a good living reporting from the sidelines. His work had brought him together with Lissy, more than making up for anything he'd lost. He had no regrets. Yet there were still times when he found himself wondering what might have been.

Let it go, Fraser.

Feeling on edge, Will turned back toward the practice field and watched the players finish one-on-one drills in the red zone. He'd been irritable all day, maybe because it was ninety-nine degrees outside and maybe because he had a beautiful fiancée whom he hadn't touched for almost three long days.

He'd come close last night to winning the bet and ending this whole thing. Then Lissy had gotten help from an old friend. He'd known the vibrator was there. Why hadn't he thrown the damn thing out or hidden it somewhere else? Well, he might have blown it last night, but he was a man who learned from his mistakes.

He'd waited until she'd walked out the door this morning, then he'd searched the guest room until he'd found it. Knowing he couldn't smash it or toss it out without giving himself away, he'd turned it on and slipped it back beneath the mattress where she'd hidden it. By the time she got home from work, the batteries would be dead—and he'd taken care to make certain there were no more AAs anywhere in the condo. If she reached for her little buzzing boyfriend tonight, she'd find him unresponsive—and Will doubted she'd go to the trouble of getting dressed and traversing the Cone Zone for replacement batteries.

Of course, she still had fingers.

The thought of her touching herself, sliding her pretty fingers between her lips and over her tasty little clit until she came, sent a rush of blood to his groin, leaving him half-hard.

"Hey, Fraser!" Coach D'Angio strolled over to him, pigskin in hand, followed by two rookies who would most likely spend the year serving an apprenticeship on the bench. "I hear you're getting hitched."

Will nodded, grinned, grateful for the distraction. "You heard right—two weeks from this past Saturday."

D'Angio slapped him on the shoulder. "Congratulations!"

The rookies nodded and smiled.

"Is she worth the ball and chain?"

Ball and chain? Will had never thought of marriage to Lissy in that way. "More than."

Coach D'Angio held up the ball. "Hey, you want to show these two clowns how to catch a damned football? Will here is more than just a pretty face," D'Angio said to the rookies. "For six years, he was the Big 12 all-time leader in receptions, receiving yardage and touchdowns."

"Do you know how long it's been since I've run a serious pattern, D'Angio? These guys are pros. I can't teach them anything." But Will was already unbuttoning his sport jacket.

From Big 12 star to former college legend.

By the time Coach D'Angio had the ball in the air, Will was far downfield. He turned in, saw the leather spiraling toward him but about two feet too far to the left and high. As it had always done, his mind emptied of everything except how much he wanted that ball. He leapt for it, thought it into his hands, pulled it against his chest. Then his feet hit turf, a sharp bite of pain in his knee the only proof he'd just done something stupid.

Back toward the fifty-yard line, D'Angio was applauding and shouting. "Softest damned hands in the Big 12, boys, and feet with wings. If it hadn't been for an interception and a linebacker with a grudge, he'd be shaking up the pros. Want to go for another one, Fraser?"

Will let himself be talked into catching three more before he pleaded deadline and retrieved his jacket. "I still have a column to write."

Only then did he realize Merrill had taped the whole thing.

"Please tell me you're going to scrap that." Will tossed his jacket over his shoulder.

"Might be fun at the employee holiday party. I do take bribes, you know."

•   •   •

Lissy picked up Chinese on the way home and tucked Will's supper in the fridge. Then she hunkered down before the television with her dinner plate and a pair of chopsticks. The station was just finishing weather, which meant sports was next. They'd probably recycle Will's live broadcast—Denver was Broncos crazy—and she'd at least get a glimpse of him. She hated it when one or the other of them had to work late.

No, it's me. I'm just—

—head-over-heels in love with a very sexy man who knows perfectly well how he affects you and is doing everything he can to make you lose the bet before he does.

Lissy hadn't been able to forget her conversation with Holly. She'd run Sunday through her mind again and again but could find no reason to believe Will was deliberately trying to seduce her. Holly had an overactive imagination.

But why had none of his friends taken off their shirts? Hmmm?

Lissy ignored the irritating voice in her head and turned up the volume.

The latest Red Sox victory over St. Louis. A doping scandal in the world of cycling. A few surprising NFL draft picks.

Thank God they were finally getting to football. No matter how much she loved Will, Lissy could only stand so much sports news. She stood and hurried to the kitchen to refill her glass of ice water, the sound of the television following her.

"At Broncos team camp this afternoon, spectators might have assumed the team had inked a new draft pick. But look closely. The man catching the ball is none other than Channel Four commentator Will Fraser, who stepped out from behind the microphone and onto the field this afternoon to catch a few passes thrown by Receivers Coach Tony D'Angio."

Lissy nearly tripped in her crazed dash from the kitchen to the sofa. She watched, thrilled, as an image of Will leaping into the air and catching a football filled the screen.

My man.

The words popped into her head, uttered by some primitive female part of her, as she savored the replay, melting into the cushions. Then they segued from the footage of him catching passes to his prerecorded analysis of the team's receivers.

It was only later that it dawned on her.

His knee, which had hurt so much last night, hadn't seemed to bother him at all.

＊　＊　＊

Will drove home feeling ready to hit someone. He'd been halfway through his column when his phone had rung and he'd found himself on the line with Lissy's mother. She obviously hadn't expected to reach him in person, had planned to leave him a message. But once she recovered from the shock of speaking with him live, she told him that she was prepared to compensate him handsomely if he signed a prenuptial agreement, which she had just faxed to him at the paper.

"You'll receive a check for fifty thousand dollars as soon as the document is legally final," she'd said, her voice all ice and clipped syllables. "Once Lissy sees you've signed it, she'll quit being ridiculous and sign it herself. The money—"

"You mean the bribe?"

"—will remain our secret."

Anger and disbelief had tied Will's tongue, but only for a moment. "I don't know how a woman as warm and loving as Lissy came from you, but for her sake I'm going to keep this conversation to myself. It would crush her to know you've gone behind her back like this."

"I will not have my daughter lose her fortune to trailer trash! You don't even know who your father was!" The ugly sharpness of her words rang between them like shattering glass.

Will fought back profanity, chose his words carefully. "I know he was a wealthy married man, like your husband, and that the young waitress he took advantage of paid the rest of her life for his irresponsibility, raising a child alone on tip money. She had more courage in her heart than he had dollars in the bank. Lissy is like her—kind, courageous, caring."

"Don't presume to tell me about my daughter!"

"Good-bye, Mrs. Charteris." He'd slammed the phone down, then retrieved the hateful document and fed it through the shredder.

Will got home just before nine to find Lissy curled up on the sofa with a pile of fashion magazines and a glass of iced tea, Seal playing over the stereo. At the sight of her, he felt his anger drain away. God, he needed her tonight.

She was wearing a skin-hugging black tank top—without a bra—and a pair of very short denim shorts. Her auburn hair was pulled back in a sleek ponytail that hung halfway down her back. She stood when he neared the sofa, raised herself onto her toes and kissed him—on the cheek. "I missed you."

He pulled her close and kissed her long and slow—on the lips. "I missed you, too."

She stepped away, started toward the kitchen. "Your dinner's in the fridge—Chinese."

"There's nothin' like my Lissy's home cookin'." He followed her, watching the feminine sway of her hips and the sexy curves of her ass, willing himself to forget the conversation he'd had with her mother.

"I saw you on TV today." She opened the refrigerator and bent over to reach inside, her shorts rising an inch to reveal the soft, rounded undersides of her ass cheeks.

His mouth watered, but not for Chinese food. "I'm always on TV, sugar."

She turned around, two take-out containers in her hands. "The receivers coach was throwing passes, and you—"

"What? Are you telling me they aired that?" Mortification followed astonishment.

She poured the containers out onto a plate and popped the plate into the microwave. "You looked really good. And, hey, you caught it every time."

Cringing on the inside, he shook his head. "Christ, that's embarrassing! I didn't even know Merrill was taping. I think he was trying to get back at that dickhead Don, but I sure wish he'd asked me first."

She took a pair of lacquered chopsticks out of the silverware drawer. "Why would that be embarrassing? Most men would give anything to be on the six o'clock news tossing the ball around with a Broncos coach."

"Most men don't have to see how much they've gone downhill or worry that everyone will think they're trying to show off." He hated the self-pity he heard in his own voice.

She looked over at him, her green eyes going soft. Then she set the chopsticks aside, walked over to him and wrapped her arms around him. "I'm sorry, Will. I'd give anything to be able to change things, to see you live the life you want to live."

He stroked and kissed her hair. "*You* are the life I want to live, Lissy. You're not someone I got stuck with because the rest of it didn't work out."

He felt her body relax, an almost imperceptible shift. "It's still hard, isn't it? Every day it's hard for you."

He pulled her closer. "Not every day."

What *was* hard was not reaching down to cup the lovely, firm breasts that pressed so temptingly against his ribs. He ran his knuckles up the warm, bare skin of her arms and cupped her silky shoulders instead. Then he ducked down and brushed his lips over hers, tasting first her upper lip, then her lower.

He heard her quick intake of breath, saw her eyes go smoky. She lifted her chin, reaching for his kiss with her luscious red mouth.

The microwave beeped.

Will bit back a groan as she slipped out of his arms, pulled his steaming chicken and vegetables out of the microwave and carried it to the table.

They shared the highlights of their day while he polished off his supper, then they snuggled on the couch to watch the ten o'clock news.

Later Will would not be able to say how it started—an innocent brush of skin against skin, a glance, a shared breath. They'd made it through the day's headlines, when he found himself brushing his lips slowly over her cheek, kissing her temple, nibbling at the whorl of her ear, sucking on her earlobe, the sound of the television a distant buzz.

Her breath came in shudders. Her lips were parted, her eyes closed, her hands clenched into fists in her lap. When her head fell back onto his shoulder, he did what he'd wanted to do all night. He kissed her full on the mouth—and she kissed him back.

It seemed like forever since they'd kissed like this with lips and tongues and teeth, and he found after the first taste that he wanted more. With a groan, he took her beneath him, pressed her back onto the cushions, kissed her harder, deeper.

She arched against him, wrapped her legs around him, moaned into his mouth, a sweet feminine sound that made every muscle in his body tense and sent his mind reeling with urgent, throbbing lust. His cock strained eagerly against his fly, seeking a way out of his pants and into her. He reached down with one hand, grasped her ass, rubbed his clothed erection between her legs, searching for relief.

She whimpered, slipped out from beneath him so that she sat on the floor, holding her hand out at arm's length as if to ward him off. "W-we have to stop. We can't!"

The goddamned bet.

Will wanted to point out that they didn't have to stop, that the best possible thing they could do right now was fuck each other's brains out, but that would mean wearing pink. He sat up, forced breath into his lungs, bit back a few choice words. "I'll bet engaged couples kissed a hundred years ago."

She seemed to consider his words, hugging her arms around herself as if that would stop whatever she was feeling. "I don't think they kissed like that."

He leaned toward her, almost touching her. "I bet they touched every way and everywhere they could—as often as they could."

She scooted backward. "But they stopped. They knew they had to stop."

"They didn't all stop." He dropped to the floor beside her, slipped an arm around her waist to halt her retreat and pressed his lips against the pulse at her throat. "Ever hear the expression 'shotgun wedding'?"

Her answer was something between a squeak and a moan.

He pressed kisses along the silky skin of her throat. "Besides, we're just kissing."

"Kissing . . . often . . . leads to . . . sex."

"Only if you want it to. I'll prove it to you." He licked the sensitive skin just beneath her ear, felt her shiver. Then he caught her hair with his fist, tilted her head back and plundered her mouth, thrusting his tongue deep, nipping and sucking her lips, taking from her mouth what he could not take from her body. He gave her no quarter.

With a muffled cry, she melted against him and met the potency of his kiss with her own ferocious hunger. He knew he was pushing her to the edge because he was being pushed right along with her. He knew he had to stop to make his point, but his body wouldn't let him. One more stroke of tongue against tongue. One more taste of her lips. One more gust of breath.

His cock hard as stone, his blood raging through his veins, he broke the kiss. "I agreed not to have sex until after the wedding. But I didn't agree not to touch you, Lissy. I intend to touch you every day. Get used to it."

She stared at him through wide green eyes, her pupils dilated, her lips swollen.

He kissed her on the forehead. "Good night, sugar. Sweet dreams."

●　　●　　●

Lissy lay in the dark, burning. She crossed her legs, squeezed her thighs tightly together, tried to ease the ache.

No, it's me. I'm just—

—head-over-heels in love with a very sexy man who knows perfectly well how he affects you and is doing everything he can to make you lose the bet before he does.

Was Holly right after all?

After tonight it certainly seemed like it. Lissy'd tried to keep their contact chaste, kissing him on the cheek, keeping her distance, trying not to add fuel to the fire. But Will had grabbed the gas can and emptied it over both of them. *Whoosh!*

He'd been just as turned on as she, his cock a hard ridge inside his pants, his breathing unsteady, his blue eyes dark like the night sky.

I agreed not to have sex until after the wedding. But I didn't agree not to touch you, Lissy. I intend to touch you every day. Get used to it.

But Lissy would never get used to it. Although she'd always enjoyed sex, nothing could compare to the way she felt when Will touched her. Will had more passion in his kisses than most men possessed in their entire bodies. His tongue alone was . . .

She couldn't think about that. She'd already found herself weighing the pros and cons of the Badgley Mischka. Swarovski crystals. Chapel-length train. Corset waist.

But she'd set out to prove to herself they could go for two weeks without sex and still have a strong relationship. She wasn't ready to give in yet.

Get a grip on yourself, Lissy!

She wanted to get a grip on Will. But that wasn't going to happen, not for twelve long days and twelve longer nights—eleven if she didn't count today. Which was almost over, so she really shouldn't count it. Then again, tonight wasn't over until she fell asleep. Twelve. Twelve long nights.

She rolled onto her belly, slid her hand beneath the mattress, pulled out her vibrator and rolled over onto her back. Then she flipped the switch—and nothing happened.

She shook it. Still nothing.

She sat up, turned on the light, saw the switch was set at Off.

"Well no wonder."

She flipped it the other way. Nothing.

And then it occurred to her that the thing had been switched to On.

The batteries were burned out.

With an aggravated sigh, she got out of bed and padded down the hallway to get fresh ones. Had she left the darned thing on all night long? No, that was impossible. It was loud enough—and strong enough—that she'd have heard and felt it. Maybe her motions had accidentally turned it on when she'd gotten up in the morning and she'd been too busy to hear it buzzing away. Yet how could that be when the switch actually required a bit of effort?

She entered the kitchen and opened the refrigerator, its light spilling across her bare legs and into the darkened room. She reached for the side shelf where they kept spare batteries—only to find it empty. She groaned.

Will must have taken them for his—

She stood bolt upright and slammed the fridge door, making glass jars and bottles clink.

That bastard!

He had turned her vibrator on and let the batteries run out. And he'd taken the rest of the pack so she'd have nothing to replace them with.

For a moment she could do nothing but fume.

He was trying to seduce her! He was trying to make her give in! He was trying to make her wear the slutty wedding gown!

Well, he was a freaking idiot if he thought an act of vibrator sabotage and battery theft would be enough to force her to come crying for him. She was more resourceful than that.

Lissy tiptoed into the living room, picked up the TV remote and opened it—only to find it took AAA batteries, not AAs.

"Damn!"

The same was true of the stereo, VCR and DVD remotes.

She wracked her brain, tried to figure out what other appliances in the house took batteries. The alarm clocks? No. They were electric. Her iPod? No, it had its own battery. The smoke detectors!

She hurried back to the kitchen, picked up a chair and carried it into the hallway. Then she climbed up and, standing on her tiptoes, tried to remove the casing. It was on tight, and as she twisted and tugged, her hand bumped the glowing red Test button.

It let out a blaring beep, making Lissy grab her ears and look toward the bedroom. The last thing she wanted was for Will to catch her scavenging for batteries. She watched for a moment, waited. All was quiet.

She reached back up and removed the cover with a quiet click. *Nine volt.*

Nine volt! The damned thing took nine-volt batteries!

"Lissy, what in hell are you doing?"

She gasped, found Will standing stark naked beside the chair. "I-it's been a while since we changed these. I was just checking to make sure it still worked."

"At one in the morning?"

"We don't want to get caught with our pants down."

"Uh, no. I guess not." He glanced down at his naked body. "Why don't you let me do that? I'm taller. Hand me the spare."

Her face flushed red. She didn't have the spare. "I-I think I forgot to grab it."

"I'll get it." He walked off, his ass muscles shifting as he moved. "You get to sleep."

Lissy swore she heard him chuckle.

Laugh all you want, Mr. Tricky Man. Two can play at this game.

* * *

On Tuesday, Lissy got up early, showered, then took her time dressing in the bedroom, being just loud enough to wake Will, but not so loud that it was obvious she was trying to wake him. As he watched from beneath sleepy lids, she slathered scented cream up the length of her newly shaved legs, across her belly and breasts, and down her arms, and over the naked mounds of her butt. She took her time doing it, massaging the cream into her skin as if she were caressing a lover, cupping her breasts, bending to give him a glimpse of her from behind.

Then she pulled a pair of garters and stockings out of her drawer of naughty lingerie and—with Will more fully awake—rolled the stockings up her legs and fastened them to the garters. Next, she put on a silk push-up bra, lifting her breasts with her hands so they filled the cups just so. Then she put on a slinky black wrap dress—but no panties.

"Where do you think you're going dressed like that?" He sounded grumpy.

"Oh!" Lissy pretended she hadn't realized he was awake. She slipped into a pair of black Manolo Blahniks. "To the paper, of course. Will you be working late again tonight?"

"No." He was grumpy.

"Have a great day at Broncos camp. I hope Don the dickhead isn't snotty to you on the air." She leaned over far enough to give him a glimpse of what he wasn't touching and kissed him on the cheek. "I love you, Will Fraser."

Then she sashayed out the door, feeling like a million bucks.

*   *   *

"She caught on to me, guys. That's the only explanation. She's fighting back. If I thought I was hurting before, I'm dying now. I'm talking balls so blue they're purple."

Will had endured three days of sheer hell and had done the only thing a man could do under such circumstances: met his buddies after work for a beer.

Devon took a drink. "What makes you say she's fighting back? What's she doing?"

Will leaned in, lowered his voice. "She's teasing me, playing stripper in reverse."

"So she's been getting dressed?" Devon looked unimpressed.

"It's more than that! She struts naked into the bedroom while

I'm still in bed. She rubs skin cream over her entire naked body like she's making love to herself. She takes extra time on all the best parts, especially her ass. I'm telling you, she greases that thing so well she could put it on the grill!"

Devon, Scott, Robert and Nick stared at him, silent and open-mouthed.

But Will had to vent, had to get it out of his system. "Then she gets dressed. Tuesday it was a push-up bra, garters and stockings—and no panties. Yesterday it was a red silk thong. This morning she wore a see-through teddy thing—white lace and ribbons."

"Whoa." Robert lifted his beer, missed his mouth.

Nick and Scott stared at him, mute.

Devon buried his face in his hands. "Man, I sense pink in my future."

"Why don't you just get up and walk out while she's dressing?" Scott asked.

"I'd like to see you try that." It wasn't that Will hadn't thought of that. But when the time had come, he'd found himself unable to move.

"You are wanking, right?" Nick had never been subtle.

"Of course I'm wanking! I'm a guy, right?"

"Just making sure you hadn't overlooked an obvious solution."

"Listen! I'm not finished." Someone had to know what he'd been going through these past three days. "Tuesday night she picked up sushi—and fed me with her own chopsticks. Last night I came home early thinking I'd beat her at her game and cook my lasagna she loves so much, only to find her setting out oysters on the half shell. And the whole time we're eating, all I can think about is that finely greased ass."

"And so you just sit there, a testosterone train wreck, and do nothing to turn the tables?" Devon glared at him as if he'd done something terrible.

"Of course not!" He couldn't tell them about running down the batteries on her vibrator. That seemed a bit too personal. Besides, she'd bought fresh batteries the next morning—and hidden the vibrator somewhere he hadn't been able to find it. "I strut around as naked as a monkey at the zoo. I've been packing boxes, lifting all kinds of heavy shit with my shirt off. I've made a point of kissing her just the way she likes to be kissed. I've brought her flowers. Last night I gave her the ultimate neck rub. She was putty in my hands!"

For a moment no one said anything, the sound of Incubus drifting through the air above the cacophony of a hundred conversations.

Will drew deeply on his brew, knowing full well he was in shit-deep trouble. He'd called Lissy from Broncos team camp to tell her he was going out with the guys and that she shouldn't wait for him for dinner.

"You're going to see them all Saturday night at your bachelor party," she'd said, clearly disappointed he was evading whatever trap she'd laid for him tonight.

But he needed to regroup, to come up with a new game plan.

"If I were you, I'd just give up," Scott offered. "Pink cummer-bunds—what's that compared to what Lissy's got cookin'?"

"I'd have given up Tuesday," Robert said, dragging a chip through dip.

Nick nodded. "I'd never have agreed to the stupid bet in the first place."

Devon placed a reassuring hand on Will's shoulder. "Don't listen to these losers, Will. You've been outclassed, that's all. But you can take her. You just got to give as good as you get. Tomorrow, when she starts to grease that fine thing, you go on over and help her out. Grease it for her."

Will nearly choked.

•   •   •

Will was awake when Lissy came tiptoeing in the next morning. When she dropped her towel and reached for the scented skin cream, he turned on the bedroom lamp. "I was wondering when you'd get here. It's time for my morning skin show."

She whirled around and saw him just as he wanted to be seen— sitting up in their bed, his arms folded behind his head, his naked body fully exposed. He watched as her gaze traveled over him, felt the satisfaction of knowing she appreciated what she saw.

She lifted her chin, looked away, removed the lid from the jar of scented cream and scooped a creamy dollop with her fingers. She rubbed the cream between her palms, lifted a long leg to rest her foot on the bed and began to work her way from ankle to thigh.

"Now the other one," Will said, already hard. "But stand at the foot of the bed—and spread your legs farther apart this time."

Her green eyes flew wide, and a crimson blush crept up her skin from her breasts to her cheeks. But she did as he asked, moving to stand at the foot of the bed, her legs shoulder-width apart. Then she scooped more cream from the jar and lifted her other leg.

"I can see your clit—just the tip of it peeking out—and your rosy inner lips. Remember what it feels like when I suck them into my mouth? Hmm?"

He heard her breathing quicken, saw her hands falter. But she said nothing.

Then she reached for the skin cream again, rubbed it between her palms and slid her hands over her hips to her ass.

"Turn around. Yeah, like that." He watched her hands slide

slowly over her rounded, white ass cheeks and felt his erection thicken. "God, I love your ass, Lissy. I want to nip it. I want to squeeze it. I want to rub my hands over it while you're bent over and I'm fucking you."

Lissy heard the bed shift, felt his feet hit the floor, and spun to face him, certain now she'd made a terrible mistake. He was taking his revenge.

"Let me help with that, sugar." His cock standing rigid against his abdomen, he strode over to her, then dragged his fingers through her scented cream.

A strong arm snaked around her waist, turned her away from him. Then his hands, hot and slick, began to move over her buttocks, cupping her, shaping her, making her shiver.

A rush of heat flared deep in her belly, leaving her wet and wanting. "This is cheating."

"Don't talk to me about cheating. You've been torturing me with this little display every morning. I'm just taking my due." His hands left her body, returned with more cream. "I wonder—are you wet, Lissy?"

His slathered hands reached around, rubbed her inner thighs, then slid slowly upward, the tips of his fingers grazing her labia, parting her, flicking her already swollen clitoris. Her knees turned to water, and she sank back into him.

"Mmmm, you are wet. You want me." Then he pressed himself against her, his cock a hard ridge against her back. "Just like I want you."

He held her against him with one arm, scooped up more cream.

"I-I can do this myself." It was a pathetic attempt, but it was the most she could do.

"You can, but I'm not going to let you. Not this time." He rubbed his hands slowly over the curves and hollows of her hips and belly, moving slowly upward, inch by agonizing inch, until her nipples puckered in anticipation of his touch.

When he finally closed his hands over her, it was heaven, his fingers tugging and teasing her slippery, aching crests, sending sharp tremors of pleasure to her belly, making her inner muscles clench and her body shake with raw, flaming lust. Her breath broke, and she moaned his name. "Oh, God, Will!"

Without warning, he released her, and she heard a drawer slide open. She turned to find him digging through delicate, lacy lingerie as if it were tube socks.

"What—?"

"Perfect." He held a black satin corset out to her, motioned for her to turn around.

She did as he demanded, raising her arms so he could tuck the satin and stays beneath her breasts, then gasping when he began to lace her with sharp tugs. Whether it was the corset or her level of arousal, she could scarcely breathe.

Next, he sat her on the edge of the bed, knelt between her parted thighs and rolled black silk stockings up her legs, fastening them in place with the garters. Then he sat back on his heels, caressed her naked inner thighs and raked her with his hungry gaze. "I bet you're wet enough to take all of me in one thrust."

Lissy's answer was a frustrated moan. She felt the flesh between her thighs pulse, every nerve in her body aching to be fucked, words of surrender on her tongue. His cock was so close, just inches away, hard and thick. She bit her lower lip, felt her inner muscles contract as she imagined how it would feel to have him inside her—the sweet stretch, the slippery friction, the velvet-steel stroke. Oh, God, she wanted him, was more than ready to take him.

One more touch, just one more, and she'd give in.

He stood, pulled her to her feet and toward her closet, then jerked a periwinkle silk dress off its hanger. "Put this on."

She bit back a disappointed groan, did as he asked, turning so he could zip her, her body thrumming with desire so intense it felt like torture.

He closed it with a jerk. "Have a good day at the paper. The coaches have some private time scheduled for the team today, so I'll probably be home early."

Then he kissed her on the cheek and walked off toward the shower looking like some kind of pagan god, bare-ass naked and still erect.

• • •

Lissy found it hard to concentrate at work. The rasp of lace against her thigh, the pinch of stays, the caress of silk against her bare bottom reminded her constantly of what Will had done this morning. Her body seemed to be in a state of constant arousal—hypersensitive, tense, burning. She'd been a single heartbeat from losing the bet. If he had pushed her any harder . . .

She was in trouble. How could she go home to him tonight when she was already wet and aching for him? How could she face him again when one touch was going to drive her over the edge? How could she possibly counter his latest strategy?

She needed help.

She cornered Holly at lunchtime and practically begged her to come over. "We'll rent any DVD you want to watch, and I'll buy your favorite ice cream. All you have to do is be there."

Holly gave her a knowing smile. "He's really gotten to you, hasn't he?"

"Oh, God, you have no idea!"

"I wish I could help, Lissy, truly, I do. But it's Friday night. I have a date. I hope to be getting laid myself."

Of course. Holly always had a date. Why hadn't Lissy thought of that?

Next she tried Sophie, but Sophie also had plans.

"I'm going to a movie with my brother—nothing exciting. Sorry, Lissy."

Lissy found Tessa at her desk, poring over police reports and sipping a designer latté. She explained her situation and pleaded for Tessa's help. "Please say you don't have a date."

"Me? Have a date? You must be joking. Sure, I'll come over."

•   •   •

Will was already home when they got there. Lissy parked next to his pickup, waited in the oppressive dry heat for Tessa to stow her car in visitor parking, then guided her through the Cone Zone, which seemed to have grown since this morning.

"What are they doing here? Prospecting for gold?" Tessa's southern deb accent had a way of making everything she said sound charming.

"I think the flyers they posted said something about working on the gas main."

Desperate to get out of the corset and stockings, Lissy hurried up the steps, unlocked the door and walked into refreshing coolness—and the delicious garlicky smell of Will's lasagna.

"I've always said the person who invented air conditioning should get the Nobel prize," Tessa said. "Mmm, what's that I smell?"

"Will's lasagna." So that had been his plan. A little homemade lasagna, probably some red wine and maybe some Italian ice. She'd have been toast. She set her briefcase aside. "Make yourself at home in the living room. What can I get you to drink?"

"Southern sweet tea if you've got it. Yankee iced tea if you don't."

"How about Yankee tea with lots of sugar in it?"

"Sounds lovely." Tessa wandered off to the living room.

Lissy went into the kitchen expecting to find Will slaving over the stove. Instead she found a sink full of dishes. Then she saw the purple orchids. They sat on the table in a crystal vase. Tucked among the glossy green leaves was a card that read only, "For my bride."

She was admiring the delicate shading of the flower petals when she heard Will striding down the hallway.

"Hey, Lissy, have you seen my—?"

She stepped out of the kitchen to find him standing just inside the living room, stark naked, a towel in hand, looking utterly astonished.

Beyond him, Tessa sat on the couch, her face pink, her eyes wide, her gaze gliding down his body to rest on his groin. She cleared her throat delicately, lifted her chin. "Yes, I believe she has seen it. And now so have I."

•   •   •

Will knew he had it coming.

Lissy was on him the moment he got back from walking Tessa to her car. She looked genuinely angry. "You did that on purpose!"

"How could I when I had no idea Tessa was coming over?"

She rolled her eyes at him, put a hand on her hip. "That's not what I mean, and you know it! You came out here naked, not knowing she was here, hoping to turn *me* on."

He gave her his most charming grin. "Did it work?"

She glared at him, but her cheeks turned pink. "No, it didn't work! It's not like I haven't see it all before, you know."

He pulled her against him, nuzzled her cheek. "Then why are you blushing?"

She pushed him away. "I'm not blushing! I'm furious! You've been doing this all week—trying to get me so turned on that I come begging. You even sabotaged my vibrator!"

He grabbed her wrist, pressed it against his lips. "And what about you, sugar, teasing me with T and A? You've slathered so much cream on that delicious ass of yours I'm surprised there isn't an oil slick on your chair at work!"

Her head dropped and she sank against him. "Oh, Will, this isn't how the bet was supposed to work. It was supposed to make things romantic, not pit us against one another."

He didn't say what he thought the bet was really about because she was already upset and because he didn't want to think about her mother. "We could just absolve one another and end the stupid bet."

She pulled back from him. "You think romance is stupid?"

"That's not what I said!"

"Kind of sounded like it to me. Maybe it's all just about sex for you."

Now he was feeling angry. "You know that's not true."

"Good night, Will." She brushed past him and disappeared into the bathroom.

He stared after her, wondering how she had managed to twist his words so thoroughly.

Women!

•   •   •

They made up over breakfast—sort of.

Will apologized for accidentally walking into the living room naked in front of Tessa when he didn't have the slightest clue she was there and for wanting so much to make love to Lissy. Lissy said she was sorry for overreacting to his apparent lack of interest in romance, something that really any woman would find irritating. Then, pretending that everything was fine, they got to work.

Lissy packed things they wouldn't need until after their honeymoon—wedding gifts, financial records, winter clothes, camping gear, Will's football memorabilia—cranking En Vogue on the stereo and singing along to "My Lovin' (You're Never Gonna Get It)."

Will seemed not to notice her or her pointed choice of music, hoisting heavy boxes onto his shoulders, carrying them outside and through the Cone Zone to his pickup and driving them to the new house without a word. But the third time she played the same song, he put on his iPod.

He was ignoring her.

She set about ignoring him, too.

They worked without speaking through the afternoon, taking a quick break over chicken curry and Thai iced teas, then showering alone, each getting ready for the night ahead. Holly was coming at seven to take Lissy to a private suite at the Adam's Mark for her bridal shower/bachelorette party, while Devon was sending a limo to pick up Will and convey him and his groomsmen to certain unnamed establishments on East Colfax.

It was only after Will had left, looking like pure sex in black jeans and a silky black T-shirt, that it hit her: She'd sent the man she loved off to spend the evening with sexy strippers angry and without so much as a kiss.

* * *

Lissy made it through the chocolate buffet, the gifts and at least ten glasses of champagne acting as if she were having the time of her life. She didn't want to ruin the evening for anyone else. They'd all gone out of their way to make the night special for her, even arranging for a trio of male strippers, whose pelvic gyrations, bare butts and flexing muscles sent some of the women—Holly among them—into estrogen meltdown and resulted in more than a few phone numbers being tucked delicately into bulging thongs along with dollar bills.

It was only after most of the guests had gone that Lissy found herself unable to hide her feelings. No sooner had Tessa asked her what was wrong, than Lissy found herself in tears.

She told them everything: how Will had tried to seduce her, how she'd tried to seduce him back, how she'd found herself on the brink of giving in and had asked Tessa to come home with her, how Will had walked into the living room, naked, right in front of Tessa, how they'd gotten into a fight and had ignored each other all day.

"And n-now he's watching b-beautiful women shake their h-hooters, and I didn't even k-kiss him good-bye!" Lissy blew her nose, sniffed, grabbed another tissue from the box Kara had handed her.

For a moment no one said anything.

Then Holly spoke. "You saw him totally naked, Tess? Is he as hot as he seems?"

"Holly!" Kara gave a disgusted snort and began to pack Lissy's gifts in bags. "Your one-track mind gets a little old sometimes."

But Sophie and Holly were staring at Tessa, clearly waiting for an answer.

Sophie cleared her throat. "Well, Tess, is he?"

Tessa nodded. "Oh, my gentle Jesus! Yeah."

Lissy had started to cry again when she felt Kara sit down beside her.

"You know what I think these tears are, Lissy?" Kara slipped a comforting arm around her shoulder. "Champagne, sexual frustration and pre-wedding jitters."

"R-really?"

"Yeah. Now let's get you home."

· · ·

"I love her so much. She's smart, and she's funny, and, God, she's so damn sexy. And she smells good and tastes good. I could taste her all day, everywhere. I really could." Will took another sip of Scotch. "And I love her—more than anything. I love just *being* with her—holding her hand, talking, watching TV or whatever. I could listen to her voice forever."

The woman he was talking to gave him an indulgent smile. "It sounds like you're really in love with her."

He nodded. "I love her so much sometimes it scares me. If Lissy were to leave me . . ."

The woman laughed. "That's not going to happen, honey. Take my word for it."

It was then Will noticed the woman wasn't wearing . . . much of anything. "Did you lose your shirt somewhere? Are you cold? Here, you can have mine."

He started to pull his shirt over his head; then he heard Devon's voice and felt strong arms yanking him to his feet. "Okay, man, time to go. On your feet. That's the way."

"Devon, there's a naked woman over there. I think we should help her."

"It's your bachelor party, Will, and she's a stripper."

The woman's voice came from behind them, a mix of laughter and cigarettes. "A stripper who's apparently losing her touch. Good night, boys. And thanks."

A stripper? His bachelor party. Loud music. An endless stream of strip bars and single malt. "I'm drunk off my ass, aren't I?"

"Oh, yeah. Watch your step. Nick, catch the door."

The floor wobbled. His stomach lurched. "Devon, I want to see Lissy."

"I know."

* * *

Lissy woke, her head pounding, her mouth full of sand. She heard someone moaning, realized it was she.

"Here, sugar."

She forced her eyes open, saw Will sitting on the edge of their bed beside her in his boxers, a glass of water and what she hoped were aspirin in his hand, though arsenic would have been fine, too. She vaguely remembered getting into bed with him, both of them too drunk to do more than fall asleep. She sat up with a groan, took the tablets, popped them into her mouth, then drank.

The water felt like salvation. She drained every drop and fell back on her pillow, in agony. "How come you're on your feet? You were in lots worse shape than I was."

"Practice. Some rumors about football players are true."

The next time she awoke, her face was pressed into Will's chest, his arms wrapped around her. She might have enjoyed being close to him had the throbbing in her head not been so terrible. It was pounding so hard, she could hear it.

Pounding. Ringing. More pounding.

Someone was at the door.

Will groaned. "Christ!"

Because he'd brought her water, she forced herself out of bed and into her robe, then stumbled through the darkened condo toward the brain-piercing noise coming from the front door. She glanced through the peephole, felt her stomach hit the floor.

More impatient pounding.

Reluctantly, she slid back the bolt and opened the door.

"Really, Melisande, did you have to keep me waiting?"

"Mother."

. . .

"We should set her up in a hotel." Will ran the comb through his wet hair, his temper only slightly worse than his hangover. "It's not like she warned us she was coming."

"But what if she really has accepted our marriage and just wants to get to know you?"

He heard the hope in Lissy's voice, and anger with Christa Charteris swirled black in his gut. He knew she hadn't changed her mind about the marriage and suspected she'd come to make trouble. But he wouldn't be able to explain his hostility toward her without also letting Lissy know the woman had tried to bribe him, and he didn't want to hurt Lissy.

"Then I guess she can stay in the guest room." He set the comb aside, pulled Lissy into his arms and kissed her forehead. "If she hurts you or tries to interfere with the wedding, I'll stuff her and her designer luggage into a cab bound for the airport. I mean that, Lissy."

"Don't worry, Will. I can handle my mother."

Will worried, but then something occurred to him. If Mrs. Charteris slept in the guest room, Lissy would have no choice but to crawl back in bed with him.

. . .

Lissy shut the door behind her, the bedroom now a refuge. She undressed, put on the old T-shirt she'd been sleeping in and hung her clothes in the closet. Then she crawled into bed and tried to relax, listening to the rumble of approaching thunder.

A part of her wished she'd followed Will's suggestion and banished her mother to a hotel. Her mother had been with them for four days, and Lissy's patience was shredded. Though her mother hadn't done anything unforgivably horrid and had even managed to be pleasant at times, she hadn't been easy to have around.

The first thing she'd done was to insist upon meeting with the wedding planner. When Lissy had assured her everything was in good hands and declined even to give her the phone number, she'd acted insulted—as if being the mother of the bride meant something after six months of trying to get the bride to call off the wedding. Then she'd watched with a knowing look on her face while Lissy had changed the sheets on the bed in the guest room.

"Sleeping apart already, I see."

"It's not what you think, Mother. Will and I are simply abstaining from sex until after the wedding in order to make things a bit more traditional and romantic."

Her mother hadn't said a word, but the look on her face hadn't changed.

After work on Monday, they'd taken her to their favorite seafood place, where they'd had a good enough time. Her mother had asked Will polite questions about his job at the paper and what it was like to do live television. Though she'd complained about her salmon and the service, she'd also complimented Will's choice of wine. But when they'd taken her for a stroll down the 16th Street Mall, she'd turned up her nose at everything from the street performers to the store displays. By the time they'd gotten home, Lissy felt ready to scream.

On Tuesday, her mother had taken the liberty of arranging a lunch for herself and Lissy at an exclusive restaurant near the federal court building, ignoring Lissy's desire to share her lunch break with Will as well. Then she'd proceeded to name every quality about Will she liked and every quality she didn't like. He was well-mannered. He was intelligent. He was articulate. He was good-looking—too good-looking. He was arrogant. He had no family. He'd grown up grasping for money. He didn't even know who his father was.

Lissy had cut her off by standing and dropping a twenty on the table. "You're forgetting the thing you hate most about him, Mother. I love him."

Then she'd walked out of the restaurant, fighting tears, leaving her mother to take a cab.

Today, Lissy had avoided her mother by pleading a busy day at work. It wasn't entirely untrue. This was her last day at the paper before leaving for three weeks of vacation, and she'd needed to make certain the fall fashion special was organized and moving forward before she walked out the door: cover design, photo shoots, articles. She and Will had enjoyed their only real time alone together since Sunday over a couple of Chicago-style hot dogs they'd bought for lunch from a vendor on the street. Being with Will for those few minutes—just sitting beside him—had been heaven.

Will had worked late taping a special Broncos team camp wrap-up and still wasn't home. She and her mother had spent an uncomfortable evening in front of the television. Lissy had tried to enjoy Will's segment, while her mother had whined about every aspect of football and sports she found disgusting. When her complaining had interrupted Will, Lissy had snapped and asked her to be quiet or leave the room. Her mother had sulked off and gone to bed early, leaving Lissy with her anger and guilt.

Through the closed curtains came a flash of blue light, followed by a peal of thunder.

Only three days.

The thought bolstered her. Tomorrow, she and her bridesmaids were spending the day at a downtown spa. Friday afternoon was the rehearsal, followed by the rehearsal dinner. Saturday morning she would become Will's wife, and they would leave for two weeks in France. Then all of this—the bet, Tessa seeing Will naked, her mother—would be far behind them.

Lissy closed her eyes and tried to sleep, listening as the bluster of wind and thunder turned at last to rain.

●   ●   ●

Will hurried through the downpour, up the steps of the darkened condo, unlocked the door and let himself in. He'd spent more time at the station than he'd intended and wasn't surprised to find Lissy and her mother already in bed. At least he wouldn't have to face his soon-to-be mother-in-law.

The woman spread poison every time she opened her mouth. She hated him—that much was clear. She rarely made eye contact with him, and when she did, her eyes were full of rage and bitterness. He knew she'd been young when she'd married Lissy's father, and that she'd desired the bank account more than the man. He knew, too, that her husband had been unfaithful almost from the start and that she had answered in kind, avenging infidelity with infidelity until she was worn and hollow. He'd have felt sorry for her if her venom hadn't been so harmful to Lissy and aimed at their marriage.

He set his briefcase aside and slipped out of his shoes, and then checked the mail before heading off to the bathroom to brush his teeth and get ready for bed. He found Lissy lying in the dark, still awake. He slipped into bed beside her, made room for her to snuggle up against his chest, pulled her close.

"What are you still doing awake, sugar?" He thought he knew.

For a moment she was quiet. "My mom and I got into a bit of a tiff."

"Do you want to talk about it?" He could feel the tension in her body.

"No. I want you to kiss me."

He traced the fullness of her lower lip with his thumb. "Well, okay, but when you kiss and make up, aren't you supposed to kiss the person you argued with?"

She gaped at him for a moment, then burst into giggles, burying her face in his chest to mute the sound. "Oh, Will, you always make me laugh!"

"No, sugar. Sometimes I make you scream." He ducked down, took her mouth with his.

He kept the kiss light, more about lips than tongues, comfort than lust. The bet was still in full force, and though going twelve days without sex had left him as randy as a frat boy, her mother's presence had left no doubt in Will's mind that there was more at stake for Lissy in this little wager of theirs than which one of them caved first. She was trying to prove something to herself about him, about their relationship. He didn't want to let her down.

But the connection between them had always been a live wire, and without meaning to, he found himself kissing her hard, cupping the fullness of her breast in his hand, teasing her hardened nipple with his thumb.

He pulled back from her, brushed the hair from her face and chuckled when she whimpered her frustration. "I'm starting to remember what it's like to be a teenager and stuck at second base—tits but no tail."

She laughed, smoothed her hands over his chest, her thumb catching one of his nipples. Then her face grew serious. "I don't know why you're putting up with her, Will."

So they were to back to her mother again.

He pressed his lips to her cheek. "I put up with her because I'm madly in love with her daughter."

Her body relaxed in his arms. "Her daughter's madly in love with you, too."

Soon, she was asleep.

*   *   *

"Surely you have some kind of mineral water that doesn't come in cheap, plastic bottles. And I'd like lemon—fresh, sliced lemon."

"I'm sorry, ma'am, but that's the only brand of bottled water we carry."

"That is simply unacceptable."

Lissy tried to ignore her mother's complaining, willing the tension to leave her shoulders as the aesthetician wrapped her hair in a towel and prepared to give her a facial. Beside her Holly, Tessa, Sophie and Kara lay on treatment tables, dressed in thick, white terry robes, their hair also wrapped in towels. Soft music drifted over the sound system like clouds, but it was no mask for the barbed wire of her mother's voice.

This was spa day. It was supposed to be fun. It was supposed to be relaxing. But her mother was ruining it for all of them with her constant criticism, her mood a chilling frost. Nothing was good enough: not the music, not the size of the dressing rooms, not the décor. Now the bottled water was below her standards, as well.

Lissy had felt obligated to bring her mother along and had been naïve enough to think this sort of pampering would make her mother happy. But it seemed nothing made her mother happy.

"When I pay for a full day at the spa, I expect to be treated like a princess!"

"You're not paying for it, Mother." Lissy tried to sound calm, as if her mother's whining weren't plucking on her last nerve. "I'm paying for it, and I like this bottled water just fine."

"Then you're wasting your money, Melisande."

An uncomfortable stillness fell over the room.

Tessa spoke in her most sophisticated Savannah drawl. "You know, the last time I visited this establishment, I found the Venetian mud bath to be most enjoyable."

"I heard they have the mud flown in straight from Venetia," chirped Holly.

"You mean Venice," Sophie corrected.

"Oh. Yeah."

"I quite enjoyed the Venetian mud bath, as well," Kara said, the tone of her voice strangely snobbish. "It was a gift from my husband, the senator, after Caitlyn was born."

"Your husband is a senator?"

"Why, yes, Mrs. Charteris. Didn't Lissy tell you? He'll likely be our next governor."

The spa offered mud baths, but not Venetian mud baths. And Kara's husband, Reece, had sworn he'd never run for governor. Lissy had no idea what they were talking about. Had they all gone wacko?

And then it hit her. She decided to play along.

"It's too bad the Venetian mud baths are available only to Platinum Spa Members. I only have a Gold membership."

"Oh, really, Lissy? What a shame!"

Lissy nearly laughed out loud at the feigned dismay in Tessa's voice.

As if on cue, her mother spoke. "Well, given the sloppiness of their service so far, I feel entitled to an upgrade in my services."

"Would you like a Venetian mud bath, ma'am? I believe I can arrange it with management."

Lissy opened her eyes to find the staff person her mother had yelled at standing by the door, a wide, beaming smile on her face.

Her mother nodded, the white towel on her head bobbing slightly. "Yes, I would."

"If you would await me in the lounge, ma'am, I'll prepare the facilities."

"I think the rest of you should insist on the same." Her mother stepped down off her treatment table and into her courtesy flip-flops, then walked out the door.

The smiling staff member looked apologetically toward Lissy. "I'm sorry she's unhappy with our services."

But it was Lissy who felt sorry. "I don't think she's happy with much of anything."

Then Tessa spoke, her eyes closed, her face covered in white goop. "There's a hundred-dollar bill in it for you if you keep her occupied for the rest of the day. Right, girls?"

Lissy, unable to help herself, burst into laughter.

• • •

Will turned onto their street and jerked the truck to a stop. "Give me a break!"

The Cone Zone had expanded while he'd been at work, reducing their street to a single, cramped lane. What in the hell was the city trying to do? If they weren't done by the time he and Lissy got back from France, getting a moving van through was going to be a bitch.

He steered carefully into the parking lot, grabbed his briefcase and picked his way through orange cones toward the front steps. He'd ended up working late again, trying to tie up loose ends so that both the paper and Channel Four would be set while he was in France with Lissy. The sports department had given him a send-off that had included putting up streamers made of hundreds of linked condom packages around his desk. Bunch of lunkheads.

He slipped his key in the lock, heard shouting coming from inside. Quietly, he opened the door and stepped into the hallway.

"You don't know him! He's nothing like my father!" Lissy's voice was trembling.

Protective rage flared in Will's gut, hot and immediate. He put down his briefcase, headed straight for the kitchen.

"They're all like your father, Melisande! You might as well plan for it now, because sooner or later he *will* cheat on you!"

"I'm sorry you think so, Mrs. Charteris." Will fought to control his temper.

Both women gasped, and he saw the blood drain from the older woman's face. Tears stained Lissy's cheeks, her grief fueling his fury.

He walked slowly toward her mother. "I'm sorry you married the wrong man for the wrong reasons. I'm sorry he hurt you by sleeping around. I'm sorry you cheapened yourself by doing the same. I'm sorry for whatever it was that made you such a heartless, miserable human being. But I'm done tolerating your poison in our home. Pack your things, and get out!"

Lissy's mother gaped at him. Then her face turned to stone, her voice to ice. "At least have the decency to call me a cab."

Will met her frigid gaze with steel. "My pleasure."

* * *

Lissy watched through the guest room window as the cab wound its way between orange cones and disappeared around the corner. Tears she didn't want to cry ran warm down her cheeks, her mind a riot of conflicting emotion. She heard the soft tread of feet on carpet and felt Will's hands against her shoulders.

"I'm sorry, sugar. I know that couldn't have been easy for you."

"Or for you." She wiped her tears away. "I really feel sorry for her, Will."

"She's to blame for her own situation. No one forced her to marry your father or to stay with him. She made those choices herself."

I'm sorry for whatever it was that made you such a heartless, miserable human being. But I'm done tolerating your poison in our home. Pack your things, and get out!

She heard Will's voice in her mind, saw the anger and hurt on her mother's face. "I wish you hadn't been so hard on her."

"Hard on her?" Will stepped back, ran a hand through his hair, shook his head. "God, Lissy! How many men would tolerate half as much as I did? I think I went pretty easy on her, considering what I heard her say. I don't care if she doesn't like me, but I won't have her standing in our kitchen, upsetting you and accusing me of fucking around on the wife I haven't married yet! I'm not that kind of man!"

She heard the rage in his voice, beneath it the hurt. "I know that, Will. You don't have to tell me that."

"I think maybe I do. That's what all this is about. Be honest, Lissy. You didn't decide to stop having sex until after the wedding for the sake of romance. You did it because some part of you doubts us—doubts me!"

Lissy felt the heat of anger rush to her face. "That's not true! But isn't it interesting that going two weeks without sex is such an issue for you that we end up fighting about it?"

"That's not why we're arguing, and you damned well know it! Don't try to turn this around." His gaze went cold, and she could tell he was truly angry with her now. "It's not the bet that bothers me—it's your lack of faith."

His words felt like a slap in the face, perhaps because some part of her knew she deserved them. But she was too overwhelmed, her emotions too raw, to think it through just now. "I defended you! I stood by you when you told her to leave. Why would I do that if I didn't trust you?"

Then, a sob caught in her throat, she ran to their bedroom and shut the door behind her.

Keys jingled, and Lissy's heart sank as she heard Will walk out the front door and lock it behind him.

* * *

Lissy woke to find she'd slept in their bed alone. She sat bolt upright, suddenly alarmed. She'd sat up waiting for him until after midnight and then had gone to bed furious. But what if something had happened to him?

Then she heard the rasp of the coffee grinder.

Will was home, but he had chosen not to sleep beside her.

The realization left her feeling almost sick. She fought the urge to dash into the kitchen to confront him or to beg for his forgiveness, instead slipping into a hot shower. When she entered the kitchen a half hour later, she found him reading the papers.

He looked up from the page, dark circles beneath his eyes. "Morning."

She stood there, looking at him, wanting so much to tell him she was sorry, wanting to shout at him for leaving her alone all night. "Morning."

They didn't talk about it at breakfast. They didn't talk about it in the car on the way to lunch with the wedding planner. They didn't talk about it while they waited for everyone to show up for the wedding rehearsal. And although the rehearsal went as smoothly as Lissy could possibly have hoped—her mother attended and didn't complain once—Lissy knew all was not as it should be.

Will was sweet and attentive, standing with his arm around her shoulders, rubbing his thumb over the bare skin of her arm, kissing her on the cheek now and again, but there was a remoteness to his affection that made the lingering pain of their argument even harder to bear. Still, it was the evening before her wedding, and Lissy was determined at least to seem as if she were having the time of her life. So she kept a smile on her face, laughed at people's jokes, chatted cheerily with friends and guests.

Rather than a formal rehearsal dinner in a restaurant, Lissy and Will had opted to have a catered buffet in the park near their condo. They'd wanted their friends to be able to bring their kids and to dress comfortably, strictly weekend casual, though Lissy had opted for a sleeveless dress of black linen and sandals. They'd all get their fill of being dressed up and formal at the wedding and reception tomorrow.

A big white tent had been set up to shelter the food and tables in case a late-afternoon thunderstorm rolled in over the mountains, as so often happened during the summer. But the sky was clear, and as their guests finished eating, they spread through the park to enjoy themselves, just as Lissy had hoped they would.

Kara's husband, Reece, was playing soccer with their son, Connor, while Kara bounced Caitlyn, their eleven-month-old baby, on her lap and talked with Lissy's mother about the trials of being a senator's wife. The groomsmen and ushers were trying their luck with a Frisbee and discovering why they preferred football. Tessa and Sophie were lost in a discussion about some investigation they were working on. Devon and Holly were . . . all over each other.

Lissy looked up at Will, expecting to share a laugh with him, only to find herself looking at his back as he walked away. He was still angry with her. They were about to be married, and they weren't even speaking.

A bleakness Lissy had never known crept into her belly. Tears pricked behind her eyes. She stood, suddenly needing to think, needing be alone. Knowing her mother would see beyond whatever lie she concocted, she threaded her way among the tables toward Tessa and Sophie.

"I've got a really nasty headache," she told them. "I'm going home for a while."

Then, before they could ask too many questions, she hurried out of the park toward the condo, tears spilling down her cheeks.

● ● ●

Will tossed the ball gently to Connor, saw a smile of surprise cross the boy's face when he caught it. "That's the way. Hug it tight, and run for the end zone."

The child ran as fast as he could on six-year-old legs toward the two trees that marked the end zone, through a gauntlet of former football players who couldn't seem to catch him.

"Whoa! Touchdown!" Devon shouted. "High five, little man! Now spike the ball!"

Will stepped out of the game and strode toward the keg, pretending to want another beer when what he really wanted was to be alone with Lissy. He'd spent all day trying to ward off his growing sense of guilt, trying not to notice the shadows in Lissy's eyes or the way she kept looking to him for some kind of reassurance.

But there was no way around it. He'd been an ass. He'd known Lissy was upset, but still he'd forced the issue, trying to make his point.

That's what all this is about. Be honest, Lissy. You didn't decide to stop having sex until after the wedding for the sake of romance. You did it because some part of you doubts us—doubts me!

She'd reacted as if he'd hit her.

I defended you! I stood by you when you told her to leave. Why would I do that if I didn't trust you?

And she had. She'd stood up to her mother for him, and she'd stood beside him when he'd kicked her mother out. She'd shown him respect, something she'd surely never seen her parents give one another, something her parents had only rarely shown her.

A voice in his mind started offering excuses. He'd only told her the truth, after all. How could he be blamed for that?

Because you hurt her, you fricking idiot!

He'd been so angry with her mother, every inch of him burning with frustration after four days of putting up with insults and innuendo. And he'd taken it out on Lissy, first by ramming his point of view down her throat, then by leaving her alone most of the night while he'd sulked and watched ESPN at a damned sports bar.

He felt a surge of regret, looked about the park for her. He needed to talk to her. He needed to apologize. Tomorrow was their wedding day. It was time to set things right.

The sun was squatting fat and orange atop the purple silhouette of the mountains, stretching long shadows across the grass. But he didn't see Lissy anywhere.

He walked up to Kara, ignoring Lissy's mother. "Have you seen Lissy?"

"I think she went home," Mrs. Charteris answered.

Kara adjusted the sleeping baby in her lap. "She told Tessa she had a headache."

"Thanks."

He could see city utility trucks parked at the edges of the Cone Zone, their yellow work lights flashing. They were working late. He was halfway down the block when he smelled it—just the faintest whiff.

Gas.

It happened as if in slow motion. A deafening blast. A rush of heat. An eruption of orange flame. Their condo exploded, spewing fire and knocking Will to the ground.

He stared for a moment in utter shock, then leapt to his feet.

"Lissy!" His heart beat like a sledgehammer in his chest. "No!"

Then he was running toward the blaze, oblivious to the heat, to the pain in his knee, to the cries of friends in the park behind him. He had to get to Lissy.

• • •

Lissy slipped the key into the lock and opened the heavy oak door. She'd been halfway back to the condo when she'd found her feet carrying her instead down the bike path to their new house. She needed to feel the future, to feel hope, to feel the life she was about to enter surrounding her.

She stepped inside, smelled the mingled scents of floor polish, new paint and moving boxes. She walked slowly through the rooms.

Here was the living room with its gleaming wood floor where they would put up their Christmas tree. They'd talked about how it would sit in front of the big bay window, where everyone could see it and feel its cheer. Here was the dining room, where they'd teach their kids to hold their forks properly and not to talk with their mouths full. Here was the kitchen, the pantry, the laundry room.

She climbed the wide staircase, her hand trailing over the polished wooden banister Will had so painstakingly restored, then walked around boxes toward the three smaller bedrooms. One day children would sleep here. Boys? Girls? She'd be happy with either. Or both.

She wandered from room to room, until she found herself standing in the master bedroom. It faced the front of the house, a wide window opening onto the branches of the cottonwood tree outside. Dappled light filtered through the leaves onto the wood floor around her feet, bringing with it a sense of contentment.

She turned, faced the empty space where their bed would go, imagined the nights—and mornings and afternoons—they would spend together there. It was there their children would be conceived. They'd already made love on the floor in that spot just to break it in—or to sanctify it, as Will liked to say. As if just by having sex they could make things pure, clean, holy.

That's certainly how it felt. Sex with him was like nothing she'd ever known before. She supposed it was because she loved him—with everything she had, she loved him.

Would it be enough?

The very walls around her seemed to wait for the answer to that question.

Her mother and father had never loved each other, not really. They'd turned marriage into misery, not only for them but for Lissy, too. How many nights had she fallen asleep to the sound of her mother's crying and her father's shouting?

That wasn't the kind of marriage Lissy wanted.

Be honest, Lissy. You didn't decide to stop having sex until after the wedding for the sake of romance. You did it because some part of you doubts us—doubts me!

The sharp edge of regret pressed in on her.

Will was right. The bet had nothing to do with romance. It was about fear. Fear that somehow she wouldn't be enough to keep Will for a lifetime. Fear that his love would wear away with time. Fear that she'd find herself bitter and old and alone.

I'm not that kind of man!

She heard the desperation in his voice, saw the plea in his eyes, and the weight of her regret doubled. She owed him an apology—

for not trusting him, for not being willing to face the truth inside herself, for putting them both through two weeks of unmitigated horniness. She'd just turned toward the stairs, eager to return to the park, when she heard it: an explosion.

She whirled toward the window, glimpsed smoke and the orange glow of fire.

The fire was a few blocks west. Near their condo.

She ran for the stairs.

● ● ●

Will stood by the fire engine, his gaze on the burning condo, an anguished cry stuck in his throat where it had died along with the rest of him the moment he'd realized he wasn't going to be able to reach her.

Lissy, oh, God, Lissy!

The fire had been hot, too damned hot. Though his mind and heart had been willing, his body had not. The heat had driven him back, even as he'd told his feet to move forward. The city utility crew had done the rest, tackling him, then dragging him off to a safe distance until the fire crews arrived.

"You crazy son of a bitch! Tryin' to get yourself killed?"

"My fiancée is in there!" he'd shouted at them.

"Not anymore, she ain't."

Will might have beaten the man's face in if his words hadn't driven the air from Will's lungs, sapping him of everything but grief and regret.

He wasn't sure why he was still standing, how he managed to say "thank you" when a fireman handed him a plastic cup of water, why he didn't simply collapse on the ground. He'd felt this bleak only once before—on the day his mother had died. No, that had been different. He'd had months to prepare himself, months to

know in his mind, if not in his heart, that the woman who'd sacri-
ficed everything out of love for him was dying.

Nothing could have prepared him to lose Lissy.

. . .

Lissy ran down the creek path, the sound of sirens echoing off the
houses and apartment buildings around her. She could see her friends
gathered at the edge of park, watching the fire. She knew before she
reached them that the condo was gone.

"Lissy!" She heard Holly shout, saw a sea of tear-streaked faces
turn her way.

Then she was surrounded, being hugged by one person after the
next, until her mother pulled her close and wouldn't let go.

"I thought . . . I thought you . . ." Her mother wept softly against
her shoulder, bringing tears to Lissy's eyes. "Oh, God, Lissy!"

They'd thought she'd gone to the condo, Lissy realized. They'd
thought she'd been caught in the fire. They'd thought—

It slammed into her with the force of a fist.

"Where's Will?"

"Oh, no! No, no!" Her mother stepped back, pressed her hands
to her face. "He went looking for you, Lissy. We all thought you'd
gone home and . . ."

"I-I went to the house. I . . ." Lissy looked toward the condo,
saw flames rolling against the sky, saw the winking lights of fire
trucks and police cars. "Will?"

The ground seemed to roll beneath her feet. She felt strong arms
encircle her waist, heard Reece's voice in her ear. "Easy, Lissy.
Come sit down."

"He can't be dead." She said it as Reece led her to a chair. She
said it when Devon put his hand on her shoulder. She said it when
Holly sat down beside her and took her hand.

Then she saw a potbellied cop making his way toward them. "Are you the folks who reported the man and woman missing in the fire?"

Reece stepped forward, gestured toward Lissy. "We found the woman, officer, but her fiancé is still missing. We're afraid he was in the building."

The cop nodded, his expression grave, and reached for the radio clipped to his shoulder.

Lissy only half-listened as the officer spoke to dispatch, her mind colliding against the terrible possibility that Will had been badly burned or perhaps even killed going after her. If only she had stayed. If only she had spoken with him earlier. If only . . .

The cop was speaking to her. "They'd gotten a report of a gas leak before the explosion and had evacuated the building. While it's possible he got past someone, the city people are telling me the building was empty when it blew."

Hope.

Lissy stood, her pulse racing. She was about to ask the officer if he would please, *please* look for Will, when a call came over his radio.

"Did you say female? Over."

"Roger that," the cop answered.

A tinny voice crackled over the speaker. "We've got a male here, approximate age thirty, named William Fraser, who says his fiancée was inside. Any chance of a match? Over."

The cop looked to Lissy for an answer, but relief had left her unable to speak. No matter. Her friends were already cheering. "Roger, we've got a match."

Lissy would have taken off running at that moment, had the cop not stopped her.

"They're bringing him around the block in a squad car. Stay

put, ma'am." Then he grinned. "I just love a goddamned happy ending."

Tears of joy streaming down her face, Lissy hurried to the edge of the park, watched and waited. And then she saw it: a black-and-white squad car, lights flashing, slowly rounding the corner. The car hadn't yet stopped when the passenger door flew open and Will leapt out.

She ran.

And then his arms were around her, lifting her off her feet, his lips kissing her hair, her cheeks, her lips, as she held him close, sobbing out her fear and happiness against his chest.

Will couldn't let go of her. She was the most precious thing he'd ever held, and he just couldn't let go. "My God, Lissy, I was sure I'd lost you!"

"Th-they told me you went in after me. I thought . . . Oh, God, Will, I'm so sorry! It's my fault! It's my fault!"

"No, sugar, I'm sorry. I should have—" But he didn't get the chance to say more because the small crowd of their friends engulfed them.

Devon drew them both to his chest in an awkward bear hug. "Next time you scare the shit out of us like that I'm going to kick both your asses."

Will endured as many handshakes, weepy kisses on the cheek and hugs as he could stand. Then Lissy's mother appeared before him, her eyes red and swollen from crying.

"You went after my daughter, Will Fraser. I saw you run toward the fire. There aren't many men who would do that." She laid her hand on his shoulder, her chin wobbling just like Lissy's did when she was on the brink of tears. "I just want you to know . . . how much that means to me."

Then she turned and walked away.

Will looked down at Lissy, saw the utter surprise on her face, and wanted desperately to be alone with her. He thanked everyone and told them as politely as he could that he and Lissy were leaving. Now.

"Let me just get my purse." Lissy hurried toward the tent.

Will grabbed Devon by the arm. "I want you to go back to the tux rental place and switch the cummerbunds."

Devon lifted his mirrored shades, his brown eyes filled with amusement. "Let me guess—pink."

"Mauve. It's what my lady wants."

"You got it, man."

• • •

Will managed to persuade the cop to drive them to their house. It took only a minute, Will sitting in the back with Lissy, holding her tightly, lost in the miracle of being beside her. They thanked the officer, and Will handed him a ten, which he refused.

"Hey, how often do I get to carry a bride and a groom in my unit?"

They found the door unlocked and left ajar.

"I guess I was in a hurry."

No sooner had he shut and locked the door behind them than they were on each other, kissing, their hands tearing at clothing, searching for soft skin. He yanked the straps of her dress down over her arms and ripped off her bra, hungrily cupping her breasts, while she tugged at his zipper and slipped her hand inside his boxers to stroke his erection.

She arched her soft breasts deeper into his hands. "Now, Will! Oh, God, now!"

He shoved her back against the door, pushed her dress up above her hips and lifted her off her feet. She wrapped her legs around his waist, kissed him as if she'd been starving for him and ground her hips against him.

He reached down, moved the irritating cloth of her panties aside, and guided his cock into her. "Jesus Christ, Lissy!"

She was already wet, and she closed around him like a fist. He thrust into her with a desperation he'd never felt before. Two weeks of wanting her. Two weeks of needing her. Long, hellish minutes of thinking her gone.

Already he was careening toward the edge, his balls drawing tight, his groin heavy and hot. He reached between them, sought between her slick folds for her perky little clitoris and stroked it. In a heartbeat, her breathing was ragged, her cries frantic. Her nails dug almost painfully into his shoulders, and her legs clamped around him like a vise.

Faster, harder. She felt so damned good. Slick. Tight. Pure heaven.

He felt her back arch, as the tension inside her peaked and shattered. Her breath caught, she cried his name. "Will!"

He pounded into her with his cock, overcome by the fierceness of his need for her, lost in the hot rush of orgasm.

For a moment, they stayed as they were, Will holding her up against the door, his cock still pulsing inside her, her body still contracting around him, wet and warm like molten honey. Then taking her full weight in his arms, he turned them so his back was against the door and sank to the floor so that Lissy straddled his lap.

Lissy couldn't help the tears that filled her eyes. To be here like this with him when she'd thought him hurt or worse . . .

"I love you, Will Fraser. I'm so sorry I ever made you feel I don't trust—"

He pressed his fingers against her lips. "Shhh! It's okay. You don't have to explain, Lissy. I shouldn't have pushed you so hard."

For a while, neither of them said anything, their mingled breathing, the feel of skin against skin, the joining of their bodies more than enough.

It was Will who broke the silence. "When my mother died, I felt so completely alone. The one person I'd known all my life was gone. But today, when I saw the condo blow and thought you were in the middle of it . . . Christ, Lissy, it nearly killed me! I never want to—"

"—feel that way again. I know." She'd felt the same blinding horror.

Lissy lifted her head from his chest, brushed her lips against his, slipped her tongue between his lips to taste him. Then she pulled his shirt over his head and tossed it aside.

The corners of his mouth turned up in a sexy smile, and he returned the favor by removing her dress, his hands returning to palm her breasts. Then he frowned.

"I guess I lost the bet. I'm the one who started this."

"I'm the one who asked for it." She lifted her hips, let him slide her panties down her thighs, then giggled as they awkwardly pulled them first off one leg and then the other. "I'm the one who should pay the price."

"We could just forget the bet." He tossed her panties aside, lifted his ass off the floor to slide his jeans down his legs, and threw them over with the rest of their clothing.

She straddled him again, ran her fingers through his hair, then pressed his mouth against a hot and aching nipple. "It was a stupid idea anyway."

He licked her, tugged her puckered bud with his lips, sucked. Heat speared through her, made her shiver.

"Do you realize that everything we own except for what's in this house is burned to a cinder?" For some reason, the thought made her laugh.

His fingers searched between her thighs, slipped inside her. "The only thing that matters to me is in my arms."

•   •   •

Lissy descended the stairs toward the lobby of the Tabor Mansion, Holly and Tessa in front of her, Kara and Sophie behind her, fussing with her train. From inside the main ballroom came the sweet strains of Bach's *Air on a G String*, played by a string quartet. When it ended, she would enter the room, and the quartet would begin to play *Jesu, Joy of Man's Desiring*. And then she would become Will's wife.

Her mother waited for her at the foot of the stairs dressed in beaded lavender silk, her eyes puffy. Her gaze traveled over Lissy's gown, her finely penciled brows lifting slightly. "You look lovely, Melisande. Truly lovely—a beautiful bride."

"Thanks, Mother." Lissy shifted her bouquet of lily of the valley to one hand and gave her mother a hug.

"I just wanted to say I might have been wrong about Will. I hope with all my heart I was." Her chin quivered, and Lissy knew she was on the brink of tears. "I'm sorry I haven't been a better mother to you. Maybe I'll be a decent grandmother."

Then, without giving Lissy a chance to respond, her mother motioned to the usher, took his arm and entered the ballroom with the bearing of a queen.

Lissy stood there for a moment, too stunned to speak.

"Don't you even think about crying, Lissy!" Holly smoothed her gown. "They haven't invented a mascara yet that's foolproof against tears."

Lissy smiled, looked into her friends' eyes. "Thank you so much for everything."

"You look truly beautiful." Sophie looked like she might cry.

"Sophie, don't!" Tessa plucked at the strap of the Badgley Mischka. "What made you change your mind about the gown?"

Lissy took a deep breath, tried to put it into words. "When I thought I'd lost Will, a lot of things went through my mind. I realized that nothing really matters but having him with me. If it makes him happy to see me in this gown, then I'll wear it. It's such an easy way to please him. This is his wedding, too, you know."

Kara smiled at her. The only married woman in the group, she understood—Lissy could see it in her eyes. "He's going to flip."

The song was drawing to its close. The bridesmaids got into line.

Holly hazarded a peek through the door, her face lighting up with a smile. "Oh, wait till you see, Lissy!"

The music ended, and for a moment there was silence, punctuated by a cough and the sound of a baby's babble.

"Sorry!" Kara whispered. "Caitlyn's a chatterbox today."

But Lissy didn't even hear, her mind on Will.

The lilting sound of a violin floated through the air, the beauty of the music making Lissy's throat tight. Ahead of her Kara walked through the door with graceful steps. Sophie went next, turning to share one last smile with Lissy.

Then Tessa turned and stared at Lissy as if seeing her for the first time. "Good God almighty, Lissy, you're getting married!"

Lissy smiled, and the tightness in her throat became a lump. "I guess I am."

Tessa turned and walked down the aisle.

"Oh, hell! I think I'm going to be the one to lose it!" Holly dabbed at the corners of her eyes with her fingertips, then turned and started after Tessa.

Clutching her bouquet to keep her hands from trembling, Lissy counted to ten, drawing deep, steadying breaths, and then stepped into the doorway.

There at the end of the aisle stood Will dressed in charcoal gray Armani—and a mauve cummerbund.

She stared at him in amazement, the sweetness of his gesture making her heart constrict, leaving her only vaguely aware that the crowd had stood and was waiting for her. She smiled at him, took one slow step after the next and felt his astonishment when he realized what she was wearing. His gaze slid over her like a ray of golden sunshine.

Then his gaze met hers, and his lips moved silently. "I love you."

And in that moment, any lingering doubts Lissy might have had melted away, leaving nothing but hope and joy and love.

So Caught Up in You

BEVERLY BRANDT

PROLOGUE

"I've heard some interesting rumors about your sister's wedding planner."

Tasha O'Shaunessey grimaced as the heels of her pointy-toed black pumps sank into the lush lawn outside the Naples Country Club. She had no idea why Celie couldn't have had her engagement party inside—away from the heat and the West Nile Virus–carrying mosquitoes here in South Florida—but she had no intention of voicing her complaints. It wasn't every day her baby sister got engaged, so Tasha kept her concerns about heatstroke and disease to herself as she turned to the woman standing next to her and smiled.

"Pardon me?" she asked, taking a sip of champagne.

"Your sister's wedding planner. Quinn Hayes. I've heard some troubling things about him." Lillian Bryson, a trim woman who looked to be in her mid- to late fifties, frowned slightly as she focused her gaze on Tasha's little sister and her fiancé, Cal Jones.

"Like what?" Tasha asked, only half-listening as she studied the woman beside her. From what Celie had told her, Lillian had been instrumental in getting Cal to propose. Her company, Rules of Engagement, was some sort of marriage preparatory academy—a business that taught women (and a handful of men) how to play the relationship game to win that all-important "I Do." When Celie had enrolled, five years after she and Cal had first started dating, Tasha had been concerned that her sister was allowing desperation to cloud her judgment. But after hunting down more than three dozen of Lillian's former clients—all of whom were satisfied with the services they'd received from Rules of Engagement, and 60 percent of whom had since been joined together in matrimonial bliss—Tasha had concluded that maybe Lillian Bryson was on to something.

Less than a month after Celie had graduated from Rules of Engagement, Cal finally popped the question. Tasha didn't believe the timing was coincidental.

So here they were, standing in the sweltering June heat, toasting the happy couple who, in less than a week, would be flying down to Costa Playa, an even more sweltering Latin American country. There, they'd tie the knot standing next to some roaring waterfall or while rafting down a raging river.

Tasha shook her head and took another sip of champagne. Celie may have been successful at getting Cal to propose, but she wasn't having much luck convincing her fiancé that she'd prefer a more traditional wedding ceremony.

Not that Tasha thought her sister had really tried. She was too happy at the prospect of finally being asked to become Mrs. Calvin Jones to raise much of a fuss. Celie had always been that way—

content to go along with other people's plans in order to avoid confrontation.

Which was why—despite the fact that she was right in the middle of a potentially career-making story as an investigative reporter at *Weekly Headline News*—Tasha was accompanying Celie and Cal to the godforsaken Latin American jungle. She planned to make sure her baby sister at least had *some* of the things that were important to her. Like a pretty wedding dress and gorgeous flowers. Not to mention professional photos and a blowout bachelorette party. All things that Cal, and the questionable wedding planner he'd hired down in Costa Playa, would no doubt forget.

What kind of man planned weddings for a living anyway?

Celie had actually giggled when she told Tasha about Quinn Hayes, who worked for a wedding planning company called Extreme I Do. According to the company's website, their wedding planners specialized in putting together ceremonies for couples who were looking for something nontraditional. Like jumping out of a helicopter and skiing down the side of a treacherous mountainside before meeting up with your friends and family to exchange vows in some picturesque hamlet in the Alps. Or white-water rafting down a Class V river in the Congo and then tying the knot while lions stalked the zebra grazing in the background.

Wasn't marriage itself frightening enough?

"He was investigated in the disappearance of Matthew and Julia Martin five years ago. It's rumored that he was the last one to see them alive," Lillian Bryson announced matter-of-factly.

"What?" Tasha's champagne sloshed over the rim of her glass as she jerked it away from her lips.

"Yes, I know. It's shocking, isn't it?" Lillian clucked her tongue like a disapproving mother at a misbehaving child. "Two of the biggest stars of our time, gone just like that. Mr. Hayes told police the couple wandered off for a moonlight swim, despite his repeated warnings that the river was full of crocodiles, sharks, and snakes. Not to mention human predators. Of course, the authorities weren't so quick to believe his story. It was said that the Martins were carrying quite a lot of cash on their honeymoon—cash that has never been recovered, I might add."

"Does Celie know about this?" Tasha asked, frowning at her sister, who seemed oblivious to anything but her fiancé.

"She thinks it'll add an air of excitement to the wedding," Lillian answered.

That sounded like Celie. She was entirely too trusting.

Good thing Tasha wasn't. Now there was an even better reason for her to accompany her baby sister and her soon-to-be brother-in-law down to Costa Playa. *Someone* had to watch over them, to make sure their wedding went off without a hitch and see that they made it back home safely. And if that meant that Tasha had to shadow their every move, then that was what she'd do.

In the meantime, she had a week to check Quinn Hayes's background. If he'd had anything to do with the Martins' disappearance, Tasha would find out about it.

Because if there was one thing she was good at, it was uncovering the truth.

With a preoccupied "nice to meet you" to Lillian Bryson, Tasha wandered over to a stone bench and sat down. She pulled a pen out of her tiny purse and set her champagne down next to her as she started making notes to herself on her cocktail napkin. First, she'd call the Extreme I Do office and see if they'd give her any information about their employee. If not, she had a contact in law enforcement who might be able to help. It would help if she could find out whether or not Mr. Hayes was (or had ever been) a U.S. citizen. With his Social Security number, there were numerous sources she could use to find out where he'd been born, where'd he'd gone to school, get his work and credit history, check out news sources, and on and on.

Gazing absently across the lawn at her sister, Tasha chewed on the end of her pen as she continued to make a mental list of things to do. And, because she was more focused on getting to the bottom of this mystery than on what was happening right in front of her, she missed the knowing wink and thumbs-up sign Lillian Bryson exchanged with the glowing bride-to-be.

CHAPTER ONE

"This last leg of our journey is the most treacherous."

Tasha gripped the thick cable overhead and silently cursed their cheerful guide. Already, they'd hiked ten miles into the hot, thick jungle and forded a rain-swollen river rumored to be full of bull sharks, man-eating crocodiles, and bushmaster snakes. She'd nearly bitten her own tongue off in fright half an hour earlier when a deadly tree frog leaped from out of nowhere and landed on the top of her head.

And *now* their journey was getting treacherous?

What was next? Cannibals? Man-eating anacondas?

No. What was next was to let go of the cable and trust the flimsy harness she was sitting in to hold her weight as she went flying above the canopy of trees, hundreds of feet above the ground.

She suddenly wished that she'd stayed back in San Pedro with

Cal, who had elected to remain at the airport to wait for their luggage, which had been misrouted to Nicaragua, according to the airline's surly lost baggage department employee.

"I don't know why you couldn't have a *normal* wedding," Tasha grumbled, swiping at a bead of sweat before it dripped into her eyes.

Next to her, Celie seemed perfectly comfortable on the five-by-five wooden platform surrounding a strangler fig, but Tasha kept a tight hold on the cable she was clipped to as she stood on the warm planks. If one of the boards had rotted through, she'd free-fall for ten stories before landing on the jungle floor with a sickening *whump*.

"Be careful," Tasha warned as Celie stepped away from the solid tree trunk. "If these boards haven't been properly treated, there could be a microscopic layer of moss growing on them that will make them slick."

This was one of the downsides of being an investigative reporter. You learned the hard way that bad things happen, mostly because people were greedy or lazy or downright evil, but sometimes just because someone didn't do the job they were supposed to do.

"Isn't it beautiful up here?" Celie, who clearly shared none of her big sister's qualms, spun in a slow circle, taking in the scene around them.

From up here, the canopy looked more like a thick carpet of grass than the leaves of trees whose branches intertwined until it was difficult to tell where one ended and another began. Brightly colored birds flew above the canopy, some gliding effortlessly toward some unknown destination and others diving back into the trees as they spotted supper. Tasha just hoped they knew how to get out of the way when the humans clipped to the zip line came zooming their way. She didn't even want to imagine the mess it would make if she slammed into a giant toucan or one of the pretty blue quetzals they'd seen earlier in the day.

Tasha looked down—*waaaay* down—to where their journey would finally end. They'd reach the final platform after zooming past a roaring waterfall that plunged more than one hundred feet to a bottomless pool below.

But first, she had to loosen her death grip on the cable, sit back in the sling, lift up her feet and let herself go.

Tasha shivered.

She was *so* not ready to do this.

"Come on, Tasha. All the amenities of a five-star hotel await you at the end of the line," Celie urged as she clipped her own harness to the cable and, without another thought, pushed off the edge of the platform and went flying above the treetops.

Tasha's eyes narrowed on her sister's retreating back. In addition to a hot meal and an even hotter shower, something even more important would be waiting for her at the end of the line. Quinn Hayes. The man police still believed had played a key role in the disappearance of Matthew and Julia Martin five years ago. But they didn't have enough evidence to hold him, so he'd escaped back to Latin America and, from everything that Tasha had discovered, was now enjoying a prosperous life here in the jungle—a prosperous life that had begun soon after the Martins vanished.

Another troubling thing that Tasha had found was that rumors of white slavery ran rampant in this part of the world—from vacationers disappearing without a trace to orphans grabbed off the streets and never heard from again. Costa Playa, a small country located near the Colombian border, touted itself as a haven for ecotourism—a safe place for travelers wishing to see the tropics in their most pure form—but despite the maniacally cheery PR efforts, the rumors persisted. It didn't help that two of America's top stars had disappeared from this very jungle five years ago.

"Time to go, miss." The cheerful guide interrupted her thoughts by prying Tasha's gloved hand from the cable and nudging her none too gently with his shoulder.

Tasha's arms flailed as she lost her balance and tripped over the edge of the platform, her feet whirling in a desperate attempt to get back to safety. As if in slow motion, she felt herself falling through the air, the tree tops rushing up toward her until she was jerked back by the line clipped to the cable overheard.

The sling was set so that the rider could spin around to get a full view of the jungle; Tasha's wild thrashing only made her spin faster as she tried to regain her bearings.

"Just relax!" she heard her sister shout from up ahead as she picked up speed.

Easy for her to say. She wasn't the one dangling upside down a hundred feet from the ground.

Tasha wished she'd spent a few more minutes of her time at the gym doing crunches as she tried to grab the line at her waist and pull herself up into a sitting position. She'd recently seen a Cirque du Soleil performance where the acrobats were suspended from the ceiling by drapes of red cloth tied around their waists. They spun faster and faster and then let go of the end of the drape, stopping only inches from the floor.

Tasha now knew how they'd felt.

Splashes of color flashed in and out of her peripheral vision as she waved her arms and legs wildly in an attempt to slow down. With a mighty effort, she finally managed to grab hold of the line and pull herself up. After wrapping her arms protectively around the cable, she glanced up to see that Celie was waving her own arms in the air. It only took her a moment to realize that her sister must have somehow lost the thick leather gloves she'd been given at the beginning of their journey. The only way to slow down was to grab the cable overhead, and Celie would need the gloves to protect her hands from being shredded by the thick wire. Without the gloves, her sister's hands would be toast. Or, rather, hamburger.

Tasha grimaced and relaxed her grip on the cable, leaning forward in an effort to gather speed. If she could catch up to Celie, she could toss her one of her gloves.

Only when she looked up again, her sister seemed to be rushing toward the final platform at alarming speed.

Tasha squinted toward the landing pad. Surely there had to be something on the end of the cable that would stop anyone from flying off it at the end? But what if the force of Celie crashing into it at top speed broke it? Tasha couldn't see any sort of pad or bumper that would cushion Celie's fall if she went careening off the end of the cable.

And that meant Celie would spend her honeymoon in a body cast. That is, if there was even qualified medical care nearby that could patch her up after such an accident.

Which, from the . . . er, *rustic* state of the airport they'd flown into that morning, Tasha doubted.

Tasha knew she had no choice. She had to protect her little sister, even if it meant endangering herself to do it.

So she let go of the line and closed her eyes as the wind whipped her hair across her face.

She had to catch up with the runaway cable car and save her sister.

•   •   •

"All we can do is hope for the best."

Quinn Hayes surveyed the motley band of human cargo that had been delivered to him moments ago before turning his attention back to the young woman standing beside him. "That's your plan?" he asked. "Just hope for the best?"

Olivia dePalma folded her hands together in front of her, as serene as the reflection pool in the hotel's grand open-air lobby—a lobby that would soon be filled with American tourists who would surely wonder what these tired, dirty peasants were doing here aside from ruining the ambience.

"You'll figure something out," Olivia said.

Quinn looked over at the group again. There were more than two dozen of them this time, when he'd only been expecting half as many. Not to mention that his contact had promised delivery of this latest "shipment" next week. Quinn had cleared his schedule, making certain that no happy couple's impending nuptials would interfere while he went about getting this latest ragtag band of workers settled into their new lives.

He should have known Rafe would do this to him. Their profits increased with each new worker, and Rafe never could turn his back on an extra buck. And getting them here faster meant that Quinn could get them to work quicker, which meant even more money in Rafe's—and Quinn's—pocket.

So he supposed he shouldn't complain.

But, still, they couldn't have arrived at a worse time.

"I don't suppose there are any empty rooms in the employee quarters where they can stay until the Americans are gone?" he asked, already knowing the answer.

"No. We're running at nearly one hundred percent capacity this week, and that means all available rooms are being taken up by guests or staff."

Quinn sighed. "We'll have to set them up in a ballroom temporarily, then. But we need to make sure they stay out of sight until I can get them out of here."

"How are we going to do that? They're going to need access to a washroom," Olivia said, raising one perfectly arched black eyebrow and giving Quinn the impression that she was secretly laughing at him.

"And here I thought that your plan of hoping for the best would take care of everything," Quinn couldn't help but toss back.

Olivia merely continued watching him calmly.

After a moment of silence, Quinn gave up. Olivia was efficient and loyal, but she always left this sort of mess to him.

Which he supposed was just as well. He had learned long ago that you could only rely on yourself anyway.

"All right. Ask the staff to see if they can rustle up some extra uniforms. No one is to leave that ballroom without a uniform on, and only then to use the restroom. If they're asked for something by any of the guests, tell them to pretend they don't speak the language."

"Anything else?"

There went that eyebrow again.

Quinn shot Olivia a look that he knew many would consider dangerous. Olivia, however, was not cowed. She never was.

"No. Just get them out of here as quickly as you can," he answered with a nod toward the eerily silent group huddled in the lobby like a herd of frightened sheep. "I'm going to call the mine and see if I can get someone to pick them up tonight, but we're going to have to do what we can to keep them out of sight of the guests until help arrives."

A quick smile dashed across Olivia's mouth, coming and going so fast that Quinn wondered if he'd imagined it. That is, until she murmured under her breath, "And hope for the best."

Quinn snorted. Yeah. Like that had ever worked.

But he didn't say what he was thinking. Instead, he dug his cell phone out of his pocket and turned toward the lobby. The cargo—he tried not to think of them as individuals; they wouldn't be around long enough for him to get attached—stood in quiet bunches of four or five, their sad, dark eyes all trained warily on him as if they half-expected him to go on a rampage and start beating them at any minute. Quinn had had enough experience to know that that sort of treatment wouldn't come as much of a surprise to them.

He blinked to cover a cringe when a girl who couldn't be more than twelve or thirteen reached out to clutch the ragged, dirty shirt-tail of the woman standing next to her. The fear was easy enough to read on her face, although she kept her shoulders straight and refused to lower her eyes.

Good for her.

Quinn turned back to Olivia after running a frustrated hand through his hair. "Take them down to the kitchen and have Javier feed them first, will you? I don't need them passing out in the lobby before I can make arrangements to get rid of them."

Olivia's lips twitched again, but she didn't do anything more than nod obediently.

Quinn started outside with his cell phone in hand, the sound of his footsteps echoing on the tile floor as he walked. He did not need this distraction right now, not with a wedding in two days that would pay twice as much as he'd make after delivering this "shipment" to the mine. The sad fact was, human life in this part of the world was cheap. Men, women, children—none carried much value around here except as symbols of power; a painful lesson Quinn had learned more than a decade ago and would never forget.

Shaking off that melancholy thought, he headed for the stairs leading to the roof.

The hotel—of which he was a part-owner—catered to wealthy Americans who claimed to want a place where they could get away from it all. To that end, there was no high-speed Internet access, no cell phone service, and the telephones in the rooms could only be used to call other guests or the front desk.

Which didn't mean that these services didn't exist, just that they were not available to guests. At least, not to those guests who weren't desperate enough to come begging for a hit on their Black-Berries. Or CrackBerries, as Quinn referred to them.

Those guests who needed a fix were shown up to the roof, where they often got four or five bars. Plenty to calm them down for another few hours. And if their families didn't believe they were at the pool or the spa or simply taking a walk on the well-marked trails in the jungle? Well, that was their problem.

Quinn only told those wild-eyed folks who came to him with their cell phones clutched desperately to their chests about the hot spot on the roof, next to the landing pad where guests arrived on the zip lines.

He chuckled to himself now as he climbed the stairs, thinking about how strange it was that guests supposedly came here to enjoy the wilderness, but that wasn't really what they wanted. No, what they *really* wanted was air-conditioned rooms, top-notch meals, cocktails with ice cubes, and hot rock massages after a few hours of white-water rafting or rappelling down cliffs. They wanted to pretend that they were staying in an unspoiled jungle where jaguars ran free and monkeys roamed the trees, unmolested by humans other than themselves, but they wanted to do so in an environment that was as similar to home as possible.

And, mostly, they wanted their cell phones to work.

Fortunately, Quinn did, too. At least in this one area of the hotel, where the addicts could hide from their loved ones while checking their e-mail and voice mail and catching up with whatever drama was going on back in their offices.

Quinn pushed open the door leading to the roof and put a hand up to shade his eyes from the noonday sun's glare. Temporarily blinded, he stepped out onto the hot tar, his boots sticking to the gummy surface.

He looked up, startled, when a shadow passed over the sun.

Only it wasn't a shadow.

It was a woman.

And she wasn't passing over the sun. Instead, she was flying through the air like a human tennis ball that had been launched from a machine.

Quinn didn't have time to think, only to react. It was only later, when he found himself lying on his back with a cute brunette lying on top of him, her small, firm breasts pressed against his chest, that he fleetingly congratulated himself for—rather than stepping out of the way like any sane person would have done—opening his arms wide and catching her as she fell.

CHAPTER TWO

Dead men don't get erections.

Tasha took comfort in that thought as she contemplated the warm, solid—yet still unmoving—man beneath her. Their legs were tangled together, his firm thighs between her own, his lean hips nestled intimately against hers. His chest rose and fell with each breath, which Tasha took as another good sign.

Dead men also don't breathe.

She raised her head. "Are you all right?" she asked.

The man's eyes opened, squinting against the sun's glare. They were a striking color, somewhere between light brown and green.

His arms tightened around her waist, his hands warm and strong on her back. Tasha resisted the urge to lay her head back down on his chest, to press her ear to his heart and let the steady beat lull her to sleep.

"I'm fine. Just don't move," he answered with a husky voice that made Tasha think of silk sheets, whiskey, and hot sex.

She blinked. Where had that thought come from?

"Why not? Is something broken?"

"No. You just feel so damn good." His voice was a whisper in her ear, his breath tickling her neck and making her shiver.

Slowly, he trailed one hand up her spine. She shivered again as goose bumps rose on her bare arms.

Tasha held her breath as he reached out and tucked a strand of hair behind her ear. She felt like they were in some sappy movie, their gazes locked together, this strange electricity passing between them. For just a moment, she relaxed and let herself feel protected in this stranger's embrace.

That fantasy died a quick death, however, when her sister's sparklingly white Keds appeared next to them. "Tasha? Mr. Hayes? Are you two all right?" Celie asked.

Tasha closed her eyes and released her disappointment on a sigh. Here she was, dreaming that this man might be her own personal dragonslayer when, instead, he was a suspected white slaver.

Figured.

Hope never lasted long when confronted with reality.

She tried to roll off her sister's wedding planner, but the firm hand he kept pressed to the small of her back didn't make it easy.

"You can let me go now. I'm fine," she protested. She was *not* going to get into some undignified struggle with the man. He'd either let her go or she'd damage a certain part of his anatomy that was still poking her in the stomach.

"Sorry. I was just . . . uh, giving myself a minute to settle down here." Quinn Hayes shot her a wicked smile that must have increased the earth's temperature about two degrees, and Tasha forced herself not to blush or stammer or react in any way except to raise her eyebrows disapprovingly.

"Yes. Well. I don't think remaining in our current position is going to help anything."

Quinn's grin only widened. "I don't know, it's making me feel pretty good."

"I can tell."

"Sorry," Quinn said again, not sounding sorry at all. Then, in one lithe movement, he rolled them both over, sprang to his feet, and tugged Tasha up beside him. He made an exaggerated show out of dusting off her rear end, which Tasha put an end to by stepping out of his reach.

"I'm fine," she said in a tone of voice that implied that she believed he might have trouble mentally processing that information. She smoothed her T-shirt and made sure it was neatly tucked back into the waistband of her khaki shorts before turning to her sister, who was eyeing them with stark curiosity.

"We're fine," Tasha repeated. "Just took a little tumble."

Celie looked back and forth between Quinn and her big sister. "Don't you hate it when that happens?" she murmured.

"Don't start," Tasha warned, scowling. If she had her way, Celie, the eternal optimist, would have Tasha and Quinn living in happily-ever-afterville before the weekend was over. But Tasha knew that things didn't work out that way, at least not for her.

She turned her scowl on Quinn Hayes, who stood watching her with a trace of that wicked smile still hovering around his mouth. "Mr. Hayes, I'm Tasha O'Shaunessey and this is my sister Celie. Her fiancé is back in San Pedro waiting for our luggage, which seems to have been misrouted. The airline assured us it would be here by this evening. I'm sorry for crashing into you like that. When I saw that Celie had come to a stop at the end of the zip line, it was too late for me to slow down. I had to unclip myself from the harness or I would have killed her."

"Don't worry about it. Let me show you to the lobby so you can get checked in. And, please, call me Quinn."

He gestured toward a flight of stairs with one large, tanned hand. Determined to do what she'd come here to do—get her baby sister safely married and back to the States—Tasha straightened her shoulders and marched across the roof, with Celie and Quinn following at a more leisurely pace. First, she'd make sure Celie got settled in her room, and then she'd do a little poking around. Someone around here had to know about Quinn's past and about his alleged role in the Martins' disappearance. People didn't just vanish without a trace.

Tasha stopped at the bottom of the stairs and pulled open the heavy metal door, then gasped at the scene laid out before her.

"It's beautiful," she whispered.

And, indeed, it was. The hotel's lobby was tiled in white travertine; dotted about the open space were couches with dark frames upholstered in white. Exposed wooden beams crisscrossed the ceiling, and in the center of the lobby was a soothing rock fountain. There were no walls on two sides of the building, which allowed a cool breeze to come in and make itself at home. Several small birds sat near the edge of the fountain, their eyes narrowed sleepily in the noontime sun.

"Worth the journey, huh?"

Tasha turned at Quinn's softly uttered question. "It's lovely," she agreed as she stepped into the lobby with Celie right behind her, a similarly impressed expression on her face.

Quinn nodded toward a dark-haired woman who was watching them from behind a large desk. "Olivia can take you from here. I've got something I need to . . . uh, take care of."

With that, he turned back to the stairs, letting the door slowly swing shut behind him.

Tasha told herself they were well rid of him and didn't even try to come up with an explanation for why she felt a sudden chill. Instead, she rubbed her arms to warm them as she and Celie made their way across the lobby.

"Good afternoon," the front desk clerk greeted them as they approached.

"Hello. We're checking in. Tasha and Celie O'Shaunessey," Tasha said.

The woman busily typed something into her computer, then frowned at the screen.

Great, Tasha thought. What now?

She waited for the clerk to tell them that there was no reservation under their names or that they were overbooked and she was going to have to send them to a Motel 6 or something.

That sort of thing happened to Tasha all the time.

"I'm sorry, Ms. O'Shaunessey . . ." the front desk clerk began, her large eyes dark and sad, as if she'd seen a lifetime of sorrow.

Tasha sighed and reached out to squeeze her little sister's arm. Everything would be all right. Tasha wouldn't let anything ruin Celie's wedding.

". . . but your room has not yet been cleared by housekeeping. The honeymoon suite is ready, but the second room is not."

Tasha blinked with surprise. She'd been prepared for much worse than an unmade bed. "Oh. That's fine. I'll just wait down here until it's okay for me to check in," she said.

"Are you sure?" Celie asked. "You could come up to my room with me."

Tasha chewed the inside of her bottom lip. This would give her the perfect opportunity to do a little snooping without Celie finding out. "No. You go. Get a little rest before Cal gets here," she answered breezily.

Celie's eyes narrowed on her sister. "Are you up to something?"

Putting a hand over her heart, Tasha blinked innocently. "Me? Why would you say that?"

"Because I know you. You're not happy if you don't have something to be nosy about."

"Nosy? I'm not nosy," Tasha protested.

Celie's only response was to raise her eyebrows.

"I'm curious. That's not the same thing."

"Uh-huh. I'm curious, too."

Tasha frowned. "About what?"

"About what was going on between you and my wedding planner just now," Celie answered with a chuckle.

Tasha turned away so her sister wouldn't see the blush heating her cheeks. "I don't know what you're talking about."

"Sure you don't," Celie muttered.

"Really. There was nothing going on. It was just . . . um . . . I mean, yeah, he's attractive. Kind of reminds me of Harrison Ford in those old *Indiana Jones* movies. But I don't even know the guy."

"And if you did, you'd find a reason to push him away."

Tasha glared at her sister. "That's not true. I always give people the benefit of the doubt."

Celie crossed her arms over her chest and tapped the toe of one of her white tennis shoes on the tile floor.

"We're not having this conversation again," Tasha said, then turned to the front desk clerk. "Can you give my sister her room key, please?"

"Certainly," the clerk said smoothly, as if she hadn't heard a word of their conversation. She handed Celie a card key and gestured toward a walkway to her left. "After you get settled, you may want to check out our restaurant. The chef prepares many daily specials for your enjoyment. Or you may just want to relax by the pool, which is open from ten A.M. to midnight every evening. You may also order room service, of course. We have a full menu, which you'll find in your room, along with a list of amenities here at Las Palmas."

Their argument forgotten, Celie took her key and asked Tasha if she was sure she didn't want to come with her to her room. Tasha, however, did not want to risk being forced to continue their conversation.

"No," she said. "I'll just hang around here until my room's ready. You go on up and get settled. No need to worry about me." She shot her sister what she hoped was a convincing smile.

Celie clutched the room key to her chest like a kid with a lollipop. "All right. But if you get bored, you know where to find me."

Tasha nodded and turned toward the nearest grouping of couches. She planned to start her investigation by chatting up the front desk clerk. As soon as her sister left, that is.

"Oh and Tasha?" Celie said.

"Yes?" Tasha paused, but didn't turn to face her sister.

"If you're going to check out my wedding planner, you'd better be careful. I understand he's got a pretty shady past."

• • •

"What do you mean you can't get here until tomorrow? I need to turn over this shipment *now*." Frustrated, Quinn pinched the bridge of his nose between his thumb and forefinger. This operation never ran as smoothly as it should. Fugitives often arrived unannounced, sometimes even when Quinn was away from the hotel trying to run his legitimate businesses.

Too bad trafficking in people was so profitable.

Not to mention important to the goals of his partners.

Quinn sighed.

Like always, he was just going to have to find some way to deal with this unexpected influx of refugees until someone from the mine was able to pick them up.

Fortunately, this latest hotel guest hadn't brought a large party of revelers to the hotel to help celebrate her wedding. Some of their more wealthy clients contracted Quinn not just to arrange the details of the ceremony itself, but for elaborate receptions, rehearsal dinners, and bachelor parties as well. But Celie O'Shaunessey and her fiancé, Cal, just wanted something simple, which made Quinn's job easy. He'd already scouted several locations for the ceremony based on his phone interviews with the happy couple. This afternoon, he'd give them a tour of the area and let them decide where they'd be most happy exchanging their vows. From there, it would be a fairly easy task to pull together everything else they'd need.

Easy, that is, once Quinn managed to get his extra "guests" off his hands.

"Fine. I'll call you tomorrow morning to arrange a rendezvous," he said to the man on the other end of the line before hanging up. There was no use protesting. He knew that if it were possible for his contact to get the refugees today, he would have done so. Quinn would simply have to make certain they remained out of sight until the next day.

That shouldn't be too difficult.

He pushed open the door leading to the lobby, intending to see how the fugitives were settling in, but froze when he heard the voice of a man he had once prayed would die a slow and painful death. He remained hidden in the shadows, his hands clenched into fists, as he strained to hear what was being said.

"—don't know what you're talking about. There's no one here

but the hotel staff and our guests," Olivia said, admirably trying to hide her fear under her usual calm.

"My men tracked Rafael Ramírez and his human cargo as far as San Pedro. Who else would harbor him but his old friend Quinn Hayes?"

"I'm sorry, Mr. Acosta, but I can assure you Rafael Ramírez has not been here."

"Liar!"

When Acosta slammed his fist down on the counter in front of Olivia, Quinn stepped away from the door leading to the roof. No way would he just stand there and allow Acosta to bully Olivia . . . or anyone else at his hotel.

The front desk clerk saw him and shook her head, as if to tell Quinn that she could handle this by herself. But she didn't know Acosta like he did. The man was a ruthless bastard who wouldn't hesitate to torture Olivia to get the answers he sought.

And because he was the head of Costa Playa's secret police and sat at the right hand of the president, he could—and did—act with impunity.

Quinn knew all too well the depths to which Acosta would sink in order to get what he wanted. He had experienced firsthand the consequences of the other man's wrath.

"Excuse me, is there a problem?" Quinn asked as he slid behind the front desk and smoothly placed himself between Acosta and Olivia.

Acosta's flat gray eyes narrowed. "Quinn Hayes. So we meet again."

Quinn half-expected Acosta to wring his hands and laugh evilly after this pronouncement, but instead he rocked back on his heels and clasped his hands behind his back.

"I'd like to say it was a pleasure, but I'd be lying," Quinn said.

"Then the pleasure is all mine."

Quinn nodded to acknowledge the truth of Acosta's statement. The guy had been a wack job when Quinn first met him ten years ago, and it didn't appear as if the ensuing years had made him any less crazy. Or any less powerful.

"Where are the fugitives?"

Quinn pretended to ponder the question for a moment before answering, "I'm sorry, to which fugitives are you referring? We get so many here at Las Palmas, where our nightly rate is double the yearly income of the average resident of Costa Playa."

A vein in Acosta's forehead bulged as the man's face reddened with anger. "I could have you killed for that," he hissed.

"Then do it." Quinn shrugged, picked up a pen that Olivia had left on the counter, and began tapping it on the marble desktop because he knew the gesture would annoy Acosta. He also knew he was poking an angry bear with a twig. If the bear chose to turn and swipe his head off, there was nothing he could do.

But he wasn't going to cower or show any weakness to the man who had once delighted in torturing him just for fun. The worst had been done to him and he had survived. He could do it again if he had to.

Apparently, however, one thing had changed from when he and Acosta had first met. And that was that Quinn was no longer a stranger in this country. He was a successful businessman with highly placed friends of his own, friends who could make trouble for Acosta if Quinn disappeared.

So Acosta had no choice but to back down. At least for now.

Quinn watched with no small satisfaction as the older man visibly swallowed his anger.

"There's no need for this unpleasantness. Simply tell me where my workers are hiding and I will take them and be off."

His "workers." Quinn clamped his teeth together to stop himself from sneering. The twenty-plus men, women, and children hiding in his hotel were not workers, but prisoners stolen from their
homes and families whenever Acosta had a need for cheap labor.
There was no way Quinn would give them up.

"You know that I'd tell you if I could, but I have no idea where
your slaves might have run off to."

Acosta glared back at him with soulless gray eyes that reminded
Quinn of a shark. "Fine, then. We'll do it your way. My men arrive
here this evening. We will all require rooms. While I'm waiting, I'll
search the premises myself."

"I'd be delighted to give you the grand tour," Quinn offered
smoothly, stepping out from behind the desk. He had to pause for
a moment to dislodge Olivia's fist from the back of his shirt, where
she was clutching him with desperation. He wished he could turn
and tell her that everything was going to be all right, but he
couldn't lie to her.

There was a very real possibility that Acosta would discover the
fugitives . . . and punish anyone he believed was responsible for
them being here.

"Where would you like to begin? The spa, perhaps? Many escaped slaves enjoy hot rock massages after traveling through the
jungle for days."

Poke. Poke.

The vein was back.

"I'm pleased that you can find some humor in the situation in
which you find yourself," Acosta said, once again reining in his an-
noyance. "I recall a time when you didn't find your life so comedic.
As a matter of fact, I seem to remember you as a broken man, begging for the pain to stop. I believe I even saw you crying a time or
two." He paused for a moment, and Quinn had to force himself

not to reach out and grab Acosta by the throat and squeeze until no more words would ever come out of the bastard's mouth.

"It's nice that you have such a different outlook on things these days." Acosta laughed lightly.

Quinn flexed his fingers and took a deep, calming breath. "Yes, well, I was a lot younger in those days. I'm not the boy I was back then."

"I'm happy to hear it."

Quinn doubted that very much. A decade ago, he had been nothing more to Acosta than a nuisance.

Now, he was a formidable opponent.

One who would not succumb quite so easily to Acosta's machinations.

"I believe I'd like to start in the kitchen. To use your logic, I would imagine that my escaped *workers*"—Acosta raised his eyebrows at that—"would enjoy a hot meal after traveling through the jungle for days."

Quinn ignored Olivia's sharp hiss from behind him. Of course Acosta would want to be shown the kitchen first. Because that's where the fugitives were.

Fuck.

All he could do was hope that Olivia would manage to get through to the kitchen and warn them before he and Acosta arrived. That is, if they picked up the phone during the busy lunch hour.

Mentally slapping his forehead with his palm, Quinn turned to Acosta and saw a flash of movement out of the corner of his eyes. Probably a bird or a dragonfly or something.

"Follow me," he said, shaking his head to clear it of everything but the ordeal ahead. "You'll soon see that I have nothing to hide."

CHAPTER THREE

Quinn Hayes was hiding something.

Tasha didn't know what it was exactly, but she intended to find out. And the first place she planned to look was in the hotel's kitchen.

She had seen the way the front desk clerk had tensed when the dark scary guy she'd called Mr. Acosta had mentioned starting his tour in the kitchen. She'd bet a million bucks that the missing people Acosta was searching for were there.

And when he found them, then what?

Tasha had done enough research on Costa Playa before coming down here to know what a slime-ball Jorge Acosta was. While Quinn Hayes's reputation wasn't exactly sterling, Acosta's was so covered with rust that it would be hard to tell if anything solid still remained. If the guy in the lobby was indeed the man she'd read about, he had his hands in everything from drug trafficking to prostitution and murder.

She hurried down the hall, the rubber soles of her hiking boots squeaking slightly on the worn tile floor. Quinn might be involved in the white slave trade, might have played a key role in the Martins' disappearance five years back, but she'd take her chances with him over this Acosta jerk any day.

She shivered as she rounded the corner and ducked under a covered walkway. At the end of the walkway, she spied a chalkboard like the kind a restaurant might use to write in the daily specials. She hoped she was right. If not, if she'd headed in the wrong direction, then she'd never find the kitchen before Quinn and Acosta did.

Tasha dashed down the hall and flung open the double doors at the end. The sound of happy diners reached her ears: the clinking of silverware against plates, the soft tinkling of glasses, the din of relaxed conversation, and the slightly censorious tone of the maître d' as he sniffed at her sudden appearance in the doorway and said, "Good afternoon, madam. Do you have a reservation?"

Ignoring him, Tasha scanned the room, looking for the entrance to the kitchen. She found it just as a waiter emerged, carrying a heavy-looking tray of steaming food.

Tasha's stomach grumbled, reminding her that she hadn't had anything to eat since finishing off a pack of salted peanuts this morning on the plane. But now was not the time to be thinking of her appetite.

There was trouble brewing here in paradise.

She sprinted toward the kitchen.

"Madam, where are you going?" the maître d' called from behind her, but Tasha didn't stop. She hit the swinging door at a full run. She'd expected it to be heavy and windmilled her arms in the air to keep from falling face-first onto the floor when it whooshed open with barely a tap.

As she skidded to a stop on the floor, all sounds of a bustling, busy kitchen during its noontime rush ceased. Tasha looked up to find that there were at least four dozen pairs of eyes locked on her in silence.

The kitchen was crowded with a mix of white-coated cooks, black-uniformed waiters, and an odd assortment of drably dressed people sitting on overturned buckets and boxes that were strewn haphazardly about the room.

These, Tasha guessed, were the missing "workers" Acosta was hunting.

"Do you know a man named Acosta?" she asked, stepping farther into the room.

One of the men sitting near the sizzling grill stood, his skin turning a sickly shade of white beneath his tan. "Acosta? Has he followed us here?"

"Yes. He's on his way down here with Mr. Hayes right now," Tasha answered.

"He can't find us. He'll kill us all." Another man leaped up from an overturned bucket and looked frantically around the kitchen, as if searching for a place to hide.

Tasha did the same, but other than the obvious walk-in refrigerator, she didn't see a place where all these people would fit.

"Is there a back entrance to the kitchen?" she asked one of the waiters, who nodded and pointed to a clearly marked exit.

"It's there," the man said, "but what if Acosta thinks of this also and comes in the back way?"

Good point.

Come on, think, she urged herself, then froze when a red telephone hanging near the grill started to ring.

On the second ring, one of the chefs reached out and picked up the receiver.

"Hello, room service," he answered.

Tasha's eyes widened. Yes, room service! That was it!

"Where are your room service carts?" she asked, whirling around, trying to spot them.

"Right here." A dark-haired woman jumped up off a box and grabbed the silver handle of a two-tiered cart.

Tasha sprang into action. "We need tablecloths to cover the carts. And give me any extra uniforms you have lying around," she ordered.

One of the chefs whipped off his own white coat and handed it to a young girl with the largest, darkest eyes Tasha had ever seen.

"Good. Hurry now. Let's try to fit two people on each cart. Give the uniforms to the ones who won't fit. You can play the part of the wait staff. We'll go out through the dining room. I passed a ballroom on the way here. We can say we're setting the room up for lunch." She grabbed a plastic bin full of silverware and grunted as she tried to lift it up onto one of the room service carts.

Damn, that was heavy.

The first man who had stood up when Tasha entered the kitchen nudged her out of the way and lifted the silverware onto the cart. He had pulled a white coat that was two sizes too small on over his dusty brown shirt and didn't look anything like a cook, but it would have to do.

Tasha yanked a white jacket over her head and smoothed it down over her hips. It came to the bottom of her khaki shorts, making it look as if she were wearing the jacket and nothing else.

"Like room service at the Playboy mansion," she muttered under her breath.

"Come. We must go," the man—who she assumed must be the leader of the refugees—said, grabbing a cart and pushing it ahead of him toward the door leading out into the restaurant.

Tasha nodded. She gripped the chilly metal handle of a cart and pushed, but the cart barely moved. With a mighty shove, she finally got the wheels to turn and smiled grimly at the two faces peering out at her from a gap in the tablecloth that had been draped over the cart. From the looks of them, these two girls weren't even in their teens. She could only imagine the life they had escaped . . . or what Quinn Hayes had planned for them now.

She had a hard time believing that the man who had put himself in harm's way to save her less than an hour ago was trafficking in human misery. And, yet, here was the proof, right before her eyes.

Tasha determinedly put all her weight behind pushing the cart over the threshold between the kitchen and the restaurant. She didn't have time to think about Quinn right now. Right now, she had to help save these poor people from Acosta.

Later, she'd ferret out the truth.

"Hurry," she urged as the man in front of her slowed to a stop.

He straightened his shoulders and shot Tasha a telling look before focusing his gaze on the main entrance to the restaurant, where two men were standing.

Tasha peeked out from around the man's back and saw Quinn and Acosta watching them from near the maître d's station. Quinn's eyes widened for a second when he saw her, but when he turned back to Acosta, his expression was blank.

"Follow me," Tasha whispered as she pushed her cart toward the front door. Fear clutched her chest, making it difficult to breathe, but she forced herself to take slow, deep breaths so she wouldn't pass out.

Acosta watched her with flat gray eyes as she approached. When she had no choice but to either stop the cart or run over the man's toes, she tugged on the handle to make the cart stop.

You can do this, she assured herself silently, then pasted a phony smile on her face. "Excuse me. We've got to get set up for a banquet," she said.

Acosta's eyes narrowed and, for a long, frightening moment, Tasha was afraid he was not going to let her pass. The seconds ticked by and she felt a bead of sweat slide down her spine, tickling her skin as it glided downward and dripped into her shorts.

Lovely.

Finally, Acosta stepped aside.

And, of course, made no move to hold the door for her.

Quinn, however, did. He pulled open the door and stepped back, gesturing for her to proceed.

Tasha gritted her teeth and tried to make it seem as if she did this sort of thing every day, when the truth was, the heaviest thing she ever pushed was a pencil.

"Thanks," she grunted as she wheeled the cart out past Quinn.

He nodded in response, but the look he shot her from beneath his thick, golden brown eyelashes was loaded with meaning.

Too bad Tasha had no idea how to interpret it.

She felt another bead of sweat drip into her shorts and had to resist the urge to squirm. She knew Quinn and Acosta were both watching her and no way was she going to scratch her butt with them staring at her. Instead, she quickened her pace, the cart now rolling easily over the stone walkway. Seven additional carts trailed out behind her, the sound of creaking and rattling silverware and dishes intruding on the quiet of the jungle surrounding them.

Tasha stopped halfway down the hall and turned right into a doorway with the word "Toucan" printed on a placard on the wall outside. She didn't know why hotels didn't just number their conference rooms instead of trying to get cutesy with the names, but that really didn't matter now. What mattered was getting these people to safety.

Not an easy task, Tasha realized, when she looked up to find that Acosta had followed them down the hall.

Damn. What now?

Tasha forced herself to remain calm as she pushed her cart over to a large circular table in the center of the room. Without waiting for it to come to a complete stop, she grabbed a tablecloth from the top of her cart and tossed it over the table. The tablecloth was nearly long enough to reach the floor, and Tasha tugged on it so that the front of the table was hidden from view. As least, it was hidden from where Acosta was standing, leaning against the doorjamb with his arms folded over his chest.

Tasha sent a wobbly smile to the leader of the fugitives. "Let's get all these tables set up and the carts emptied," she said brightly, hoping he'd get the message.

The man nodded curtly, then said something in rapid Spanish to the rest of the refugees.

Turning her attention back to her own cart, Tasha made a big show out of fishing for matching silverware with one hand while reaching underneath with the other to signal that her human cargo should take this opportunity to scoot under the table.

She held back a grimace when the heel of one girl's hand landed on her foot as she tried to extricate herself from the cart, then dropped a handful of silverware back into the bin to cover a loud *thunk* as the other girl's head banged against the top of the cart.

Tasha winced. That had to hurt.

She scattered the silverware on the surface of the table and then, after testing the weight of the cart with her foot and satisfying herself that the bottom was empty, she rolled the cart to another table to help cover the noise of yet another extraction.

She refused to look over at Quinn, who stood next to Acosta and silently watched the activity.

He had to know what they were doing.

Tasha swiped an arm across her face. She didn't know if it was the humidity or her nerves that were making her sweat like a glass of iced tea left out in the sun, but she was fricking melting here. When this was all over, she wanted nothing more than a long, cool shower and an intimate moment with a big glass of wine.

"Enough!" Acosta shouted suddenly.

Startled, Tasha dropped a knife, which clattered to the floor.

Doing her best not to look as terrified as she felt, she warily watched as Acosta stalked toward her. Quinn uncoiled himself from where he'd been leaning against the wall, his jaw tightening in anticipation of what might happen next. Tasha saw his right hand move slowly to his side, as if reaching for a weapon and, for a moment, she closed her eyes and prayed that her sister's wedding planner was also a crack shot.

She opened her eyes and drew in a calming breath as Acosta stopped in front of her.

"Is something wrong?" she asked.

Acosta's nostrils flared as he inhaled and Tasha found herself thinking that this guy should take up yoga.

"Yes, you people are up to something. I can feel it," he answered.

Tasha blinked several times. "I don't know what you mean. We're just setting up for a banquet this evening. That's all."

"You're lying to me. I can tell," Acosta hissed, grabbing her upper arm and squeezing until Tasha winced.

"Hey, that hurts."

"Tell me what's going on here or I'll show you what real pain is."

Tasha batted his hand, but he still didn't let go. She looked up to find that Quinn had drawn a gun and was aiming it at Acosta's head. After meeting Quinn's gaze, she shivered. She may not be an expert at reading people's expressions, but the dead calm in Quinn's eyes was impossible to miss.

Funny. She'd never met a dangerous wedding planner before.

Tasha winced as Acosta strengthened his grip, then shook her head almost imperceptibly as she felt rather than saw Quinn's finger tighten on the trigger. Acosta ran in some dangerous circles, and if Quinn killed him, she was certain that retribution would be vicious and swift.

She didn't quite know why that bothered her, but it did. She wasn't going to let this man get himself killed over her.

So she shook her head again and stopped struggling to get herself out of Acosta's grasp.

"Okay, okay. Let go and I'll tell you what's going on," she said, ignoring the gasps from the people behind her.

Acosta loosened his grip but didn't let her go. Tasha figured that was as good as she was going to get.

Quinn's eyes narrowed as he slowly lowered his gun.

"We didn't want Mr. Hayes to find out because . . . well, because we're using the hotel's resources. It's the maître d's birthday and we were going to throw him a surprise party. That's why we're not dressed properly. We're all here on our day off."

Acosta's eyes bored into hers for what seemed like an hour, but Tasha didn't so much as blink.

Finally, he let her go and stepped back, and then surveyed the room full of fugitives, who were doing their best to look sheepish as they hung their heads and nodded agreement with Tasha's confession.

"Very well, then. But I hope Mr. Hayes punishes you all for your thievery," Acosta announced, then strode from the room without a backward glance.

Tasha let out a relieved breath and looked up to find Quinn studying her intently.

"You're either very brave or very stupid," he said.

Tasha dipped her head in acknowledgment. "I could say the same about you," she countered.

Quinn snorted and then, with one hand holding the door open, turned back to her and said softly, "Sometimes, bravery and stupidity are the same thing."

As the door swung shut behind him, Tasha's mouth curled up into a half-smile. "Wedding planner. White slaver. Philosopher. Will the real Quinn Hayes please stand up?" she murmured to herself.

Then she turned back toward the fugitives, who were all looking at her as if she had just snatched a helpless baby from the jaws of a hungry crocodile.

She crossed her arms over her chest and rocked back on her heels.

"Now," she began. "Would someone like to tell me what's going on here?"

The leader of the fugitives exchanged a wary glance with another man, who Tasha took to be the second-in-command. "We mustn't. All I can do is to assure you that we're in good hands with Mr. Hayes."

"And how do you know that?" Tasha asked with a skeptical tilt of her head.

"He's a good man," the leader said.

"How can you be sure?"

"Because," a young girl said, poking her head out from underneath the table in the center of the room. "My brother knows him. They met long ago." She paused for a second, then looked up at Tasha with her soft brown eyes and added, "When they were both in prison."

CHAPTER FOUR

The wedding planner was a suspect in the disappearance of two people, was trafficking in human beings, and—as Tasha had just discovered—was also an ex-con.

This did not bode well for her little sister's wedding.

She had to find Celie and warn her to stay away from Quinn until Tasha had a chance to determine what was going on here. Even more important, she needed to caution Celie to stay out of Acosta's path. No way did she want her baby sister exposed to a creep like him.

"Celie? Are you in there?" she called, tapping on the door of her sister's suite.

There was no answer from inside.

"Must be in the shower," Tasha muttered to herself.

Well, she might as well get checked in to her own room and see if Cal had arrived. She'd suggest that they try to leave this cursed hotel right now, but knew it would be pointless. There was no way they could get back to San Pedro before dark, and traveling in the jungle at night wasn't smart. They'd just have to wait it out until tomorrow morning.

She took the stairs down to the main floor, careful to watch for any snakes or scorpions or deadly frogs that might be lurking in the stairwell.

As she turned the corner on the first floor, she nearly collided with a dark-haired woman who was running down the hall.

"Oh, pardon me," the woman said, reaching out a hand to steady Tasha as she leaped back out of the way.

It was the front desk clerk who had checked them in. What was her name again? Tasha glanced at the woman's name tag. Olivia.

"I'm sorry. That was my fault. I was coming to see if my room was ready. You wouldn't happen to know if I can check in now, would you?"

Olivia smoothed her shiny black hair over one shoulder before answering. "Yes. I tried to find you when housekeeping called down to tell me your room was done, but you were gone."

"I had an . . . um, errand to run," Tasha said.

"Hmm," Olivia answered as if she didn't believe her, then said, "If you'll follow me, I'll get you your room key."

Obediently, Tasha followed the front desk clerk back into the soothing lobby of the hotel. The plump birds were right where she'd left them an hour ago, sunning themselves at the edge of the fountain.

Olivia seated herself on a stool behind the desk and clacked away at some computer keys. Then, after a whirring set of clicks, she slid a key card over the marble counter.

"There you are. Room 214. That's back up the stairs and to your left."

"Thank you," Tasha said, pocketing the card. She had turned to leave when Olivia's voice stopped her.

"Oh, and I see here that you have a message."

Tasha turned back to face the front desk clerk and raised her eyebrows questioningly.

"Your sister called down about fifteen minutes ago. She wanted to let you know that she and Quinn were going out to scout locations for her wedding."

Tasha's hand fluttered to her chest. What? Her sister had gone out with Quinn? Into the jungle? Alone?

"Where did they go? Were they on foot?"

Olivia smoothed a hand over her hair again, a habit that was beginning to annoy Tasha. The woman's hair was beautiful, black and shiny and smooth, not a hair out of place. So why did she keep fiddling with it?

"No, they used the zip line," Olivia answered, nodding her chin in the direction of the landing pad on the roof, where Celie and Tasha had first arrived.

Tasha turned on her heel. She was not going to leave her little sister alone with a suspected slave trader. God only knew what might happen. He might kidnap her and try to sell her into the sex trade. With Celie's trusting nature, she could be halfway to Venezuela before realizing that Quinn's motives weren't exactly pure.

"They would have taken the blue route," Olivia called after her as she hurried across the lobby toward the stairs leading to the roof.

Tasha yanked open the door and pounded up the steps. After recovering from her not-quite-ten-point landing this morning, she had looked around and seen other landing pads dotted about the roof. Now, she headed toward the one with a blue marker, assuming from Olivia's comment that this was the line Celie and Quinn had taken.

As she clipped herself into a harness and stepped to the edge of the platform in preparation for takeoff, Tasha forced herself not to look down at the jungle floor thirty feet below.

She didn't have time to be scared. She had to save her baby sister.

• • •

Jorge Acosta slowly lowered the newspaper he had raised a moment ago to shield his face from view of the women in the lobby. He dismissed the front desk clerk—she was of no consequence—and, instead, focused his attention on the woman with the light brown hair.

She had lied to him.

She was not a hotel employee, but, rather, a guest.

The question was, why had she lied?

The answer was easy. She had to be involved with the workers that had been stolen from him. It could not be a coincidence.

And now she was off to meet Quinn Hayes somewhere in the jungle.

Again, he added two and two together and came up with four. This must have something to do with his workers.

He got to his feet as the woman disappeared through the doorway, easily escaping the notice of the harried front desk clerk who had turned her attention to another task.

For years, his workers had been mysteriously vanishing—usually in small groups of three or four several times a year. His second-in-command, Luis Ortega, had said there were rumors that they had help in escaping, but Acosta refused to believe that anyone would be foolish enough to risk their lives to bring a few worthless slaves to freedom. That is, until this latest batch disappeared. Not in a small group of three or four, but nearly two dozen men, women, and children, who were in the guarded barracks one evening and gone by morning. Even he had to admit that this could not have been accomplished without outside assistance.

When Luis tracked the fugitives as far as San Pedro and Quinn Hayes was mentioned, Acosta knew Hayes had to be involved. He didn't know yet whether Hayes was motivated by revenge or profit, but that didn't really matter.

Either way, Acosta now believed he had enough evidence to kill Hayes . . . and the woman who had just left to find him.

Her lies could mean only one thing: Quinn and this woman were hiding the fugitives.

Now they would have to die.

As he turned to follow the woman, a half a dozen blue-gray tanagers suddenly took flight. He closed his eyes and raised his hands instinctively to protect himself. The birds soon settled down to roost and Acosta cursed them under his breath as he strode to the stairwell, not realizing that the birds had been spooked by the young, dark-haired girl hiding in the shadows.

CHAPTER FIVE

Quinn unclipped his harness from the zip line and stepped away from the landing platform to await his client's arrival. While he waited, he looked around the clearing with a critical eye. It was not a large space—perhaps enough for twenty people, no more—but it was beautiful. The clearing was flanked by lush trees and bushes heavy with brightly blooming flowers. Through the foliage at the edge of the clearing, he could see the sparkling water of a small river and hear the soothing sound of it rushing over the cliff forty feet below. It wasn't a large waterfall, so the noise wasn't bad. The bride and groom would have to speak up to be heard, but they wouldn't need to yell.

All in all, it would be a lovely place to—

Quinn's thoughts were interrupted by the raucous chirps and

howls of a small band of monkeys that suddenly came flying out from behind him.

"Omigod, what's that?"

Quinn turned to find Celie O'Shaunessey clinging to her harness as she watched, wide-eyed, as the monkeys stopped on the opposite side of the clearing, their bright beady eyes staring intently at the intruders.

Quinn frowned. "Monkeys," he answered. "And it looks like they're staking this place out as their own for the time being."

Celie stepped out of her harness and walked farther into the clearing. "They're so cute," she breathed.

"They can also be dangerous," Quinn warned, putting a hand out to stop Celie from going any farther. Monkeys had been known to pelt unwary travelers with nuts and sticks, or even feces, if they felt they were being threatened.

He studied the group of small tan-and-orange faces and saw several babies—yet another reason to keep his client out of their way. Monkeys, like most animals, would kill to protect their young.

"Aw, but they're like little wizened old people," Celie cooed.

Quinn swallowed a sigh and kept a firm grasp on his client's arm when she would have taken another step toward the howling monkeys. These were not cuddly cartoon animals. They were wild creatures with strong limbs and razor-sharp teeth.

"Yes. Well, I think we should move on to the second location I wanted to show you. You don't want your wedding disrupted by a gang of shrieking monkeys, do you?"

"Oh, but it's so beautiful here." Celie turned to him with a beatific smile and Quinn blinked. Before this moment, he hadn't realized how much she looked like her sister, but there was something in his client's almond-shaped blue eyes just now that reminded him of the way Tasha had looked when she'd first seen the lobby of the hotel. Something that had told him the world-weary attitude she wore was nothing more than a cloak she used to shield herself from hurt.

Quinn snorted. Where the hell had that thought come from?

He had enough to deal with without waxing poetic about a woman he had just met.

Even if she was cute.

And smart.

And incredibly brave.

"Unhand my sister, you . . . you slave trader, you."

Huh? Quinn spun around to see the woman he had just been thinking about flying down the zip line straight toward him.

He wasn't going through this again.

He stepped away from the landing platform as Tasha jerked to a halt at the end of the line, grunting as the cable bit painfully into her chest.

He might be a gentleman—though even that was questionable— but he damn sure wasn't a martyr.

Quinn rubbed the spot at the back of his head that was still sore from this morning's tumble to the rooftop. No. He wasn't going to get rammed into again.

Not even for the cute, smart, incredibly brave woman who just happened to be glaring holes through him at the moment.

He stepped back and crossed his arms over his chest. "Is there something I can help you with?" he asked, and then leaped into action when he spied something out of the corner of his eye.

"Yes, you—" Tasha broke off as Quinn lunged at her, his hands grasping for the waistband of her shorts like some deranged rapist.

"Stop it!" she ordered and slapped ineffectually at his searching fingers.

Quinn grabbed her by the front of her shirt and yanked her hard against his chest. Tasha felt the air whoosh out of her lungs as she stared up at him, unsure whether her reaction was in response to being manhandled or from the sudden way her heart started fluttering as they once again made full body contact.

God, he smelled good.

And felt good, all pressed up against her, his body hard in all the right places.

Tasha blinked.

No. No, no, no. She could not feel this way about someone like Quinn Hayes.

She struggled against him, trying to get him to let her go, but he just kept fumbling at her waistband with one hand while the other held her pressed to his chest.

"Stop squirming, damn it," he said roughly as Tasha became uncomfortably aware that he had another hard-on.

"Are you on Viagra?" she muttered.

She felt his arms go around her waist then, and her feet came off the ground as he took a step backward, away from the landing platform. Startled, she squealed and wrapped her arms around Quinn's neck to keep from falling as she realized that rather than trying to unzip her shorts, he'd unclipped her from the zip line.

Tasha looked up into his greenish brown eyes and felt as if her heart had stopped. The same force that had sucker punched her this morning hit her again and she shivered against the force of it.

She couldn't be attracted to him. He was a bad, bad man.

But her warning to herself dissipated like mist in the morning sunlight when Quinn leaned into her, his firm, warm body pressing into hers as his mouth stopped just a breath away from hers.

"Who needs Viagra? I've got you," he said softly.

Then, as if he couldn't stop himself, he lowered his head that last inch, his eyes on hers the whole time. Tasha knew she should let go of him. Move her head back. Anything. Especially since her little sister was standing right there, gaping at them.

Instead, she licked her bottom lip in an age-old come-on, her mouth opening in anticipation of Quinn's kiss.

And, omigod, he might be a bad, bad man, but he was a good, good kisser.

Tasha heard herself let out a noise that sounded like a purr as Quinn's tongue touched hers, then the purr turned to a breathy moan when he sucked her into his mouth. She felt her entire body go limp and hot and wet and, without even thinking about where she was or what she was doing or who was watching, she let her hands slide down Quinn's back until his tight, firm butt was filling her palms. She'd always been a sucker for a guy with a cute ass and, even through the fabric of Quinn's khakis, she could feel that his was world-class.

Unable to help herself, Tasha squeezed, and his hips pulsed forward, his erection letting her know that he was just as affected by her as she was by him.

With his hands still splayed against her back, pressing her to him, Quinn lifted his head.

"I've never been more happy to own a hotel as I am at this moment," he said, sliding one hand up her back to bury his fingers in the hair at the base of her neck.

Tasha shivered and swallowed, trying to get a few brain cells to start firing again. "Why's that?" she asked.

"Because when this is all over we need to get a room." With his mouth quirked up into a half-grin, Quinn leaned down again and kissed the tip of her nose, then slowly let his arms fall to his sides.

Bemused, Tasha blinked, trying to process what he'd just said.

They needed to get a room?

When *what* was over?

She looked up, intending to ask just that, then clamped her mouth closed when Quinn turned his attention to the landing platform. She hissed in a breath when she realized that she had been followed.

As Jorge Acosta unclipped himself from the zip line, Tasha suddenly realized what Quinn had been doing earlier. He hadn't been fumbling with her shorts. He was merely trying to get her out of the way so Acosta wouldn't land on top of her.

And she'd misread it as a pass.

She was such an idiot.

Soon to be a *dead* idiot, because Acosta would surely recognize her from this morning, and he didn't seem like the type to appreciate a good joke. Especially not when the joke was on him.

"I'll take care of this," Quinn said in a voice that made Tasha shiver.

Acosta stepped off the platform and Quinn strode forward to meet him. Tasha wished she knew what to do.

Running and hiding in the jungle was an appealing option.

"Who's that?" Celie whispered as she sidestepped over a dead vine to reach Tasha's side.

"Jorge Acosta," Tasha answered shortly. "He's rumored to be the corrupt leader of a secret police force here in Costa Playa that does the president's dirty work. Not a nice guy."

As Celie shuffled closer, Tasha scanned the clearing, looking for anything she might use as a weapon if Acosta attacked. There were several small rocks and twigs on the jungle floor, but nothing that looked too lethal.

She was about to bend down and pick up a rock that was lying at her feet when Acosta lunged for her. Tasha leaped back, ignoring the strange squealing noises and sudden burst of activity behind her.

Her feet scrambled on the loosely packed earth. She ducked, but she wasn't quick enough. Acosta managed to grab her arm and stop her before she could get away.

"Where are my workers?" he spat, his face just inches from hers.

"I don't know what you're talking about," Tasha said.

"She has nothing to do with this. Let her go back to the hotel and you and I can work this out, man to man."

Tasha twisted her head to see that Quinn had raised his palms up, as if in surrender. She wouldn't trust him. She doubted Acosta would either.

When she felt the tip of a knife digging into her stomach, she knew she was right.

"Turn around," Acosta ordered.

She had no choice but to obey. As she turned, Acosta raised his right arm and rested it against her shoulder, the knife in his hand now pressed against the soft skin of her neck.

Quinn's eyes flashed with anger. "I don't even know this woman. Why do you think that torturing her will make me give you what you want?"

Tasha felt her flesh crawl as Acosta pushed the tip of his knife into her neck. His breath was hot on her skin as he leaned toward her and laughed.

"I have a very good memory, Mr. Hayes. You may wish to forget the circumstances under which we met, but I have not."

"What does he mean by that?" Tasha asked with a frown, pulling as far away from Acosta's knife as she could get.

"Nothing," Quinn answered.

Acosta laughed again, caressing Tasha's upper arm with his

thumb as he did so. "So, you don't know the details of this man's past. And, yet, you allied yourself with him against me. Not a smart move, Ms.—O'Shaunessey, is it?"

Tasha swallowed. All right. This guy was giving her the creeps.

She didn't know how to respond, but was saved from having to answer when—for God's sake, was this the Grand Central Station of landing platforms?—the jangle of another traveler coming down the zip line reached her ears.

When one of the girls that Tasha had helped rescue from the kitchen that morning appeared, Tasha grimaced.

What was *she* doing here?

The girl landed on the platform with an ungraceful *oomph*, but she was out of the harness before Quinn could stop her.

She neatly sidestepped Quinn's arm as she dashed toward Acosta, brandishing a stick she must have picked up on the other end of the line.

"You let go of her," the girl ordered in a voice that belied her shaking hands.

"It's okay, honey. Go back to the hotel," Tasha said, sending Quinn a look that pleaded with him to get this poor kid out of here.

Quinn tried to grab her, but the girl was too fast. He lunged right and she dashed left, circling around Acosta's back, where she managed—even as frightened as she must have been—to land a blow across the man's shoulders.

Acosta growled, but didn't loosen his grip on Tasha, instead jabbing the knife into her neck until she felt the sticky wetness of blood dripping into her T-shirt.

"Do it again and I'll kill her," Acosta said, whirling around to show the girl what he had done.

"Leave her alone!" the girl shouted.

The chattering sound that Tasha had heard earlier was growing louder by the second and she looked up to see that the trees seemed to be coming to life, their branches shaking, leaves falling to the ground, as the noise increased.

"Stop!" Quinn yelled.

Tasha looked back at the girl just in time to see her reach her arm back. Thinking the girl was going to throw something at Acosta, Tasha figured now was her chance. She shoved her heel down as hard as she could on Acosta's instep and ducked out of the way just as a barrage of projectiles came flying through the air, as if the trees were launching an attack.

Tasha rolled away from Acosta and covered her head as the air filled with flying objects—rocks and sticks and God only knew what else.

Acosta's howl of pain stopped abruptly as Tasha rolled over and over on the warm dirt, thinking only of getting to Quinn and the girl and getting the hell out of here before Acosta could kill them all.

It was only when the jungle became eerily silent that Tasha stopped and peered between her fingers at the scene before her.

Celie stood at the edge of the clearing, her jaw hanging open. The girl who had followed them was standing right where Tasha had left her, one hand still holding the stick, the other closed around a handful of dirt that was seeping out from between her fingers.

Quinn loomed over the prone form of Jorge Acosta, who was lying on his back, staring up at the cloudless sky.

Slowly, Tasha lowered her hands and pushed herself up into a sitting position.

"Is he . . ."

She looked at Quinn, who looked back at her and nodded.

"Yeah."

"But who?" Tasha asked.

Quinn glanced up into the trees, then shook his head, as if baffled.

"Acosta's dead," he announced, and then added, "The monkeys killed him."

CHAPTER SIX

"What the hell is going on here?"

Tasha stood in the center of the clearing, looking from Quinn to Acosta to the trees and back. She wasn't budging until he told her the truth about his involvement with the fugitives . . . and his history with Jorge Acosta.

"I don't have time to explain," Quinn answered. Then he bent down and grabbed Acosta under the arms. "Somebody get his feet. We've got to get him back to the hotel as soon as possible. His men are arriving later today."

"Why don't we just leave him here?" Celie asked.

"Because if he's not there when his men arrive, they'll torture us all to find out where he is. If they find him out here like this, they'll never believe we didn't kill him."

"How is getting him back to the hotel going to help?" Tasha asked.

Quinn grunted as he lifted Acosta and dragged him one step, then another, toward the zip line. "I don't know yet. But we can't leave him out here."

Tasha chewed the inside of her cheek as she contemplated their situation. Quinn was right. There's no way anyone would believe that a rogue band of monkeys was responsible for Acosta's death— not when Quinn, Tasha, and even the girl who had followed them had a motive to kill him. Celie was the only one who didn't have reason to fear Acosta, and one could reason that she might have done the deed in order to save her sister. God knew, if Celie was in trouble, Tasha would do the same.

"Look, you can either trust me or take your chances with Acosta's men," Quinn said, grunting again as he struggled to haul Acosta's dead weight by himself. "And I can assure you from personal experience that they don't know the meaning of the word *mercy*."

The girl dropped her stick and ran over to pick up one of Acosta's booted feet. Her glance back at Tasha was filled with fear. "He's right. We must hurry."

When Tasha hesitated, the girl let go of Acosta's foot and, with one hand, pulled the shoulder of her ragged shirt down to expose the skin of her back. Tasha gasped at the welts she saw there—a few white ones that had healed over time, and some more recent ones that were still ugly and red.

That spurred Tasha into motion.

She nudged the girl out of the way and picked up Acosta's feet. It wasn't easy clipping the dead man into a harness, but with all of them helping, they managed.

"I'll go first and make sure the coast is clear," Quinn said, clipping his own belt to the zip line in front of Acosta.

"And I'll ride right behind him and make sure he stays upright, just in case anyone's watching," Tasha said. They had tied him to the cable running from his waist to the line overhead, but it was possible that the rope might come loose during the ride. If that happened, he'd arrive at the hotel spinning wildly out of control, the way Tasha had that morning.

Tasha got into place behind Acosta, looping her legs around his waist to hold them together. She avoided looking into his eyes, even though they didn't look any more flat and dead than they had when the man was alive.

Even dead, he gave her the creeps.

"I'm ready," Tasha said.

"Let's go," Quinn ordered. And then he was gone.

Tasha looked back at Celie and the girl, who was clipped to the line behind her. "You guys get out of sight as soon as we get to the hotel," she said.

Celie nodded and waved in the direction that Quinn had just gone. "Be careful," she cautioned.

"I will. You, too."

She let go of the line overhead and was soon flying over the canopy of trees, her legs wrapped around a dead man.

Definitely not how she had imagined this vacation turning out.

• • •

This day had become a never-ending nightmare.

Quinn swiped a palm over his face and tried to come up with a plan of what to do with Acosta's body, but every idea he came up with was flawed.

By the time he spotted the roof of the hotel up ahead, the only conclusion he had come to was that there was no way they were all going to make it out of this alive.

Or, rather, no way *he* was going to make it out of this alive. If someone had to take the blame for Acosta's death, it would have to be him. At least he would be prepared for the punishment Acosta's men dished out.

Even now, a decade later, he couldn't forget the endless days and nights of pain.

Absently, he rubbed his left kneecap, the one Acosta himself had pried loose with his own fingers. It still ached whenever it was about to rain.

Quinn grimaced and shook his head to clear his mind of memories of those days. He wouldn't give up hope, not yet.

He reached up with one gloved hand to slow his descent and looked up to see that Olivia was waiting for him on the landing pad.

Great. Now what?

Olivia's voice reached his ears even before his feet hit the white-painted square on the roof.

"Acosta's men are here. They're looking for him," she said.

Quinn unclipped the harness from around his waist and glanced around the roof. "Where are they? And how many are here?"

"Just three," Olivia answered. "They tried his room, but he wasn't there. They're waiting for him in the lobby right now. I told them I didn't know where he had gone."

Quinn wiped the sweat from his brow with his sleeve. It had cooled down somewhat now that evening was approaching, but it was still hot out here. What he wouldn't give for a cool shower, a cold beer, and for this nightmare to be over.

"He followed us out to the waterfall," Quinn said. "And the less you know about what happened out there, the better. Go stall them. Offer them a drink or something. But whatever you do, don't let them leave the lobby for the next fifteen minutes or so. You got that?"

Olivia's gaze swept to the zip line, her solemn brown eyes not registering shock or anything else, even though Quinn knew she had to see Tasha and Acosta; they were only a hundred feet behind him.

She nodded once, then turned to leave without another word.

"Oh, and have someone leave a key outside Acosta's room for me," Quinn called after her retreating back.

Olivia nodded again as she disappeared down the stairs.

Quinn sighed and rubbed his throbbing forehead with his hand. Things were going to get pretty ugly from here.

But there was nothing he could do about it. The wheels had already been set in motion.

Hell, he'd probably been doomed to this fate ten years ago, when he'd been sitting in that open-air bar, having his fifth tequila shooter, and seen those girls' faces pressed against the dirty windows of that van. In that moment, if he had just turned away, just poured the liquid gold down his throat and shrugged off what he had seen, he wouldn't have spent three years in the prison where he'd had the extreme displeasure of meeting Jorge Acosta.

And Acosta wouldn't be dead now.

But Quinn guessed those girls would be.

He sighed again, then turned when he heard the zip line start to hum at Tasha's approach. He stood at the edge of the landing pad, watching her chew her bottom lip as she concentrated intently on getting safely to the platform.

He had to hand it to her—she had *cojones*. Ironclad ones.

Any other woman he'd ever known would have run screaming from Acosta. Hell, they wouldn't have gotten themselves involved in this mess to begin with.

Which, considering that Acosta had gotten himself killed because he had followed Tasha out into the jungle, might not have been such a bad thing. Still, he had to admire her motives. She'd only interfered to begin with because she was trying to help keep the fugitives safe.

"Acosta's men are here. We're going to have to get him up to his

room. Quick," Quinn said with a grunt as Tasha overshot the red
X in the center of the landing pad and whacked into his gut with
her knees.

She nodded, already hurrying to untie Acosta from the cable.

"Should we put him between us? So we can pretend he's been
drinking if we get caught?" she added.

"No, that'll just slow us down. I'll put him over my shoulder,"
Quinn answered. He crouched down and put his shoulder against
Acosta's stomach. "Go ahead and unclip him," he said.

Acosta's body slumped forward when Tasha did as he asked,
and Quinn sweated with the effort to lift the man's dead weight
onto his shoulder. He took a wobbling step, thankful that Acosta's
room was on the second floor and that he wouldn't have to climb
up any stairs with the man on his back.

He heard Tasha's footsteps behind him and considered telling
her to go to her room now so as not to risk them being seen together. But he didn't for two reasons. First, he wasn't certain he
could make it all the way with Acosta's two hundred lifeless pounds
on his back and he might need her help to get him there. Second, he
didn't think she'd listen anyway, so why bother?

"I'm sorry I'm not much help," Tasha said as she trotted to
keep up with him.

Quinn just grunted and kept putting one foot in front of the
other.

By the time they reached the hall leading to Acosta's room,
Quinn was staggering like a drunk under Acosta's weight.

"What room is he in?" Tasha asked, nervously glancing up and
down the hall to make sure they were alone.

"Two thirty-three," Quinn answered shortly, then added,
"Should be a key card in the door."

Tasha hurried past him and stopped when she reached the door to Room 233. Quinn half-expected the key to be missing—or for it not to work even if it was there—but Tasha was holding the door open by the time he managed to lurch his way to the room.

"Thanks," he ground out as he stumbled over the threshold and unceremoniously dumped Acosta's body on the king-size bed.

"Can we make it look like a heart attack?" Tasha asked, leaning over Quinn's shoulder with a frown creasing her forehead.

Quinn frowned, too, but more because the feel of her breasts pressed into his back was doing things to him that shouldn't be happening right now.

Focus on the dead guy, he admonished himself.

"How would that explain the bruises on his forehead?" Quinn asked.

"Hmm. Good point," Tasha answered.

They stood in silence for a moment, neither able to come up with a scenario that might make Acosta's death look natural. Finally, Quinn just shook his head. The bottom line was, they were totally screwed. They could leave Acosta here and try to pretend they had no idea what had happened, but Acosta's men wouldn't be satisfied with that. They'd start with Quinn—who wouldn't tell them anything, no matter what they did to him—and then move on to the rest of the staff. No matter how loyal his employees were, Quinn knew that when the pain got too bad, most people would give up their own mothers to make it stop. Acosta's men would find out about the fugitives, and that would lead them to the girl and, thus, to Tasha and her sister.

Not only would the fugitives be returned to captivity, but there was no telling what Acosta's men might do to the O'Shaunesseys.

Which meant that Quinn had no choice. He was going to have to face this. Alone.

"You should go back to your room now," he said, allowing

himself a moment of pleasure as he leaned back into Tasha's warm body.

She caught her lower lip between her teeth and looked up at him with doubt shining from her eyes. "Are you sure? If I stay, I could back up whatever story we come up with."

Quinn smiled sadly. Ah, the world's last optimist.

"No, it'll be better if I handle this alone," he said.

Tasha surprised him then by raising her hand and gently smoothing a lock of his hair off his forehead. "I'm starting to think I might have been wrong about you," she murmured.

Quinn caught her hand in his and, slowly, his eyes on hers the whole time, lowered her palm to his mouth. He kissed her, tasting the salt on her skin. Then he folded her fingers into a fist, as if she could hold his kiss forever that way.

"Sometimes, things aren't always what they seem," he said.

"No," Tasha agreed, then stepped back with a small sigh. "Usually they're much worse."

So much for her being an optimist.

"You'd better go," he said.

Tasha took another step toward the door, as if reluctant to leave.

"Go," Quinn ordered. Then, because he suspected she would stay if only he asked—and because he found himself tempted to do just that—he raised his head, leveled an even look at her, and said, "All the rumors you've heard about me are true. I trade in human flesh. I've served time in prison. And," he added, as if that weren't enough, "Julia and Matthew Martin didn't just vanish. I helped them plan their wedding . . . and then I made them disappear."

CHAPTER SEVEN

"There has to be another side of the story," Celie insisted after her sister wearily plopped down in the chair next to the bed and told her what Quinn had said.

"Tell that to Julia and Matthew Martin."

"I just can't believe it. Quinn seems like such a nice man."

Tasha shot her sister a skeptical look. "You've got to be kidding. He flat-out admitted that he's a white slaver. That's not exactly the profession of someone who's 'nice.'"

"I don't believe the rumors are true. I mean, I knew about them, of course. To be honest, I was the one who hatched the whole plan to have Lillian Bryson tell you about Quinn's questionable past." Celie sat down on the edge of her bed and stared glumly at the wide-planked hardwood floor.

"You what?" Tasha asked, sitting up straight in her chair.

"When I first heard about Quinn and this hotel, I looked him up on the Internet. He was so cute, and since we were all going to be down here for the wedding I thought it might be cool if you and he, er, hooked up. I knew you wouldn't give him a second thought if he was just a regular guy, so I had Lillian tell you about the rumors to make you pay him some attention. I never once thought the rumors might be true." Celie continued studying the floor as her cheeks took on a rosy hue.

"You can't be serious." Tasha knew her mouth was hanging open, but she couldn't seem to close it. They were in this mess because her sister had been trying to fix her up with her wedding planner?

"It's just . . . I want you to be happy," Celie said, finally looking up to meet Tasha's gaze.

"I'm happy," Tasha protested.

"Right. That's why you never date. Because you're happy by yourself."

"I'm by myself because every man I get involved with turns out to be secretly married, is a complete asshole, or lives with his mother."

"I know. But Quinn's none of those things. That's why I thought you guys might hit it off," Celie said.

"He sells people for money, Celie. I think that trumps being married, a jerk, or living with Mom."

"I still think there's something he's not telling you—something that proves he's not the man you think he is."

Tasha shook her head with disbelief. Could her sister *really* be that naïve? "You're too trusting," she said.

"And you're a cynic," Celie countered.

"You don't understand. People do bad things."

"They do good things, too," Celie said softly. "You spend your entire life searching for the worst in every situation. Why not try looking for the best just this once?"

Tasha blinked and hugged the overstuffed pillow she'd been holding to her chest. That wasn't true. She didn't always look for the worst.

Did she?

"I mean, did it occur to you to ask Quinn why he was in prison?"

"Well, no. I just assumed that he got caught selling slaves," Tasha said.

Celie snorted and stood up to pace the room. "I talked to Elise—that's the name of the girl who tried to protect you from Acosta—while we were on the zip line coming back to the hotel. Want to know what she said?"

Tasha hugged the pillow tighter. She wasn't sure she did want to know. Her entire belief system was at stake here.

She cleared her throat. "What'd she say?"

Celie stopped pacing and turned around, spearing her sister with her gaze. "She told me that Quinn was down in Costa Playa on spring break during his senior year of college. He was at this open-air bar, drinking with some friends, when a van full of women who had been kidnapped parked across the street. The driver got out, and some of the girls tried to get the attention of people walking by, but no one wanted to get involved. That is, until Quinn happened to look up and see them."

"Oh, God," Tasha breathed. *Please don't let this story end how I think it will.*

Celie nodded. "Yeah. He could have turned away, but he didn't. Here he was, this dumb kid on spring break with his whole life ahead of him. And you know what he did?"

Numb, Tasha shook her head.

"Yes, you do," Celie admonished. "He got up from his stool, went over to the van and smashed in the driver's side window. While his friends were urging him to come back to the bar, he freed all those women. They probably owe their lives to him."

"But he got arrested," Tasha said with a sick feeling in the pit of her stomach.

"The police were being paid off by the slave trader. They got to him before he could leave town."

"And no one in the U.S. could help?" Tasha asked.

"His parents tried, but the police moved him to a prison outside of San Pedro and wouldn't tell them where their son was being held. It took nearly a year for them to locate him. They finally came during the rainy season to visit him and tell him they were doing everything they could to get him out when a stretch of road washed right out from under them. No one ever saw them again."

Tasha tried to breathe around the tightness in her chest. She couldn't imagine being twenty-one, trapped in some hellhole of a jail, not knowing if anyone even knew you were alive. Quinn had to have been terrified.

How had he held on to hope all that time when no one—not his friends or his parents—was able to contact him? How had he managed to stay sane?

And if she'd been so wrong about that so-called fact, was it possible that there were other things she was wrong about, too?

"I left him to face Acosta's men alone," Tasha whispered.

"Maybe that's for the best," Celie answered evenly.

But Tasha knew it wasn't. He shouldn't have to deal with this by himself.

She stood up and tossed the pillow to the floor. "I'm going back there," she announced.

Then, without waiting to see if her sister would try to stop her, she hurried out the door.

·   ·   ·

When the knock sounded at the door, Quinn straightened his shoulders and took a deep, steadying breath.

This was it. His last moment of freedom.

"Come in," he called, remaining seated in the chair next to the bed where Acosta's body was sprawled out.

He expected to see three uniformed men with the hardened faces—and muscles—of thugs. He was surprised, instead, to see Tasha O'Shaunessey step quickly through the doorway and pull the door shut behind her.

"Tell me again why we can't just leave him here alone," she said by way of greeting, watching him intently as if the rest of her life hinged on his answer.

Quinn propped one foot up on the bed frame. "Because too many people know he came after us. If Acosta's men start probing, suspicion will fall on you and your sister. And they'll find out about the girl and the other runaways. I can't let that happen."

"Your people would betray you?" she asked.

"I know how ruthless these men can be. It wouldn't be easy, but they would find out eventually."

"You were going to tell them that you killed him, weren't you?"

"Yes," he answered calmly. No sense lying about it.

Tasha crossed her arms over her chest and leaned back against the door. After a long moment, she let her breath out slowly, as if she had come to some sort of conclusion.

"I think I can buy us some time to figure out a better plan," she announced.

Quinn quirked one eyebrow at her. "Oh?"

"Help me get Acosta into the bathtub and get him undressed. I'll tell you my idea while we work."

"You're kidding, right?"

Tasha unfolded her arms and walked toward him. Or, rather, toward the bed. "Got any other ideas?" she asked, turning to look at him over her shoulder.

Quinn thought for a moment, then slowly stood up. "No," he admitted.

"All right, then. Let's hurry. We're going to have to make this look good."

CHAPTER EIGHT

When the first knock sounded, Quinn raised himself up on one elbow and quirked an eyebrow at her.

"Are you sure you can do this?" he asked.

Tasha shuddered, and then took a deep breath and nodded. "I'm a woman. I've been doing this since I was eighteen," she assured him with a hell of a lot more confidence than she felt.

"That's the spirit."

From the opposite end of the bed, Quinn shot her the briefest of wicked grins before diving under the sheet. Tasha shivered again when she felt the warm touch of his hand on her thigh.

All right. It was showtime.

She leaned back on the fluffy white pillows and forced the muscles in her jaw to relax. She closed her eyes and tried to forget about the naked dead guy in the bathtub and the fact that she was being felt up by a handsome stranger with questionable morals. Pretty tough to forget about that, though, as his work-roughened fingers skimmed down the smooth skin of her inner thigh.

Wow, that felt good.

Tasha moaned low in her throat and was surprised at how easily it slipped out. She moaned again when Quinn's hands slid down to cup her feet in his palms. He massaged her insteps with his thumbs and Tasha felt her entire body relax.

Mmm. Feet as an erogenous zone. Who knew?

"Yes," she murmured, pressing her toes into his fingers so he wouldn't stop.

He made slow, lazy circles on the balls of her feet while Tasha continued to purr. Then, as the door slowly creaked open, he moved up, trailing hot, wet kisses behind her knees as he parted her thighs with his hands.

"Oh, Jorge," she breathed as Quinn's tongue traced a line up her inner thigh, following his strong fingers as they caressed her skin.

And suddenly she wasn't thinking about Jorge Acosta or the stage they'd carefully set for his men—not the clothes they'd strategically tossed over chairs or the phony love scene they'd choreographed to make it appear that it was Acosta in bed with her and not Quinn.

No. She wasn't thinking at all.

Instead, she was just feeling, reveling in sensation as Quinn's mouth moved up, up, toward her waiting, wanting flesh. Her subconscious registered the soft click of the lock as the hotel room door closed, but she was past caring.

"Don't stop," she pleaded, unmindful of the desperation in her voice.

And Quinn, gentleman that he was, didn't stop. He slid his

thumbs into the hot, slick folds at the juncture of her thighs and groaned. God, she was wet.

He tried reminding himself that this was just for show, hoping that the reminder would soothe the ache at his own crotch.

It didn't.

Tasha's toes brushed against his erection and Quinn nearly screamed with frustration. Okay. So he'd had a king-size hard-on for her since he'd first opened his eyes and found her lying on top of him. That didn't mean anything. He was a guy. Guys got hard-ons for pretty women all the time.

It didn't mean he felt anything for her, didn't mean that the hope stirring in his gut was for real. It was just sex.

He couldn't let himself dream that it might be more than that.

No, she was only here with him because of Acosta's men. And if they were listening outside the door, hoping for a good show, then, by God, he'd give them one.

He glanced up then and found Tasha watching him through half-lidded eyes filled with a mixture of desire and fear. Lazily, Quinn circled his thumbs around her heat, burying himself in her slick wetness. Then, with their gazes locked together, he brought one thumb to his mouth and sucked the taste of her into his mouth.

"Oh Q— Jorge," Tasha corrected before his name slipped out from between her lips.

With a self-satisfied smile, Quinn went in for the kill. He slid Tasha's white silk panties down past her knees with one hand, while slipping one finger slowly, tauntingly, into her. When her panties were gone, he settled himself between her knees, flicked his tongue over her swollen clitoris and then sucked her into his mouth as she writhed beneath him, her breath coming in panting gasps as he felt the tension mount, mount, mount. Then, with a strangled groan, she tensed, her legs pressing against his skin.

And then it was over, her legs sprawled at his sides as she re-laxed in a boneless heap.

It was a long moment before Tasha opened her eyes, a moment Quinn used to rearrange himself and move into a more comfort-able position with his hips resting between her legs, his hands splayed across her stomach.

"I'm . . . uh, sorry about that," she whispered, two spots of pink staining her cheeks.

Quinn couldn't help but grin. No woman should ever apologize about having an orgasm. He reached up and smoothed a lock of hair behind her ear before placing a warm, wet kiss on her stom-ach.

"You know what I'm sorry for?" he asked softly.

Tasha pulled her bottom lip into her mouth and shook her head.

"That it wasn't *my* name you screamed when you came." Quinn paused for a moment, then added with a wolfish grin, "But don't worry. You can make up for that next time."

•   •   •

"So, tell me about the Martins," Tasha said hours later, when dusk had been replaced by a soft shimmering moon. She didn't know if Acosta's second-in-command was still listening by the door—when their room service order of champagne and chocolate-dipped straw-berries had arrived half an hour ago, she'd flung the hotel room door open wide and come face-to-face with the man. With a half-feigned shriek, she'd pulled her robe closed and yelled, "Jorge! There's someone skulking out in the hall."

To which Quinn had shouted back an unintelligible response from behind the bathroom door.

Acting as an interpreter, Tasha grabbed the tray of food from the room service waiter, told Luis Ortega to go away, and slammed the door in the man's face. Then she'd pressed her back to the door, panting with fright as she waited for him to break down the door and shoot her.

He hadn't, but Tasha was too scared to crack open the door to see if Ortega was still out there.

Instead, she'd snuggled back under the covers, where Quinn's large, hard body was waiting.

She trailed her fingers down his chest, feeling the rumble beneath her palms as he chuckled softly. "You probably won't believe me if I tell you," he said.

Tasha draped herself over Quinn's chest and looked him straight in the eyes. "Try me."

He studied her intently for a moment before reaching over to the nightstand for the glass of champagne he'd set there earlier. He took a long sip of the golden liquid. Then, with the flute still in his hand, he said, "Ten years ago, I came down to Costa Playa with some friends on spring break. On the day before we were supposed to leave, we were hanging out in this bar when I spotted a van full of young women. They were trying to get my attention, trying to get me to help them."

Quinn told the story dispassionately, as if it had happened to someone else and not him. Tasha didn't interrupt, didn't tell him that she already knew about this part of his past. She wanted to hear it from him.

Her hand stilled on his chest as she nodded for him to continue.

"So I, uh, I did. I broke into the van and found out that they'd been kidnapped. Most of the girls had been taken from their homes, but I later found out that one of them was an American who was down in Costa Playa with her church group. She'd strayed from the group during a shopping trip, and the kidnappers plucked her off the street. That girl . . ." Quinn paused, took another sip of champagne and continued. "She was Julia Martin's sister."

"You saved her. Saved all of them," Tasha said softly.

Quinn didn't bother denying it. "Like I said, I didn't know who she was. I just . . . let them all out of that van and got the hell out of there as fast as I could. Unfortunately, I wasn't fast enough. The local cops found out what I'd done and tossed me into jail. I didn't know it at the time, but they were all on Acosta's payroll. I didn't find out until much later that Julia's sister never stopped looking for me—or forgot what might have been."

Tasha waited for the puzzle pieces to fall into place. She was starting to see the outlines of a picture, but right now, it was still out of focus. Most stories she worked on were like this. You'd find a piece of sky here, a few blades of grass there. Then, suddenly, someone would reveal a key fact that made it a complete landscape.

"Then, five years ago, after *Newsweek* did an article about Extreme I Do and the types of services we offer, Julia Martin called me. Her sister had apparently seen my picture and recognized me from all those years ago. Julia and Matthew were about to get married. They had amassed a huge fortune, and they wanted out of the Hollywood life, wanted to give something back. And Julia's sister had a plan for how they could do just that."

"Yes?" Tasha asked eagerly. The truth was about to be revealed. She could feel it.

"They wanted to help others who had been kidnapped, but not in the usual way." Quinn snorted and shook his head. "This is where it gets complicated."

Tasha reached up to caress Quinn's cheek. "We've got all night."

"Good thing," Quinn muttered, then put his hand over hers and turned to place a kiss on her palm. "To put it simply, the Martins wanted more than just to save a few innocent victims from Acosta's reign of terror. They wanted to topple the government, but in a peaceful way."

It was Tasha's turn to snort. Right. Like that ever happened.

"With their financial resources, they've been able to set up a very lucrative mining operation deep in the jungle. We have a network in place to steal Acosta's slaves and move them to the mine. It's not an ideal life, but at least they're paid for their work and given homes and schools for their children. In the meantime, the company profits are being used to educate politicians in the U.S. about the plight of the people of Costa Playa. They're hoping— *we're* hoping—that this regime will be gone by next year."

"But I don't understand. Why did the Martins have to disappear?"

"Because they couldn't have accomplished anything with reporters from *Entertainment Tonight* or the *National Enquirer* following them around. They needed secrecy and . . ."

". . . and you knew where to buy it, because when you got out of prison, you didn't just go back to the U.S. and live a nice, safe life, did you? You stayed here in Costa Playa and tried to save everyone you could."

Quinn stared up at the ceiling while one hand absently tickled the skin of Tasha's naked back. "There have been rumors over the years that I might be involved in something like that," he answered.

Tasha laid her head down on Quinn's chest and closed her eyes.

Celie was right. People did good things, too. Tasha had just let herself forget that for a while.

"How are we going to get the fugitives to safety with Acosta's men sniffing around?" she asked.

Quinn's hand tightened on her lower back. "Well, I did have an idea . . ." he began.

"Oh?"

"But it's risky," he cautioned.

"And this wasn't?" Tasha asked dryly, waving one hand toward the hotel room littered with clothes and smelling of raw sex.

Quinn shot her a wicked grin, then hauled her up so that she was lying sprawled on top of him, her hips cradling his intimately.

"Risky, but fun," he corrected, running his hands down the length of her spine and making Tasha shiver.

"Tell me your plan before we both get distracted."

Quinn nudged her thighs open with his knee and Tasha felt his erection rubbing against her. He reached up and caught her face between his hands, his fingers tender as he held her, their gazes locked together as he slowly lowered her mouth to his, stopping when they were only a breath apart.

"Too late," Quinn whispered.

Then he proceeded to prove just how good *distracted* could be.

CHAPTER NINE

When the pounding on the door started the next morning, Tasha and Quinn were prepared. Or, rather, Tasha was prepared. Quinn had silently slipped out the sliding glass doors and dropped onto the balcony of the room below, leaving her alone with the dead guy in the bathtub.

Tasha left the bathroom door slightly ajar as she went to answer the summons.

She took a deep breath, mustering the last vestiges of her courage. If Quinn's plan worked, this would all be over in less than two hours.

She could do this.

"Good morning," she said, pulling open the door.

Luis Ortega, a commanding man with a lean body and hard, dark eyes pushed past her into the room. "Who are you?" he asked harshly.

Tasha refused to act intimidated. She held out her right hand. "Tasha O'Shaunessey. Pleased to meet you."

Ortega scowled at her but didn't take her hand.

She hurried on, knowing that if he took a closer look into the bathroom, all would be lost. "Jorge's in the bathtub right now, getting ready for my sister's wedding this morning. You're welcome to come if you'd like. Jorge told me that when it's over, he needed to meet with you. I hope you don't mind me monopolizing his attention until then." Tasha clutched her bathrobe closed at the neck and did her best to giggle.

Ortega didn't look convinced.

Tasha swallowed and crossed her fingers under the lapel of her robe. "I could get him if you want. He said he needed to, uh, relax for a little bit after last night, but maybe he wouldn't mind being disturbed." She turned toward the bathroom and pushed the door open an inch.

The sweet smell of a burning cigar wafted out on a cloud of steam. From where she was standing, she could see Acosta's head resting on a towel at the deep end of the tub. Water flowed from the spigot and Tasha prayed that Ortega would leave before the tub overflowed.

Her eyes widened when Acosta's head slid down a bit.

Holy crap. He was starting to float.

Tasha giggled nervously and turned to look back at Ortega. "I think he might have fallen asleep," she whispered.

Ortega's dark eyes bored into hers.

The silence ticked on.

Tasha's hand flew to her throat when a bird screeched outside the window. "You have such interesting wildlife here in Costa Playa," she said.

"Yes, don't we?" Ortega agreed with a scowl.

She held her breath as he strode toward the bathroom door. *Please, don't let him go in there,* she prayed. He paused, pushed the door open another inch.

Then, as if satisfied that his leader was safe in her company, he left her without another word.

Tasha let out a relieved breath and hurried into the bathroom to unplug the bathtub drain before Acosta floated away.

Phase two of Operation Dead Guy was about to begin.

She only hoped her sister wouldn't mind a few uninvited guests at the wedding . . .

•   •   •

There was no way this plan could possibly work.

Quinn rubbed his aching forehead and squinted against the morning sun's cheerful glare as he watched one person after another disappear into the trees.

His contact was to meet them at the waterfall in an hour. The fugitives had all bathed and been given clean clothes to wear. Supplies were being hauled to the clearing right now, his employees on the other end fully prepared to make it look as if a real wedding was taking place.

And yet . . .

Quinn could not quite believe that this day would not end in disaster.

"Where's Tasha?" Celie O'Shaunessey asked, panting a bit under the heavy weight of her fancy wedding dress.

Quinn found it amusing that so many of his clients wanted extreme weddings with all the trappings of a more traditional ceremony. The exotic setting was great . . . as long as there was chilled champagne, elaborate bouquets, and men in tuxes.

"I'm going to get her right now," Quinn said. He'd just seen Luis

Ortega and his henchmen cross the lobby, presumably to get some breakfast while their boss was taking a bath. Now was their chance to get Acosta out of his room and on his way to the clearing.

Once he was there, all they could do was hope that Ortega took the bait. If not . . . Well, Quinn didn't exactly have a Plan B just yet.

"You and Cal get out to the clearing and take your places. We'll need to be ready when Acosta's men arrive."

Celie nodded and looked around the crowded roof for her fiancé, who had arrived yesterday evening, just after dark. He had accepted the explanation of their current predicament with much more equanimity than Celie had expected. His only comment after hearing the whole story was the somewhat crude, "Your sister gets in more tight spots than Hugh Hefner's cock." This had been accompanied by a wry shake of his head, as if to say, yes, he did know what sort of family he was marrying into.

Celie found Cal helping secure equipment to the zip line and relayed that it was their turn to go. They held hands and had just pushed off the landing platform when Quinn hit the hallway outside Acosta's room.

Warily, he checked to make sure the coast was clear before rapping once, then again on the door. He'd been smart this time and brought a luggage cart so they wouldn't have to lug Acosta's dead weight through the hotel. The less time this took, the better.

"Tasha, it's me," he whispered.

She yanked open the door almost immediately. "Let's get out of here. I managed to get his clothes back on him, but it wasn't easy."

"I can imagine," Quinn said, striding toward the bathroom where he found that she had, indeed, managed to get Acosta stuffed back into his uniform. "Grab a blanket, would you? We're going to need to cover him up."

Tasha helped him maneuver Acosta onto the luggage cart, then tossed one of the blankets from the bed on top of him. It was only as they pushed him out into the hall that Quinn realized one of Acosta's booted feet was hanging off the side of the cart.

Which wouldn't have mattered had Ortega and his men not rounded the corner at that exact moment.

"Shit," Quinn muttered.

"What do we do now?" Tasha mumbled out of the side of her mouth as the three men marched toward them.

"Hell if I know," Quinn answered.

"Keep moving."

"Yeah. Good plan. Harder to hit a moving target, right?"

Tasha didn't answer that. Instead, she turned her brightest smile on Acosta's men. "I'm afraid you just missed Jorge. He's on his way to the wedding."

Luis gave her his patented scowl. "What are you doing?"

Tasha glanced down at the lifeless lump on the luggage cart and grimaced. "You guys get *60 Minutes* down here, don't you? You've heard how they never wash the blankets in hotels? All those germs from all those guests who've come—sometimes quite literally, I'm afraid—before you?" She gave a realistic shudder.

Luis merely continued to scowl, so Tasha continued as if he had encouraged her to do so.

"Well, so after last night and all of our, er, activity, Jorge got out of the bathtub and had a giant rash on his, um, you know, his backside?" She smiled sweetly. "So I asked if someone could please wash the bedding before we, um, *used* it again. Mr. Hayes volunteered to take care of it because so many other staff members are busy with my sister's wedding."

"You know how it is. Everyone has to pitch in around here." Quinn shrugged and hoped like hell that no one saw the boot sticking out from beneath the covers.

"Fine. Whatever. You, girl, take us to Acosta. Now," Luis ordered, grabbing Tasha by the arm.

While it was tempting to think about kneeing him in the balls and reintroducing herself properly, Tasha didn't figure that would be the best course of action. Instead, she kept the phony smile plastered on her face as she turned and walked away from Quinn . . . and the landing pad.

She managed to take them the long way around the hotel, hoping to buy Quinn some time to get Acosta out of the way, before leading them up to the now-empty roof.

"It's the blue line," she murmured.

"Get on," Ortega ordered after one of his men clipped a harness to the cable in front of her.

Tasha did as she was told, grateful that for the next ten minutes at least, she'd have a little peace.

Only, that didn't happen. Ortega kept close to her, crowding her whenever she tried to slow down. By the time the clearing came into sight, Tasha was ready to scream with frustration.

She didn't like being bullied.

Which was probably why she'd taken up investigative journalism—to take on the bullies of this world the only way she knew how.

Tasha found herself searching for Quinn's face in the crowd. Rows of chairs had been set up at the edge of the clearing and the seats were filled with brightly dressed guests, who Tasha knew were actually the fugitives who were running from Acosta's men.

She had to hand it to Quinn and his staff, they'd worked a miracle on this place. There were flowers everywhere—brilliant corals, pinks, reds, and yellows. A flower-covered trellis had been set up near the trees where the monkeys had been roosting yesterday. Tasha could only hope that they were gone by now. The last thing they needed was another murder-by-monkey.

A long table sat off to the right with a three-tiered wedding cake iced in white and a silver champagne fountain bubbling brightly on the cloth-covered top.

"Amazing," she whispered, catching Quinn's eye as her feet touched down on the landing pad.

He stood next to Acosta behind the back row of seats, sunlight glistening off his golden brown hair. She felt an odd tightening in her chest when he smiled at her, and had to force her feet to move as Ortega shoved her out of the way.

Quinn scowled and started toward them, but Tasha shook her head for him to stay where he was. They needed to remain calm if this crazy plan had any hope of working.

Quinn slowly rocked back on his heels. He'd arranged it so that there would be no free seats near him and Acosta—but, as he'd suspected, Ortega was striding toward them, obviously intending to force people to move to accommodate his men. Fortunately, Quinn had anticipated that move.

He nodded to the leader of the band, who nodded back and then began to play the first strains of the Wedding March.

On cue, Celie started up the aisle, her white dress billowing out behind her.

As one, the crowd stood, their low murmurs of approval rippling through the morning air.

Quinn did his best to hide Acosta from view while keeping watch on Ortega. The uniformed men had stopped near an empty smattering of seats nearest the landing pad. He hated leaving Tasha anywhere near Ortega, but there was nothing more he could do. He had to keep them away from Acosta until the time was right.

Quinn kept his gaze focused on the couple beneath the trellis as the ceremony began.

As the faux minister made up some nonsense about the rings

representing never-ending circles of love, Quinn wiped a bead of
sweat from his brow. The tricky part was coming.

"I now pronounce you man and wife. You may kiss the bride,"
his maître d' said.

"Come on. Hurry it up," Quinn urged under his breath as the
smooching commenced.

Out of the corner of his eye, he saw Ortega and his men stand.

"Throw the bouquet, Celie," he whispered, as Tasha ducked
out from under Ortega's grasp and raced toward him.

This had to look perfect.

That's why Quinn hadn't told Tasha the last part of his plan.

Because if she knew . . . Well, let's just say she might not be
such an eager participant.

For a split second, Quinn let his gaze wander among the scared
and hopeful faces of the refugees. Nearly two dozen innocents who
had had their lives brutally stolen from them and now—at last—
were on the verge of finding freedom.

Would he risk it all to save them as he had a decade ago; this
time *knowing* the price he might have to pay?

That was the problem with being an idealist, he supposed.
Sometimes you had to back up those ideals with sacrifices beyond
what you thought you could bear.

He pushed his chair back and stood up, searching the crowd for
Celie.

"Throw it," he mouthed when their eyes met.

She reached her arm back and threw the bouquet, the brightly
colored flowers flying through the air toward the cliff's edge.

Quinn slid the gutting knife from his pocket, its wicked blade
flashing in the sun.

"What's th—" Tasha began as she reached his side.

"Trust me?" Quinn interrupted. They had no time for this. Ortega was bearing down on them. He put his blade against the rope holding Acosta upright.

"What? Yes, of course I do."

"Good, then catch," he ordered, pushing her toward the bouquet that had begun its downward arch just past the edge of the clearing.

He cut the rope and, with fear for what he was about to do nearly choking the breath from his throat, he stepped back out of the way as Tasha grappled to catch the bouquet. Her fingers closed on the ribbon trailing out behind the flowers and she reeled it in, turning with a smile to show him that she'd caught it—her smile turning to a startled scream as Jorge Acosta toppled against her, his weight pushing her over the edge of the cliff and toward the ground forty feet below.

CHAPTER TEN

"I can't believe you pushed me off that cliff."

Tasha indignantly brushed the dirt off the seat of her shorts and shot Quinn a bruised glare from over the top of her wineglass.

Quinn reached out and traced the line of her jaw with his index finger. "I'm sorry, honey. I told you, I had to make it look like Acosta was trying to save you. To look authentic, it had to appear that you believed you really were going over that cliff."

"Yeah, well, you're lucky it worked." Still hurt, Tasha turned away from Quinn's caress. Indeed, his plan had worked perfectly. Acosta's men could hardly believe anything was amiss—after all, they had witnessed the accident that killed their boss with their own eyes. An added bonus was that they were too distracted with trying to recover Acosta's broken and battered body to notice that the wedding party was short two dozen people by the time they climbed back up the cliff.

The fugitives had been safely handed over to the human resources manager at the Martins' mine, Acosta's death had been accurately faked, and Celie and Cal had been married by the maître d'.

Oh, and Tasha had survived her near-fall over the cliff because Quinn—after letting Acosta crash into her—had reached out and caught her.

Or, rather, he'd pulled her out of the way before Acosta's dead weight could push her over the cliff.

She had never really been in danger.

But, still, it hurt that he hadn't told her what he had planned to do.

Quinn wrapped his arms around her waist as the band he'd brought out for Celie and Cal's wedding struck up their rendition of "I Will Always Love You."

"I'm sorry," he said again, this time without the half-quirked smile that told her he thought she was overreacting. "I know you don't trust me yet, and I guess I can't say that I blame you. I was just doing what I thought was best. For you. For me. But mostly for the people who had escaped Acosta's grasp. As arrogant as it might sound, I felt like I was their last hope. I couldn't let them down."

Well. Didn't that make her feel like a selfish brat? Here she was, annoyed that she'd been scared for half a second, when the whole time he'd been trying to save them all.

Tasha stared at the firm line of Quinn's jaw.

"Okay. Maybe I'll get over it," she mumbled.

Quinn chuckled. "Good. Do you think you'll forgive me in time for your sister's wedding? I could really use a date."

Tasha looked up at him then and smiled. "Yeah, I think I'll forgive you by then. But don't ask me to catch any more bouquets."

"It's a deal," Quinn said. And, as the happy laughter and sounds of music seemed to melt away, he added, "Because really, who needs a bouquet when you've already made your catch of the day?"

The Wedding Party

WHITNEY LYLES

CHAPTER ONE

Meg was standing by the chip and dip platter when she received the bad news.

"I don't think he's coming," Claire said.

She held a tortilla chip midair. "What? Why?"

"Ben said he missed his flight out of San Francisco, and the next one to San Diego is full."

She could feel the edges of her mouth falling, and she tried to hide her disappointment from Claire. The purpose of the party wasn't for her to rekindle her relationship with Mason Strout. She was here for Claire's engagement party, to celebrate the future marriage of two of her closest friends.

"Oh well," she said. "It's not a big deal. I'll see him in a few weeks at the wedding." She pretended like her heart wasn't sinking like a ship on fire.

"Good. I'm glad you're not too bummed. And guess what?" Claire beamed. "We rented a karaoke machine! So, get ready to have some fun." She waved to some new arrivals. "I gotta go say hi."

I won't let this ruin my night. I won't let this ruin my night, Meg thought. She tried to convince herself that she wasn't disappointed that her ex-boyfriend wasn't coming. Claire's mom's scalloped potatoes were on the buffet and Prince was playing on the stereo. Though she'd have to be very drunk to hit the karaoke machine, she had a long entertaining night of watching everyone else sing their hearts out to look forward to. It would still be a great party.

Who was she kidding? She was devastated. She'd been waiting months for this evening. Last year, when Claire had asked her to be a bridesmaid, she was so honored she'd almost cried. However, when she'd found out that Claire's fiancé, Ben, was asking Mason to be a groomsman, she thought she might be happier than Claire and Ben about their summer wedding. It might be a little selfish, but their marriage really meant more to her than free champagne and the electric slide.

The realization that she'd made a huge mistake when she let Mason go had hit her months before the engagement. Since he lived in San Francisco now, she knew that her chances to correct her life-changing mistake were going to be scarce. This wedding was her beacon of hope to see him again.

However, shortly after Claire and Ben were engaged, Ben left San Diego for FBI training in Quantico, Virginia. There hadn't been time for an engagement party, and since Claire had her heart set on one they decided to postpone the party until he returned. She'd been worried sick that Mason would find a new girlfriend while Ben was learning to negotiate hostage situations and profile serial killers. There had even been a scare when Mason started dating someone else, but from what Meg understood it hadn't lasted. She'd been waiting months for this and had been dining on solid protein to shed a few pounds from her five-three frame. And now he wasn't even coming.

Twenty minutes later she was still standing alone in the same spot, digging through her purse for her cell phone. Loners should always look busy. Preoccupied with something, so it appeared as if she chose to be alone. The task at hand, whatever it might be, was so overwhelming she couldn't find the time to chat with anyone else. She was too busy to socialize, and she needed her phone immediately. Only she had no idea who she was going to call. Ever since her sister had given birth to twins she rarely answered the phone. Her best friend, Simone, was on a date with a fireman, and her neighbor, Dana, was in France. Meg had been feeding her cat.

So she stood alone in her vintage Dolce pumps watching Claire's gay uncle Albert sing "Mandy" on the karaoke microphone. Meg wasn't sure why he'd worn a tux to the party. Everyone else had understood that this backyard soiree was cocktail attire.

"Oh, Maaaandyyyy," he sang as he twirled to a few of Claire's parents' neighbors. She watched as he serenaded a little girl, before making his way to Claire's sister, Avril. He sang to Avril as if she'd been Barry Manilow's muse when he'd written the song. He tilted her chin up with his index finger.

If he came anywhere near Meg she'd slap him. Okay, she wouldn't slap him. But she definitely didn't want him serenading her. She looked down at her shoes, the same way one would pretend to look for a pencil when they didn't want the teacher calling on them.

She'd battled ruthlessly for her size-five black pumps on eBay. Vintage Dolce and Gabbana, the rhinestone brooches on the front of them had made her lose sleep until the end of the auction. She admired the way the stones glittered beneath the patio lights until she felt it was safe to look up again.

Except for Avril, Meg was the only bridesmaid who had attended the engagement party. The rest of the girls were from Los Angeles, and couldn't make it to the party in San Diego. Claire's bachelorette party in Mexico was only a weekend away, and they'd all be attending. Meg had heard so much about the other bridesmaids, and she couldn't wait to meet them.

She spotted Avril rummaging through her purse as well. Her bottle-blond hair hung over the collar of her fur coat, and she wore pink pants with white patent heels. Her real name was April Caridini, but she had started going by Avril Carie a couple years ago when she had decided to pursue a modeling career. The results were far from glamorous, as she ended up posing in spandex atop treadmills and stationary bikes for a brochure for Slim Gym, where she worked as a receptionist. Like Meg, she appeared to be dateless—and friendless, for that matter. Meg headed her way.

"Avril, it's great to see you." She couldn't help it, but her eyes immediately wandered to Avril's hairless eyebrows. Penciled lines resided above each eye, and Meg wondered what had possessed her to do this. Maybe she'd accidentally plucked too many, and when she tried to correct the situation it snowballed? Perhaps some nuclear hair removal cream? Or was this her idea of a new look? She wore a fur coat in San Diego in June, so one had to wonder.

"Hi, Meg." Her smile was tight.

"So, how is your job? At the gym. Right?"

"It's fine." She paused. "What do you do again?"

"I'm a movie critic and entertainment writer for *San Diego Weekly*."

How many years had they known each other? Five? Six, maybe. Every single time Meg saw her she asked what she did for a living.

"Hmmm," she said. This was the part of the conversation when Avril could now return with a question for Meg. Keep the conversation going. Instead, Avril checked *herself* out in the reflection from the sliding-glass door.

She was the type of woman that some guys probably thought was gorgeous. The same type of guy that hung out at Hooters and smelled like beer on Sunday afternoons. But she tampered with herself too much. If she would let things be she might be naturally pretty. Her brown hair had been dyed blond so many times that it looked like it was covered in rough gold semigloss spray paint. She always overdid it with the makeup, looking as if she used chestnut-colored crayons for lip liner and petroleum as gloss.

Meg scanned the room for others to chat with, but the scene was bleak and so she made another attempt to connect with Avril.

"So, how is your love life? Dating anyone these days?"

"It's okay." She paused, then looked down at Meg. "Isn't Mason coming?"

Claire must've told her that she was hoping to see him. This irked Meg a tad, because she didn't want it spreading like wildfire that she was still in love with him. It was kind of personal. Personal in the same way she didn't want everyone to know she'd been fired from her last job because she'd told her psychotic boss to go to hell. It was fine if everyone assumed she'd quit.

"No. I heard his flight's been cancelled." Meg tried to keep her tone cool and nonchalant.

"You can't ever go back." Avril sounded like Meg's mother, using one of her trite phrases like, "You lie down with dogs, you're going to get fleas."

"What do you mean?"

"I mean, it's really hard to get back together with an ex. There are always reasons for breaking up with someone and people don't really change. I'm just saying it's usually impossible to go back. At least in my experience."

Well, you don't know Mason and me, Meg wanted to say. *You don't know our situation and you hardly know me, you dummy.* But instead she decided to let Avril rattle off her hollow wisdom. They stood in silence for several more seconds before Meg excused herself. Wasn't there always one bad bridesmaid in every bunch?

Meg decided her best bet for excitement was by the Brie platter. Cheese always excited her, and if dairy didn't make her butt blossom like a magnolia in springtime she could and would eat an entire block of sharp cheddar in one sitting. She popped a slice of Brie into her mouth.

"Hey. You dateless too?" She turned to a guy who appeared to be no more than eighteen and looked as if his last haircut had been given with a pair of garden shears. He had hoops in both ears, and she thought she saw traces of eyeliner beneath his eyes.

She finished chewing. "Well, uh, yes. As a matter of fact I am."

"Yeah. Me too. I don't have a date either." He held his hands to the side and said, "I just plan on getting drunk."

She chuckled. "Nice attitude." She probably could've been his babysitter at some point and wanted to tell him that she was twenty-seven years old, but he seemed harmless and just as lonely as her. "So how do you know Claire and Ben?"

"I'm Ben's cousin. Matt. I'm in the wedding."

She extended her hand. "Nice to meet you, Matt. I'm Meg. Are you a groomsman?"

"No. I'm doing a reading. My brother is a groomsman."

"Oh. Who's your brother?"

"Bill. There he is right now!" Just as he pointed, "The Devil Went Down to Georgia" blasted from the karaoke machine, the shrill fiddle descending over the party like confetti.

"Him?" She pointed at the guy who stood behind the microphone, rolling up the sleeves of his untucked shirt.

"Yeah! That's my brother!" Matt shouted over the music.

Bill began to sing as if he'd been moonlighting in country bars his whole life. He was attractive in an outdoorsy type of way, deeply bronzed skin, with a prominent tan line where a large watch must've resided on his wrist. She sensed that his khaki pants and loose, button-down shirt were probably his dressiest clothes.

He jumped on top of the Jacuzzi, stood on the cover and began to speak the words of the song as if he were Charlie Daniels himself. She watched as women flocked to the foot of the hot tub.

When the fiddle part of the song sped up, he hopped from the spa, grabbed Claire's grandmother, linked elbows with her and began to do-si-do around the barbecue. Meg watched as Claire's parents did the same.

Ben came from a huge family so it was no wonder she had never met these particular cousins. It was hard enough to keep track of his siblings half the time. He had twelve groomsmen, most of whom she'd never even met.

As soon as Bill finished his song the entire party roared with applause and Claire's mom immediately grabbed the mic. A line began to form for the karaoke machine.

Matt grabbed her arm. "Let's sing something."

She shook her head. "Oh no." She laughed. "I can't sing. Nooo way."

"So what? C'mon. It'll be fun." He tugged on her arm.

"I can't. I'm not kidding." Not only did she not want to sing, but she was having way too much fun watching Claire's mother sing "Build Me Up, Buttercup." She was one of the only people Meg knew who still wore a beehive. Meg suspected she went through a bottle of hairspray a week. When Mrs. C moved, her blond hair didn't. She kicked her foot out in front of her as she sang, "I need you!" She proceeded to throw a foot out in front of her with each "build me up" chorus.

She hardly noticed when Matt's brother joined them. "Nice job," Matt said as he patted his brother on the back. "Bill, this is Meg."

When she reached to shake his hand she noticed small beads of sweat around his temples. His loose dark hair hung over his ears.

"Meg Thomlinson?" he asked.

"Yeah." She was pretty sure they had never met before. He would be hard to forget, and she started to feel a little embarrassed that she didn't recognize him.

"I've heard Claire and Ben talk about you quite a bit," he said. "I just moved here from Santa Barbara, so I'm still getting to know everyone. I read *San Diego Weekly* too, and I saw your latest review on the Peter Jackson movie."

She hadn't experienced this kind of flattery in ages. While *San Diego Weekly* was a popular magazine, it was pretty rare that anyone paid attention to her byline.

"What do you do?" she asked.

"I'm trying to start my own surfing camp for kids, but mostly I teach private lessons right now."

"You're entirely responsible for getting this party started," Meg said.

"Someone had to do it." He laughed. Matt excused himself and headed for the karaoke line.

"You want to grab a drink with me?" Bill asked. They both glanced at her empty wineglass.

"Sure." He filled both their glasses with merlot and they stood near the wine table talking about movies and his recent move to San Diego. Meg had never met anyone like him. Surfers by nature were usually carefree to the point of being careless. They were nomadic and so laid-back that they lacked ambition to do anything other than surf. But he seemed to be ambitious and curious about everything.

Matt returned with a twinkle in his eye. "We're singing 'Mony Mony.' I've signed us up. All you have to do is the background. Bill is doing it with us. You know the 'so good' parts. Or 'like a pony'? Just sing those lines."

"I'm not doing it." She was definitely not drunk enough for this. But even as she protested she was dying to get up there. It looked like so much fun.

"And now. Bill, Matt and Meg Jagger!" Mrs. C boomed from the microphone. It was going to be hard to argue with someone whose head butt could knock her out.

"Meg Jagger?" She laughed nervously. "I'm hardly Mick Jagger and if you think I can sing like him you're insane." She stayed put.

"Come on, Meg!" Claire yelled from the back. She looked around the room. They were all watching her. It was subtle at first, like the sound of crickets, but then the chanting became louder and louder with each passing second. She was sure Claire had started it and she wanted to kill her as they all chanted, "Meg! Meg! Meg!"

What the hell? she figured. It wasn't like Mason was here to see her.

"All right," she said before downing the remaining contents of her drink.

"Good girl." Bill patted her on the back.

She was shaking when they got to the mic. Why? She wasn't sure. It was just an engagement party. Everyone was drunk anyway. Mrs. C had just sung "New York, New York" and had almost backed into the pool when she hit the high notes. She'd even seen Avril browsing the karaoke book.

Meg and Bill positioned themselves on either side of Matt. At first they all hovered around the mic and when she heard her own voice bellow out Billy Idol she didn't think she sounded all that bad. Several seconds into the song Matt ripped the mic from its post, jumped into the crowd and knelt on one knee while he screeched out the words. Then, to her horror, he looked up and tossed the mic back to her. Clumsily, she fumbled with it, and for a moment felt like tossing it back. But Bill elbowed her and yelled, "Sing!"

"You make me feel!" she belted out. She could feel Bill's warm breath on her face as he moved in closer and sang the chorus. She looked out at the crowd, the glee in their eyes as they danced to her song, her singing. She felt like Janis Joplin and couldn't control herself when the lyrics burst from inside her chest. She opened her arms and let her pashmina fall to the ground as she performed like a born diva. Matt and Bill scrunched in closer and picked up the background.

It only felt natural to do the pony. She grabbed each side of her red skirt and bounced up and down while lightly kicking each foot in front of her. She was in perfect sync with the music, and bounced higher, kicked harder with every chorus. She threw her head back and even shimmied a little.

She was a rock star, and she felt her adrenaline surge when she noticed the first three rows of the dance floor doing the pony with her. She gave her foot its hardest kick yet, and felt the bliss that surged through her veins turn to ice-cold terror as her Dolce pump slipped off her heel and soared over the crowd. She screamed, but everyone was too busy doing the pony to notice. Everyone except for the guy standing next to Avril in the back row. The guy who looked a lot like Mason. The guy who—holy shit—*was* Mason. Mason! She watched as his placid face became contorted and her pump headed like a shooting star toward his head. She stood frozen as his hand shot up and caught her shoe.

• • •

Meg hobbled off the Jacuzzi, plucked her remaining shoe from her foot and darted for the ladies' room. She passed Claire on the way.

"That was aweslum!" Claire said, notes of intoxication in her voice. "Oh and hey." She winked. "Maaaason. Apparently, he flew standby and lucked out." She high-fived her.

"I almost hit him with my shoe."

"Don't worry. I'm sure you'll get it back."

Actually, getting her shoe back was the least of Meg's worries. She was supposed to look beautiful, make him instantly take a pleasant trip down memory lane—not thank God for unanswered prayers. She'd been doing the pony to "Mony Mony." Her shoe had nearly taken his eye.

She felt like she'd woken up after a long night of drinking, sick with regret and filled with memories of all the idiotic things she'd said and done. Only she wasn't hungover, or drunk. She was pretty sober, which gave her no excuse to be singing Billy Idol in front of a crowd of fifty strangers. At least if she'd been drunk she'd have a reason for all this.

Her dark hair had frizzed in the fresh air, and if she had known he was going to come she would've avoided the karaoke machine at all costs. She did her best to smooth her hair, and felt somewhat comfortable with the soft wavy look she was stuck with when she left the bathroom.

Should she approach him? Or should she wait for him to find her? She didn't think she'd have the courage to approach him. What if he noticed that her hands were shaking?

She waited by the wine table, collecting her wits while he chatted with some of the other groomsmen. She stole glances in his direction and even from where she stood she could see his huge smile. He looked wonderful, absolutely gorgeous. He'd quit gelling his hair, and his natural dark curls looked loose and boyish around his forehead. The slicked look had never done much for him; on many occasions she'd gently tried to convince him to bail the Mafia hit man appearance for a more relaxed image. But he'd been attached to his hair gel the same way her mother was attached to nude stockings.

She'd broken up with him sixteen months ago because she'd needed to figure out exactly what she wanted. He'd brought up marriage, but at the time she wasn't exactly dying to race to the altar with him. There were a few things about him that bothered her. Though he was a wonderful boyfriend, he could be a little uptight. *Selfish* was the word she had used at the time. She knew she could never change him. People just don't change based on some coercion from their significant other. Though she loved him, she didn't feel it was fair to string him along while she tried to figure out if she could live with the things she didn't like about him.

She remembered how he'd called her five times a day for a month, trying to convince her to give their relationship another chance, and how hard it had been to resist him. He'd finally given up and moved to San Francisco to pursue pharmaceutical sales.

She'd had this dreamy notion that there was some perfect soul waiting for her to find him. Someone with everything she wanted and more, someone who did nothing to annoy her. Oh, how horribly wrong she'd been. Six months in the dating pool and she couldn't even remember what Mason had done to bug her. She appreciated him more than ever.

There would never be another Mason. There would never be someone who made frames from driftwood, or bought them tickets to Las Vegas two hours before their plane took off. He was creative and spontaneous and after all her bad dates she realized that Mason's flaws paled in comparison to the yetis she'd been exposed to.

Now she wanted him more than ever. She figured it was partially because breaking up with him had been her decision. She couldn't stand living with the thought that she had made such a drastic mistake.

After a godawful blind date with a musician who actually turned out to be a church choir director she had summoned up the nerve to call Mason. He'd been friendly but distant, and who could blame him? She had nearly broken the man. A week later he'd called her drunk, crying, wanting to know how she could dangle his emotions on a string. She had created more of a mess than she realized when she'd taken her break, and the damage was nearly irreparable.

She was rummaging for a piece of gum in her purse when she heard his voice. "There you are!" His tone was too friendly, the same tone of voice she would use with one of her girlfriends. He was holding her shoe. "Lose something?" Even though she wanted to die of embarrassment she couldn't help but laugh with him.

"I'm just thankful you don't have a black eye," she said. "I'm so sorry."

He opened his arms.

"I heard you weren't coming," she said, giving him a hug. His body felt warm, but stiff and unfamiliar as if he were hugging his Aunt Beatrice whom he saw every ten years at a family holiday.

"I couldn't miss the engagement party, so I waited on standby and I got lucky." Naturally she began to fantasize that he'd perhaps waited standby so he could see her. "It's not often that one of your best friends gets married. Or that you see your ex-girlfriend shimmying to Billy Idol." His tone was playful but she couldn't control the fire that was burning her cheeks.

"Who were those guys you were dancing with anyway?" he asked. His tone was still playful, but she thought she detected a tiny little hint of jealousy. He'd always been protective of her. At times she'd loved it. It had excited her when he'd asked fifty questions about her cute UPS guy, or told drunken stragglers at the bar to beat it when they hit on her. Sometimes it had been sexy. Other times it had driven her crazy. Like the time she'd come out of the shower to find him going through her wallet.

"They're Ben's cousins. Matt and Bill."

"Ah yes." He nodded. "I've heard all about them."

They caught up, chatting about their jobs and families. She asked questions only to be polite. The truth was, she knew everything about his parents and job from Claire. His father had remarried, and Mason's job couldn't be better. He'd bought a brand-new Lexus; rumor had it he was in the highest tax bracket in California.

"I heard you got a dog," he said.

"How'd you know?"

"Claire told me."

He'd been asking about her, and Claire had forgotten to mention this? She couldn't blame her, with the wedding and everything. But for God's sake, if Mason was asking about her she needed to be notified at once. "She's adorable. You'll have to see her sometime." She hadn't meant to say the last part. The words had slipped out, but she was sort of glad she had suggested he meet Katie. His reaction would be telling.

"Yeah, that would be great." Not a bad reaction, but was he just being nice? They spent several more minutes catching up and she started to feel disappointed when she saw people leaving. The evening would come to an end soon and she would have to say good-bye to him until the next event.

"Where are you staying tonight?" she asked.

"I have a reservation at the Hilton down the street. I should probably call a cab."

"Why don't I drop you off at your hotel?" she offered. "We're in the middle of suburbia—you'll end up waiting hours for a cab. I'll be going right past your hotel."

"Are you hungry?" he asked.

She wasn't, but sensed this question might lead to something more. "I could eat."

"You mind if we stop for Mexican food?"

She'd always believed in fate. Things always worked out for a reason. Missing his flight may have been the best thing that had ever happened. It was the work of God. If he'd made his flight he would've arrived when all the food was still out on the buffet, but since he was late he had missed dinner. The food had long since been wrapped and refrigerated, and Mrs. Caradini had been too caught up in Frank Sinatra to bring it back out. Not only would she get to spend more time with him, but they'd be alone. She reached for her car keys.

•   •   •

If they were in her neighborhood near the beach they would've found a dozen places that catered to night owls. But they were in Rancho Bernardo, an upscale community with golf courses every two miles. He suggested they eat at the hotel after a half-hour of hunting for a twenty-four-hour Alberto's.

She doubted there would be a restaurant open this late at his hotel, but if it meant spending more time with him she was willing to play along.

He checked into his room, and the bellman told him that all the restaurants were closed but they could try room service.

"Why don't you come up for a midnight snack?"

This was going better than she had ever imagined.

She wasn't very hungry, and ordered French onion soup. She watched him devour a club sandwich with fries, and a garden salad drenched in blue cheese. He had the metabolism of a high-performance athlete. But as far as she knew he only lifted weights a few days a week. He was truly blessed with the luxury of pigging out at one A.M. whenever he pleased, and never gaining an ounce on his perfectly sculpted body. It was a gift from God that she had definitely been deprived of. She worked hard to keep her small butt. If she ate the way he did, her back end would be the size of a dump truck.

He kicked off his loafers and tossed his blazer over a chair, and she wished she were staying with him. She longed to peel off her uncomfortable clothes and slip into one of his oversized T-shirts like she used to.

He pulled a bottled water for each of them from the minibar and they sipped and chatted about all the things he loved to do in San Francisco. Conan O'Brien cracked jokes in the background, but they hardly paid attention to the show.

Listening to him talk about how much he loved the Bay Area made her feel discouraged. She'd sort of been hoping that he'd say how much he missed San Diego. Hearing how settled he was didn't provide much hope.

However, hope came quickly when he leaned over and kissed her. Tasting him made her feel as if he'd left yesterday. She felt as if no time had passed. He was the kind of guy who found more pleasure in pleasing her than in meeting his own needs first. He knew all the right places to touch her. He had been in long relationships before, and she'd found that men who were in longer, more secure relationships seemed to know more about women as opposed to men who just had casual flings. He moved his hand up her shirt and barely touched the tip of her nipple with his fingertip, lightly brushing his skin over hers. She felt herself explode with need. He then unbuttoned her skirt and pulled it down her thighs.

The evening rapidly shot above any previous expectations. She'd hoped for a good solid conversation with him at the party—that he'd notice how fit and tan she was. She wanted him to leave San Diego wanting more of her. So far they'd practically had a date and now they were headed for sex. This wasn't going badly, but having sex with him was also sending him back to San Francisco with little to desire. Physically, she was dying to feel his naked body move over hers. But her mind knew that giving him everything was giving him too much. It could be the last word as far as he was concerned. She was the one who had broken it off and it might give him the satisfaction of knowing that he could get her back whenever he wanted.

"Wait," she said.

He hovered over her.

"I just . . . I'm not ready for this yet. It might complicate everything." She said this partly because she was afraid it *would* complicate everything and partly because she wanted to see what his reaction would be.

He pulled back, and she wondered if he had lost his erection as quickly as the playful look faded from his face. "Yeah. You're right. I don't want to complicate anything either." He stood and reached for his pants.

This wasn't exactly the reaction she'd hoped for. She'd sort of wished he'd said, "Complicate what? We're together again and that's all that matters. Love is never complicated."

She wanted to know what he thought was so complicated.

What did he fear? Or not fear? And did he miss her too? But she didn't know how to ask him all these things without coming on too strong.

"Do you ever think about me?" he asked.

She was grateful that he had opened the door for discussion. "Yes. All the time." He was silent, so she continued: "What about you?"

"Sometimes." He looked down at his feet.

"Well, what do you think about?"

"I don't know. Sometimes I miss you."

Fantastic! She tried to keep from laying kisses all over his face and telling him how much she had missed him, and to go grab a condom after all. "I miss you—"

He cut her off. "But sometimes I wonder . . . I don't know. I have a lot of questions."

Something about his tone made her heart sink. "Questions about what?"

"I just wonder if . . . if maybe we are supposed to be together, or maybe we're not."

"I do too," she said. "You have no idea. Sometimes I think I made the biggest mistake."

"Do you know how hard those months were for me after we broke up?"

"I'm sorry." She suddenly felt conscious of her exposed breast. The moment had been ruined. She pulled her shirt back on. "I thought I was doing the right thing at the time."

"I know you did. And I would've taken you back in a second if you had just given me the chance. But you wouldn't. A lot of time has passed now."

"I know. But it doesn't seem that long."

"Maybe not to you. But I've changed, and you've probably changed too. I just . . . What I'm saying is that I miss you too, but

I can't jump back into anything with you. Look, I'm sorry. It may have been a mistake for me to bring you back here tonight."

"No. It wasn't." She felt a lump in her throat, and for a moment thought that she actually might start crying. If he felt that seeing her was a mistake, there was no way he was going to be prepared for what she had in mind—kick-starting their relationship within the next week or two.

He squeezed her knee. "I'm not saying that it's over for good. I'm just saying that seeing you is really confusing and I don't know what I want. You've been out of my life for over a year. But on the other hand I don't know if you were ever really out of my life. I just think we both need time to think. It's probably best that we don't rush into anything yet."

Yet was the key word in his sentence. *Yet* meant that he wasn't completely writing her off. This she could live with. If it took him time to figure it out, she'd wait.

CHAPTER TWO

"Eye yi yyi yi yiiiiii! Palooooma." She sang with a Spanish accent as she drove to her parents' house in Torrey Pines. As soon as she dropped Katie off she would be on her way to Mexico. Margaritas. Mariachi singers serenading her poolside. Cheap quesadillas. And a splendid girls' weekend of fun was what she looked forward to. She was already wearing her bikini under her shorts and tank top.

Her father was swinging a golf club in the foyer when she entered. "There's my girl!" Meg smiled at him, but quickly realized he was referring to the dog.

"Oh! Would you look at how precious she is?" Her mother beamed as she entered holding a bone-shaped cookie. She was glad her parents liked her dog. But, hello?

Her father let Katie lick his face for a moment before turning to

Meg. "Make sure you get insurance," he said. "The *federales* down there will take all your money and jewelry if you don't."

"I'm actually not driving in Mexico. We're all meeting at Claire's and some of her friends are driving, but I'll make sure whoever drives stops for Mexican insurance."

"I don't know why you girls would even want to go to Mexico," her mother said. "It's just so dangerous. Lemme show you something." She hurried off.

While Meg waited, her father gave her a long lecture about all the hazards she might encounter south of the border. "It's not like San Diego. You're going into a foreign country. Borderline Third World down there and the police are extremely corrupt."

Little did they know she'd snuck out of her bedroom window on a regular basis during her senior year of high school so she could go drink in Tijuana with all her wild friends. She'd been there more times than them.

"Read this," her mother said when she returned, holding out a newspaper clipping dated three days earlier.

The headline read "Kidnapping Rampant Along Borders." The article proceeded to explain that hundreds of innocent Americans had been kidnapped at U.S. borders and held for ransom by drug cartels.

"Okay, *now* you are scaring me."

"Good. Why don't you just tell Claire you're not feeling well?"

"I can't cancel. It's Claire's bachelorette party. And besides, we're not walking across the border. We're driving. And we're staying in a really nice hotel near Ensenada. It's not like I'll be hanging out in the heart of TJ." However, she was a little concerned for Mason, who was camping on the Ensenada coast with the rest of the groomsmen. Ben was having his bachelor weekend in Mexico as well. They'd be right outdoors for anyone to rob or kidnap them. Her anxiety suddenly felt overwhelming. Again, she remembered there was a big difference between poverty-stricken Tijuana and the foamy remote coast of Ensenada. They'd be miles from crime.

She decided it was time for good-byes, then continued on to Pacific Beach to meet Claire and the rest of her friends. She knew Mason was probably in San Diego by now, getting ready to head to Mexico as well for the bachelor party. It made her heart ache to know that he'd probably flown in that morning, or even worse, the night before and hadn't called her. She hadn't heard a peep from him ever since the engagement party. If he wanted to get back together with her, he definitely wasn't racing into anything. Claire had said he probably just needed time and that he'd told Ben he'd enjoyed seeing her. But if he'd *enjoyed* it so much, why hadn't he called her?

She knew it was going to drive her crazy knowing he'd be minutes away all weekend and she wouldn't be able to see him. Couldn't Claire and Ben have a coed weekend?

She'd been a bridesmaid in two other weddings and had concluded that most of the fun of being in them was meeting the rest of the wedding party. With the engagement party, the shower, the bachelorette, all the gown fittings, and the rehearsal dinner, by the time everyone reached the wedding it was if they had traveled around the globe together. Meg had never met Claire's friends from college. In fact, she hadn't met Claire until after college, through Mason and Ben. They'd gotten pedicures and had girl talk while the boys watched basketball.

The screen door was unlocked at Claire's condo so she let herself in. Several girls occupied Claire's couch and were so engrossed in their conversation that they hardly noticed Meg when she stepped inside. "Ahem." She jingled her keys while shoving them in her purse.

A couple of them glanced at her, but continued chatting away. They were earthy girls with freckled skin and hair spun from wheat-toned threads. They possessed a J. Crew type of beauty. Like the models in the clothing catalogue, they were simple and boyish. There probably wasn't a drop of concealer in the room except on Meg's face and the stash she had in her makeup bag. She felt girly and small around them. They all had long legs, and she noticed that a couple didn't even shave.

"You would not believe how awesome Greece was," one girl said. Where was Claire?

"Oh, Greece is fabulous, but nothing like backpacking around Thailand," another replied.

"Hi, everyone," Meg said. She wasn't sure why she hid her Coach tote behind her calves. "I'm Meg." She felt as if she would have something to add to this conversation, as she had done some traveling back in college. But not one of them looked up. Instead they all looked at her red flip-flops.

"I've heard so much about all you guys, and I've been waiting to meet you—"

She heard the sound of a toilet flush and was relieved when the bathroom door swung open and Claire emerged. "Meg! Yeah! You're here." She greeted her with a hug. "Let me introduce you to everyone. You guys, this is Meg!"

There was Joss and Cassie and Allie and Sagie, who apparently had been named after her birth sign, Sagittarius, and went by Sagie for short. She lost track after that. She'd heard all about most of them, and they were probably nice once you got to know them. She was just so surprised by how different they were from Claire. Joss, a tall, muscular brunette with long hair and freckles covering her nose, bounced a volleyball on her knees. Her sandals top-fastened with Velcro straps and looked as if they could safely ski over nails. Backpacks in natural shades of pine green and granite rested around the couch, and their jean shorts were faded and slightly outdated. She noticed a couple Grateful Dead patches on a dirt brown backpack. Meg wondered if Claire had been spinning to Jerry Garcia at one point.

"Now we're just waiting for Cynthia and then we can go," Claire said. "She doesn't know anyone either, so I've put you two in the same hotel room together. Oh, but you do know someone! Avril. I practically forgot. She's staying in your room too, and you guys can ride down together."

"Great."

She was relieved when Cynthia arrived. A tiny little thing, she looked as if she could probably fit into a child's size 6X. Her strawberry blond hair was pulled into a wispy French twist and she had an eye for summer pastels in her lavender shorts and white sandals. She was a coworker of Claire's who'd missed the engagement party because she was visiting relatives.

Meg rode in Avril's Honda with Cynthia and Sagie to Mexico. Driving in Tijuana was like driving among a bunch of blind people. Drivers paid little attention to lanes, or even center dividers for that matter. Everyone herded together in one mass and sped toward the same direction. It was a little nerve-racking to know that Avril was shepherding them through this, and she felt much better once they were out of Tijuana and heading down the coast.

Cynthia talked for most of the two-hour drive, speaking mostly of herself. She rambled on about her boyfriend who played for a minor league baseball team and how she was getting promoted at her job.

"What do you do?" Cynthia asked Meg.

"I'm a movie critic and entertainment writer for *San Diego Weekly*."

"Hmmm. So, you go to lots of movies?"

"All the time."

"Oh." Cynthia looked out the window and commented on all the dead dogs they'd passed on the side of the highway. Road kill was part of the scenery in Mexico, and Meg had never been sure why.

• • •

There was a wedding at the hotel. A bride and groom were taking photos on a veranda overlooking the ocean, the wind blowing her veil in a loose billowy cloud behind them. It was a nice place for a wedding, emerald lawns and sprawling cliffs overlooking turquoise waves. Modern and spacious; Meg thought she could really get used to this place. When she heard there was a spa, she decided she might have to splurge on a massage, or something more budget-friendly like a pedicure.

She could hardly wait to get to the pool but faced a minor setback when they had to check in. Claire's maid of honor, Cassie, had already assigned people to rooms, and it felt a little like summer camp, bunking up with strangers. A problem arose when Cassie informed them that someone had to put down a credit card for each room. She'd made the reservation with her credit card, but didn't want to be responsible for the rest of the weekend.

"I thought we were paying in cash," Cynthia piped up.

"We are. But we have to put down a credit card for a deposit and then we can pay in cash when we leave and they won't charge the card," Claire said. "I promise."

Naturally, volunteers were scarce. No one jumped at the opportunity to be financially responsible. Avril pretended to look at a Mexican tour booklet, and Cynthia said she didn't have a credit card on her.

The other girl, Sagie, who was staying in their room was too busy chatting with her pals to notice.

"I'll put mine down for our room and then everyone can just pay cash when we check out," Meg said. Someone had to do it.

All she wanted to do was get to the pool. She waited for the other girls to change into their suits before heading there with the whole group. She ordered a piña colada from a waitress and sprawled on a lounge chair. There were no mariachi singers, but they could hear plenty of brassy Mexican music from the wedding reception several yards away.

Chilly breezes made it difficult to warm up, but she figured if she sat long enough beneath the sun she'd eventually heat up. She was barely starting to get comfortable when Sagie came over spinning a volleyball on her fingertip. The sun was bright and the light revealed a fuzzy patch of dark hair above Sagie's lip. "Does anyone want to play volleyball?"

"I would totally be into that!" Cynthia screeched.

Meg looked around and prayed some of the other girls would say no. She remembered the time in eighth grade when she'd been forced to play volleyball in PE. When the ball came hurtling toward her she had struggled to hit it with the inside of her wrists. She hadn't even hit it that hard, but it was enough to break blood vessels; the memory made her shudder every time she saw Gabrielle Reece on television. But she couldn't let them know this. She had to be a good sport. She wanted to click with them. She wanted them to like her and she wished she was athletic, but the truth was that she sucked at sports.

She ended up on the same team as her roommates and a few other girls, including Claire. She felt self-conscious standing in the sand wearing only a bikini. The last time she'd felt comfortable playing sports in a bathing suit was in the third grade.

She prayed that no one would hit the ball in her direction. All the girls were so tall, she wondered if she could hide behind someone. She was doing a pretty good job using Sagie as a barricade until they decided to rotate positions. She figured the best way to handle the situation was to stay put, and maybe no one would notice.

"What are you doing?" Avril asked. "You're in the front row now."

"Oh." She slowly moved to her position. Every time the ball came over the net she thought her heart was going to spring into her throat. The one time it did come spinning straight toward her she attempted to hit it, but missed and sliced the air with her arms. Sagie, however, came to the rescue; she jumped in front of Meg and whacked the ball over the net before sliding onto the ground. When she popped back up she had a sand burn on her right thigh.

"Way to go, Sagie!" Whoever yelled sounded like a man. "Way to take one for the team!" It was Cynthia.

Meg said a silent prayer that they would rotate again. Her prayer was answered sooner than she thought. They rotated all right. This time, Meg's position was front row, dead center. She prayed that the ball would sail over her head, all the while wondering how long volleyball games lasted. She'd always skipped watching this event during the summer Olympics and had tuned into gymnastics and diving. She was wondering whatever happened to Greg Louganis when the ball came flying toward her. She assumed the position just as she had been taught in P.E. and hit the thing as hard as she could. She was so happy she'd made contact that it took her a minute to realize she'd hit the ball in the wrong direction. Her victory dance ended as soon as she noticed the ball heading straight for the Mexican wedding reception.

Someone catch it! Please someone catch it! God, someone catch it! No one caught it. She could hear the shrieks over the seagulls. What she assumed were Spanish swearwords fell like grenades over the hotel grounds. It was hard to tell what kind of damage she'd done. However, it only took a few seconds for the groom to come storming toward them, holding their volleyball like a weapon. She didn't need to speak Spanish to know the guy was pissed.

Claire covered her mouth, and they all watched as the tuxedo-clad man hurled their ball on the ground. He was backed by the hotel concierge, who pointed out in broken English the white and pink frosting on Sagie's ball. "You destroy wedding cake." They all looked at Meg.

She wanted to bury herself in the sand. She could only think of one thing to say. "I'm *so* sorry. I am *sooooo* sorry."

Volleyball ended after that. The concierge took their ball and told them they could pick it up at the front desk after the wedding was over. No one said much to make Meg feel better. Instead they all went to their rooms to shower. Claire was the only one who didn't act as if Meg should be tossed into the rough waters below.

"I feel like the biggest asshole in the world," Meg said, thinking of the way the white cake had looked on the ball.

"Forget about it. Any one of us could've done the same thing. It was an accident." Then Claire began to chuckle. "Did you see how pissed that guy was?"

"Oh, my God. I thought he was gonna kill me." They burst into laughter.

• • •

During dinner Meg was seated between Cynthia and Joss. "What do you do?" Meg asked Joss.

"I'm the assistant to the assistant director for a movie coming out next year starring Keanu Reeves."

"Oh!" Cynthia shrieked. "I have totally been wanting to talk to someone who is into movies all month because there are so many good movies out right now, and I've been dying to know which ones to go see. What's good? What do you recommend?"

Um, hello? Am I the invisible, imaginary movie critic and entertainment reporter, or do I look like my opinion is worthless? Just because I like to paint my toenails and wax my upper lip doesn't mean I'm a complete airhead, Meg wanted to shout.

She listened as Joss answered. Her suggestions were decent ones, but Meg could think of better movies. When she spoke they looked at her.

"Thanks, Meg," Cynthia said. "I'll keep it in mind." Then she smiled and looked around the table. "So everyone tells me I look like Nicole Kidman. I get that all the time."

Nicole Kidman with a gummy smile and huge nostrils, Meg thought.

"I could see that." Cassie nodded.

"You totally do," Joss chimed in.

The rest of the table nodded in unison.

After dinner they hung out in the hotel bar. Some of the girls flirted with a group of guys who looked as if they had come to Mexico on a military leave of absence so they could legally drink. They couldn't be older than twenty and were as red as hot sauce. Their sunburns looked painful.

It seemed like an eternity before everyone was ready to retire. Meg had been dying to go to bed all night, but once under the covers she couldn't sleep. She had bunked up with Cynthia, and it felt awkward sharing a double bed with a stranger. It seemed as if there were some kind of imaginary line through the mattress that separated her side of the bed from Cynthia's. If crossed, she would be electrocuted or scratched by one of Cynthia's toenails.

She lay on her side, facing away from Cynthia. She couldn't sleep with their noses practically touching. She needed to adjust her body, but she had already rolled around three times and she was afraid that if she moved again she'd keep the other three girls awake with all her shuffling around. The more she thought about the need to roll onto her stomach, the more uncomfortable she became. So she lay as rigid as a curtain rod.

CHAPTER THREE

The following morning she woke with a stiff neck, and a long strawberry blond hair stuck to her cheek. The other girls were still sleeping, so she decided to get up and head to Claire's suite early. Cassie had made a trip to Costco before they'd left and stocked up on breakfast for the weekend. Some of the L.A. girls were already sitting around the room, eating granola and playing a card game. No one said hello to her.

"Good morning," Meg said cheerily.

Each grunted without looking up from their cards. She wondered why they were so rude. Had Claire said something about her to them? Not an option. Claire was one of her closest friends, not a backstabber. Did they not like her clothes? Her hair? She felt like she was in junior high again. She sat down at a small table by the window and ate a piece of peanut butter toast by herself.

"What are you guys playing?" she finally asked with a hint of enthusiasm in her voice.

"Poker."

"I love poker!" Her brother-in-law had taught her to play a couple Christmases ago. It had taken her a few games to catch on, but now she was a regular Kenny Rogers.

"We might play volleyball later this afternoon," Allie said. "Are you in?"

"I'm definitely in!" Cynthia shouted as she banged her way into the room. "I love volleyball!"

"Awesome. You can be on my team," Joss said.

Meg secretly hoped there would be a group going into town to do some shopping.

After eating her toast she strolled back to the room alone, and was totally overjoyed when she felt a drop on her face. Rain! No volleyball. However, this meant that she would probably be stranded inside with them for the rest of the afternoon. She suddenly felt homesick. She thought of Katie at her parents' house and wondered if she was waiting by the front door for her as she sometimes did when Meg went away.

Then she thought of Mason, only minutes away, and how much she wished she was with him at the moment. He was probably having a blast.

After she returned to her room she watched a snowy CNN on television and mentally calculated how many hours she had left here.

Their phone rang and Avril answered it. "That was Claire," she said. "Since it's raining she wants us all to come to her room to play Jenga." Yes! "Then when it clears up we'll go to the pool."

Meg could handle Jenga. It was the game where a tower was built from dozens of blocks and each player took a turn pulling a block from the stack. The object was to prevent the whole stack from falling over. She could keep a tower from crashing, no problem.

Rain was coming down heavily as they headed to the suite, and the girls had to run to keep from getting wet. She wondered how Mason was doing in the rain—if his tent was waterproof. Perhaps they would call the camping trip off and join them at the hotel for a coed bachelor/bachelorette weekend. She knew this fantasy was far-fetched, but she couldn't help but imagine.

When they got to the room all the seats around the coffee table were taken, so Meg made herself comfortable on the floor.

Allie handed her a pen. "Make some blocks."

"What do you mean?"

"Write something on the blocks. You know. Something funny." She handed her a block. "Like this." Meg looked down at the block and read the scrawled handwriting: *Run to the balcony and shout I love big dicks.* "Whoever pulls that block from the stack has to do that. So make some of your own up. Or you can just write 'drink ten drinks,' or something like that."

"What if they don't do it?"

"They have to do a shot of tequila."

She looked through the pile. *Snort like a pig while crawling on the ground. Sit on someone's lap and sing something by Air Supply while bouncing up and down.* As she held a block between her fingers she wanted revenge. She'd make them all do things that would embarrass the living crap out of them. But then she remembered she ran the risk of pulling out embarrassing blocks too. There was only one solution.

She'd have to mark the blocks. She'd put a tiny black dot on the side of the ones that were intended for them, and a minuscule X on the side of the ones that were intended for her.

She glanced at her red flip-flops. *Bow down and kiss the feet of anyone wearing red*, she wrote on her first block. Two other girls were wearing red. They'd never know who wrote it.

Suddenly, she felt as if she couldn't get her hands on enough blocks. She wrote on them as if she were being timed. Dotted ones said things like, *Go make refreshments for the entire group, and pound two beers while you're at it.* She'd get them all hammered too.

Starred ones said things like, *Choose four people who must only refer to you with Queen before your name for the rest of the day.* There were already quite a few that had been filled out by the girls, and she managed to sneak some dots on those as well.

She hadn't realized she was laughing out loud while writing *Do three shots of tequila, then remain mute for the duration of the game* until Sagie elbowed her.

"What's so funny? Did you put something really twisted on there?" The twinkle in her eye was alarming.

Meg winked. "You bet." She decided she better start disguising her handwriting.

"Look at mine," Sagie said gleefully. *Squeeze your tits five times while mooing like a cow!*

Who the hell were these people?

Claire pulled the first block and was forced to howl like a dog while moving around the room like a belly dancer. Meg had not come up with this idea, but recalled marking it with a dot. Cynthia went next. She carefully slid a block from the tower then read her task.

"Who is wearing red?" The dread in her voice put a smile on Meg's face.

She watched as Cynthia kissed Cassie's dirty toes, then moved on to Claire, who had some sand stuck on her feet. Meg was last. Cynthia's lips felt dry.

Sagie's turn was next and she jumped at the chance to flash her breasts at the Mexican bartender by the pool below the balcony.

When it was Avril's turn Meg felt triumphant. "I have to make snacks for everyone?" Avril asked, her voice heavy with disappointment. "*And* pound two beers?"

"That's brilliant! Who wrote that one?" Cynthia asked.

Meg pretended to fix a button on her blouse.

"Meg, it's your turn," Claire said.

She carefully selected a block and slid it with slow precision from the tower.

"What is it?" Allie asked.

She read the block then selected her three roommates and the girl who had served her the volleyball the day before to now refer to her only as Queen Meg.

●   ●   ●

The best part of her day was the stiff margarita she had with dinner. The girls who were sober enough to make it to the restaurant went back to the bar afterward and found the same Marines they had been flirting with the night before. Avril got wasted and passed out on a barstool. Meg graciously offered to put her to bed. It was the perfect excuse to get out of there, and she could go to bed too. Sleeping through the rest of the trip sounded like the best way to deal with them.

However, getting Avril back to the room was difficult. She had to balance her, and Avril's head kept rolling over onto Meg's shoulder. Meg was much smaller than Avril and dealing with her weight slowed them down a bit.

"Thanks for sporting me, Queen Meg," she slurred.

Putting her to bed was much easier. Avril face-planted on the comforter and was out within two minutes.

Meg was just drifting off to sleep when she heard a gentle thud on the balcony, like a shoe dropping from the edge of the bed. She figured it was the wind and closed her eyes. The same thud again. She sat up and waited. Silence. Just as she began to lie down again she heard it. Soft, but definitely something. Her first thought was that someone was breaking in. Quickly she went to the door, pulled back the curtain a mere inch and peeked outside. The moon cast a dim shadow over the patio furniture and she watched as something sailed over the railing of their balcony and landed right next to the sliding door. It was a tiny package of Chiclets. The gum was sold by homeless people on every street corner in Mexico. One could buy a box of two hundred rainbow-colored packets for less than three dollars if they had the right bargaining skills. As a child she'd thought of Mexico as a sacred place. It was the capital of cheap, fruit-flavored gum.

Who the hell was throwing gum on their balcony? What if it was the salsa-complected Marine from Alabama that Avril had been eyeing all night? She debated calling hotel security. Then she decided she'd get rid of the little Romeo herself. She slid the door open, thinking of what she would say.

Oh, you're here for Avril? She's passed out. Quite a lightweight. She'd be more than happy to tell him to leave. Something small and pink soared over the railing, and she ducked to avoid being hit. "Don't throw," she called as she slowly peered over the ledge. "Mason?"

"Hey." He smiled. Her first thought was that she needed to find out what brand of teeth-whitening strips he used. His smile glowed like something from the aerospace museum in Balboa Park. Then she realized it wasn't because his teeth were bleached. It was because his face was so dirty. "What are you doing?"

"Shhh!" He held a finger to his lips. "Don't let anyone know I'm here. I snuck away to see you."

She felt like clapping her hands with glee and doing the Macarena right there on the patio. "How did you sneak away from the guys?"

"I managed. Come down here."

It didn't take much convincing. "Coming."

He was sprawled out on a lounge chair when she found him. Dusty black streaks covered his face and clothes. When he stood up to hug her a few packets of gum fell from his pockets. He smelled like a Ball Park frank peppered with beer, suntan lotion and a little body odor. "What's all over your face?" she asked.

"Probably charcoal. I helped keep the fire going tonight, and I've barbecued like ten hot dogs."

He kissed her and she didn't care if she looked like a coal miner too. She loved the feeling of his face next to hers.

"What's with the gum?" she asked.

He looked at the little packets on the ground. "I bought a whole stash from some guy with like ten kids on the beach. I think I cleaned him out. Made their whole month."

She wanted to elope. Not only was it great to be with him again, but he'd also changed. The old Mason would've tossed a nickel at the man and told him to take his gum to some other campers.

"I've been thinking about you all weekend," he said softly before taking her face in his hands. "You still feel the same way every time I touch you. I miss you. So much, Meg. You have no idea."

Every nerve in her body came alive with happiness. She no longer felt irritated with all the L.A. girls. These were the words she'd been waiting to hear. This made the whole weekend wonderful.

They sat down on the lounge chair and kissed again. "I couldn't imagine making the trip all the way down here and not seeing you when you were only a few minutes away."

"That's exactly how I felt all weekend. I'm so glad you came," Meg said.

"I want you to come to San Francisco and stay with me next weekend."

She felt her heart plunge. "I can't. It's the weekend of the couple's shower." Her life could be summed up in four simple words. Claire and Ben's Wedding. "It seems like this whole month is pretty much booked with wedding events."

"I know. Tell me about it. I would come to the couple's shower, but I just can't take the time to be traveling back and forth the whole month. Why don't you come the following weekend? I'll pay for your ticket."

"Okay."

They kissed again and he pulled her into his arms. They lay on the lounge chair for a while, the scent of salt water climbing over the cliff top, and the brilliant glow of millions of tiny stars above them. "I've been thinking *a lot*," he said.

"About what?"

"About us." He kissed her forehead. "I really started to convince myself that I was over you. But seeing you last weekend made me realize that I don't know if I can be without you anymore. I'm willing to see if we can give this another chance."

She kissed his dusty forehead. "I feel the same way."

"There is only one Meg," he sighed. "There is nobody else like you."

They lay there for quite a while. She didn't want him to leave, wasn't thrilled with the idea of him walking all the way to his campsite in the middle of the night. "You better start back," she said. "Be careful."

"I'll be fine." He walked her back to her room and quickly kissed her before she closed the door.

CHAPTER FOUR

The following morning she awakened to the sound of a blaring phone. All she could think about was going back to Katie and her bed with her clean jersey-knit sheets and abundance of throw pillows. She'd call Mason, then eat graham crackers and Cool Whip in bed, cuddled up to her pup, in front of *Fried Green Tomatoes* and she wouldn't have to deal with these people again until the wedding, and by that point she'd be officially back together with Mason and spending all her time with him anyway, so—

Her fantasy was interrupted when Sagie answered the phone. "Yeah, that sounds great. I'd totally be down with staying till tonight. I've got nothing to do. I'm sure everyone else feels the same way. Volleyball? Of course. Count me in."

God, why?

Meg wondered why she hadn't thought of throwing their volleyball into the Pacific while they all slept the night before.

After Sagie hung up she turned to the group. "That was Joss and she wants to know if anyone is up for volleyball. I guess they've all decided to stay today since the sun is out. They're going to drive home later."

This wasn't exactly the way she wanted to wake up, but she was so happy about her rendezvous with Mason and her upcoming trip to San Francisco that she didn't care. She should've brought her own car, so she wasn't at their mercy. She would just skip volleyball. She didn't care if she was a poor sport.

"I'm sooo hungover," Avril moaned. She sat up and Meg noticed that one of her eyebrows was gone. It must've rubbed off on her pillow. *Unibrow* now had a new meaning. "There is no way I can play. I don't even think I can get out of bed."

Even though Meg could think of a million other people she'd rather hang out with than Unibrow, she was glad that Avril nixed volleyball. She didn't want to be the only one. Meg's plan was to head to the pool, and remain there until it was time to go. If anyone wanted to join her, fine. She was in the bathroom, nude on the bottom and tying the straps of her string bikini when the phone rang again. She heard Sagie's voice. "Hey, Claire. Oh. Okay. I'll ask. Hold on. It's Claire and she said one of Ben's friends is here because he's driving back to San Diego and has an empty car and wants to know if anyone wants to ride with him."

Meg almost ran into the room nude. She accidentally knocked the towel rack from its mount when she yanked a towel down to cover her body. If this person had offered a ride to San Diego on the handlebars of his bicycle she probably would've accepted. "Tell him I'll be down in five minutes," she yelled.

She looked for something to wear and realized that she hadn't packed well. Since the weather had been so crappy she'd been lay-ering her clothes to keep warm. She was going to have to wear something semidirty. She grabbed the shirt from the night before. She'd only worn it for a couple hours, and figured it was probably the cleanest thing she had.

"Later," Sagie said as she passed Meg.

"'Bye, you guys." Meg smiled. "Have fun playing volleyball." They were just outside the door when she remembered that the room was in her name, under her credit card. She needed to collect the cash from the girls and check out.

"Oh, hey you guys, I hate to be a pain. I know it's early but do you think you could all pay me for the room now because I'm leav-ing and I need to make sure they don't charge my card."

"I'm so hungover," Avril groaned.

"Can you hand me my wallet?" Cynthia asked from the door-way. "It's on top of the TV."

"Sure. My wallet is in Claire's room," Sagie said. "Can you stop by there on the way out?"

"Not a problem."

Cynthia opened her wallet and began to count through some bills. "Oh shit. I only have seventy-five and the room is eighty, right?"

"Yeah."

"Well, can I just pay you the other five next time I see you?"

The only other time Meg would see her would be at the wed-ding. Something told her Cynthia wasn't going to remember five dollars. But what was she supposed to do? Be the stingy, uncool bridesmaid who interrupted volleyball to send Cynthia to the ATM for five dollars? It was only five dollars, she told herself. If losing a little money meant leaving earlier, it was a good deal. "It's fine. Just pay me *next* time you see me."

"I'm dying," Avril breathed as soon as they were gone.

"I know. I'm sorry. It's just that I need to make sure my card isn't charged. Here. I'll tell you what. I'll go check out and then I'll come back to get my luggage and you can pay me then. How does that sound? That way you don't have to walk to your wallet right this second."

"It's okay." She sounded annoyed. "Just hand me my wallet. It's in my jeans."

Meg rummaged through a mountain of clothes next to Avril's suitcase before she found the wallet. "Here you go."

She sounded annoyed when she opened it. "I have eighty dollars exactly, which means I'll have to go to the ATM if I want to eat today."

What did she look like? A giant ten-percent-off coupon? Avril was going to fork over the cash, even if she had to walk to Venezuela for lunch money. "Here," she snapped before thrusting the cash at Meg and rolling over onto her side.

She quickly headed to the lobby. Bill was standing outside.

"Hey!" he said as soon as he noticed her. "You riding back with me?"

"Yes!" After spending the past seventy-two hours with The Bitch Squad she couldn't have been happier to see his friendly face.

"Awesome." He looked as if he had been camping, hair thick with grease and dirt beneath his fingernails. "My car is kind of a mess with sleeping bags and whatnot, but I'll make some room for you."

"I don't mind a little mess," she said. "But do you mind if I run to Claire's room really quick? I need to grab something."

"No. Not at all."

He followed her to the suite. Only two girls sat in the room, still gearing up for a day of beach sports. Sagie was nowhere to be found. "Hi, is Sagie here?" Meg said.

"No, she already went to play volleyball. What's on your shirt?" Allie asked.

She glanced down at her white cotton top. It looked clean to her. "What do you mean? Where?"

"On the sleeve." Cassie pointed.

She looked at her sleeve and noticed a big brown blotch. She immediately thought of Mason and his dirty face, but she hadn't worn this shirt when she saw him. Then she remembered Avril, her big, heavy head leaning on her for support. She was wearing Avril's eyebrow on her sleeve. "It's just a little makeup," she said, covering her disgust. What if she had been making out with a guy and her eyebrows ended up on his face?

At any rate, she had eighty dollars to collect. If she had to go call time-out to collect the money, she would. "I'm sorry, Bill. But I have to collect for the room because it's under my name."

"No problem. I'll tell you what, I had to park kind of far so I'll pull up to the front of the hotel while you're doing that."

"Thanks."

She found them grunting and baring their teeth like animals while they slammed the ball back and forth. For some strange reason, they looked even taller and more ominous than before. She felt like a nerd doing the hand signal for time-out, so she decided to wait for one of them to whack the ball out of bounds. The moment came sooner than she thought as the ball went hurling over her head. "Uh, Sagie," she called. "I'm getting ready to leave."

"Oh," Sagie said as she caught the ball. "I looked in my wallet. I don't even have one dollar right now. So, do you think you could wait until I go to town later? Or I can pay you at the wedding."

"No, I can't wait. Bill's waiting for me." Her tone was agitated, but she didn't care. Again, she had a bad feeling she would never see the money. "Just pay me at the wedding. Eighty dollars. Thanks."

When she checked out there was a fifty-dollar phone tab on the bill. "Fifty dollars? What's this for? We didn't use the phone."

The desk clerk pointed to three long-distance phone calls to Los Angeles and Meg instantly remembered Sagie talking on the phone.

She paid the balance with the cash received and put one hundred and thirty-five dollars on her credit card. She tried not to fume, and blamed only herself for agreeing to be the credit card martyr. She should've known better. Someone always got screwed in these situations. She should've insisted that one of them put their card down. She would've given them their eighty dollars, as *she* hadn't irresponsibly spent all her hotel money over the weekend.

She found Bill at his Suburban, tossing a bag of hamburger buns into the backseat of his car.

"So how was the weekend?" he asked.

"Great," she lied. "And how was camping?"

"It was *a blast*." His enthusiasm made her wish she'd been with the guys all weekend.

"What did you guys do?"

"Surfed all day. Then hung around the campfire at night, or went into town for fish tacos and some drinks. It was great, really relaxing. Great group of people too."

He handed her a CD case. "Here. Pick out whatever you want."

She thumbed through his CDs. He had good taste in music, a lot of classics like Elton John and Marvin Gaye, but also some new ones. She selected Jet's CD. They listened to the music and she felt so comfortable in his car that she could've propped her feet up on the dashboard and sung along to "Are You Gonna Be My Girl."

"You hungry?" he asked as they passed signs for Puerto Nuevo.

She wanted to get home to Katie, but she *was* hungry and enjoying this part of the trip so much that she could be up for stopping in the lobster capital of the Baja peninsula. Except for Mason's surprise appearance the night before, she was having the best time she'd had all weekend—plus, how often did she get the opportunity to eat a lobster meal for ten dollars?

They pulled into the tiny village. The cobblestone streets were covered in thick, rust-colored dust, and weeds sprouted between the stones. Tons of vendors lined the sidewalk, selling everything from silver jewelry to piñatas. It was crowded in Puerto Nuevo, mostly because of all the San Diegans who crossed the border on the weekends to come to the rustic Mexican town for cheap lobster.

After parking they walked to a three-story building painted orange with white trim. Inside, a hostess wearing a ruffled shirt and matching full skirt took two menus. "You want to sit up?" She pointed to the staircase.

They followed her up a dark, winding, tiled staircase that reminded Meg of the inside of a lighthouse. They took a seat right next to the window. Beyond the decrepit rooftops below rose a jagged cliff. She could see the never-ending line of the horizon. The sun was bright and felt hot against her face and shoulders, and the ocean appeared bronze with gold-crested waves. She ordered one lobster tail with rice, beans and flour tortillas. He ordered two tails and the same side dishes.

The food was delicious and she was more than glad they had decided to stop. She dipped each piece of warm salty lobster into a bowl of melted butter that they shared. They chatted about their weekends and she wondered if he had spent much time with Mason. They didn't seem like two people who would have much in common. Mason didn't surf and he would've never allowed his car to get as sandy as Bill did.

He told her about his family. Meg only had one sister, and she always felt a little envious of people who came from giant-size families like Bill. He had five siblings and was in the middle.

She went to the bathroom and when she returned he had paid for their meal. As they left the restaurant he refused to take her money.

"Where did we park?" he asked as they headed to the car. "I thought it was just a little ways down this road, but I don't see my car."

"Yeah, it is down this street. We probably can't see it." She looked down at her toes, which were covered in a fine layer of dust.

"I'm positive I parked next to that truck." His voice sounded alarmed.

When she glanced at the truck she became worried as well. "I thought you parked there too. But maybe there are two red trucks."

"Two red trucks with Hawaii stickers on the back?"

They both gazed at the empty spot where his Suburban had been, the pile of shattered glass that lay next to what should've been the driver's side of the car. "My car is gone," he said, stunned.

She had no idea what to say. It was obvious by the glass that someone had busted a window and taken off with his SUV. "Bill, I feel terrible. I'm so sorry."

"Why? It's not your fault." He released a stunned chuckle. "I can't believe my damn car was stolen in broad daylight."

"Please tell me you got Mexican insurance."

"Of course." He shook his head. "All your stuff is in there, though."

"Don't worry about my stuff," she said, and meant it. "It's all replaceable, and at least I've got my purse with my cell phone and money."

He shook his head. "Only in Mexico. Only in flipping Mexico.

I swear." He revealed a weak smile, and his cheeks looked rosy. He seemed embarrassed, but it wasn't his fault. She tried to think of ways to make him feel better. "Well, we've gotta find a ride back," he said.

"Maybe we can call the girls at the hotel and they can grab us on the way out," she suggested.

She pulled out her cell phone, and then remembered that she had not signed up for an international plan. "Do you have your phone?"

"It's charging in my car right now."

"All right," she said calmly. "Let's find a pay phone."

They spent a solid twenty minutes trying to figure out how to use the pay phone. Once they were finally connected to the hotel she spent another ten minutes trying to communicate with the same woman who had explained the phone bill. Eventually, she learned that the girls had checked out.

"Crap," she muttered. "They're gone."

"No worries," he said. "We're going to get out of here one way or another. I'll call one of my buddies at home. Someone will come get us."

She remembered her parents, who were probably waiting by the window with Katie for her safe return. "I should call my parents," she said. "I'm sure they'll come get us, and besides, they're going to start worrying if I don't come pick up my dog soon."

"All right." He moved to the next pay phone. "I'll try making some calls too."

Dialing international took even more effort than calling locally. After three attempts and several chats with a Spanish operator she finally got through—to her parents' machine.

"Mom. Dad. It's Meg. I'm in Mexico and I'm okay. We stopped in Puerto Nuevo for lobster and my ride's car was stolen. I won't be back as early as I had planned and I was hoping you guys might be able to come pick us up. But my cell phone doesn't work down here and I don't know how you're going to be able to get ahold of me, so I'll have to call you back later. Don't worry, though. Everything is okay. Give Katie a kiss for me, and talk to you soon."

Bill was leaving a message as well when she hung up. She called her sister, and her best friend and was about to attempt her parents again when she realized she was out of change. "I'm so sorry," he said.

"Why are *you* sorry?"

"I just feel like I got you stranded here. It was my idea to stop for lobster."

"Look, it's not your fault. How could you have known this was going to happen? You couldn't. And, hey, it's an exciting story to tell our friends. It's not every day your car gets stolen in Mexico."

He laughed. "Well, let's just give it a rest and go have a margarita somewhere. I'm not driving, so at least I can drink now," he said.

She laughed. "That's right. At least you can drink." For some reason she wasn't panicked or wanting to call every single person she could possibly think of to come rescue them. Something about his presence made her feel as if everything was going to be okay.

She couldn't wait to tell Mason this story. Stranded in Mexico. A stolen car. She'd heard about stolen cars in Mexico, especially SUVs. They were a hot commodity, because bigger cars made it easier to smuggle people across the border.

They walked around Puerto Nuevo and were drawn to a bar with the festive sound of brass instruments. It was warm inside and the first thing she noticed was a quartet of mariachi singers. They wore cowboy boots and sombreros, and ruffled shirts with jackets that matched their Spanish-styled pants.

"I'm really sorry about your car," she said after they ordered drinks.

"It's okay. The car is insured. I'm more upset about my surfboard. I've traveled around the world with it and I can't ever replace that."

She wished she could think of something poignant and wise to say, but she knew that losing his surfboard was the same as Slash losing his guitar. It was irreplaceable. "I wish there was some way to get all your stuff back," she said.

"It's just stuff." He shrugged. "It could be worse. Now it gives me an excuse to travel around the world again. I'll have to break my next one in."

One drink turned into two and then three and soon they were requesting songs from the band.

"Guantanamera," she said, feeling buzzed.

Maybe it was the alcohol, but she thought the mariachi singers were the best she'd ever heard. "I feel like dancing," she said as they played her song.

"Sounds great." They stood up. Bill turned to one of the mariachi singers and pointed to his pocket. "For the señorita," he said.

The singer nodded and Bill pulled two maracas from the musician's pocket. He handed them to Meg.

"You keep one!" she shouted over the music, as she pulled one from his hand.

She shook the instrument as she danced, not caring if she was completely out of sync with the band. She was having a blast shaking her maraca. They danced to three more songs until someone in the restaurant requested "Bésame Mucho."

It was a slow song and she was forced to abandon her maraca. She had no idea what the singer was saying but his voice was passionate and beautiful and she wondered if they sold CDs. She thought of Mason and wished he were here. She watched as couples swayed together around the bar.

"Pretty song, isn't it?" Bill said as he held out his hand. "You want to dance?"

When she moved close to him she caught a whiff of campfire. The top of her head came up to his chest and the side of his shirt felt soft against her cheek. When the song ended, neither one of them pulled away from the other.

"Cielito Lindo," he said to the band. They continued with another beautiful song. One she had never heard. If these three old mariachis sold their music she would've definitely bought it, because she was quite sure she would never hear music like this again. Their voices were strong and thick with longing. They sang in perfect harmony. She could feel the rise and fall of Bill's chest beneath her face. They kept moving after the song ended.

"I should try calling my parents again," she said. "It's getting late and I'd hate for them to have to drive all the way down here in the middle of the night."

The sun was setting and a soft red glow had settled over the town. On the way back to the phones they passed all kinds of vendors. They stopped to look at some silver jewelry. She pulled a ring with a blue stone from the cart. She had tiny hands and it was rare that she found rings in her size.

"Is this real?" she asked the squat little man behind the stand.

"Yes. One hunred pear cent real silver, señorita. For you, I give you nice price."

"How much?" she asked.

"For that one. Twenty dollar."

"Twenty dollars?" She pulled it off. "No, thank you."

"How much you willing to pay?"

"Five."

He laughed and shook his head. "Five? These is real silver. Can't do it." He folded his arms over his chest. "Ten dollar."

"Seven."

"Seven dollar? This is the best silver you will find. You want to pay seven dollar for these?"

"How 'bout two for fourteen?" Bill's voice came over her shoulder. "I'll get one too." He rolled a plain silver band with a black line etched through the middle of it into the palm of his hand.

"Deal," the man said.

Bill handed the guy a twenty.

Meg handed Bill fourteen dollars. "You bought lunch. Please let me buy these."

Don't worry about it," he said as he collected his change. "It's a souvenir on me." She shoved the money in his pocket.

When she called her parents again there was no answer. Bill tried a few more friends and she tried a couple people as well. The funny thing was she didn't feel that frustrated, and when Bill suggested looking for fish tacos she agreed.

• • •

They had no luck reaching anyone after dinner, and she really began to feel stranded when she realized they might not find a ride home that night. Except for her wallet and useless cell phone she had no possessions. They had no transportation, and they were in a foreign country. However, for some reason she kind of liked the excitement, and thought of how uninteresting the rest of her day would've been if Bill's car hadn't been stolen. Returning to her everyday life, her furniture that she'd looked at every day for five years, the computer she sat in front of for eight hours a day. She probably would've ended up eating from a can of tuna in her pantry rather than dining on lobster.

"Listen, why don't we grab a hotel?" he suggested. "We can crash. I can shower and no one will have to drive down here in the dark."

They checked into a run-down motel. It was a busy weekend and their options were limited. They could share a room with a king-size bed, or they could each get their own room. She wasn't concerned about the cost. She feared more for her own safety. Staying in a decrepit motel room in Mexico was a little unsettling, especially after the crime that had occurred earlier that day. Bill looked at her. "Whatever you want to do," he said. "I'll try not to snore."

"I promise I'll stay on my side of the bed and I won't hog the covers," she said. She wanted to make it clear that her decision to share a room with him didn't mean that she wanted him groping her in the middle of the night for some action. But he didn't seem like the type of guy who would take advantage of the situation. She used a pay phone at the motel to call her parents again.

"Mom!" she said when she heard her mother's voice.

"Megan! What's going on? Where are you?"

"I'm still in Mexico." She explained their situation. Naturally, her mother had a million questions. They set a time for her parents to pick them up the following morning before she said good-bye.

Their room was clean enough, but old. The plain blue blanket on the bed looked as if it had been around for seven decades and the paint was peeling from the walls.

"Do you mind if I hop in the shower?" he asked. "I haven't bathed in three days and the smell of campfire is starting to get a little stale."

"Not a problem."

The television in their room got two stations. One featured what appeared to be a Mexican Justin Timberlake, dancing in an *American Idol* type of setting to lively Spanish pop. What made the show so interesting was that there was a giant white Easter bunny character clapping on the side of the stage and an MC who looked like a cross between Liberace and Rosie O'Donnell. Meg was pretty sure it was a man.

The other channel played a *telenovela*, the type of show where half of the female cast looked like American supermodels, only they all spoke rapid, fluent Spanish. Their behavior was so engaging, their looks so stunning, that Meg found herself sucked in even though she had no idea what the hell was going on.

She could hear the sound of water running and for a moment wondered what Bill looked like without his clothes on. She couldn't help it. He was a cute guy. Even though her heart was full of Mason, she couldn't help but wonder what it would be like to kiss Bill, to lie next to him in bed all night. Was he a good kisser? She bet he liked to spoon.

For God's sake, she hadn't expected him to come out of the bathroom wet and wearing only his shorts! His chest was far more toned than she had thought and he was tan, lusciously bronzed, and a little red on his shoulders. She couldn't believe he didn't have a girlfriend. He was a blast to be around, and the rare breed of male who had no idea how cute he was.

"So what do you feel like doing?" he said as he sat down on the edge of the bed.

"I really would like to take a shower too."

"I was thinking about walking to a liquor store and grabbing some Coronas. Maybe I'll head over there while you're showering."

She took a hot shower and wished she had her makeup bag and blow-dryer with her. She felt a need to look her best in front of him, not because she wanted him to be attracted to her. Well, yes, she did. For reasons she couldn't explain. Maybe it was her ego. Maybe she was attracted to him. Either way it didn't matter. As soon as she returned to San Diego she was booking a flight to San

Francisco; she was pretty much back together with Mason. Bill was a hottie, and she didn't want to feel like a pale frizzy-haired troll in his presence.

She had no choice but to let her hair air dry and make do with what she had as far as makeup went. She found a nearly empty tube of concealer in the depths of her purse. There was gum stuck to the tube, and the actual makeup had an interesting odor, but she stretched the contents thinly under her eyes and over a few zits she'd been picking at all weekend. She also found a tiny stick of lip liner. It was down to the last millimeter of makeup and when she rubbed the pencil over her lips the wood felt scratchy and she worried about splinters. The end result wasn't bad and her lips actually looked pretty red from pressing the hell out of them with the pencil. She watched a few more minutes of Spanish soap opera before he returned wearing a poncho.

"I see you bought some new clothes while you were away," she said.

"Yeah, and a deck of cards too."

"Cool. What do you feel like playing?"

"I was thinking poker, but we'll have to come up with something to use as chips. I bought some peanuts. Maybe we can use the shells."

They played poker on the bed, peanut shells leaving crumbs all over the comforter. She didn't care about the shells, because she planned to remove the blankets before they went to bed anyway.

He was good, but she was better and if they'd been playing for money she'd have been able to afford new shoes. He was a risky player and liked to throw in everything just so he could see what kind of hand she had. It made the game more fun that way.

Eventually they were too tired to play. They propped themselves against pillows and watched a variety show with a bunch of

Mexican line dancers dressed as Little Bo Peep performing to music rich with accordions. She eventually fell asleep.

She slept deep and hard and when she woke the television was turned off and the room was dark. She had no idea what time it was, but guessed three or four in the morning. The room was cold and she was tempted to pull the gross hotel blanket up to her waist.

Bill stirred and when he rolled over she felt his calves brush against her own. It had been ages since she'd felt a rough leg touch hers. She hadn't even wanted to touch another man since she'd started missing Mason.

She had to pee but didn't want to get up. She was comfortable and exhausted and didn't want to wake Bill. She was completely stunned when he pulled her into his arms, released a deep sigh and spooned against her. She didn't push him away, partially because the sound of his ragged breath behind her indicated that he was asleep and that he wasn't trying to get some action, and partially because he felt so warm. She wondered if he was so deep in slumber that he'd forgotten who she was. Perhaps he'd reached out for her, assuming she was someone else. Someone he felt comfortable with, and spooned with often.

She lay there for a moment, taking in the scent of his hair and his skin. She felt warm and eventually fell back to sleep. They woke again in the wee hours of the morning and he groggily rolled back to his side of the bed, as if they were a couple who had been dating for several years. She slept for another hour and when she woke that final time, their feet were touching.

He yawned and turned to her, his warm feet still resting on hers. He smiled. "We better get up. Your parents are going to be here soon."

•   •   •

When Meg returned home there were flowers waiting on her doorstep. Her heart leapt as she pulled out the card.

Looking forward to seeing you in a couple weeks. Your flight has been taken care of. Love, Mason.

CHAPTER FIVE

The first thing she noticed when she pulled up to Claire's Uncle Albert's for the couple's shower was the vintage black T-bird convertible parked in front of the house. She admired people who owned vintage cars, because she'd always wanted one for herself. However, every time she'd been on the verge of purchasing one her parents talked her into something more sensible, like the trustworthy Toyota Corolla she currently drove. She pulled up next to the T-bird and saw Bill getting out from the driver's side.

"Is this your gift to the bride and groom?" she asked.

He laughed. "Yep. Bought it yesterday."

"Seriously, is this yours?"

"It is."

"It's gorgeous. What made you decide to get this?"

"It's easy to throw my surfboard in when the top is down."

He looked at the package in her hand. "What did you get them?"

"Their cheese board and matching cutter. You?"

"Beer mugs."

After an hour at the shower she realized two things. One, men should never be allowed to attend any kind of bridal shower under any circumstances. For heaven's sake, showers were boring enough for women. For men, it had to be torture. She figured most of them had been dragged there by their significant others. The rest probably had no idea what they were getting themselves into. She watched as her former karaoke partner, Matt, dozed in the corner. The only male who seemed to be enjoying the event was Uncle Albert, who had a scarf tied around his neck and had been serving mint juleps in dainty little glasses since Meg had arrived.

The other thing she noticed was a certain individual with fake eyebrows and a taste for white patent leather hitting on Bill. She'd noticed it the second they'd entered the house. Avril had been following him all night, laughing loud at everything he said. For some reason this bothered her. She liked Bill, as a friend. He was a good guy and she didn't want to see him with someone like Avril. At least that was what she told herself.

Halfway through the gift opening she ducked into the bathroom. She was about to close the door behind her when she felt it push a little as if someone was trying to come in. She spun around and faced Bill. He closed the door behind him.

"What are you doing?" she whispered. Several yards away Claire and Ben were holding up their soup ladle for everyone to admire.

Without another word he took her face in his hands and kissed her on the lips. She surprised herself when she didn't stop him right away. He was the perfect kisser. However, when she felt her panties turn warm she pushed him away. "Bill? This isn't a—"

"Listen, I know this is really forward, but I figure why should I waste any time, right? I'm just going to say it. I like you, Meg. I haven't stopped thinking about you since Mexico."

She was speechless—partly because she hadn't really stopped thinking about him either. But she didn't want to be with him. Sure, he was fun to hang out with and cute and genuine but she was in love with Mason. *Love.* Bill could just be a passing infatuation for all she knew. Mason was someone she could marry; why Bill had come along right when she was about to mend the fences with the love of her life, she had no idea. It was a cruel twist of fate. Like when she was skinny and there were no sales on. But when she was feeling fat right before her period there were screaming deals on every designer brand at the mall. It was life, and unfortunately Bill was going to fall into the fateful abyss of irony.

"Bill, I'm sorry. But I, uh . . . I like you too, but it wouldn't be fair to string you along. I . . . well, you see, I used to date one of the other groomsmen in the wedding party, and well to be honest with you I'm not over him," she finished in a rush of words.

"I know. Claire told me."

"She did?"

"Yeah. But I mean, how serious are you about this guy? I mean, is he serious too?"

She swallowed. "I love him."

He nodded. "All right. Well, I guess I have to respect that." Part of her was relieved and part of her wondered if she had just made a huge mistake.

CHAPTER SIX

She brought a book for the flight, but was too fidgety to read. She opened to where her bookmark was but found that she had read the same paragraph three times before they had even taken off. She just wanted to get there. She wanted to deplane and be with him. For two solid days. She wondered if he felt the same. An hour and a half in the sky seemed like an eternity and she tried to keep herself occupied by flipping through *SkyMall* magazine.

She wondered if he would pick her up curbside, or would he be waiting for her at baggage claim? They hadn't been clear on this. She wondered what they would do that evening, but realized she didn't even care. She wanted to be with him. He was The One. She was sure of it now. She'd never craved someone like this before, never had such a need to feel a pair of arms around her. The

thought of continuing the rest of her life without him was unfath-
omable. She'd pushed Bill and their rendezvous in the bathroom
from her mind, and reasoned that she enjoyed the flattery of knowing that a hot, nice, fun guy was attracted to her. That was the only
reason she had kissed him back. It was her ego, nothing more.

When she walked into the airport she immediately spotted him
peering through a sea of faces. He was tall, almost six-three, and
his gorgeous features made him stand out amid the average-looking
crowd of people in the terminal.

She expected him to be in a suit and tie, having come from
work, but he was wearing sweatpants, tennis shoes and a T-shirt.

He pulled her off her feet and planted a warm kiss on her cheek.
She laughed. It felt good to be picked up, and she had no doubt
that he was excited to see her too.

"I came from the gym," he said as he set her down. "So I've
gotta go home and shower before we go out to eat. Is that okay?
Are you hungry now?"

"I can wait." He grabbed her suitcase and even though it had
wheels he carried it by the handle, the muscle in his forearm tight
and sinewy as they headed for the escalator.

She wasn't familiar with San Francisco, but knew it was an expensive place to live. Rent was outrageous and mortgages were
even worse. So when they pulled into Mason's apartment complex
she knew right away that he must be doing well. He owned the
two-bedroom apartment on the top floor of this building, complete
with a sprawling view of city lights and rooftops. She was further
impressed by the mirrored halls, hardwood floors and touches of
modern art. "Did you decorate yourself?" she asked.

"I hired someone." He opened the fridge. Inside were strawber-
ries, banana yogurt, a block of cheddar cheese and Choco Top—
the kind of chocolate syrup that hardens when you pour it on ice

cream. He'd stocked up on all her favorite foods. "You got Choco Top," she said, amazed.

"I sure did. And open the freezer."

She pulled the freezer open and found a brand-new tub of vanilla ice cream sitting inside.

"I can't believe how sweet you are." She kissed him on the cheek.

"I want you to feel at home."

She did feel at home, and she felt like suggesting they have Choco Top for dinner followed with some long-overdue lovemaking.

"Do you mind if I take a shower?" he asked.

"No. Not at all. I'll just make myself comfortable."

"Oh, I TiVo'd Oprah for you," he said. "I know you missed it because you had to hop on the plane." Why had she ever broken up with him?

He reached for a remote. "You just take a seat," he said.

He messed around with the remote before a menu of selections popped onto the screen. He showed her where to click to start Oprah. "So, you're all set."

She started the show and two minutes into what appeared to be a makeover program the screen froze. She grabbed the remote, clicked exactly what he'd pressed and tried to unfreeze the show but it didn't work. She tried again and again to get Oprah back, but she was gone.

She heard the shower running and realized she was stuck watching the frozen image of a middle-aged woman with feathered bangs and blue eye shadow. She looked around for some magazines. She settled on a huge coffee-table book of San Francisco.

The book was heavy and felt awkward when she set it on her lap. She'd use it to get some sightseeing ideas for their weekend. She was thinking about all the pictures of Alcatraz she'd browse when she opened the book. A card slipped from inside the front cover and fell to the floor.

Whenever she went into a male's house she expected to be startled by a pubic hair in the bathroom sink, or a dirty sock under the sheets. Upon setting foot in the domain of the opposite sex she knew opportunity was abundant to meet with a wet toilet seat or a foul odor from the garbage disposal. However, it never occurred to her that she would encounter remnants of the woman who had been there before her.

The second she looked at the card she knew it had come from the female species. Mason's name was scrawled in loopy, springy feminine writing on the outside of the envelope.

She said a few quick prayers that it was signed by his mother or late grandmother. Would reading the card be snooping? She had, after all, stumbled upon it. It wasn't like she had been looking for evidence of another woman. It had fallen into her lap, literally. She looked over each shoulder before slowly pulling the card out. Before she had even cracked it open something slipped from inside. She thought her heart might pound right out of her chest and land on the coffee table when she realized it was a photograph—a picture of Mason cheek-to-cheek with some girl.

She had curly shoulder-length hair and a nose sprinkled with freckles. Her playful smile revealed straight, white teeth. At this point ending the investigation was out of the question so Meg proceeded to read:

Dear Mason,
These past few months have been amazing! *You are* such *an* incredible *person and you deserve the best birthday. I look forward to many more happy memories, and I thought we could explore the city together.*
Love,
Kristen

So *this* was Kristen. This was the girl he'd dated *briefly* after they had broken up. Meg'd heard about her from Claire and had spent many nights wondering what she looked like. But now she wished she'd never seen the picture. She hadn't realized how hard it would be to see Mason with another woman. To see him smiling with another woman. To know that at one point he'd felt happy with another woman.

Suddenly, the book was not as cool or interesting as it had seemed when she picked it up. *What a lame gift.*

She studied the picture, and hated the fact that Mason looked happy.

Kristen is gone, she thought as she stuffed the card back into the envelope. *Her days of excessive underlining are over. You are here. You broke up with him, and he dated other people. Let it go.*

She wondered what he would do if he knew that she had seen the photo. Would he lament over it, tuck it in between his birth certificate and college diploma in his filing cabinet? Or rip it in two before tossing it in the trash can with all his other garbage? She hoped for the second option.

She tucked the envelope back in the book before going to the kitchen for vodka.

While she poured liquor into a glass Mason returned, wearing khaki slacks and a black T-shirt.

It was strange, but seeing that photo of Kristen made her want to strip him right there and have mad passionate sex with him on the kitchen floor. She truly felt aroused. She'd never felt a need to claim anyone, but she felt sexually territorial, and it frightened her a bit.

His stomach growled loudly and she was so preoccupied that she hardly even noticed. He laughed. "Excuse me. Sorry for all my bodily noises."

"Oh. Ha." She faked laughter. "That's okay."

"You hungry?"

"Yeah."

"Great. I have the perfect restaurant in mind. We can walk from here." He touched her back as they moved toward the front door. "You okay?"

"Oh. Of course. I'm fine."

The air outside was chilly and she wrapped her arms around her chest. "Is it always like this in the summer?"

"Usually, but we get some warm days too." He pulled off his coat. "Here. You take my jacket."

"That's okay. I don't want you to freeze."

"No. I'm used to it."

When he wrapped the coat over her shoulders she could feel the warmth he'd left inside. They walked down one of the steepest hills she'd ever seen in her life, and she wondered how anyone managed to drive a stick shift or parallel park without rolling into something behind them.

Nonetheless, she loved the old San Francisco buildings. They were so full of charm and character, and she thought of how different San Diego was with its sprawling developments of modern tract homes. Except for a few historic neighborhoods almost all the homes in San Diego were built after the sixties.

The neighborhood seemed safe and clean, but they passed at least a dozen homeless people. Some were huddled in corners, hiding their faces beneath the high collars of dirty jackets just to stay warm. Others picked through trash cans.

They walked to a small Italian restaurant and she realized how wonderful it was to be with him again. However, she couldn't help but wonder if he had been to this restaurant with Kristen. While he ordered a bottle of Chianti she realized that if she wanted to move forward she was going to have to erase the whole image of Kristen's face and the book and everything about them from her memory. When they did get back together she could "accidentally" slip the book into a box headed for Goodwill.

"I think we should start with beef carpaccio and we'll each have a salad," he told the waiter. He looked at Meg. "Caesar for you?"

"Please."

"I'll have a green salad with Italian dressing." Though being with him again seemed new, it was as if no time had passed. He still knew exactly what she liked to eat and she felt a sense of security. Dinner was delicious and they ate and chatted about old times and new times and the upcoming wedding. Afterward they walked to a jazz bar a few doors down. The inside looked like it could be the dimly lit, swanky living room of a close friend. Soft, comfortable couches in front of candlelit coffee tables covered the floor. They made themselves comfortable on a red velvet sofa and ordered martinis. The music was low and sexy and he drew her into his arms, cuddling against her body as if they were curled up on his couch watching live music. "So, you think you could live in San Francisco?"

The question took her by surprise. She'd never thought of relocating. Furthermore, she had never thought he would ask her so fast. They'd had a few drinks and maybe this was just his tipsy side talking. However, she loved this moment and wanted to believe he was serious.

She smiled. "I hadn't thought of it. But so far I'm in love with San Francisco."

"Good."

After they finished their martinis she could hardly wait to get to his place. She could practically feel the warmth of his skin through his clothes and she couldn't wait to feel their bare skin touching, the way his body felt against hers when they slept.

They held hands on the way back to his apartment. They were a couple blocks from his building when a homeless man, wearing a muscle shirt and a green top hat, approached them. He held a green cane with a shamrock on top. "Hey, you two lovebirds. You want me to sing you a song?"

"Sure," Meg said, open to spontaneous and strange entertainment.

"No." Mason picked up his pace, but the homeless man kept following them. He began to sing an Irish song for them before doing a little jig in their path.

"You mind sparing some change? I got no food. I'm starvin'."

Meg reached for her purse. She liked this little leprechaun. He had a warm smile and he danced well. "Here. I think I have some extra change," she said. Mason grabbed her elbow.

"What are you doing?" The grimace on his face spoke volumes. "Don't give him any money."

"Mason?" She looked up at him, surprised by his anger, as he pulled her away.

"Oh c'mon, man. Spare a brother some change." The homeless man followed them. "C'mon, man. I'm hungry."

"Don't give him any money, Meg."

"Mason, let go of my elbow."

"Listen, you can't pay any attention to these crackheads. They all—"

The man's voice boomed behind them. "You gonna die with all yo' money, man! You gonna die with it. You greedy prick, you gonna die with all yo' money!" Though the elfin little man had given up, she could hear his voice echoing behind them all the way down the block.

"For God's sake, Mason, let go of me."

"Look. I'm sorry," he said. "Those freakin' bums are everywhere and if you give one of them money they all want money. They're dirty and they're on drugs. Just ignore them from now on."

She knew Mason had a tendency to be cold, but this cold? She wanted to tell him that it was her change, and that yes he was probably right. The man probably would go buy crack, but if it made him feel better for one night she could care less. Suddenly she remembered the time they were on the freeway and had seen an abandoned dog, frightened and nearly getting run over by oncoming traffic. Mason had refused to stop, saying the animal probably had ringworm.

At the time she had wondered how she could be with such a prick. It was the beginning of the end. She couldn't believe she had forgotten about this side of him. *Loneliness does this to people*, she thought. *They can forget all the bad stuff, and focus on the things that made them secure—the things that made them feel like they weren't alone.*

"What's wrong?" he asked, taking her hand.

"Nothing, it's just that, well . . . I felt bad for that homeless man."

"Forget about him. Trust me. He'll make a ton of money tonight." He kissed her on the forehead. She had to admit, she was still attracted to him. Perhaps she was being overly sensitive about the homeless man. Everyone was entitled to their opinion.

His apartment felt as cold as the outdoors when they returned.

•   •   •

She wasn't sure how it happened but they ended up kissing on top of his bed. It was strange, but she felt like a schoolgirl around him, unsure if she wanted him to see her naked. Something about kissing him fully clothed seemed to make her feel more comfortable. But when he pulled her top over her head she let him. When his lips latched on to one of her nipples, she didn't stop him. Partially because his touch had made every nerve in her body turn to water. She felt as if she were melting and the feeling of his lips lightly pulsing in and out over her breast made her want her pants off as well. He kicked his pants off then he moved his hand up her thigh. He rubbed the outside of her panties with his fingertips. With his other hand he took one of hers and moved it to his erection. She rubbed her hand over him, noticing that he was still wearing socks.

"Do you have a condom?" she whispered. For a fleeting second she wondered if it was too soon for sex. He'd pretty much invited her to move in with him, but something still felt *unofficial* to her. However, it wasn't as if he was a stranger. They'd done it thousands of times and she was dying to feel him inside her, to release the tension she had felt building up ever since she had seen him at the engagement party.

On the other hand, she'd had a funny feeling ever since they'd walked home from the bar. It was the same feeling she'd had right before she was getting ready to break up with him. She couldn't put her finger on exactly what she felt, and tried to dismiss it.

This was what she wanted. She wanted to be with him. She wanted to start her life with him.

"The condoms are in my dresser," he moaned.

"I'll be right back," she whispered. His eyes looked glassy with need when they made eye contact.

"Thank you," he said, pointing to the top drawer of his dresser across the room.

When she returned he still had the same look in his eyes. His legs were two toned from a farmer's tan, and the tops of his thighs looked pale and hairy in the dim light.

She was afraid his drunken passion would fade into disappointment when he noticed she was holding the bottle of lotion she'd packed instead of a Trojan. She didn't give him a chance to figure it out, but rather began to stroke his erection. Moments later he climaxed, the sound of his voice echoing off the walls. "I'm sorry," he said. "You didn't get to finish." He stretched his arms behind his head and released a long sigh. "You got me so worked up I couldn't help it."

"It's okay." She smiled and kissed him on the cheek. "Maybe we'll have to try again later." As she said the words she wondered if he could sense that she wasn't sincere. The sheets were cold when they climbed into bed and as he drifted off to sleep she felt as if she had just escaped . . . something. After several hours of listening to the sound of his heavy breathing she realized what it was that she felt when they returned from the restaurant. Trapped.

●   ●   ●

When she woke the following morning they were spooning. He kissed her when she looked at him and she instantly recognized the taste of his mouth in the morning. It was neither bad nor good, a little sweet mixed with sour. He'd always tasted this way and something about it made her feel at home again. A night of sleep had made her less angry about his reaction to the homeless man and she felt as if she were doing the right thing by being here. She rationalized that she had probably overreacted to everything that had happened the night before. He dealt with the homeless on a regular basis and was probably fed up. Furthermore, it was only natural for her to be analyzing his every mood. If she got back together with him she knew the commitment would be much stronger this time around. Probably for life. It wasn't as if he were some guy she had met and they were in the getting-to-know-each-other phase. The phase where she could simply see where things went and if there would even be a relationship. Perhaps sensing that this was a step toward making things permanent with Mason was why she couldn't stop thinking about Bill.

They spent the afternoon shopping in Union Square, dodging animal rights activists outside Neiman Marcus and perusing Tiffany. She could afford nothing in any of these stores and wondered why he had brought her there.

Everything she looked at, she saw Bill. When she looked at clothes, she saw the poncho Bill bought in Mexico. When she looked at jewelry, she remembered the rings they'd purchased. When a car sped past, she saw his new Thunderbird. When Mason reached for her hand, she thought about Bill taking her hand when they'd danced in Mexico.

It was during lunch that things became weird. "So you never told me everything about the rest of your trip in Mexico," Mason said.

They were seated in the restaurant at the top of Neiman Marcus. For some reason the view made her nauseous and she wondered if it was because she had an empty stomach and it was taking so long for her risotto to come.

"What do you mean?" she asked. "I told you. I got stranded with Bill. We grabbed a hotel and my parents picked us up the next morning."

"I mean, did you hook up with Bill that night?"

"No. We were *stranded* there."

"Yeah right," he muttered.

He was eerily psychic this way. Like when she was attracted to the food critic from *San Diego Weekly*. She was stunned when, out of the blue, he'd started grilling her about him. There was no way he could've known that she'd been thinking about Bill all day.

"I just don't believe a guy and a girl could sleep next to each other all night and not touch each other."

"Mason, what are you talking about? Why are you doing this?"

There were times when his jealousy was sexy, and times when it was a total turnoff. This was the latter.

"I'm doing this because I'm not stupid, Meg. You spend the night in a hotel with a guy like Bill—in the same bed, no less—and you expect me to believe you didn't hook up with him. That he didn't even try."

She'd always wondered if all the other girls he dated had been sluts, because he had this notion that she was some out-of-control sex maniac that could never resist the urge to screw around. It was like he didn't know her.

"Mason, you're being weird. Really weird. I'm going to say this once. I did not hook up with Bill in Mexico."

"Just tell me if you did, so I don't look like a total ass at the wedding."

"If you want to know the truth, I told him I love *you*." Well, she'd actually said that at the couples shower when Bill had kissed her in the bathroom, not in Mexico. But it was still true. Wasn't it?

"Yeah right."

"Look, if you don't let this go, I'm leaving." She meant it.

"All right. Sorry, Meg. Look, I'm sorry. I don't mean to be this way. It's just that I'm so afraid of getting hurt again—I have to make sure that this is for real."

"Fine, but Mason, you know I've never cheated on you."

"I know."

They spent the remainder of the day walking around; by evening she just wanted a nap. Like the bachelorette party in Mexico, she wanted to sleep off the rest of her trip. And that was pretty much what she did.

CHAPTER SEVEN

"I've made a terrible mistake," Meg said as she wrapped cellophane around her fiftieth glass apple.

Claire reached for the scissors. "Why?"

"I've led Mason on. I don't want to get back together with him."

Claire was quiet. It was the day of the rehearsal and they were sitting in Claire's kitchen preparing three hundred wedding favors: glass apples that read *Apple of my eye, Claire and Ben's Wedding.* Each one would be individually wrapped in iridescent cellophane, then tied with peach and gold ribbons—Claire's colors. Meg wrapped. Claire cut and tied. Meg still wasn't clear about what you were supposed to do with the apple after receiving it. Use it as a paperweight? A decoration on the kitchen table? She didn't want to ask, as she knew Claire had put hours of thought and consideration into the hand-blown fruit, so she remained quiet and hoped the purpose of the apples would be revealed at the wedding.

"Really? I thought you were just having doubts again. How did you leave things with him?"

"Very vague. I took a long nap, then woke the next morning to catch my flight."

"So, he has no idea?"

"No. But I know for sure now. We're two different people. We were very different when we dated, but being around him again made me realize how much we've grown apart. I feel terrible. I've led him on again, but I can't be with him. I felt so trapped all weekend. Like I was caught in the same horrible role with him, always overlooking how cold and selfish he can be. And his possessiveness. I don't know how I could have forgotten about it."

"Do you want to know what I think?"

"Of course."

"Well, I didn't want to say anything before because who am I to interfere? It's your life." She paused to snip a ribbon. "I've never thought he was right for you. Ben's never said anything, but I think guys who are as possessive as Mason are usually insecure because *they* can't be trusted. I've always wondered how honest he is."

Meg herself had often wondered if Mason was so worried because he had a guilty conscience. If he was cheating, it must mean she was too. But Mason wasn't a cheater. His love had been genuine, and he'd called so often that she always knew his whereabouts.

"I'm going to be around him all weekend and I have to tell him."

"He's going to be crushed."

"I know," Meg said quietly. She noticed that Claire was adjusting the cellophane that she had wrapped around her last apple.

"I'm sorry. I don't mean to . . . It's just that . . . never mind. I'm being totally selfish. Thinking about my own wedding when you have all this stuff going on."

"What? What were you going to say?"

"I was going to say that he is such a huge part of our wedding. A groomsman, plus doing one of our readings, and I'm afraid he'd be so upset during the ceremony. But it's so selfish of me. In fact, I feel like a real bridezilla for even thinking it."

"No. Don't feel that way. You're right. I'll wait to talk to him about all this until after the wedding. Okay?"

· · ·

The rehearsal dinner was at Napa Valley Grill, a nice gourmet restaurant on the top floor of a large shopping mall in the heart of downtown San Diego. She was heading into the restaurant when she heard the muffled sound of a woman singing "New York, New York."

Odd, she hadn't remembered Napa Valley Grill having live music. She entered and was escorted by the hostess into a separate room for the wedding party. As soon as she stepped inside she realized that the music was coming from their party. Someone had brought the karaoke machine to the rehearsal dinner. Mrs. Caridini was taking full advantage of the microphone. Meg watched as she sat down in Matt's lap and sang to him, her sequined jacket sending off sparkles across the room. As she twirled away she grabbed a champagne glass from a tray and downed the contents before landing in her husband's lap.

Mason wasn't there yet, which was a good thing. She was going to need a couple of drinks before she found the courage to face him. She was going to have to put a front on until after the wedding. Fake it. He'd been calling her all week and she'd avoided him as much as she possibly could. She'd also told him that she had volunteered her apartment for a bunch of Claire's out-of-town friends and there wouldn't be room for him there.

As Mrs. C reached the end of the song she saw Bill walk in. He looked fantastic and she wished more than anything she could corner him right there and tell him that she wasn't in love with Mason and that she had feelings for him. Her heart dropped in her chest when she noticed Avril, her arm linked with his.

Avril? April Caridini, or Avril Carie, or whatever the hell her name was? She knew that Avril had been throwing herself at him at the couple's shower, but he'd actually fallen for it? For a moment Meg locked eyes with him, but he turned away before she did. She headed to the bar for a drink.

"How was San Francisco?" The voice came from behind and she knew it was Bill.

"It was okay," she said as she faced him. He was wearing the ring she'd bought him in Mexico. "But—" She was about to tell him it was not that great when Mason swooped in and kissed her on the cheek.

"There you are!" he said.

Her smile was forced. "Hi. How was your flight?"

"Wonderful." He held her hand, and she wanted to take it away from him, but she knew that would be cruel.

She sat next to him at dinner. Bill was across the room with Avril and it killed her to see them having a good time. She could tell Mason was drunk by the time they got to the main course and couldn't understand how he had gotten so tanked.

Mrs. Caridini dominated the karaoke machine. Finally Claire and Ben sang "At Last" by Etta James: their wedding song. What shocked the hell out of Meg was when Mason got behind the microphone.

"Anything by Elton John," he yelled.

She immediately recognized "Philadelphia Freedom." He was surprisingly good. He sounded a lot like Elton John and he even did the air splits at one point. She thought he might stop after one song, but apparently his liquid courage had led him to believe that he was actually doing a concert. He sang "Tiny Dancer" next and half the party joined him.

Shortly after his musical debut he passed out at one of the tables. "It must be jet lag," Mrs. Caridini said as she danced past Meg. Meg snorted. He'd flown down from San Francisco, in the same time zone. Plus the flight was only an hour and a half.

She couldn't believe what a lightweight he was. Well, at least he wouldn't want to go home with her. She'd been worried about how she was going to dodge that bullet. All she had to do was put him in a cab with someone else who was staying at the hotel.

She was standing alone when Bill grabbed her arm and led her to the microphone. "Come sing with me," he said.

It was Kid Rock and Sheryl Crow's "Picture." At first she felt uncomfortable. There was no way she was going to be able to sing the Sheryl Crow parts. This was a slow, serious song. She was just gaining the courage when Avril came bopping up. "Mind if I join you guys?" She was much friendlier when she was trying to impress someone.

"Sure," Bill said.

Apparently joining them meant butting in between the two of them and hogging the microphone.

• • •

At the end of the night she helped Mason into a cab with some of the L.A. bridesmaids who were also staying at his hotel. "Can you make sure he gets to his room?" Meg asked.

"Sure," Sagie said.

"Oh, and do you think you could pay me for your share of the hotel? There was also a fifty-dollar phone charge on our bill."

"I don't know what you're talking about," Sagie said.

"Didn't you use the phone?"

"No."

What a liar. "Really? Because I thought for sure I saw you using it."

She shrugged. "I didn't, but I'll have to pay you tomorrow. Okay? I left my wallet at the hotel."

Of course.

Mason stirred and began to sing an extremely slurred version of "Candle in the Wind" from the backseat of the cab. "Could you please make sure you remember your wallet? I really need the money. And I'll show you the phone bill."

"Fine." Sagie slammed the cab door behind her.

Meg waved good-bye to them, and could've sworn she saw Mason's tie fly from the window.

CHAPTER EIGHT

The following morning she arrived at the hotel on time, holding her peach bridesmaid dress on a hanger, doing everything she could to make sure it didn't drag on the ground. All twelve bridesmaids were packed in one hotel room, waiting for their turn with the hairdresser. The only armchair was occupied by Sagie, who was currently getting her hair done. Meg found it interesting that she could afford an expensive updo, but could never seem to come up with the money for her share of the hotel.

Meg went straight to Claire and hugged her. "Are you excited?"

She took a deep breath. "Yes, but very nervous."

"Don't worry. Everything will be fine. I know it."

"I keep thinking of all these things that can go wrong."

Meg rubbed her arm. "Listen, nothing is going to go wrong. And if anything does, you just tell me and I'll deal with it. Okay?"

Claire smiled. "Thank you."

Meg ended up sitting on the floor, watching while a hairdresser who looked like she had recently celebrated her senior prom did Sagie's hair. The girl wore the highest platform flip-flops Meg had ever seen and had purple toenails with little flowers painted on each big toe, and a gold toe ring on her left pinky toe. Meg guessed she could call her capri pants jeans because they were the color of denim and had pockets in all the right places. But they were as tight and stretchy as leggings. Her hair was a platinum mullet.

Meg turned to Claire. "Where did you find her?" Her nonchalant tone masked her burning desire to ask Claire what the hell she'd been thinking when she'd entrusted this girl with not only her appearance as a bride, but the entire bridal party.

"My salon recommended her."

"Oh. Did you go in for a trial run?" *Please tell me you did. Please.* She kept her tone pleasant, but was truly dying to get to the bottom of this.

"Oh yes. Last week." She handed Meg a page from a magazine. "This is how I'm having it done."

The clipping gave Meg some reassurance. She gazed at the portrait of a bride with a clean sweep of bangs over her forehead and a romantic chignon at the base of her neck. If Claire had gone in for a trial run, then she had to be okay. "How are you going to do your hair?" Claire asked as she took her picture back.

"I think I just want a simple, classic French twist."

"That will look really pretty on you."

She watched as the hairdresser took a thin piece of Sagie's hair from a high ponytail. She wrapped the strand around a curling iron, then slid it off the hot stick before spraying it to death with hairspray. She proceeded to repeat this procedure over and over.

The style looked alarming in a bad, early nineties homecoming type of way. But Meg tried to be optimistic. She wasn't done yet. She must have a vision. Soon all Sagie's hair was pinned up, each ringlet springing from her head like seasoned curly fries. More alarming, she'd left a strand of hair dangling by each of her temples and was in the process of curling those as well. Apparently, she intended to leave the ringlets there because she preserved them with hairspray on either side of her face. It was *North and South* meets Homecoming Queen. Meg really felt someone should fire this girl before she went any further.

Meg watched with anticipation as she gave Sagie a hand mirror. She expected Sagie to burst into tears, but she smiled. "I like it," she said. Her tone was genuine.

Strangely, this put Meg at ease. Perhaps it meant that Sagie had asked for this hairdo. She wanted to look this way. Meg would have to make sure she also gave specific instructions.

She watched as Sagie left the chair and grabbed her purse. She listened while she told Claire she was heading to the vending machine for a soda. Cynthia joined Sagie, and Meg took the opportunity to follow them.

She trotted down the hall to catch up. "Uh, Sagie," she called, "Cynthia, wait up."

Sagie spun around, her ringlets bobbing like pigs' tails.

They stopped walking and Meg caught up to them. Asking for money was never easy. However, Meg's patience had worn thin and she was over being polite. She glanced at Sagie's wallet. "I noticed you finally have your wallet today, so it's the perfect time for you to pay me back. You owe me a hundred and thirty dollars."

"I don't know what you're talking about. I might owe you eighty, but I never used the phone."

"Gosh, Meg," Cynthia snapped. "Couldn't you have waited for a better time? It's Claire's wedding."

Meg felt an anger unlike any she had ever experienced. Slowly, she turned to face the little troll. "No." She spoke slowly, and her tone was as firm as the diamond Claire wore on her ring finger. "Actually, *Cynthia*, I couldn't have waited for a better time. You see, I've been waiting for over two weeks. I need my money, and come to think of it, you owe me five dollars." This shut her up quickly. Meg watched her wilt like a flower in desert heat. She turned back to the other troll. She didn't look as frightened yet. "Sagie, you did use the phone. I saw you."

"Whatever. I used my calling card. It must've been someone else. Are you sure you didn't use the phone too?"

Meg pulled the bill and her cell phone from her purse. "I have the numbers right here. How 'bout we call them and I'll ask whoever answers if they know you? How does that sound?" Meg began to dial the first Los Angeles area code.

"All right. Stop. I'll pay you. Jeez, I didn't know you would be such a . . . so uptight." She sighed. "I have to go to the ATM, though."

"That's fine. We can all walk together. There's one in the lobby. I checked on my way in." She turned to Cynthia. "Do you have your five dollars? Or do you need to join us at the ATM?"

Cynthia slapped a bill into her palm.

•　　•　　•

One hundred and thirty-five dollars richer, Meg returned to Claire's room. A couple of other girls had gotten their hair done and she noticed that they all had gone for the same look. The hairdresser was finishing up Avril's hair when the maid of honor grabbed Meg by the elbow. "Is it just me or does everyone's hair look like shit?" Her whisper felt like a Santa Ana inside Meg's ear.

Meg lowered her voice. "I know. Are they telling her to do their hair like that, or is she taking the liberty to do it that way?"

"I think she's just doing it that way. I mean, look at the girl. She's like sixteen. I will freak out if she does my hair that way."

"Who's next?" Claire called. "Lindy is ready for someone."

For some reason they all looked at Meg. The hairdresser waited for her, armed with a curling iron. And for one moment Meg imagined being chased around the hotel by Lindy and her curling iron. "I guess I'm going." Meg forced a smile.

She sat down in the chair. "So, I really just want something simple. A French twist. Think Audrey Hepburn. Very *Breakfast at Tiffany's*."

Lindy said nothing in return, but instead pulled pieces of Meg's hair up, as if she were rifling through fabrics trying to pick out the best material to upholster a couch with. Then she nodded. "Okay. Not a problem."

Meg's shoulders were rigid at first, as if she were waiting for her to pull out a syringe and inject her with a flu vaccine. But she became so engrossed in a movie about Betty Broderick that the other girls were watching on Lifetime that she eventually relaxed. It was during a commercial when she realized that Lindy was using the curling iron. Why? There was no need for a curling iron with a French twist. She wanted to convince herself that there was some step involved that required a curling iron, but her instinct told her otherwise. *Speak up*, she told herself. *Say something now or you'll live to regret it once the whole wedding is caught on film and you have to remember your bad hairdo for decades to come.*

"Um," she started in her sweetest, most tactful voice. "I like curls, but I think I'd rather go for a smoother look. You know. A French twist?"

"Oh, yeah, yeah. I know. Don't worry," she said enthusiastically. "I'm not doing yours loose like the other girls."

Meg breathed a sigh of relief. "Okay. I just wanted to double-check. Sorry."

Just as the movie ended Lindy thrust a hand mirror in her face. At first glance the front of her hair wasn't *bad*. It wasn't exactly the swept-over-the-forehead, Holly Golightly look she had wanted to achieve. Rather, it was parted severely on the right side of her head, the line on her scalp resembling a long, skinny earthworm. However, Lindy hadn't lied. Her curls weren't boingy like the rest of the gang. Instead, she had taken each curl and wrapped it tightly into its own bun. There were dozens of them, pinned to her head like mini cinnamon rolls. For crying out loud, didn't everyone know who Audrey Hepburn was? And wasn't a French twist as standard as bangs for a hairdresser?

"Your hair looks cute, Meg," Avril said, cocking her head to the side. This was the confirmation she needed to know that her hair looked like shit. Absolute shit.

"Yeah, Meg. It's so cute," some others chimed in. All she could think about was how she was going to redo it. Should she ask Lindy for help? No. Several other girls had to go and the bride's hair wasn't even done yet. She didn't want to interfere with the whole schedule, so she wrote a check for fifty dollars and fled to the bathroom.

There wasn't much she could do to remedy the situation. She was going to have to take the whole thing out and start from scratch. Dismantling Lindy's creation could make things worse. "Damn," she muttered. She was not only going to look like an Easter cupcake in her peach dress, but she was also going to look like one with a bad frosting job.

She returned to the main room and watched while the rest of

the girls went under attack. One by one, they all began to look the same. Ugly. When it was finally Claire's turn she said a silent prayer that this woman who called herself an updo specialist knew what she was doing. Claire's hair was wet, so Lindy would be starting from scratch, which was frightening.

She was so lost in thought about Mason and how drunk he'd been the night before that she hardly paid attention to the different conversations. However, when she heard the mention of Bill's name her ears scoped out the voice like a spy satellite. "So what's going on with you two?" The question came from Joss.

She watched Avril smile. "I don't know yet."

"Did you guys go home together last night?"

The smile again, and then Lindy's blow-dryer went on and she missed the answer. Dammit. Did they hook up? Would Bill hook up with someone like her?

• • •

When the time came to change into her dress she felt like she was preparing to wait in line at the DMV. A dreaded task, but part of life. She had to do it, so she may as well do it with a smile. She slipped into her long peach gown. It had a sweeping train and several layers of thin wispy fabric down the skirt. She couldn't have looked worse.

Two limos waited outside for them. Half the girls were to ride in one, and half in the other. Meg was actually happy to be climbing into the one with Avril. She might find out more about her night with Bill. Meg was the last in. Joss got ahold of the volume control on the stereo and cranked the radio so loud that conversation was out of the question.

She sat in the limo, listening to "Big Pimpin'" by Jay-Z, and felt sick to her stomach thinking about how she was going to break it off with Mason. They were driving along when Meg glanced out her window and noticed Claire's limo driving right alongside theirs, as if it were racing. Cassie's head popped through the sunroof of the other limo. She yelled something and all the girls waved back. But the glass was tinted so she couldn't see them. Cassie pointed to their limo, then pointed to her dress and they thought maybe her dress was getting ruined from hanging out the sunroof so they all waved good-bye. But Cassie didn't go back in.

"She wants something," Cynthia said. "I'll find out what it is. Open the sunroof." They were going seventy on the freeway.

"Maybe you should just wait till we get there," Meg said.

"No. I'll be fine." She popped up. "What?" she yelled as she cupped a hand over her ear. "I don't understand!" Her scream competed with the wind. She finally gave up and sat back down. Her hair actually looked better after being thrashed by the wind. "I don't know what she wants. She keeps pointing to her dress and then down."

Sagie shrugged and cranked up the music again.

They pulled up to the church in La Jolla. Meg was the closest to the door; instead of waiting for the chauffeur she reached for the handle and the second she did she realized what all the daredevil stunts from the sunroof were about. Her peach dress had been slammed in the door. It had been dragging and flapping over asphalt for at least fifteen miles.

"Oh shit," she breathed. She kicked the door open and immediately noticed how dirty and tattered the bottom was. The girls from the other limo immediately raced over. "We were trying to tell you! The chauffeur slammed your dress in the door!"

"We're cutting it off," Claire said.

"Cutting what off?"

"The bottom part of your dress."

This was fine with her because her dress had looked terrible to begin with. Now it looked like it had been run over by a tractor. The wedding coordinator found a pair of scissors and within minutes they were snipping the train off. She overestimated and ended up cutting the dress mid-calf. The long bow in the back dangled beneath the hem. She looked like a total jackass. There was no easier way to put it. This really was the epitome of bridesmaid hell. What could possibly get worse from here?

She excused herself to use the ladies' room. She moved quickly and stealthily, hoping she wouldn't run into anyone. She could practically reach out and touch the door when she felt a hand grab her arm. She spun around and faced him.

"You look hot," Mason said.

Instantly, she knew he was wasted. It wasn't even two o'clock yet.

"Uh, thanks." He lowered his head to kiss her and she found it remarkable that he didn't reek of alcohol.

"Come here," he slurred. "Kiss me."

"Um, Mason. Now is not the best time. Are you okay? You look like you could use some water."

"Now that you say it, I am a little thirsty." He took one step toward the drinking fountain and fell. "Ah fuck!" he yelled.

"Shhh. Guests are arriving. Let me help you up."

Matt came around the corner. She hadn't seen him since the engagement party and he had dyed his hair blue. "Thank God," he said. "I couldn't find him anywhere. He's been a mess all afternoon."

"Why? How did this happen? Is anyone else drunk?" Meg demanded.

He shook his head. "He's not drunk. Apparently he bought some Valium while he was in Mexico. I guess he was sort of nervous about doing a reading and he took three."

"Holy shit."

"Yeah, I know."

"He's supposed to do a reading. There is no way he is going to be able to read. We have to find someone to fill in for him."

"He'll be lucky if he can even walk down the aisle."

"Matt, you have to do his reading."

"I don't even know what he's reading. They gave us all that stuff last night and he doesn't have his."

"Well, we need to tell someone. The priest?"

She could hear violins coming from inside the chapel and knew they were minutes from starting.

"I'll find the wedding coordinator. You wait here with him."

She returned to the bridal room and was thrilled to see the wedding coordinator. "Listen," Meg began.

"There isn't time to listen, dear. The wedding is starting. You need to get in your place in line."

"But there's a drunk groomsman—drugged groomsman—who is supposed to do a reading and he can't because—"

"Don't worry. Just take your place in line."

Meg popped into line and the next thing she knew they were moving. Under normal circumstances she would've been nervous to head down the aisle wearing a dress that made her calves look like a pair of chicken legs and a hairdo suited for a female rapper from the eighties. But she was too worried about Mason to care. The first thing she looked at was the row of groomsmen. Mason stood at the end. He waved to Meg when he noticed her. *Holy fuck, don't wave.* Then he blew her a kiss. She wanted to hit him over the head with her bouquet. What was he thinking? She took her place at the altar and cringed when she heard him howl. Luckily, the music was so loud and the audience so focused on the next bridesmaid that few people noticed.

Meg knew the priest had one foot in the grave, but it soon became clear that he also had Alzheimer's.

He lifted his thin arms and raised his wrinkled hands to the ceiling. He couldn't be taller than Meg. The decrepit little man started the ceremony by saying, "We are gathered here today in honor of Claire and Beth."

"It's Ben," Claire whispered.

"What?"

"It's Ben." Her voice became a little louder.

"Huh?"

"His name is Ben! Not Beth."

He forgot part of his opening prayer twice, and Claire and Ben had to whisper some of the passages to him.

When it came time for Mason to do his reading, one of the groomsmen nudged him. He skipped onto the altar before crashing into the podium. He saved himself and the Bible from falling to the ground and stayed balanced by gripping each side of a cloth that dangled from the podium. "Well, here is my reading," he said. "O holy art thou. You are older than us. You're a star in the sky. Do you still feel the pain? Or the scars . . ."

For crying out loud, it was "Daniel." He was reciting the words to "Daniel." The lines from the song were in the wrong order and the words jumbled, but thank God the priest was too clueless to realize. She prayed that they made it through the rest of the reading without the entire congregation breaking out in chorus.

Except for the priest forgetting most of the vows, the rest of the ceremony was uneventful. Meg headed back down the aisle with Mason, who curtsied when they reached the end of the aisle. Why he did that, she had no idea. Bill came toward them and she honestly couldn't remember being happier to see anyone.

"How is he holding up?" Bill asked.

"Fine. But I think we should put him to bed before the reception."

"I'm riding back with him in the limo. I can take him to his room," he offered. "Then you can take care of him if you want."

"Thank you."

•   •   •   •

If Mason had been coherent, she would've beaten him over the head with her bouquet. How could he have done this? Drugs? At Ben and Claire's wedding? When he was doing a reading? What the hell was wrong with him? Nonetheless she still felt sorry for him. He was going to feel like the biggest ass in wedding history after he woke up tomorrow. She wondered if Ben and Claire would ever forgive him. Clearly, he had some real problems he needed to work through if he'd resorted to popping pills from a Mexican pharmacy when the pressure was on.

It was shortly after cocktail hour that she began to worry about him. Bill had said he'd tucked him into bed, but what if he overdosed or something? What if he was choking on his own vomit while she was ordering a Cosmopolitan? She decided to go check on him.

His door was cracked open. It seemed out of character for Bill to be so irresponsible. He didn't seem careless enough to leave Mason drugged and incoherent in a hotel room with the door open for any nut to come along and rob him. Or worse—what if Mason wandered from his room, out of the hotel and into oncoming traffic? However, once she caught sight of the peach-colored heel wedged in the crack of the doorframe, she stopped worrying about Mason being hurt and started worrying about who else was here.

She pushed the door open and followed a trail beginning with another shoe and a bouquet similar to the one Meg had been carrying. Apparently they had been in such a hurry to undress they'd scattered their clothes all over the place and hadn't noticed the shoe wedged in the door. She almost laughed out loud when she reached the bed. However, she also felt like screaming.

Avril Carawhatthefuck—buck naked, riding Mason. He was neither incoherent nor fully clothed, but seemed perfectly happy listening to Avril shout, "You bronco!"

Meg couldn't help but notice that he still wore his socks. His thighs looked exceptionally hairy. She watched for a moment as Avril threw her head back and shouted, "Give me the ride of my life, cowboy!"

"Meg!" He sat up. His hair was a mess, and he had waxy brown smears streaked across his forehead.

Avril jumped from the bed, and immediately covered her privates with her hands.

"Shit!" Mason sprang up and reached for his pants. "She came on to me," were the next words out of his mouth.

Avril's jaw dropped quicker than his penis probably went limp.

Strangely, Meg wanted to hug Avril. Not only had she saved her from a huge and messy breakup at her friend's wedding, but by hooking up with Mason she'd also just confirmed that she wasn't shagging Bill.

"Avril, can you please give us a minute?" Meg said, calmly.

She slipped into her dress before flipping Meg the bird and storming from the room. Meg waited until she heard the door click behind her.

"Look," Mason said. "It's not what you think."

"Oh, I think I know what it is."

"I've never been that into her." Which sounded as if this wasn't the first time he'd been rolling around in the sheets with her. And as soon as the words came from his mouth, he realized how bad they sounded too. "I mean, I've never found—"

"This is why you're so possessive," she said. "I should've known it all along. You're possessive because you were always fooling around behind my back, and you assumed I did the same. Did Claire know about this?" She wanted to get away from Mason, but she also wanted to know if her friend had been keeping Mason and Avril a secret.

"Know about what? There is nothing to know. I told you, she forced herself on me."

"Mason, look, no matter what you say I'm not coming back. For many reasons."

"I love you, Meg. It's always just been you."

"We're two different people, Mason. We're not meant for each other, and you know it as well as I do. I planned on telling you this after the wedding. But since I, well, walked in on you and Avril I'm telling you now. So just tell me, did Claire know?"

He was silent then shook his head. "Claire never knew. I swear."

•   •   •

She set out to find Bill as soon as she left Mason's room. She didn't have to go too far because she found him hanging out near the elevator in the lobby.

"Hey," he said. "I was going to come find you."

"You were?"

"Yeah, is everything okay?

"Mason's fine, but I broke—"

"I know. Avril told me. I just passed her. I wanted to go up there to make sure you were okay, but I thought I'd give you a minute."

"Bill, I've been fine for a week. In fact, I think I've been fine since we got stranded in Mexico." She took his hands.

She could tell by the way he pulled her closer that he understood.

"I knew the second I left you in the bathroom at the couple's shower that I was over Mason. I feel like such a fool now."

She could hear Mrs. Caridini singing. She had brought the karaoke machine to the wedding. Then she heard her singing in Spanish. She knew Spanish? "It's that song, 'Bésame Mucho.' The one in Mexico. What does *bésame mucho* mean anyway?"

"Kiss me a lot." Then Bill leaned in and kissed her. He pulled her into his chest and she closed her eyes as they danced in the middle of the lobby, her peach bow hanging down to her calves.

She'd always known that once a bridesmaid reached the wedding reception she felt as if she'd made several friends in the wedding party. She'd found something better than friends. She'd found love.